Also by Matthew J. Kirby

The Clockwork Three

Icefall

The Lost Kingdom

Infinity Ring Book 5: *Cave of Wonders*

The Quantum League: *Spell Robbers*

The Dark Gravity Sequence #1: *The Arctic Code*

The Dark Gravity Sequence #2: *Island of the Sun*

Last Descendants: An Assassin's Creed Novel

A TASTE FOR MONSTERS

MATTHEW J. KIRBY

SCHOLASTIC PRESS / NEW YORK

All rights reserved. Published by Scholastic Press, an imprint of Scholastic Inc., *Publishers since 1920.* SCHOLASTIC, SCHOLASTIC PRESS, and associated logos are trademarks and/or registered trademarks of Scholastic Inc.

The publisher does not have any control over and does not assume any responsibility for author or third-party websites or their content.

Library of Congress Cataloging-in-Publication Data

Names: Kirby, Matthew J., 1976– author.
Title: A taste for monsters / Matthew J. Kirby.
Description: First edition. | New York : Scholastic Press, 2016. | Summary: In 1888 seventeen-year-old Evelyn Fallow, herself disfigured by the phosphorus in the match factory where she worked, has been hired as a maid to Joseph Merrick, the Elephant Man—but when the Jack the Ripper murders begin she and Merrick find themselves haunted by the ghosts of the slain women, and Evelyn is caught up in the mystery of Jack's identity.
Identifiers: LCCN 2015048826 | ISBN 9780545817844
Subjects: LCSH: Merrick, Joseph Carey, 1862-1890—Juvenile fiction. | Jack, the Ripper—Juvenile fiction. | Phosphorus—Physiological effect—Juvenile fiction. | Neurofibromatosis—Juvenile fiction. | Ghost stories. | Serial murders—England—London—History—19th century—Juvenile fiction. | Murder—Investigation—England—London—History—19th century—Juvenile fiction. | London (England)—History—19th century—Juvenile fiction. | CYAC: Merrick, Joseph Carey, 1862-1890—Fiction. | Jack, the Ripper—Fiction. | Disfigured persons—Fiction. | Neurofibromatosis—Fiction. | Ghosts—Fiction. | Serial murderers—Fiction. | Murder—Fiction. | London (England)—History—19th century—Fiction. | Great Britain—History—Victoria, 1837-1901—Fiction.
Classification: LCC PZ7.K633528 Tas 2016 | DDC 813.6 [Fic] —dc23 LC record available at https://lccn.loc.gov/2015048826

10 9 8 7 6 5 4 3 2 1   16 17 18 19 20

Printed in the U.S.A.   23

First edition, October 2016
Book design by Ellen Duda

For Sophie

CHAPTER 1

I woke up next to a dead woman. A black fly rested on her open left eye, straddling her lashes, and in my fear and disgust I leapt from the bed without first making certain the straps of my carpet-bag were still entwined in my arms. The bag fell to the floor as I reached my feet, and I snatched it up with the brief, daily moment of relief that it hadn't been stolen in the night.

"Who was she?" asked a dollymop from the bed next to me, the paint on her cheek a smeared bruise, crudely applied to hide how young she was.

"I never asked her name," I said, though I had been forced to share the bed with her when the doss-house filled to overflowing the night before.

"Best notify the manager," the girl said, and flopped onto her back.

I stared at the dead woman and wondered when in the night she had passed away. Her body lay on its side, utterly still, facing the empty half of the soiled bed I had just fled, her gray hair filled with grease and dirt, the toil of her life in evidence. She was of dizzy age, her face rutted with deep lines, her nails chipped away and fingertips blunted by hard labor. I had no idea what color her dress had been before the back slums got to it, but it was ratty enough now that it wasn't worth taking.

I turned away from her and opened my bag, then pulled out the nicer of my own two dresses, the one I kept away from the fleas and grime. My skin turned to gooseflesh as I undressed to my corset and pulled on the dress, and afterward I placed around my neck the silver locket bearing twin portraits of my parents, painted when they were still happy.

"Ain't you fine and large," said the prostitute. "Off to the palace today, are we?"

I ignored her. This clean dress had been my mother's, one of the few pieces of finery my father hadn't sold off. It was ten years old, its fuller shape now out of fashion, but still lovely and respectable, and clean, which were all I required.

"You're enough to make a stuffed bird laugh," the girl said. "You can change your dress but not your face, now can you." She chuckled.

I held myself still against the familiar pain, for I could not show a whit of weakness. To do so invited the cannibals to descend upon me. They waited for any opportunity to plunder the living and the dead, and if I tarried here, I would see it again. There would be someone who would take the dead woman's dress.

It helped if I allowed the pain to become anger, to let it scorch the backs of my eyes for several moments, and then unleash it like the phosphor I once handled so carefully. To survive, I had to always be a savage fire-in-waiting.

I put that flame into my voice. "I can't change my looks, and you can't change the number of times you've spread your legs. Can you even count that high?"

That stunned her eyes and mouth open wide. "Who you think you are?" she said, but I could see that my appearance and my tone had unsteadied her.

I pulled my shawl out of the bag, draped it over the top of my head, and wrapped it around the lower half of my face. "Keep to your own business, church-bell."

She didn't utter another word as I snatched up my bag and left her in the cramped room. My anger burned out and left me shaking as I bumped down the narrow corridor. I did not relish having said that to her, nor any of the far worse things I'd had to do in the last few years. That was not me. I hadn't yet let the streets change me deep down, though they had surely tried.

In the kitchen, several women sat along the benches against the wall, sipping weak tea and eating their breakfast. When the manager saw me come in, she left her stove and offered me bread, but I could see that mold had got into it and declined. She shrugged.

"The woman who shared my bed last night is dead," I said.

She put her red hands on her hips, her arms huge. "Another one, eh?"

I nodded. She shrugged once more and went back to stirring whatever she had in the pot that would be served as supper that night. But I would not be coming back for it. Even if my plan today failed, I didn't have the coin for another night's lodging.

I checked the placement of my shawl and stepped outside, where I found it had rained the night before, turning the streets into a foul mire. I kept carefully to the sidewalk as horse hooves and carriages slipped in the muck, and set off down Wentworth

Street toward Osborn. Before I reached Whitechapel High Street, mud had caked my boots above the soles and clung to the hems of my skirts, while rough, gray clouds shouldered the city, threatening to rain again. It was early enough and the weather dour enough that the streets weren't yet swarming, but were coming to life with oystermen, milk boys, organ grinders, and tinkers.

I made my way eastward a half mile on foot, wishing I had but one more farthing to make the two required to ride the omnibus down the street. I passed storefronts as they opened, the lurid signs for Thomas Barry's Live Entertainments, the Red Lion pub, and the Star and Garter, until I stood opposite the black gates and porters' lodges of the London Hospital.

Behind me, an aproned greengrocer stood next to his bushels and crates, muttering curses at the sky in Irish, and next to his shop, a boarded-up waxworks suggested former horrors. The smell of souring fruit cut through the odors of manure and soot.

Beyond the iron fence, set back from the commotion of the street, the hospital's high arches and columns presented a severe and imposing edifice. It seemed almost scornful of me, daring me in my impudence to attempt what I was about to do. But I could not be dissuaded or intimidated, for I had no choice.

"Pardon me, miss?"

I turned to my left.

A costermonger with a door-knocker beard had his wheelbarrow of eels and herring up on the sidewalk, out of the mud, chancing the ire of a passing copper. He flinched when he saw my face, his revulsion apparent, and I realized my shawl had slipped.

I hurried to adjust it as his gaze dropped hard to his wares and stayed there.

"Out of the way," he said.

I stepped aside. "Good day to you."

He trundled past me, eyes downward, shoulders rounded. "Filthy strum," I think he may have said, but the rumble of the wheelbarrow flattened his words.

He wasn't a threat to me, and I was exhausted, so I let the affront slip by me as he walked on. A moment later, the greengrocer cleared his throat behind me. I turned, and he stared at me before nodding his head toward the hospital.

"Can they help you, then?" he asked.

He had seen the slip of my shawl, too. "That is my hope."

His nod was quick. "Best be off. Gates open soon, and there'll be a crowd already."

I thanked him, then dove through an opening in the traffic and hastened across the wide street. My boots collected more mud along the way and grew heavy before I reached the gate, where I found the greengrocer had been right. A crowd had already gathered.

Among them was a young woman, about my age, clutching a sunken-eyed little boy, his chestnut hair lank with sweat. I could tell his mother had endured a sleepless night, and I pitied her.

"Can I give you something?" I asked the boy.

He cast me a shy look from against his mother's bosom, the hope in his eyes somewhat tarnished. His mother eyed me with suspicion, so I waited until she nodded her permission.

Then I leaned in close to the boy and pulled out my last farthing. "This coin is charmed with luck. You hang on to it whilst your mother speaks with the doctor, and you'll be feeling better in no time. I've got all the luck I need, you see. Will you take care of it for me?"

He came out from hiding a bit and nodded, with a smile, and I pressed the coin into his dirty little palm.

"You hold tight to that, now," I said, and his mother mouthed a silent thank-you.

Near us, a dandy fellow swayed on his feet, his eyelids fluttering, clutching an arm that bent in the wrong place. He was supported by several other young men, and by the look of them they all suffered, to a far lesser degree than their comrade, from the excesses of their night. They regarded me with their lewd and bleary eyes, and I checked the placement of my shawl.

We all waited in grim silence for the hospital gates to open. This was the red-slicked eddy where the city's currents collected its maimed and diseased. It had carried me here today for the second time in my life.

A doctor and a nurse soon came with two porters to open the gates. Before doing so, their practiced eyes surveyed us, and I imagined them cataloging and sorting the afflictions before them.

"The broken arm will most likely need surgery," the doctor said to the porters. His blond hair had as much wave as a silk ribbon, and his face was shaven. "Take him up to the operating theater. The rest of them can wait in the receiving room."

One of the porters nodded. "Yes, Doctor."

The doctor exchanged a look with the nurse and turned away, but he gave me a parting glance that held curiosity, and perhaps even a brush of admiration for the part of my face I didn't hide. I was accustomed to that and took no more flattery from it than the fruiterer takes in the few ripe apples he uses to hide the worm-ridden.

I made use of the boot brush as the porters unlocked the squealing gate, and then we all shuffled through, first into the hospital's foyer and then into the receiving room.

It remained as I remembered it. The austere benches waited in rows, the wooden floor beneath them an open testament to mortal suffering, written in stains that would never lift out. The fronds and leaves of potted plants reached out from the room's corners, while the sweet, almost burnt scent of carbolic permeated the air.

All the other wretches who had been waiting outside took seats, but I inhaled deeply and approached the attending nurse sitting behind her broad desk. This was a scene I had rehearsed again and again, but had no true confidence it would unfold as I had envisioned it.

"I would like to speak with Matron Luckes," I said.

The nurse looked up from a wide ledger. "Pardon me?" She had a few gray hairs and wore a blue dress, white apron, and a small white bonnet.

"I would like to speak with the matron." I bowed my head a little. "Please."

"The matron does not see patients. What is your complaint?" She swept me with a quick glance. "Are you ill?"

"No, ma'am. I wish to speak with her about becoming a probationer."

"Oh." Now she scrutinized me as if through a different lens, and I felt myself standing straighter. Though I had worn the better of my two dresses, I still felt shabby. "You wish to be a nurse?" she asked.

"Yes, ma'am."

"And what is your name?"

I gave my voice a gentle clearing. "Evelyn Fallow, ma'am."

She rose from her desk. "Please wait here, Miss Fallow," she said, and left through a nearby door.

I waited and watched as nurses moved down the rows of patients, documenting illnesses and injuries, and doctors summoned the poor souls in order of urgency for further examination. I admired them all for their charitable work, and wished that I could say the same about my own reasons for being there.

The nurse returned. "Matron Luckes will see you." She extended her hand to usher me through. "This way."

We left the receiving room and entered a wide hall. Glass doors at one end opened onto the hospital's gardens, but we turned to the right down a corridor into the west wing. Nurses glided by us with gentle nods, entering and exiting the wards we passed. I tried not to be overt about peering inward, and thus caught only a glimpse of the rows of patients in metal beds.

At the next intersecting hallway, we turned right again and came into an area of offices. We passed a few doors, until we arrived at one labeled MATRON in brass. The nurse knocked with the back of a knuckle.

"Enter," came a voice from within.

The nurse opened the door and gestured for me to go through, which I did, and then heard the door shut behind me. Here in the west wing, direct sunlight had not yet reached the well-appointed office. Matron Luckes stood behind her desk, a very sturdy woman, her complexion the color of boiled sheets, fingertips on her desk, her arms spread like flying buttresses. She appeared to be in her thirties and wore a black dress, white lace at her collar and cuffs, and she had a round moon of a face. Papers covered the desk in neat stacks, an inkwell and pen nearby. Behind her, shelves displayed books, plaques, pictures in frames, and other objets d'art.

"Miss Fallow?" she asked, her voice imperious.

I stepped farther into the room, which smelled delicately of violet. "Yes, ma'am. Thank you for seeing me, ma'am."

"It is customary for requests such as yours to be put in writing and delivered. But I like to recognize initiative, and I see no reason for you to have wasted a journey here. From where do you come?"

"Spitalfields, ma'am."

"Oh." She paused. "I see."

I thought I heard disappointment in her words and feared in that moment she had set her mind against me. Nurses came from far better places than the godforsaken East End. But she lowered herself into her chair and motioned me toward one of the seats in front of her desk with an elegant flick of her wrist.

"Please, Miss Fallow."

I sat forward on the edge of the cushion and laid my bag close by.

"Tell me." The matron propped her elbows on the desk and looked at me over the steeple of her fingers, each of which bore a jeweled ring. "Why do you wish to become a nurse?"

This, too, I had rehearsed. "To help others, ma'am. To do some good in the world."

"A noble intent," she said. "And why do you wish to do good?"

I hadn't expected that question, and it seemed to contain its own answer. "Aren't we all supposed to do good?"

"Yes. But some do good even when others would not expect it. Take this hospital, for example, which operates by the charity of others. There are those who think our patients bring their misfortunes on themselves, and are both deserving of the consequences and undeserving of our mercy. How would you respond to such people?"

My first thought was that such people might think me undeserving. "I'd point them to the Bible, ma'am. If I remember correctly, Jesus did not hold much company with the toffs and swells. He ministered to the sick and afflicted."

"True. You have read the Bible?"

"I have, ma'am."

"Remove your shawl, please."

"Ma'am?" The sudden request came at me like a hansom cab charging out of the fog, and left me frantic.

"It seems to me you are hiding something." Her eyes shone. "I must know what it is if we are to go any further with this interview."

"Yes, ma'am." I looked down at my lap. I'd known this moment would come, and I had tried to prepare for it, but when confronted with its reality, I faltered in the fear that the matron would treat me no different than the streets I'd come here to escape. Perhaps my purpose had been a failure before the first step taken.

"Miss Fallow," Matron Luckes said, "please remove your shawl."

I reached up and pulled the fabric away from my head. I felt some of my hairs fly loose, and felt the air against my scars.

The matron was silent for several moments. "You poor girl. You worked in a match factory, if I am not mistaken."

I nodded. "Bryant and May's."

"Were you party to their strike last month?"

"No, ma'am. My jaw had already started to ache by the end of April, and I haven't worked there since."

"Phosphorus necrosis."

"Yes, ma'am."

"You have fared very well, considering. You are lucky to have a lower jaw at all."

"I didn't ignore the signs, and a doctor here in the hospital got to it early. He performed surgery and saved much of the bone and some of my teeth. I had already quit the factory when the strike started, but I'm glad for the reforms, for the sake of those still working there."

"The reforms did not go far enough." The matron shook her head, scowling. "White phosphorous is a poison. There is simply no justification for its continued use over red phosphorous, other than greed."

That was true, and the greed of the match factory owners had left me disfigured, unable to find good work or to marry a good husband. But the doctor and nurses who had cared for me had inspired a single possibility for a decent life, and now that I was here, I was determined not to let the opportunity pass without an attempt to take hold of it.

"I am aware of my appearance," I said. "More acutely than any-one else, I assure you. But I can read and write. I can do sums and figures. I will make a fine nurse if you but give me the chance."

My revelations seemed to surprise her. "Where were you educated?"

"I did not come from the East End, ma'am. I went to school. I had tutors. My father was once a quite prosperous silk merchant. But he lost his fortune speculating, and the financial ruin proved too much for him. He took to the bottle and the bottle took his life." I didn't tell her about the countless times I'd pleaded with him to leave the drink alone, or how he'd left me crying and alone that last night, and I hadn't seen him again until I was called to identify his body at the inquest.

"And your mother?" the matron asked.

"She died when I was eight while giving birth to my sister, who lived but five days."

"I see." The matron looked down at her desk, drumming a tat-too with her fingertips, and a delicate hope fluttered inside me. Several moments passed with maddening slowness, counted by the ticking of the wall clock. But then she looked up abruptly, and by the serious expression she wore, I knew my hope had been false.

"I'm sorry, Miss Fallow. I truly sympathize with your plight. But here are the facts, which cannot be ignored. Our patients come to us in the extremities of pain and despair. A nurse is engaged in divine work, and to be of comfort and benefit, she must possess an angelic countenance. Your disfigurement would cause shock and discomfort, I am afraid. There is also the matter of maturity. How old are you?"

"Seventeen, ma'am."

She sighed. "There we are. Probationers must be at least twenty-one. You have my deepest pity. Had I the power, I would—"

"Begging your pardon, Matron, but I did not come here for your pity." I swallowed to keep my voice steady and strong. "I came for a position, and if I'm to be perfectly honest, it wasn't out of charity, either. I came because I have nowhere else I can go. I have no money, but I refuse to debase myself with men. I do not want to die in a doss-house, but I am terrified that is my fate, or something worse. Please, ma'am. I'll accept anything. Just allow me—"

She held up a hand to stop me from speaking. "You have strength of character, and I admire it," she said. "But it does not change the facts I have already stated. I am sorry, Miss Fallow, but there is nothing I can do."

"I see." I felt my whole being collapsing inward, but forced myself to my feet. "Thank you for your time, Matron." I managed a curtsy, reclaimed my bag, then turned and crossed her office, eyes downward on the Persian rug, attempting to scrape together a desperate plan for where I would go and what I would do outside the hospital walls. I reached the door and grasped its cold handle.

"Miss Fallow," the matron said.

I turned to face her. "Ma'am?"

"A possibility has just occurred to me." She came around from behind her desk and approached me, joining her bejeweled hands in front of her waist. "It is actually your condition, as well as the strength you have shown, that may render you suitable to the task I have in mind. But I must warn you. The patient has proven too much for even the most seasoned and accomplished on my staff."

I forged my voice of adamant. "Whatever the duty, ma'am, I accept it."

"You will be a maid, but also the patient's attendant. You will light his fire, bring his food, and you will assist him with whatever he requires."

I would not have to return to the streets, after all. I had escaped the city and what it had tried to make out of me, the life and death that waited for me there. "You have my deepest gratitude, ma'am. I know I am capable, and I won't disappoint you."

"But this duty is different from whatever it is you are expecting, I assure you. This patient is quite singular."

"How so, ma'am?"

"His name is Joseph Merrick. You may have heard him referred to as the Elephant Man."

CHAPTER 2

Matron Luckes was right. I knew of the Elephant Man. Girls from the match factory had seen him on display as a great freak of nature some few years earlier. One of them had apparently run screaming at the sight of him, and another had simply fainted on the spot from the shock. The grotesque images they had conjured in my mind at that time rose up now to haunt me. I felt crushed in a vise, desperate not to return to the streets, but terrified of this new spectre.

The Elephant Man.

"Ma'am . . . I . . ."

"You have heard of him, I see. I warned you, Miss Fallow. He is quite singular. If you do not think you have it in you to undertake this, I urge you to say so now."

As frightened as I was by this unknown, I was more frightened by what I knew full well awaited me in the streets at night. There were worse ways to die in Whitechapel than in the bed of a doss-house. "I have it in me, ma'am."

"You are certain?" She fixed me with a blade of a stare that transformed her from hospital monarch to inquisitor. "You are *quite* certain?"

Though I had once faced down a huge longshoreman crazed with drink, I found myself unable to combat her gaze and lowered mine. "I am quite certain, ma'am. I am sorry for my hesitation."

"When you are introduced to Mr. Merrick," she said, her voice as honed as her eyes, "no matter what your inward reaction might be upon seeing him, you *will* maintain a pleasant and compassionate demeanor. He must see no outward sign of your discomfort, whatsoever. Do you understand?"

"I do, ma'am."

"Good." She looked at my carpetbag. "Shall I have a porter assist you with your other things?"

"This is all I have, ma'am."

"Very well. I shall escort you to the maids' dormitory, and later, you'll be introduced to Mr. Merrick. Provided that goes well, you will begin your duties tomorrow. Your wages are six shillings a week." She reached around me and opened the door. "Please, after you."

I hesitated leaving the office, because my face lay exposed, and moved to lift my shawl. Matron Luckes waited patiently until I had it adjusted before ushering me out into the corridor.

"Under the circumstances," she said as she led me back down the wing, "I will allow you to wear your shawl when moving about the hospital. But when you are in Mr. Merrick's presence, you will refrain from covering your face."

"Yes, ma'am," I said, then risked an impertinence. "May I ask why, ma'am?"

"To do so would undermine the very reason I selected you. It would not do him good to see someone of vastly better circumstances ashamed of her disfigurement."

"I see." It seemed I was there to show the Elephant Man that he was not the only monster in the world. Only I wasn't a monster, in spite of how I looked and what I'd done, and ordinarily I would have been angry, but in that moment I was much more worried about seeing him than I was about being seen by him.

The matron moved along with a rigid grace lessened somewhat by a slight swivel at her hips, like a barrel walking. When we reached the main hallway near the receiving room, we turned toward the garden doors I had seen earlier.

"That is a fine locket you are wearing," she said. "Beginning tomorrow, when in uniform, you must not wear it at any time. I do not permit anyone on my staff to wear jewelry."

I thought of her many rings, sparkling on her fingers even now as we stepped outside and down a set of stone steps to a gravel path. "Why is that, Matron?" I asked.

"It invites distraction and risks offense. A crucifix, for example, might cause discomfort for our Jewish patients and benefactors."

"I see," I said, but resolved to wear it under my clothes where it wouldn't be seen, for it was my talisman of better times.

The hospital's garden filled in the wide space between its west and east wings, the dense flower beds having already begun to shed the last of their blossoms and color with the coming of autumn. On the garden's far side, beyond the ends of the building, lay a shady lawn and a tennis court.

Matron Luckes led me down a path that skirted the eastern wing, which towered over us several stories, until about halfway along its length we came to a set of stairs leading up to another pair of doors. We entered through them into an open lobby with two wards on each side, to the right and left. We paused here, allowing for a longer glance through their double doors than I'd previously been given. Some of the patients were sitting up in their beds, while others reclined. Some had bandages wrapping various parts of their bodies, the injuries and maladies of the others not plainly visible.

"Gloucester and Bowley wards on your left," the matron said. "Cambridge and Albert on your right. Your regular duties will not require you to enter any of the wards. You will refrain from doing so unless directed otherwise."

"Yes, ma'am," I said.

We crossed the lobby and exited from the opposite side of the wing onto an open square, where women were washing and scrubbing iron bed frames, the smell of carbolic more pungent in the air than it had been inside the hospital. Additional bed frames that appeared in need of paint or repair waited in forlorn stacks in the corners of the courtyard. A third hospital wing enclosed the square on the opposite side and to the left, and a somewhat forsaken quality oppressed the space.

"That is the Grocers Wing." Matron Luckes pointed across the way, and then nodded toward the women at work. "And this is commonly referred to as Bedstead Square, for obvious reasons."

We descended a few steps and turned to the right, strolling down the length of the square, and a short distance later we reached another flight of concrete steps, these leading downward to a low wooden door into what appeared to be the basement of the east wing.

Matron Luckes halted before the top of the stairs. "That door leads to Mr. Merrick's quarters."

I looked again, suddenly fearful, and a mite curious. The door had a fanlight above it, and a narrow sash-window at its side, through which I wondered if the Elephant Man was watching us even then, just on the other side of the darkened glass. At that thought, I felt a prickly coating of unease spread over my scalp.

"We will return here later," the matron said, and strolled on in the direction we'd been going. "When we do so, you will curtsy upon your introduction to Mr. Merrick. You may offer him your hand to shake, if you wish, but as a maid that is not expected of you. I can, however, say that he would deeply appreciate it, and he may extend his hand to you. When it comes to members of our sex, he has a kind of general infatuation. But it is naive and quite innocent, I assure you."

"Then . . . I shall take his hand," I said, though the thought unsettled me. But I did wish to be kind to him.

"Good. I've not found a way to adequately prepare a person for their first encounter with Mr. Merrick. His appearance is quite extraordinary, and his deformity renders his speech difficult to understand."

"I'm sure I'll grow accustomed."

"Most people do, with time. Dr. Treves—you will meet him later this evening—now understands his speech completely, and though I still have some difficulty in that area, Mr. Merrick's appearance strikes me but little."

That offered me a measure of reassurance, though I remembered there had been others before me for whom he had proved too much. We approached the end of the hospital's east wing, where it joined with another building perpendicular to it, and climbed a few steps to another set of doors. Through them, we came into a small, wainscoted foyer decorated with vases and plants, and from which a corridor reached outward and a stair-case climbed both upward and downward.

"This building opened two years ago to better meet the needs of our staff, and you will find it equipped with all modern conve-niences. To your right, down that corridor, you will find my rooms and those of my assistant." She gestured to the left. "Nurses and sisters have their rooms that way. Above us are the nurses' sitting and dining rooms. Servants are below."

I followed her down the staircase to the basement floor, where the air smelled of roasting mutton and potatoes, and having skipped the doss-house breakfast, the aromas wet my mouth. The sound of pots clanging and women's laughter carried down a hall-way toward us on a draft of heat and steam.

"The kitchens," the matron said, "where you will take your meals and collect Mr. Merrick's." She turned in the opposite direc-tion. "And this way you will find the servants' dormitories."

She guided me down a dark and narrow hallway lined with doors to either side, and stopped at the third to the right. "There is an unoccupied bed in this room, I believe." We entered without knocking and found the room empty.

A single high window let in light from what I guessed to be the back side of the building, toward Oxford Street if my orientation was true, but there was a gas lamp in the wall and oil lamps as well, all currently unlit. The plain walls were painted white, the floor made of wood. A tall bureau and three beds occupied the space, the iron bedsteads similar to those I had just seen being scrubbed. Two of the beds had been made, while the third lay bare to the mattress. It was by far the cleanest bolster I had seen in years.

"That one will be yours," the matron said. "You may take one of the empty drawers in the bureau as well. I shall have bedding brought to you momentarily, in addition to your uniform."

"Thank you, ma'am."

"You will keep both in a state of great cleanliness, as well as your person. Once you have your uniform, you will wash yourself and put it on."

"Yes, ma'am."

She waited a moment before speaking again. "Miss Fallow, I can see that life has been quite hard for you. Please feel free to take some hours' reprieve to settle in. Later this evening, I shall come for you and make your introduction to Mr. Merrick."

"Yes, ma'am."

She nodded and had the door halfway closed before I managed to call to her, "Matron Luckes?"

She leaned back into the room. "Yes?"

"Thank you," I said, but had insufficient words for my gratitude. "Thank you very much, ma'am."

She smiled with a warmth that rounded the edges of her regality. "You are welcome. I pray this arrangement will prove mutually beneficial." She nodded again, and this time the door closed all the way, and then I was alone.

I crossed to the bureau and opened the drawers until I found one that was empty. Into this I laid the contents of my bag, all the possessions in the world I owned. There was my other dress, redolent of every inch of street I had walked and every doss-house in which I had slept; a hairbrush; a hand glass I rarely looked in; a couple of frayed ribbons and hairpins; spare stockings and chemise; and finally, my treasured copy of *Emma* by the author Jane Austen.

The book had been my mother's. Miss Austen had delighted her, and before my mother died I spent many evenings with my cheek against her knee as she read aloud to me. I understood little of it, of course, and I believe my mother knew that, but she read the books to me nevertheless, perhaps believing the words would simply soak into me as milk and honey soak into bread. Through everything I'd done, I had not and could not part with this last book of hers, which I had managed to preserve.

A gentle sentimentality prompted me to carry the book to my new bed, where I lay down very slowly. The mattress gave beneath me, and even though I knew it to be of only modest quality, I luxuriated. I could not smell any of its previous occupants, and there were no fleas attacking me from within it.

I reclined on my back and held the book above me. I could not remember the last time I had opened its cover, but did so now, and at the sight and sound of the first sentences I recalled my mother with such clarity that I wondered where she had been hiding all those years. Her voice echoed in my ears and her scent filled the room, that of neroli, the citrus perfume recipe her mother had passed down to her. The power of the memory soon overcame me, and I felt myself suffocating on it, for it did not offer me the nourishment of real air, but merely the illusion of it.

I sat up gasping, the wet sting of tears in my eyes both frightening and rare. I wiped at them furiously, but then realized I had no reason to fear them there, so I lay back down and set them loose. It wasn't a violent sobbing that followed, but rather a slow and careful release of innumerable pains ignored and denied.

I don't know how long I cried there, but a terrible exhaustion followed, which seized me and dragged me down further into the mattress. I closed my sore, spent eyes and slept deeply enough it felt nearly final—

"Miss Fallow?"

I awoke.

A young black woman about my age stood near the bed, wearing the black dress and white apron and cap of a maid. She wore the tight curls of her raven hair pulled up, her features full and smooth, and she smiled when I raised my head.

"Evelyn, is it?" she asked, her voice gentle.

"Yes." I imagine it would've been as difficult to climb from my own grave as it was to rise from that bed, but I somehow reached my feet. "I didn't mean to sleep."

"I won't tell. You slept right through luncheon, though. You must've been awful tired." She held out a neat pile of sheets, atop which were folded a dress, apron, and cap like the ones she wore. "Matron Luckes asked me to bring you these."

I accepted them from her. "Thank you," I said, and turned to put them all down upon the mattress.

When I faced her again, I saw she'd picked up my mother's book. "What are you reading?" she asked.

"That's mine!" I said, and before I could bridle my instinct I snatched it back from her with such force she flinched. I realized then how hard it might be to break the habits of survival I had adopted on the streets. "I'm sorry," I said, and turned the book so she could see its spine. "*Emma*, by Jane Austen. It was my mother's. I don't have much left that was hers."

She peered warily at the gold leaf lettering, which had almost been rubbed away. "You miss her? Your mother, I mean."

"Yes. Very much."

"I miss my mother." She still stared at the book. "She died last spring."

"I'm so very sorry," I said.

"It were cancer took her. Cancer of the lungs. She were in service, too."

"I'm very sorry," I said again.

She bobbed her head and sighed. "I'm Becky Dods. That's my bed." She pointed to the one farthest from mine, then fixed her eyes back on my book, and I wondered if she perhaps wanted to read it, but then I realized she was simply avoiding looking someplace else. My shawl lay on the bed where it had fallen as I slept.

I retrieved it and moved to cover my face. "Forgive me."

"What for?" Becky asked. "Can't help how you look, now can you?"

"No. I suppose not," I said, grateful for the rare kindness, and I presumed she knew something about how people are disposed to judge appearances. My father had employed blacks and lascars alike in the shipping aspects of his business. As a young boy, he'd seen Pablo Fanque's renowned circus, and so deeply impressed was he by Mr. Fanque, he'd told me numerous times that if a man of color could rise to such prominence in reputation and abilities, there seemed no reason to think the black race inferior in any regard. But others did not hold the same opinion.

"Does it hurt?" she asked, and I knew she meant my scars.

"Yes," I said. When the weather changed, it was an ache at the roots of my teeth, and sometimes a pinch in the tight skin at the surface. "On occasion."

She winced, and then said, "Are you really Mr. Merrick's new maid?"

"I am."

"Well, I say that's very Christian of you."

I decided not to argue that. "Thank you, Becky."

"Want help making up your bed?"

"I believe I can manage."

"Suit yourself." She turned toward the door. "I best get back to work. Matron says for you to wash and dress. She'll come for you in a couple of hours." She paused. "You should know that's right generous for her."

"I guessed as much."

"A pleasure meeting you, then." She smiled again and left the room.

After Becky had gone, I pulled the sheets tight over the mattress, along with the quilt, and then went in search of the bathroom. I found one at the end of the hallway not too far from the bedroom. It was clean, tiled in black and white, with a standing sink in one corner and a sloping bathtub on brass feet against the wall. Hot water poured steaming from the spigot after a short wait, and while the tub filled I undressed.

It was a rarity for me to stand naked as a needle, shivering, for I'd seldom found a place where I felt safe enough to do so. But I felt safe there in the hospital, just as I had hoped I would. As I dipped my toe, then my calf into the hot water, a chill climbed up my back and down my arms, and after I'd lowered myself fully into the tub, the surface of the water kissing my chin, my knees like two pale islands, the experience of that simple pleasure nearly set me crying again.

I used the lavender soaps there in the bathroom to clean my skin and hair, clouding the water with my grime, scouring away the streets from my flesh until it turned red and angry. I stayed in there much too long, until the bath was the same temperature as my body. Outside the tub, the drain gurgling behind me, I dried with clean towels and dressed in my new clothes. I returned to the bedroom and brushed my hair, then read from *Emma* until it had dried a little, and afterward risked using the small mirror above the bureau to braid it and pin it up beneath my bonnet. Mirrors were perilous for me, for some blemishes can't be washed away. There'd been many times my reflection had shown me someone I didn't even recognize as myself, but this time, with all the questions about what awaited me filling my mind, I managed to escape without much anguish, and returned to my bed, where I sat and waited.

Though the streets had driven me and battered me and done their best to break me, they hadn't succeeded. Instead, *I* had succeeded in finding a safe place where I could live and hide.

A short while later, there came a knock at the door.

"Miss Fallow?" the matron called through it.

I rose from the bed and smoothed my apron. "Yes, ma'am."

The door opened and in she swept. "Ah, good. You are ready. I trust you find your living quarters comfortable?"

"Quite, ma'am."

She brought her hands together in a silent clap. "Excellent. Then let us go to Mr. Merrick, shall we?"

"Yes, ma'am, of course." I tried to sound pleasant and walk calmly from my room, but I did not feel at all calm.

CHAPTER 3

We stood at the top of the stairwell Matron Luckes had earlier pointed out to me, the same wooden door and darkened windows waiting for us below. I was afraid, even terrified, and my awareness of the hypocrisy in my fear did nothing to assuage it.

"Miss Fallow, your shawl," the matron said.

I nodded and pulled it slowly from my face, feeling my color go with it, draping the cloth instead over my shoulders. Matron Luckes nodded her approval and descended the cement steps. I followed behind her, my heart rattling my ribs.

We arrived before the door, and as the matron reached for the handle, I wanted to tell her to wait before opening it but could not think of a reason for the delay. I only knew I did not want to go into that room. Nothing could have induced me to do so, but for the fact that without this position, I would've been out searching the streets that very moment for a place to spend the night. Thus, as the matron twisted the knob and opened the door, I inhaled and followed her through, my head down.

We came into a dim, plain sitting room, heated by a small fireplace with a wooden mantel lined with pictures and greeting cards. A table bore even more of the cards, as well as a phonograph and a partially completed card model of a church. There was also an especially wide and sloping armchair, a door into a second room, and over in one of the corners, which I avoided looking at directly, a bed with a lumpen figure sitting up in it.

Near the center of the room stood a man of robust build, and he turned toward us when we entered. He appeared to be in his thirties, well dressed, and he wore his thinning hair cropped short, his mustache in wide, twin blades that stabbed toward his jawline. Through his spectacles, his eyes, somewhat small and deep set, regarded me with an intense and intelligent curiosity.

"Matron Luckes," he said, his voice neither deep nor high, but full. "Is this the new attendant you spoke of?"

A sour, cheese-like odor in the room had begun to faintly suggest its presence to me.

"Yes, Dr. Treves," the matron said, with a deference in her voice that diminished her seeming supremacy. "This is Miss Fallow."

Dr. Treves nodded. "Miss Fallow. May I present Mr. Merrick." He gestured with his open palm toward the bed.

I could not avoid looking in that direction any longer, and when I did, something looked back at me.

It was a man only in the most obscure and fundamental sense of the word. A massive and irregular swelling of flesh sat atop its shoulders, approximating a head, with sparse and languid hair, eyes, nose, and, beneath the folds of skin and tissue, a mouth. Its left arm appeared completely normal, slender hinting at delicate, while the other struck out from within the sleeve of its shirt like some kind of anarchistic root intent on bringing down a wall. The rest of its figure lay blessedly hidden from my view beneath the blanket, but I could imagine the subterranean contours of its terrible, fungal form.

I do not know how I managed to keep from instantly fleeing that room, but before I could, the monster spoke, and the gentleness in his voice so opposed the harshness of his appearance, I stood baffled for the moment it took Dr. Treves to translate.

"He said it is a pleasure to meet you," the doctor said.

"I know, sir," I said, for I did. The figure's speech was very slow, but it had struck a bell of recognition in my mind, even wrapped as it was in the loose wool of my confusion and shock. "I understood him, sir."

"You did?" the matron asked.

"Yes, ma'am."

The figure spoke again, and again I struggled to reconcile the musical sound with its source. "How is it you understand me when so many cannot?" he asked.

"I suppose . . ." I touched the puckered scar that lined my altered jaw. "During my convalescence, my own speech suffered terribly, and I was on a ward with others in similar conditions, who likewise found it difficult to speak. We had to learn to understand one another if we wanted companionship."

"Well, this is a rare discovery," Dr. Treves said, his voice rising with jovial enthusiasm. "What do you think of that, John?"

The Elephant Man nodded his great head.

I had thought his name was Joseph, and I turned to Matron Luckes in puzzlement, but Dr. Treves intercepted my question.

"John is the nickname I've given Mr. Merrick," he said, "after so many generous souls made donations to secure his future here at the hospital. John the Beloved, you see. Beloved of London."

"I see," I said, though I believed this nickname to be an exaggeration for the Elephant Man's benefit, for I had never heard him mentioned in the context of any kind of love. In point of fact, the nickname seemed somewhat patronizing.

"Dr. Treves is much too kind," the Elephant Man said, with a ferryman's evenness. "You may call me Joseph, Miss Fallow."

"And you may call me Evelyn," I said.

"Is that acceptable to you, Matron?" Dr. Treves asked.

"She is not a nurse or even a probationer," the matron said. "I see no reason to stand on ceremony."

"Evelyn, then," the Elephant Man said. I looked a bit more closely at the assemblage of folds and flesh that made up his face, for I thought I heard a smile in his voice, but the weight and toughness of his skin did not seem to allow for any outward expression. "I would take your hand in greeting, Evelyn, if my arm were long enough to reach it," he said.

"Oh." I had decided I would let him, so against my revulsion I moved to break the distance between us, the sour odor growing stronger as I approached his bed. He extended his left hand, his good hand, mercifully, and I gave him mine. His skin felt warm and supple, quite unlike the hand of any man I had ever known, or even many of the women. He raised my knuckles to his rough lips in a charming gesture that seemed a deliberate, gentlemanly performance, but not one for my benefit. Rather, it appeared to satisfy Mr. Merrick that he had adequately played a part.

"You appear to have many admirers," I said, glancing around us at all the cards.

"Oh yes," he said, his beautiful voice gaining excitement even as his miscreated face remained rigid. "There are many from Madge Kendal, the famed actress, who is an acquaintance of mine, though we have not had the pleasure to meet in person. The phonograph was a gift from her. On the mantel, you will even find a portrait of Alexandra, the Princess of Wales, which she signed for me."

I peered more closely and discovered the picture of the princess to be but one of a dozen or so different portraits, from many beautiful and highborn women, each signed by its sender. If I hadn't known who occupied this room, I would have suspected it the trophy hoard of some gal-sneaker.

"John the Beloved, indeed," I said, not intending to mock him, but still unsure of the meaning of all the attention lavished on him. I wondered if it had become a kind of game among society women to tease this poor creature with gifts and portraits.

"Many women come to see me," he said. "I am very fortunate to have such friends."

"Indeed you are," Dr. Treves said, pronouncing it as if the matter were settled beyond any further debate.

"May I ask you a question?" Mr. Merrick said to me.

"Of course," I replied.

"What happened to your face?"

It wasn't his directness that surprised me, but rather that I had actually forgotten my shawl was down.

Dr. Treves grunted. "John, she may not want to speak of that. You should wait until you are better acquainted to ask such a question."

"Oh," Mr. Merrick said, with such dismay his whole person seemed to wither. "I'm sorry. I meant no offense. My manners are poor."

"Your manners are very fine," I said. "Think nothing of it."

"I was born with my deformity," he said. "My mother got frightened by an elephant in her pregnancy. It was during a fair, and the beast nearly trampled her."

"That's awful," I said. A moment passed, and I realized he meant for there to follow an exchange, his story for mine, and I resolved to deal as plainly as he had. "I worked in a match factory. The white phosphor poisoned my jawbone, and some of it had to be cut out."

"That's dreadful," Mr. Merrick said. "Why do they use such poison if it hurts the factory workers?"

The question cut a clear path through the bramble of the problem. "I suppose it's more important they make a match that can strike anywhere."

He was silent a moment, and then he closed his eyes. "I am very sorry for you."

Despite his words, it wasn't pity I felt from him, but understanding, and his sincerity touched me, for in spite of the vast chasm between his disfigurement and mine, he seemed in that moment to be as concerned for me, if not more so, than he was for himself.

"That is kind of you," I said.

There came a knock at the door, and two nurses entered the room. They curtsied. "Dr. Treves, Matron Luckes," they said, nearly in unison.

"Ah," the matron said. "My stalwarts, Miss Flemming and Miss Doyle."

"It is time for Mr. Merrick's bath, ma'am," the nurse on the left said.

"So it is," Dr. Treves said. "I shall leave you to it. Good evening, John. See you tomorrow."

"Good evening, Dr. Treves," Joseph said.

"Matron Luckes," Dr. Treves said, "good evening to you. You as well, Miss Flemming. Miss Doyle." He looked at me. "Welcome aboard, Miss Fallow."

"Thank you, sir," I said.

He plowed from the room headfirst, hands clasped behind his back, and after he had gone, Matron Luckes seemed to reclaim her full dominion. "It seems this introduction has gone quite well. Miss Fallow, while the nurses are bathing Mr. Merrick, why don't you see if his dinner is ready."

"Yes, ma'am." I nodded as the nurses helped Mr. Merrick rise from his bed, grateful I would not have to stay and help wash him, for I was not yet accustomed to the sight of his face, to say nothing of the rest of him. Once standing, he teetered a bit on his wide, pachydermic feet, the weight of his head robbing him of balance.

"When Mr. Merrick is finished eating," the matron continued, "clear his dishes and see to any of his other needs before you go to bed. Tomorrow, Miss Dods shall take you through your daily duties."

"Yes, ma'am," I said again.

"I am pleased you are here," the matron said.

"As am I, ma'am."

She nodded and left the room.

Mr. Merrick had steadied himself and now labored on his own toward the inner doorway, followed by the two nurses. He moved by means of a slow and plodding limp, which appeared to cause him considerable difficulty, and perhaps pain, but he managed it. "I shall see you shortly, Evelyn," he said.

"Yes, Mr. Merrick."

He walked through the door, and for a terrible moment I imagined the disrobing soon to take place on the other side, the hideous revelation of his whole person, but I squeezed my eyes shut against the vision and fled the room before I might chance to see it.

Outside, I breathed the carbolic-scented air of Bedstead Square, listening to the scuffing of brush bristles against the bed frames and the distant sounds of the city just reaching over the hospital rooftops. I then replaced my shawl and turned up toward the nurses' house and the kitchens the matron had earlier shown me, the smells of which set my hungry stomach complaining.

Once there, it was a simple matter to identify the cook, a narrow rolling pin of a woman, and wait as she prepared a tray with a glass of water, a glass of beer, and a covered plate.

"You're new," she said as she handed it to me. "Off to the Elephant House, are you?"

"Yes."

"Look here," she said. "You wash his dishes, eh? No one in my kitchen wants to catch whatever it is he's got."

It hadn't occurred to me that his deformity might be contagious. I looked at my hand where he had kissed it, and for a brief,

irrational moment felt the urge to wash. But then I considered
that neither the doctor nor the matron had taken any precautions that way.

"He was born with his condition," I said. "I doubt it's
contagious."

"Oh! Are you a doctor, then?"

Her sarcasm irritated me. "Of course not."

"A nurse, surely."

"No."

"Then shut your sauce-box." She seemed prepared to flatten
me. "I'm in charge here. You wash his dishes, and yours. That's the
end of it. Hear me?"

"Yes, Cook," I said. Back on the street, I would not have let
myself be so cowed, but I wasn't on the street anymore. "I hear you."

"Good. Now get out of my kitchen." She turned her back on
me, and I left with the tray.

When I returned to Mr. Merrick's room, I found him in a dressing gown, seated at his table. His grotesque appearance struck me
anew, not as roughly as it had the first time, but still hard, and it
took me a moment to recover. The nurses, Miss Flemming and
Miss Doyle, were gone, and I noticed the room smelled better, the
sour odor replaced by the fragrance of lavender soap.

I carried the tray to the table and presented Mr. Merrick his
food by lifting the cover from the plate. There were boiled potatoes with parsley, a chunk of roast lamb covered in brown gravy,
and a slice of bread and butter.

Mr. Merrick had already picked up his fork with his left hand,
but he held it aloft, staring at the plate.

"Is something the matter?" I asked. "The food not to your liking?"

"No, it's not that. It's just . . . the cook forgot to cut it again."

I realized then that with his deformed right hand incapable of holding a knife, or any other implement, he needed someone to carve his food.

"Allow me." I took his fork and used his knife to cut up both the potatoes and meat into morsels.

He thanked me after I'd finished and proceeded to eat, and while he focused on his food, I was able to study him with a more careful and deliberate scrutiny than I had been able to before. The girth of his head was incredible, and I wasn't convinced I would've had the span in my arms to take his measurement for a hat. The excess growth of skin appeared to have the quality of a sponge in places, elsewhere that of thickened callus, or even hard bone. These outcroppings had entirely overcome and ruined one side of his face, and the protrusion over his mouth and lips made it impossible for him to eat without smacking and drooling, which I did my best to ignore.

"How do you like the hospital?" he asked.

"I like it very much," I said. "It is far superior to where I've been living."

"And where was that?"

"Wherever I could afford."

He put down his fork. "It was once the same for me. I've slept in the meanest of places. I've lived in that hell on earth they call a workhouse, but I don't like to think on it. The hospital is immeasurably better."

I had long ago resolved never to go to the workhouse. Anyone I'd known desperate enough to do so came out of that infernal place worse for it and refused to ever go back, even if it meant dying in the gutter. What horrors must Mr. Merrick have endured there?

He returned to his meal, and the two of us sat there together as evening fell about us and the room darkened. Try as I might to disregard it, the sight and sound of his eating were enough to turn my stomach, and it was difficult not to contemplate the reality of my position. I was to sit with this monstrous man, cutting his food, watching him attempt to eat it, three times a day, until such a time as Matron Luckes might deem me capable of other work.

A gob of partially chewed lamb tumbled from his mouth to the table. My gorge rose with a swell of nausea at the sight of it, and I felt the need to flee from that room once again, but I stayed in my chair.

"Pardon me," he said.

I shook my head. "No need for pardons, Mr. Merrick."

He wiped at his mouth with the napkin. "I am finished."

"Very good." I rose from the table. "Shall I tend the fire?"

He, too, stood and hobbled the few feet over to his bed. "Yes, if you would."

I crossed the room and knelt before the hearth in the embers' bloody light. The coal hod was nearly empty, but I used the tongs to add more fuel, enough to keep the heat up for several hours. By the time I stood and turned around, Mr. Merrick had climbed back into his bed and was sitting under the covers, his pillows behind his back.

"Would you like me to help you lie down?" I asked.

"I can't sleep that way."

"Why not?"

"The weight of my head. It twists my neck so I can't breathe."

"Then how do you sleep?"

He brought his legs up nearly to his chest and wrapped his arms around his shins, and then laid his forehead upon his knees. "Like so."

"That doesn't look very comfortable."

"Some nights, I rest well. Other nights, I start to think I might be willing to trade breathing for sleep."

"I'm sorry."

"Don't be. Good night, Evelyn. I shall see you in the morning."

"Good night, Mr. Merrick." I took up the tray with his plate and left his quarters.

Outside, the night sky was starless and colorless over the empty square. I turned toward the nurses' house and found my way back to the kitchen, where I washed Mr. Merrick's dishes, though the cook wasn't there to compel me. After that, I went to my room, where I undressed and climbed into my bed. Thoughts of Mr. Merrick kept me awake until Becky came in with another servant she introduced as Martha.

"Where you been?" Becky asked. "You eat supper?"

"No," I said. I'd not given a real thought to my own food, incredibly hungry though I was. It was far from the first night I had gone to bed with an empty stomach, but I hoped it would be the last.

"You been with the Elephant Man?" Martha asked. She had rust-colored hair, an abundance of freckles that stood out against her pale skin, and a sharp voice like that of a coster's boy, used for barking wares.

"Yes, I have," I said.

Becky sat down on her bed, leaning toward me. "What's he like?"

I didn't know if she meant his appearance or his character, but I did not want to talk about the former. "He is very gracious and polite, actually."

"Gracious and polite?" Martha flopped onto her own bed. "That freak of nature?"

"Yes," I said. "He is very well mannered."

"That so? Did he doff his cap and kiss your hand?" Becky said.

"Course he did," Martha said. "He's a proper gentleman, that one."

They both giggled.

"He *is* well mannered," I said, raising my voice, and their laughter ceased. "And undeserving of your mockery."

"Easy now, Evelyn," Becky said. "We meant no harm."

"Just a bit of fun," Martha said.

"Just a bit of fun." I shook my head, a bit surprised at my sudden defensiveness of Mr. Merrick. It's not as though the girls had said anything truly vulgar, and I was sure Mr. Merrick had endured much, much worse. But I did not like to hear them laughing at his expense. "He is a pitiable person," I said.

Becky stared at her hands clasped in her lap. "I suppose . . . you know what that's like."

She referred to my own disfigurement, but did so with the same innocence as before. "Yes, I suppose I do," I said.

"Were it phossy jaw what did it?" Martha asked.

"Yes," I said.

She shook her head. "Well, that's two ends and the middle of a bad lot."

She may well have been sincere in her sympathy, but I wasn't yet prepared to show my back to her, especially considering the way they'd been speaking of Mr. Merrick. Earlier that same day, I might have met these two on the street as enemies.

"Get you some rest, Evelyn," Becky said. "I'm to show you the lay of things tomorrow."

I nodded. "Good night, then." And I lay back down, facing away from them, trying not to listen to their whispers, which continued well into the night. I tried also to ignore the sense that I was defended only by a cold wall of brick and mortar against the patient and merciless streets that waited nearby to reclaim me.

CHAPTER 4

The next morning, I rose, washed, dressed, and sat down for a breakfast of tea and buttered toast with the other servants, all women, before the sun was up. We ate with our elbows touching at a couple of long tables near the kitchen. I tried to keep my shawl in place to hide my jaw as best I could, but eating made that difficult. It seemed news of my appearance had spread quickly among the staff, at any rate, for those at my table either avoided looking at me altogether or gave me sidelong stares.

Near me, a stout barge of a woman with ruddy cheeks named Beatrice read from a newspaper and seemed to believe it her duty to relate the contents to everyone else. "Did you know that Martha Tabram woman was stabbed thirty-nine times?" she said, phrasing as a question what she clearly wanted to state. "Thirty-nine times! A lot of hate behind that knife, I'd wager."

"I hope it were the first strike that killed her," Becky said.

"Remember that Emma Smith?" Martha asked. "She didn't go quick. Poor girl."

Becky shook her head. "I don't like to think on it."

Beatrice let the newspaper topple and peeked overtop of it. "I remember that Smith girl. Someone brought her to the hospital, oh, back in April was it? A gang had got hold of her and—"

"Please." Becky's voice had gained some urgency. "I don't like talking about the departed. The ones what died here in the hospital, leastwise."

Martha turned toward me. "Becky's afeared of ghosts."

"We all got a soul, ain't we?" Becky said.

"Bah! Superstition." Beatrice raised her paper wall of gossip, but she said nothing more about the ignominies and tragedies written there.

I was glad for her silence, for I could have easily been one of the women whose brutal murders they talked about. I'd openly feared for my life so many times, and I shuddered to think how close I had come to such an end, without even knowing it, at the hands of one who prowled the shadows. As for ghosts, I was already haunted by too much of the living world to worry over the spirits of the dead.

A few moments passed before normal conversation resumed, and from it I gleaned a bit about the hierarchy of the hospital. It seemed I was more fortunate in my position than I'd realized. Those servants who lived on the hospital premises were only the highest ranking, attending to the matron, the hospital governor, or the young men training to be doctors and surgeons at the nearby college. Likewise, the women around me all had experience in service, while I had none. I knew myself and my abilities to be much closer to those of the scrubbers and porters who were forced to make their homes out in the city. My assignment to Mr. Merrick was the only reason I was sitting at that table. My scars, it seemed, had at once driven me to the hospital and also secured my place here.

"We'd best hurry," Becky said, tipping back the last of her tea.

I swallowed my final bite of toast, and we rose from the table.

First, Becky showed me where to find the laundry and linens for changing Mr. Merrick's bedding, along with the necessaries for cleaning his rooms. Then, I learned where I could find the small coal and kindling with which to build his fire. Next, she instructed me on his mealtimes for breakfast, luncheon, tea, and dinner.

"And most days the nurses bathe him twice," she said. "Once in the morning, and again in the evening. For the smell."

"I gathered that."

"That's all I was asked to show you," she said as we stood in Bedstead Square. Beyond her basic instruction, she hadn't offered to assist me with my tasks, but from the way she cast a wary eye in the direction of Mr. Merrick's rooms, I guessed that to be in hopes of avoiding him. "You have any more questions, you come find me," she said. "All right?"

"Yes, thank you," I said.

She turned away and hurried toward the hospital's door, while I turned toward Mr. Merrick's, remembering to remove my shawl before I entered.

Inside his room, I found him still asleep in that awkward position of his, and I wondered for a moment how anyone could be comfortable in that manner. I took his coal hod to refill it, and he did not stir until I had returned and begun to kindle the fire back to life.

"Good morning, Evelyn," he said, lifting his great head.

"Good morning, sir," I said. "Did you sleep well?"

"Not until the small hours."

"I'm sorry to hear that."

"Not to worry. I'm accustomed to it. At least I got some rest."

"Shall I fetch your breakfast?"

"Yes, but before you go, could you help me out of bed? I must go to the water closet to relieve myself."

"Oh, um, certainly." I assumed the frankness of his statement was owed to his living in a hospital, where the functions of the body were a common matter, but it was also true that I had heard men speak openly of much worse.

I went to his bedside and pulled and supported him as he stood, momentarily taking from him a measure of the strain his body placed on him constantly. After he had gained his feet and shuffled to the inner door toward his bathroom, I left and retrieved his breakfast from the kitchen.

When I returned, I found him at his table turning over pieces of the card model church.

I placed the tray of food before him. "That's coming along nicely."

"It's the Mainz Cathedral in Germany. I can't work at it alone. The nurses help me with it when they have the time, which isn't very often."

His hinting came with a childlike innocence. "I could help you with it sometime, if you like."

"I would like that very much. Thank you." He put down the piece of card and turned toward his breakfast. In addition to tea, the cook had sent eggs, a sweet bun, toast, and a slice of cold meat, none of which required my help in carving it.

He took a bite of crispy toast. "Evelyn," he asked, "are we better acquainted?"

I wasn't sure what he meant by that question. "Better than what?"

"Better than we were yesterday." He ate some of his eggs. "Dr. Treves said I ought not to ask you about you until we are better acquainted."

Again it was a child's question, and a child's way of asking it, which I would not have expected from a grown man. "How old are you, Mr. Merrick?"

"Twenty-six," he said.

A grown man, to be sure. But he had not lived the life of a man, at least not an ordinary one. "Well," I said. "You may rest assured that we are acquainted well enough for you to ask what you wish."

"Have you also come to the hospital to hide? Like me?" He took another bite of eggs.

His sudden perceptiveness disoriented me; it seemed he had found the kinship in me Matron Luckes had hoped for. "I . . . yes, Mr. Merrick."

"I thought you might," he said. "Hiding is difficult to manage, isn't it? I don't want to be seen. But at the same time, I do want to be seen. Truly seen, that is, beneath my deformity. Did you know I used to stand on a stage, and people would pay twopence to gawk at me? It was right across the street from the hospital, next to a greengrocer's. That was the opposite of hiding, but not one of them truly saw me. Now I am hiding here."

I gestured toward the cards on the mantel and smiled at him. "It doesn't seem you've been hiding very well."

He laughed. "I suppose you are right about that. But at least people finally see me."

There came a knock at the door.

Mr. Merrick asked the caller to enter, and in strutted a very fine young man carrying a violin case, which he set down on the floor. He was tanned, wore common clothes: wool trousers, vest and coat, scuffed leather shoes, and a bowler cap he removed once he'd closed the door behind him. He wore his brown hair short and flashed a smile that could catch a fish in the filthy Thames. I fought a powerful desire to raise my shawl.

"Charles, how good to see you," Mr. Merrick said, and I heard genuine joy in his voice.

"Joseph!" The young man Charles nearly bounded across the room to Mr. Merrick's side. "My ugly bloke, how are you? It's been too long." He clapped Mr. Merrick on the back.

"Too long," Mr. Merrick said. "What have you been doing?"

"Oh, you know me. Some of this, a little of that. I keep telling you to come out with me sometime. I know where to find the jammiest bits of jam." He winked at Mr. Merrick, and then looked at me, directly into my eyes. "But maybe you don't need my help, eh? Who's this? Got yourself a girl, have you?"

"No, not at all." Mr. Merrick spoke with all seriousness. "This is Miss Evelyn Fallow, my new maid. Evelyn, this is Charles Weaver."

"It's a pleasure to meet you, Mr. Weaver," I said.

"Pleasure is mine, Miss Fallow, to be sure. And please, call me Charles." He smiled that fishing lure smile again and then looked back at Mr. Merrick with such ease it seemed he hadn't noticed my scars at all, though they lay bare. "I don't have long today, so what say you? Care for a tune?"

"If you would be so kind," Mr. Merrick said.

"Let me help you to your chair, then." Charles took Mr. Merrick by his arm and around his back, then helped him to his feet. Mr. Merrick shuffled over to his armchair by the fireplace, and Charles supported him as he sat down. I noticed, then, how odd the chair was, canted backward at an angle by ebonized front legs nearly three times as long as its rear feet. This arrangement seemed to allow Mr. Merrick to comfortably recline and rest his head while sitting nearly upright.

Charles went for his violin case, opened it, and pulled out his instrument, a battered old violin. "How about 'The Lights o' London Town'?"

"I shall be pleased with whatever you play, as always," Mr. Merrick said.

Charles nodded, then lifted the violin to his chin and set about tuning it.

"Do you come and play for Mr. Merrick often?" I asked. Something about him spread unease through me, though I could not say what it was.

"When I can," Charles said, between discordant notes and without taking his eyes from the violin's strings. "Not as often as we'd like, eh, Joseph?"

"To be sure," Mr. Merrick said.

A moment later, Charles plucked at the violin and nodded to himself as if satisfied at the sound. "Right, here we go," he said.

The riotous tone that then leapt out of the instrument as he pulled the bow across it filled Mr. Merrick's room to the top and ran over the sides, the sound of the violin exquisite in spite of its shabby appearance, and the song was a familiar one heard in all the music halls. It called to mind the exuberant noise and crowd of a London market at night, with its hawkers selling hot potatoes, ice cream, ale, winkles and oysters and other relishes, cheap medicines, and jewelry.

Mr. Merrick tapped his toe in time with the rhythm, as did Charles as he played with his eyes closed. He was obviously an accomplished and talented musician, with a performer's grace and natural charm that captured his audience's attention and held it.

When he finished, Mr. Merrick applauded, as did I.

"Delightful!" Mr. Merrick said, manifesting the greatest degree of emotion I had yet seen upon his face. "Wonderful!"

"Thank you very much, Joseph." Charles bowed, then looked at me, once again directly into my eyes and not at my jaw some inches lower. "And you, Miss Fallow? What think you of my entertainment?"

"I find it quite diverting," I said.

He bowed once more. "You're a penn'orth o' treacle, you are. How about another?"

"I'd like that," Mr. Merrick said, though the question had been directed at me.

"'Afton Water,' then," Charles said, and began a second song, this one of a gentler inclination, and after the violin had sung some lovely notes, Charles offered his own voice in complement to his instrument.

> *Flow gently, sweet Afton, among thy green braes,*
> *Flow gently, I'll sing thee a song in thy praise.*

His voice had the solidity of old wood with deep grain, dark stain, and smooth varnish, and he employed it with the same skill as he did his violin.

> *My Mary's asleep by thy murmuring stream,*
> *Flow gently, sweet Afton, disturb not her dream.*

The tune was another I'd heard before, a love song about a woman as much as an ode to a waterway, and it was exactly the sort of music I had long since dismissed.

> *Thy crystal stream, Afton, how lovely it glides,*
> *And winds by the cot where my Mary resides,*
> *How wanton thy waters her snowy feet lave*
> *As gathering sweet flowrets she stems thy clear wave.*

I knew no man would ever make me the object of such praise or adoration, and it seemed a fantasy to imagine it otherwise, yet that seemed to be the lie that every man singing upon a stage wanted me to believe. Well, I was determined not to be so deceived, and when this performance was finished I followed it with less applause than I had given Charles for the previous song.

"Another?" Mr. Merrick asked.

"Afraid I must be off," Charles said, tucking the violin in the crook of his arm. "But I'll try to visit again later in the week. Will I see you again, Miss Fallow?"

"That's quite possible," I said, "even if unintentional."

"And what if I intend it?" Charles asked as he stooped to replace his violin in its case.

In that moment I began to suspect him of mocking me. I couldn't imagine why he would intend to see me at all. "I can do nothing about your intentions, Mr. Weaver, even if I had the desire."

"Charles," he said.

"You're quite a performer, Mr. Weaver." I decided to tease his vanity with a false compliment of my own. "Clearly you belong on the stage."

"I thank you for that," he said. "Yes, I've played many a music hall."

"Then I'm sure you'll have no trouble finding yourself another audience besides me. Good day, Mr. Weaver."

He smiled, then shrugged, before putting his bowler back on. "Good day to you, Miss Fallow." He strode to the door, opened it, and turned back. "'Til next time, Joseph, my ugly bloke."

"Until next time, Charles," Joseph said.

The door shut, and Charles's shadow passed across the window as he climbed the cement stairway.

"I wish I could go to a music hall," Joseph said. "Or the theater. I would so love to watch a pantomime. Perhaps my friend Mrs. Kendal could arrange it?"

"Perhaps," I said, my ear divided between what Mr. Merrick said and the echo of Charles's presence in the room. I still had trouble identifying why he unsettled me.

"I hear there are amazing spectacles to behold on the stage," Mr. Merrick said.

"I've never been."

"Amazing spectacles, they say."

"How did you come to meet Charles?" I asked.

"Oh, his father was a bricklayer working on the new Grocers Wing of the hospital. Charles came to see him one day with his violin, and Dr. Treves asked if he might play for me. We have been friends ever since."

"I see." At least the affection Charles showed for Mr. Merrick appeared genuine.

Mr. Merrick remained in his chair for the rest of that morning as I changed his sheets, which needed to be cleaned as frequently as his person. When the nurses came to give him his first bath, I went to fetch his luncheon, and he asked if I might also bring him a book from the hospital's library.

"Certainly," I said. "Do you have a title in mind?"

"I've recently enjoyed the novels of Miss Jane Austen," he said.

"Miss Austen? But she's a favorite of mine, as well! My own copy of *Emma* is one of my dearest possessions."

"I've read it!" Mr. Merrick said. "Oh, do you ever wonder what Emma and Mr. Knightley are doing? I think they must've had children by now, don't you? A son and a daughter, I imagine. I wonder what they named them."

I didn't know what to make of those questions. It pleased me to know he and I shared this in common, but he spoke almost as though the characters in the book were real people, rather than figments. I chose to say nothing to dispute that.

"Are there any of Miss Austen's novels you haven't read?" I asked.

"*Northanger Abbey*," he said.

"Then I shall see if they have a copy of it."

With that, I left the room and found my way to the hospital's library by asking for directions from the staff I encountered, and discovered it in the medical college at the southwest corner of the hospital grounds. The library was a long, open room, with towers of bookshelves and many desks where several students hunched over their studies. A wide alcove of windows looked out over the large garden field in which the hospital's vegetables and fruits were grown. Before I could venture deeper into the room, a bald, bespectacled man appeared before me, short and round as a cabbage.

"Can I help you?" he asked.

"Yes, sir," I said. "Mr. Merrick would like to know if you have a copy of *Northanger Abbey*. By Miss Jane Austen."

"Oh." He sniffed. "A *novel*."

"Yes, I—"

"We have a small collection of those for the patients. Wait here." He turned away before I could finish speaking and disappeared between two banks of shelves, returning a few minutes later with a volume in his hand. "There you are, for Mr. Merrick. I noticed it has never been loaned before." His tone and mild smirk suggested this pleased him.

I accepted the book from him. "Thank you. I—"

"Is there anything else?"

"No, sir, that—"

"Then, good day."

He blinked at me, clearly waiting for me to leave, which I did, and crossed the hospital grounds to the kitchens. There I claimed Mr. Merrick's luncheon and returned to his rooms with both his meal and his book. The nurses had finished bathing him and gone, and I set his food before him at the table.

While he ate, he asked, "Would you read the novel aloud to me?"

"Of course," I said, delighted, and soon found myself engrossed in it such that several hours passed and I forgot to fetch Mr. Merrick's tea, only giving a thought to his dinner when the nurses came to offer him his evening bath. He didn't seem to mind my lapse, and asked that I read to him again the next day, and the day after that.

We passed several days this way. I read to him at the table, at his bedside, and near the fireplace as he sat in his peculiar chair, breaking from this diversion only for our discussions of the book, his meals, and washing, as well as his occasional visitors. Dr. Treves came to see him daily, and Matron Luckes every few days. I wasn't certain the matron approved of my reading Mr. Merrick a novel, but I supposed she likely disapproved of novels in general, and anyway she said nothing to discourage it.

The novel was quite different from *Emma*, and—Mr. Merrick agreed—from any of Miss Austen's novels he had previously read. It was eerie and spoke of ghosts and vampires, which seemed to thrill Mr. Merrick, but which I tried to scoff at inwardly.

Yet late one Thursday evening after dinner, while reading the second volume of the novel, our heroine, Catherine, finally came to the abbey for which the book was named, a storm descended upon that gothic estate, and I felt the first tingle of fear at the base of my neck. The novel's gloomy, drafty corridors along which murmurs crept, and its distant moans and rattling locks, all vividly described by Miss Austen, insinuated a sinister air into the immensity and oppressiveness of the hospital, and I recalled with dread what Becky had suggested about the ghosts of the dead.

Such was my fear, I found myself reluctant to turn each page and keep reading, and when the door to Mr. Merrick's room opened suddenly, both he and I startled and gasped.

"I'm sorry to be late for your bath," Miss Doyle said, slightly short of breath, a flush reddening her porcelain cheeks. She had come by herself, but I hadn't thought of her tardiness until that moment.

"Where is Miss Flemming?" I asked.

"In the receiving room. There's a terrible fire down at the docks, and most of the staff are standing ready for any wounded." She brushed past me toward the inner door. "You are to help me wash Mr. Merrick."

My fear at the thought of ghosts suddenly fled before a fear of something much more real.

CHAPTER 5

I stammered a bit in protest. "Miss Doyle, I don't believe I'm qualified—"

"There is no one else," the nurse said. "The matron said you are to assist me, and we are to be as quick about it as possible so I can return to my post." She disappeared through the doorway, I heard the echo of water pouring into a tub, and then she returned. "Sorry to rush, Mr. Merrick. Are you ready?"

"Of course," he said, sitting forward in his chair. "If you would kindly help me up."

As Miss Doyle took his arm and gently pulled him to his feet, I felt immobilized by a sudden and growing pain in my stomach, and stupefied by the scattering of my panicked thoughts. I did not want to wash him. Though I had grown somewhat accustomed to his face, I desperately did not want to see his body exposed, nor touch it, and I felt terribly guilty about that.

As Mr. Merrick limped toward the inner door, Miss Doyle called to me and roused me from my stupor. "Miss Fallow, please. You are needed."

"I . . . might I have word with you, Miss Doyle?"

She scowled but sent Mr. Merrick on his own through the doorway and returned to me. "What is it?" she asked.

"I don't think I can do this," I said.

"Do what?"

"*Bathe* him," I said.

She took me by the arm in a firm grip and lowered her voice to a menacing whisper. "Do you suppose this is an easy task for me, Miss Fallow? Because it is not. It is my Christian duty, and I would think a person in your *condition* would show more compassion."

My burden of guilt grew heavier.

She continued, "And let's not forget your status here, should the matron learn you have failed in your duties. Do I make myself clear enough on that point?"

The open threat in her words carried sufficient force. I couldn't lose my position. "Clear enough," I said.

"Good. Then let us do our duty."

She led the way and I followed her through the inner doorway, down a short passage, into Mr. Merrick's bathroom. In it he had a water closet and a bathtub similar to the one I had used in the maids' dormitories. A single, flickering gas lamp lit the room from one wall, and Mr. Merrick stood undressing in its glow and the steam from the hot water, his back mercifully toward me.

I balled my hands into fists and tightened the muscles in my limbs against the shaking that had begun to seize them, then forced myself to cross the room toward him. Miss Doyle reached him before I did and helped him remove his shirt, trousers, and drawers, exposing the extent of the devastation wrought by his disorder, while I could only stand in horror and watch. The same growths that had claimed his head and his arm had obliterated his back and his sides, with somewhat lesser destruction of his legs. I averted my eyes from the fleshen drapes of his buttocks and noted the cruel curvature of his spine, like a wet rag someone had wrung out and left twisted.

Miss Doyle gently took his left arm, his untainted arm, and turned to glare at me over Mr. Merrick's shoulder. "Miss Fallow, take his other arm and we'll help him into the bath." Her voice remained pleasant, even if her eyes did not.

"Yes, Miss Doyle," I said, then stepped up beside Mr. Merrick and locked arms with him in a ghastly imitation of a Sunday stroll. I kept my gaze up and forward, so as to avoid seeing his manhood, and did my best to adopt Miss Doyle's expression of decorum.

Together, she and I walked him to the tub and steadied him as he climbed in, his smell sharp in my nose, his skin rough and trembling beneath my fingers. Once he was submerged in the water, leaning forward, Miss Doyle handed me a sponge and bar of soap, and then she went to work, first softening her own sponge in the bathwater, then lathering it with soap and scrubbing Mr. Merrick's back. I did the same, slowly and reluctantly, the pleasantness of the warm water and smell of lavender from the soap doing little to calm my nerves. After we'd finished with his back, Miss Doyle moved to cleaning his head, from which patches of dark hair sprouted like weeds from between the crags of his flesh.

I'd so far managed to contain my revulsion, but felt myself on the verge of losing restraint, assaulted as I was by thoughts I knew to be irrational and fears I knew to be false. Mr. Merrick was not contagious nor was he cursed, and yet I couldn't reassure myself of these things; I was overwhelmingly repelled. When Mr. Merrick leaned suddenly backward, I caught a glimpse of his manhood beneath the water. The sight of it was too much for me and I recoiled, staggering away from the bathtub with my eyes clenched shut, forearms dripping water.

"Evelyn?" Mr. Merrick asked with his soft voice.

"Miss Fallow?" asked Miss Doyle with a great deal more hardness.

I opened my eyes and my mouth. "I . . ." But nothing could have brought me back to that bathtub, so I turned away from them, toward the door. "I must go," I mumbled, and hurried from the room.

"Miss Fallow!" I heard Miss Doyle call, but I ignored her and fled Mr. Merrick's quarters, rushing up the flight of steps into the square.

There I paused briefly, the image still clinging to my eyes, before rushing along the wing through smoke-laden air toward my room. Once there, I found Becky and Martha already preparing for bed, having finished their duties. Both of them stared as I burst in and threw myself onto my bed, where I let the trembling take me. I knew very well the consequences of what I had done. This life I had only just found would be taken from me.

"What is it?" Becky asked, coming over.

I covered my face and shook my head.

"There now," Martha said. "We're your friends, ain't we?"

I looked at her. I hadn't called any woman friend since I'd worked in the match factory. I hadn't even let myself hope for that here.

"I can't," I said.

"Yes, you can." Becky spoke as if coaxing a cat from a barrel. "We've all had our share. You'll feel better."

I shook my head again, but then said, "I had to bathe Mr. Merrick."

They were both silent for a moment, looking at each other.

"But that's the nurses' job," Becky said.

"Miss Doyle made me help. But I ran away. And now Matron Luckes will sack me."

Becky frowned a moment. "I don't think the matron will sack you. She got no one else for the job, does she? Most don't last more than a day. And the way you been reading to him and everything?"

I tried to take comfort in what she said, but I didn't dare to hope she was right.

"So you saw him, then?" Martha asked. "Whiles he was naked?"

I could only nod, still at the mercy of those memories.

"So did you see it?" Martha asked.

"See what?" I asked.

"You know," she said. "His tackle."

Becky gasped. "Martha, you devil!"

"What, me?" Martha opened her hands wide in a shrug. "I'm rightful curious, is all. Ain't you?"

Becky shook her head, and I sat upright in my bed. "I am *not* going to talk about that," I said.

"Oh, come on, we won't tell," Martha said. "Is it like an elephant's trunk? Just say whether—"

"No!" I allowed some of the street back into my voice. "You know what's good for you, you'll drop it."

"Easy there," Martha said. "I meant no harm. Becky, tell her—"

"I'm with Evelyn," Becky said. "It weren't a proper question."

"Couple of nuns, the both of you," Martha said, chuckling as she walked over to her bed.

Becky scowled at her, but then smiled at me and reached out to take my hands in hers. "You'll sort it out with the matron in the morning. You'll see. Try not to worry."

I nodded, but the matron was only a part of my concern. I'd likely insulted Mr. Merrick deeply with my escape. He seemed so fragile, and it pained me to think that I'd caused him any degree of hurt. I knew what it was to have someone recoil from me, and yet I had just done the same to him. But there also remained a splinter I couldn't quite pinch as I first prepared for bed and then lay there in the darkness while Martha snored.

"You awake, Evelyn?" Becky whispered, sometime later.

I thought about leaving her unanswered, but whispered, "Yes."

"What did it look like? Mr. Merrick, I mean? Sorry to ask, but I can't sleep for thinking about it. Blast her."

Unlike Martha, I knew Becky's question was innocent, and I answered her honestly. "It was perfectly ordinary."

"Really?" she said.

"Yes."

"Well, that's . . . good for him, then." She paused, and her voice took on a shade of mischief. "How you know what common looks like, anyway?"

I smiled in the darkness. "I've seen enough drunkards pissing in the street, or tending to other . . . needs. With ladybirds."

"Men are all the same, ain't they?"

"I . . . suppose," I said, but her words had just got the splinter out. Until tonight, I hadn't truly seen Mr. Merrick as a man. If he'd been deformed down there as I'd expected him to be, he could have remained in my estimation nothing but the pitiable, child-like creature I'd thus far known.

"Think I can sleep now," Becky said. "Night, Evelyn."

"Good night," I said, but then I couldn't sleep. My guilt redoubled at what I'd done. I still worried for my own position, but I felt a greater distress at knowing that Mr. Merrick may have suffered at my hands. I needed to make amends to both him and the matron.

In the early hours of the morning, I rose, washed, and dressed. The kitchen had only begun to stir, so I made myself a cup of tea under the stern eye of the cook and had it with a buttered slice of the previous day's bread. When finished, I stepped out into Bedstead Square, where I found the sky still dark and full of storm clouds, and the odor of smoke from the dock fire still sharpening the chilled air. I thought it might be too early in the morning to go to Mr. Merrick and apologize, but I worried that if I was going to be sacked, I wouldn't have another chance to speak with him again.

I decided to risk the hour, thinking he might be awake in his sleeplessness, and strode in the direction of his quarters through the utterly quiet and lonely courtyard. On the streets, I'd made it a habit to avoid such empty places, for they seldom truly were, and I felt a familiar apprehension unsettling my nerves as I recalled the haunted Northanger Abbey. The sound of my footsteps echoed up the walls and along the east wing, and the shadows of broken bed frames clawed upward around me. I hurried my pace and had nearly reached Mr. Merrick's door when the sight of something stopped me.

A woman stood absolutely still at the top of his stairs, her back toward me, pale as a statue. I had no idea where she might have come from so suddenly. I had heard no other footsteps in the courtyard but mine.

"H-hello?" I called to her.

She ignored me.

As I drew closer to her, my heart pounded. A sensation of wrongness scraped my bones and set a terrible ache in my jaw.

She wore what might have been a wedding gown, though why she should be so dressed, in that place, at that hour, I could not say. She was short, perhaps five feet, and still she hadn't turned toward me.

I called to her again, and this time she turned her head slowly toward me. She was young, perhaps twenty years old, her skin like pale cambric, her eyes gray hollows filled with such sadness they stole my breath. I took a step backward, nearly choking. She then descended the cement stairs, without a sound, and Mr. Merrick's door creaked opened without her touching it.

"No," I said, my voice weak. "You can't—"

She stepped through into the darkness and the door closed, leaving behind the unrelenting chill of a winter fog, though it was not yet autumn.

I didn't know what to do. I believed—I *feared*—that I'd just seen a ghost. I tried to tell myself I was wrong, that it must have sprung from the novel I'd been reading to Mr. Merrick, as well as Becky's suggestion. But I had no other explanation for what I'd seen, nor for what I had felt.

I resolved to go into Mr. Merrick's room to make sure he was safe, although that was the last thing I wanted to do. For several moments, I couldn't make my feet obey and move a single step. By the time I did reach the top of the stairs, a new doubt arose and weakened my intention.

I heard Becky's voice echo in my mind. *Men are all the same, ain't they?*

There was another possibility, more believable than a ghost. I wondered if I had simply witnessed a clandestine tryst between Mr. Merrick and a willing young woman. Though I found the idea scandalous, it seemed possible that for the right price he might be able to pay for certain services. His musician friend, Charles, could no doubt arrange such a thing. If that were the case, I most assuredly did not want to enter his room and witness it. So I stepped away from the staircase, desperate to believe the woman I had seen was actually flesh and bone.

Rather than go back to my room, I went instead into the main hospital, with my face hidden behind my shawl, and passed the silent, sleeping wards of the east wing, into the main entry and receiving room. There, I beheld and smelled some of the aftermath of the dock fire. Porters and scrubbers worked on cleaning blood and black from the floors, while a few of the conflagration's more fortunate, less injured victims still waited for treatment, many of them lascars. There was a blood-streaked midwife there, a leathery old hag with a frown that would drive a saint to confession, and I wondered if a pregnant woman had somehow been caught up in the accident. As I walked over to the attending nurse's desk, my shawl slipped open, and the midwife gasped.

"That's a pretty scar you've got," she said, her voice a croak.

I ignored her and spoke to the attendant. "Excuse me, is Miss Doyle somewhere nearby?"

"She is quite busy," the nurse said, eyes bruised with exhaustion. "And has been all night."

"I know," I said, but felt my position depended upon my speaking to her before she went to the matron. "I must speak with her about Mr. Merrick."

"Oh," the nurse said, leaning back. I'd gambled on the effect of his name and won, for she clearly did not want to deal with matters relating to the Elephant Man. "In that case, I best get her for you. Wait here." She left me and went into one of the examination rooms. A moment later, she returned with Miss Doyle.

"Yes, Miss Fallow?" Miss Doyle said, followed by the kind of sigh that left no breath inside her. Her apron below her bosom had not a bit of white showing and had gone rigid with blood.

"Miss Doyle," I said. "I wanted to speak to you about Mr. Merrick."

She blinked, as if bringing me into focus. "Mr. Merrick?"

"Yes. I must apologize. Last night, I didn't mean—"

"Stop." She closed her bloodshot eyes and laid the back of her hand against her glistening forehead. "Have you not looked around you? Do you not suppose there are more important matters to worry about?"

"I . . . I'm sorry. It's just that—"

"Evelyn, listen to me. I was angry with you, I admit, but after the night we've all just had, I am tired, and I've lost any inclination to carry the matter further."

"Truly?" I stepped toward her in gratitude and relief. "Thank you, Miss Doyle, I—"

"Though your coming here, taking me away from my patients, is most inappropriate. My inclination might easily change. If you fail again in the least regard, the matron shall hear of it. Do we have an understanding?"

"Yes, we do, and I'm ever so grateful—"

"Good." She shook her head. "I must get back." And she left without another word.

I stood there a moment longer, and then ventured out into the hospital's gardens feeling slightly stunned at my fortunes. The shy sun had finally allowed a blush of first light, and I strolled among the flower beds until it reached a full glow, feeling a tremendous relief that I would not be sacked. At least, not yet. But I was now indebted to Miss Doyle, and that was a condition I had never before permitted myself. Debts were dangerous.

I waited until I felt it safe to return to Mr. Merrick's room, and even then I knocked before entering. I found him alone, abed in much the same state as every other morning I'd gone to him, but he nevertheless appeared differently to me now, and I trusted less in his innocence. Even so, I apologized to him for the way I'd fled his room the night before.

"I don't know what came over me," I said. "I think it was the heat and steam from the bath, perhaps. I felt dizzy."

"That's quite all right," he said, yawning. "I'm just glad to see you are well. I worried about you." A dourness weighed down his musical voice.

"Thank you, Mr. Merrick." I went to tend his fire, and when I'd finished with that, I turned back to him. "Shall I bring your breakfast?"

"Thank you," he said, yawning again.

"You seem tired." I was divided between wanting an answer to the question of his night visitor, and not wanting to know. By that point, I'd fully convinced myself the woman could not have been a spirit. "Did you . . . sleep well?"

"Not so well, no."

"Oh?"

"No. But perhaps tonight I shall not be disturbed."

"You were disturbed?" I thought that an odd choice of word for an assignation.

"I—" He stopped and stared at the door for a moment. "Never mind. I'm well enough."

"Would you like to sleep longer? I could bring your breakfast at a later time."

"No, bring it now, please," he said.

He apparently did not want to speak of the young woman who'd entered his room, and I accepted that.

"As you wish, Mr. Merrick."

He said nothing, and appeared to have withdrawn very far into his own thoughts, staring in my direction as I left his room, but not, it seemed, at me. Rather, his eyes were still fixed on the door.

CHAPTER 6

When I returned with his breakfast, I found Mr. Merrick still weighed under by a darkened spirit, and it did not lift from him as we went about the day's routine of his bath—late, by an exhausted yet indefatigably cheerful Miss Doyle and Miss Flemming—and my changing his bedding. Afterward, when I asked if he'd like to resume our reading of *Northanger Abbey*, he quickly and firmly declined.

"Very well," I said. "Perhaps another day, then."

"No," he said. "I find I'm not enjoying it as much as I'd hoped. You may return it to the library, with my apologies to Miss Austen."

"Very well," I said, and put the novel aside. "What shall we do, then?"

"Would you mind helping me with my card church?"

"Not at all," I said.

So we went to the table and worked together on the cathedral he had partially assembled. It was a rather complicated model, with a central structure comprised of many delicate pieces, its six spires, with buttresses and windows, all printed with the color and lines of masoned stone. We sorted it all out, largely without speaking, and went to work folding and fixing the paper edges together with glue. During the process, I tried as much as possible to let Mr. Merrick handle the construction, and merely offered him assistance when he required a second hand. Before long, we had made some headway, having raised one of the towers, and it was time for me to fetch his luncheon.

When I returned, I found Charles had come back to visit Mr. Merrick, and I greeted the violinist with apprehension and some irritation.

"Miss Fallow," he said, flashing that smile. "I was hoping to see you."

"Were you?" I said, keeping my back stiff and my voice even as I placed Mr. Merrick's meal on the table.

"Of course," Charles said. "I thought I made my intentions clear the last time we spoke. Come, take off your scarf and enjoy some music. I was just about to play for Joseph here."

I hadn't yet removed my shawl after my walk from the kitchens, and aside from Matron Luckes, no one had ever invited me to do so before. I'd long since learned that most people would rather I keep it in place, but I lowered it for Charles hesitantly, feeling exposed and somewhat disarmed by the casualness of his request.

"This one's called 'Bloomsbury Square,'" he said, and proceeded to play and sing.

> *I'm a good-natured fellow, pray let me confess,*
> *And I can't bear to see a female in distress.*
> *While crawling up west a few weeks since, I met*
> *with a little adventure I'll not soon forget . . .*

From there, the song told of how a rather gullible gentleman got swindled out of ten pounds by a woman claiming to have

forgotten her purse at home—a home in Bloomsbury Square, naturally, at an address occupied only by an old codger—and he paid
not only her cab fare but the cost of a new silk dress. I'd heard the
song played in beer houses, and it was customary for the whole
drunken lot inside to join discordantly in singing the chorus:
"Bloomsbury Square! Bloomsbury Square!" Neither Mr. Merrick
nor I did so, which was likely a disappointment to Charles.

In fact, when the song ended, not only did Mr. Merrick not
laugh, he sounded quite agitated. "Well, what—what happened to
the young lady?" he asked.

Charles chuckled. "She was given six months reflection by
the law."

Mr. Merrick sputtered. "She went to jail?"

"Of course, man!" Charles said. "That's the point! You'd like it
better if she got away with it?"

"But surely there must have been some misunderstanding."
Mr. Merrick shook his head. "Perhaps the gentleman misunder-
stood the address she gave, or he failed to remember it correctly."

"She wrote it down for him," Charles said. "The song said as
much. Weren't you listening?"

"But—"

"She swindled him! Trust me, there's women will take your
very last farthing and curse you for a miser whilst doing it."

"I can't believe it," Mr. Merrick said. He seemed genuinely
affronted on behalf of the girl in the song. It endeared him to
me once again, and I wondered if I'd been wrong in my suspi-
cions. "Such a lovely young lady would never do a thing like that,"
he said.

"Suit yourself, my ugly bloke," Charles said, pointing an accusing finger at Mr. Merrick. "But don't you say I never did warn you about women."

"I doubt I'll ever have cause to say that," Mr. Merrick said. "For . . . many reasons. Some of which I think are quite obvious."

I heard a caged pain break through the bars of those last few words. I'd only truly learned for myself Mr. Merrick was a proper man the previous night, and just then I realized he was also quite aware that no woman would ever have him as such.

"Easy, there, Joseph. Have a look at that there mantel." Charles had let down his jolly bravado and now spoke gently. "You've got a treasure hoard of cards and lovelies would make any man green with envy, and you can count me one of 'em."

Mr. Merrick kept his eyes downward, clearly still frustrated. "I still think you got it wrong about the young lady in the song."

"Perhaps I did get it wrong." Charles nodded with his nose pointed at the floor. "Perhaps I did. No stranger to mistakes am I, that's for certain." I'd heard the song before and knew he hadn't mistaken its lyrics, but I appreciated his kindness to Mr. Merrick. "I'll pick a better tune next time, eh?" Charles bent to put his violin away.

"I meant no offense, Charles," Mr. Merrick said.

"Well, that lets me off the hook, then, 'cause I took none." It seemed his bravado didn't stay down for long. "'Til next time."

"Wait," Mr. Merrick said. "Before you go . . . might I ask you a question?"

"As sure as the river reeks," he said. "Ask me."

"Do you believe in spirits?"

The image of the pale woman crept into my imagination. The cold hollow in my chest returned at the memory of her, and Mr. Merrick's question seemed to confirm my fears.

"What?" Charles said. "Ghosts, you mean?"

Mr. Merrick nodded. "Yes."

Charles rubbed his chin, and I heard the scratch of his stubble. "That's an odd question," he said. "I reckon I do. Them Spiritualists is mighty convincing."

"I see," Mr. Merrick said. "Thank you. It was good to see you."

Charles blinked, then nodded. "Right. Pleasure to see you, too." Then he turned to me. "Miss Fallow, might I have a word with you outside?"

His request startled me a little, and I agreed before I'd given it a real thought. A moment later I stood outside with him on the cement stairs. "Yes, Mr. Weaver, what is—"

"Call me Charles."

I could not help but give him a slight glare. "I have work to do," I said. "What did you wish to speak with me about?"

"First, you call me Charles."

His bravado had swelled to impudence. "You think you're in a position to bargain?"

He smiled. "I think you want to know why I asked you out here."

"Not particularly," I said, though that wasn't entirely true, but I refused to let him think he had got the better of me. "However, if calling you *Charles* will get me off these steps that much quicker, I'm happy to oblige."

"There, that weren't so hard. That's music to my ears, that is."

"But it's a tune I fear is going out of fashion very soon."

"Then I best enjoy it whiles I can." He removed his bowler cap with a flourish. "Do me the honor of walking with me this Sunday?"

"I . . ." I had not expected that at all. "You mean . . ."

"Surely I do. A walk to a park, or maybe even to church. Lord knows I could do with a spot of church. Afterward, perhaps we could eat some ice cream."

I didn't know how to suppress the rising storm of panic and confusion inside me. Surely he mocked me, for why else would he ask me that? Yet his demeanor seemed earnest. Still, I could not fathom going with him anywhere, least of all out in the very streets I'd come into the refuge of the hospital to escape. He would offer no protection from what I knew lay beyond the hospital walls.

"No, thank you," I said. "I'm afraid I must work."

"When you get your day off, then?"

"It's not just that. I don't . . . go walking. With anyone."

"Why not?"

He knew exactly why, and his feigned ignorance angered me. "Do *not* mock me."

"I'm not mocking you," he said. "Upon my sivvy, I'm not."

My anger multiplied. "You are. You know very well why I don't go walking about—"

"Wear your shawl, then, if you like."

"No." I turned away from him and descended the steps to Mr. Merrick's door. "My answer is no, Mr. Weaver."

"Ah," he said, frowning. "The song is ended."

I said nothing more as I opened the door and went back inside, where I breathed deeply and tried to hide my frightened and angry quivering, but Mr. Merrick noticed.

"Are you all right, Evelyn?" he asked.

"Yes, Mr. Merrick," I said.

"What did Charles want? Or is it impolite of me to ask?"

"I take no offense at you, Mr. Merrick. He asked if I would go for a stroll with him."

He was silent for some time. "And will you?"

"No."

"Because of your scars?"

"Yes," I said, though it was more complicated than that simple answer.

"I should like to go walking, if I could. I used to walk about the hospital gardens at night, when I wouldn't disturb anyone."

Charles had to realize what he was asking, and the easy way he'd asked it, as if it would be nothing for me, made me angry. Even if I'd had no ambivalence about him as a man, I had no desire to go strolling about to once again be the subject of ridicule and hatred. I decided to change the subject away from myself, toward the thing I wanted and yet feared to know.

"Mr. Merrick, may I ask you a question?"

"Of course," he said. "I've certainly asked questions of you."

My voice fell to a whisper without my meaning it to, and my heart beat apace. "Was it a . . . a ghost that came into your room early this morning?"

Though his face remained rigid, I saw him swallow, and his gaze darted about the room, everywhere and anywhere but my face. "No one came into my room," he said.

"But I saw a young woman. She was—"

"No," he said, raising his voice. "No one came into my room."

I decided not to press him, for it obviously caused him distress, perhaps even fear, which made my own fear even worse. "Very well, then," I said. "Would you, um, like to eat? I believe cook made a sandwich."

"No," he said. "I am not hungry."

"Very well. Would you like to work on your model?"

"No."

He was sounding like a petulant child, and in my state I didn't have much patience for it. "Mr. Merrick, is there anything else you need from me?"

"No."

"In that case, I shall see to your bedding."

He made no reply to that, so I gladly left him and took his soiled sheets to the hospital's laundry, where I overheard the washerwomen gossiping in the steam about another murder the previous night but one street away from the hospital, on a narrow alleyway called Buck's Row. The washers knew little beyond rumor—a prostitute, they said, like the Tabram woman who'd been stabbed—but at breakfast the next morning Beatrice held the *East London Advertiser* before her and gladly related all the known aspects of the crime. I didn't want to listen, but Beatrice's voice forced some of the details in.

"Throat cut ear to ear," she said. "Abdomen was completely ripped open, with the bowels protruding. They don't know who she is, poor soul. Age thirty-five to forty. Five feet two inches in height."

"That's awful," Martha said.

"Dreadful business, to be sure," Beatrice said. "There be a demon at work in Whitechapel, and mark me, the police won't do nothing about it."

"Don't say that," Becky said. "'Course they will."

"What, fuss over a couple of dead prostitutes?" Beatrice folded her newspaper and slapped it on the table. "Not likely."

I agreed with her on that point at least, for aside from the Salvation Army and other such Christian missions, the world seemed willing to leave the East End festering unto itself. While the rest of London brightened with electric lamps, gaslit Whitechapel remained the city's black shadow. Nobody thinks or cares about their shadow.

I turned toward Becky and whispered to her, "Has a young bride died recently in the hospital?"

She lowered the dark skin of her brow. "That's a strange question."

"Has one?"

"Not that I've heard," she said.

Following my breakfast, I brought Mr. Merrick his and found him in somewhat better spirits than the day before, though he ate but little of his food. Miss Doyle and Miss Flemming came shortly to bathe him, and afterward I worked with him again on his church model for a time, and we raised another of its towers. Through it all, I felt as though the ghost of the young bride haunted our interactions.

"Would you read to me again?" he asked as we surveyed our craftsmanship.

"Certainly," I said.

"Perhaps your copy of *Emma*?"

"Of course," I said.

"You mentioned it was dear to you."

I nodded. "It was my mother's. She used to read it to me."

"I wish that I had one of my mother's books," he said. "She was a Sunday school teacher, you know. She was educated and very beautiful." He pointed toward the mantel. "There is a small portrait next to the picture from the Princess of Wales. Would you bring it to me?"

"Of course." I went and found the painting. It was small, just two or three inches on a side, and quite battered, but the woman it portrayed was indeed lovely. "Is this your mother?" I said, handing it to him.

He accepted it reverently with both hands, in the manner of a prayer book, appearing utterly mesmerized by the image. "Yes. She died shortly before I turned eleven. Since then I've kept this portrait with me at all times. It has been with me through all my travails."

"I did the same with my mother's book," I said. "And also this." I withdrew my locket from inside my uniform and unclasped it from around my neck. "These are my parents," I said as I opened it and showed him the pictures inside, feeling a sharper than usual stab of grief at the sight of them. Sometimes, the portrait of my father reminded me not of who he once was, but who he became. "You won't tell Matron I wear this, will you?"

"No. Never," he said in seriousness. "Your mother was also quite beautiful."

I smiled. "And my father's kindness back then made him handsomer than he was."

That brought Mr. Merrick's eyes up to mine. "Kindness can make someone handsome?"

"In a manner of speaking. It can make a person more attractive, at any rate."

"What else can make a man more handsome?"

"Many things. Courage. Honesty. Loyalty." Qualities my father had ceased to show me, in the end. I would never understand why.

"Honesty?"

"Certainly."

I thought I could guess what he was thinking then about his own attractiveness, but he said nothing more and I let go of the matter, for I knew very well there was a degree of ugliness against which no amount of kindness or virtue could balance the scale.

"I think your mother must have loved you very much," I said, to change the direction of our conversation.

He nodded and returned his devoted gaze to the portrait. "She did."

"And what of your father? Do you have brothers or sisters?"

"No," he said, with a cold and vast emptiness in his voice.

"Oh," I said. "I was also left all alone. It seems we have much in common, Mr. Merrick."

He stared at the portrait a moment longer, sighed, and handed it back for me to replace on the mantel. "I want to be honest," he said. "So I must confess something."

"What is that?" I asked, though I knew what he was about to say, and I thought of hollow, mournful eyes.

"I lied to you."

I swallowed. "Oh?"

"When I told you no one came into my room the night before last. Someone did come."

My heart cantered, driven by a rising dread at the memory of the young woman, and I winced at a twinge of pain in my jaw. "Who was it?"

He hesitated and glanced toward the door. "I don't know."

"You didn't know her?"

He shook his head. "She didn't speak. She simply stood there, by the mantel, looking at my pictures and cards. I think she . . ."

I waited, but he never finished his statement. "You think she what, Mr. Merrick?"

"I think she may have been . . . a spirit."

The word, coming from him, was a cold, wet eel coiling in my stomach. "A ghost?"

"Am I mad to think so?" he asked.

"No, I don't think you're mad. I admit I had the same thought when I saw her."

"You did? I am relieved by that, at least." Fear then frayed the hem of his voice. "She came again this morning also and stood at the foot of my bed. I . . . I believe she will come tonight."

If I had not seen the phantasm for myself, I would have doubted Mr. Merrick's ghostly visitations as the product of his dreams, and I wished I could so disregard them. To acknowledge them as supernatural rendered me powerless and terrified.

"I am afraid of her," he said. "I don't want to see her alone."

I knew, then, what he was about to ask me, and I wanted to leave his room before he could.

"Will you be here with me?" he said. "When she comes?"

"Mr. Merrick . . ."

"Please, Evelyn."

His voice had such a plaintive vulnerability that I couldn't help but agree to return in the early morning, at half past three, the hour at which the ghost had manifested the last two nights. A rising dread grasped at my heels the rest of that day, and later drained away my appetite as I sat with the staff at dinner. That was just as well, since Beatrice had acquired a copy of the evening *Star* and read aloud what the police had learned about the murder of that poor woman the morning before, whether any of us wanted her to.

"They say the killer must be some cool, cunning man with a mania for murder," she said. "That's three women, now, each of 'em with an abandoned character. All were killed on ill-lighted off-turnings from Whitechapel Road. Clues to the murders are entirely lacking. But one—"

"What's her name?" Becky asked.

Beatrice appeared irritated at the interruption. "Whose name?"

"The murdered woman."

"Oh." Beatrice scanned the paper. "Mary Ann Nichols. Sometimes called Polly. Says she was a prostitute, a drunkard, and a thief."

Becky tapped her chin with her index finger. "I like the name Polly."

"Oh, you do, do you?" Beatrice leaned away from Becky a bit and stared hard at her. "That all you're thinking about after what I've been reading?"

"No." Becky scowled at the older woman. "What's it to you, anyhow?"

Polly.

The name made the woman's death more real to me. I didn't want to hear the argument going around at the table, so I rose and went to my room. There, I lay down on my bed still clothed, for I knew I would be getting up in a few hours to go to Mr. Merrick as promised, and tried not to think about the ghostly young woman. A short while later, Becky and Martha returned to the room shivering with gossip and speculation over the murders.

"A maniac, he is," Martha said. "One of the porters told me the police is looking for a man called Leather Apron."

"Leather Apron?" Becky said. "He wear one or something?"

"Yeah. Been ill-treating judys on the street for weeks, apparently. Bashing them up something fierce."

"Leather Apron," Becky said again, and shuddered.

I thought better of telling them about Mr. Merrick's visitor, especially Becky, and before long, they had gone easily to sleep, while fearful thoughts spurred my wakefulness late into the night. I didn't have any notion of what to say or do in the presence of a ghost, and I hoped to God Almighty the apparition didn't come, and if she did, that she'd prove somehow to be nothing but a mortal woman of flesh and bone.

The sleepless hours passed more quickly than I'd have liked, and at the agreed-upon time I rose from my bed and slipped out of the dormitory into what was becoming an increasingly sinister Bedstead Square. It was a cold, desolate night, the kind that wouldn't just turn its back on terrible goings-on, but would stand by and watch. I trembled as much from the chill as from my trepidation while I crossed the courtyard, quick as I could. I did my utmost to make little sound, as if to avoid drawing attention to my passage and keep from stirring dark things from slumber, and even so imagined eyes upon me from within the shadows.

When I reached Mr. Merrick's door, for the first time I felt his room was not a place from which to flee, but a place to escape from the square, and I entered gratefully, even knowing what it was I might yet face there.

CHAPTER 7

"I wondered if you would come," Mr. Merrick said, sitting in his peculiar armchair near the fireplace, the embers low and red.

"I gave you my word," I said. "I wouldn't break it."

"Thank you, Evelyn," he said.

I pulled a chair over from the table and placed it next to him, where I then sat, and we both faced the door.

"Did you believe in spirits before now?" Mr. Merrick asked.

"No," I said. "Well, not the haunting kind, leastwise. I do hope the spirits of my mother and my sister are in heaven, wherever that is."

"And your father?"

That was a difficult question to answer. "I hope he has found peace, too," I said. I certainly hadn't been able to provide him any, though I had tried. I had hidden his drink, and failing that, I had washed his clothes and cleaned him up. I had done my best to care for him, but it hadn't been enough.

"Do you think your family has been watching you?" Mr. Merrick asked.

It took a moment for me to answer him. "I hope not," I whispered.

He seemed not to have heard me. "My mother is an angel now," he said. "She died of pneumonia."

A few coals slumped to ash in the fireplace, and the ruddy room dimmed by a degree. I rose and went to add more fuel from the coal hod but found it nearly empty. It seemed my earlier nervousness had so distracted me I'd neglected to fill it. The room had a gas lamp on one wall, so I lit that, and felt somewhat comforted by the increase in light, a fevered yellow though it was.

"That's better," I said.

"Angels watch over us," he said. "That's what they say."

"That's what they say."

"It was my mother brought me here. Away from the workhouses. The beatings. The hunger."

"The exhibitions?"

"That wasn't always bad," he said, staring into the fire. "The Silver King treated me well, and I made friends among the other freaks of nature. Sam Roper had these two midgets, Dooley and Bramley, and they looked after me." He paused and chuckled. "Those two could make a mockery of anything. But . . ." His laughter abruptly ceased. "London's taste for monsters changed. The police shut us down, and I went to Belgium. Then that man robbed me . . . I had nothing. I don't know how I made it back to Liverpool. But that was as far as I could go. The crowd at the station . . . pressing in, shouting at me, kicking me. I was nearly senseless. I collapsed, and I thought they would tear me apart. And then I found it." He turned toward me, his eyes aglow. "Dr. Treves had given me his card, you see, a year earlier. Truthfully, I'd long forgotten it, and I still cannot explain how it came to be in my pocket that day. But I showed it, and Dr. Treves came for me, and now I'm here."

His story had robbed me of breath.

"It was my mother," he said, returning his gaze to the coals. "She put that card in my pocket."

I could not have disputed him even had I not partly believed he was right.

"Perhaps this spirit coming to visit me is an angel like my mother," he said.

I did not believe an angel would cause the disquiet I had felt upon seeing her, but I still could not dispute him, and we both fell silent after that in the gentle warmth of the fire.

"Perhaps she will not come," Mr. Merrick finally said, after some time had passed.

"Perhaps it's because I'm here," I said.

"You think she—"

The gas lamp dimmed, or seemed to dim. I could not say if it was my eyes failing or the light, but a spreading darkness choked the corners of the room, and then I felt an ache in my jaw. It was the same pain I had experienced upon seeing the ghost the first time. Then a devastating sadness fell upon me, followed by a terror that shoved ice into the deepest reaches of my body.

I gasped.

"Evelyn?" Mr. Merrick said, sounding in every way like a child.

I fixed my eyes on the door, which seemed suddenly insubstantial, straining to see through the barrel of tar that was now my vision. "Mr. Merrick," I whispered, my voice nearly impossible to find, "I think she's here."

I heard him swallow hard, and then whimper.

Having sensed what lurked outside, I expected the door to be thrown open, or to splinter apart, and I waited for that to happen. But it didn't. Instead, after an endless moment, the door handle moved. I watched it, fighting the urge to rush and grab it and hold it fast, but I knew no mortal hand could prevent its turning.

Mr. Merrick covered his face with his hand and shook. "She's coming. She's coming," he said.

The latch clicked, the door swung slowly open without a sound, and then I saw her.

It was the same pale woman, the same ghost, wearing her wedding gown, her gray eyes hollowed out by despair. Her presence extinguished the last flame of heat in my body, leaving me light-less and cold, my jaw throbbing with blinding pain.

She entered the room, and I leapt to my feet, fighting the panic that urged me to run as she drew nearer. I'd heard stories of violent, vengeful spirits that clawed and beat and even dragged people across the floor. The only thing that kept me there in that room was the realization that Mr. Merrick could not run, and I would not leave him alone with that *thing*.

She reached the far edge of the mantel and there she stopped, looking about the room, paying particular attention, it seemed, to Mr. Merrick's cards and pictures.

Mr. Merrick finally brought his hand down from his eyes and looked up, tears glistening in the firelight on his cheeks. "Wh-who are you?" he asked, his musical voice sounding nearly undone. "What is it you want? Can—can I help you?"

The ghost turned to regard him, and then closed the distance between us, standing near enough I could have reached out my hand to touch her, though that was an utterly horrifying thought.

Instead, it was she who bent down toward Mr. Merrick and extended her hand toward him. He couldn't move away, and I could do nothing but watch as she laid her palm against his cheek, after which a visible tremor worked its way down through him.

"There is light here," she said, her voice as forceful and ephemeral as the wind. "All is dark. But here there is light."

"Who are you?" he asked again.

"Polly," she said.

The name struck me all of a heap. It was the same name as the woman murdered but two nights ago, and it occurred to me then that these visitations had started the morning after the dock fire, the same morning Polly Nichols had been killed. But the living Polly had been a woman in her forties, and this ghost appeared not much older than twenty.

I marshaled my voice. "Were you murdered, Polly? Is that who you are?"

She ignored me, just as she had the first night I saw her.

"Polly," Mr. Merrick said. "Why are you here? Why have you come?"

The ghost withdrew her hand from Mr. Merrick's face and stood upright. "I don't know. I . . . I'm getting married."

"I can see your dress," Mr. Merrick said, his voice strengthening. "It's lovely."

"It's the first happy day in me life."

"Oh?" Mr. Merrick said. "Why is that?"

She seemed to shrink then, with a fading away like scattering smoke.

"Polly," Mr. Merrick said, "don't go. Please. We won't hurt you."

"My father will," she said, her voice smaller. "If I tell. It weren't natural what he did to me. It weren't what a father ought to do to his daughter. William don't know, or he wouldn't have me, I know it. But he's marrying me. He's taking me away, and it will all be better."

I'd known girls and women whose fathers had ill-used them, and I counted myself blessed to have had a father who, until he left me, had loved me exactly as a father should. My heart broke for Polly, and suddenly I didn't feel so afraid.

Mr. Merrick shook his head. "I am very sorry."

"But William don't know it, see?" she said. "He don't know he's saving me. I want to tell him, but I'm so afeared he'll toss me over."

"He wouldn't do that," Mr. Merrick said.

"Yes, he will. I know it. Any man would do the same." She shook her head. "I won't tell him. I won't." Then she looked down and smoothed her wedding gown. "We'll just marry, and all will be well. You'll see."

Mr. Merrick was silent for a moment. "Then . . . my congratulations to you," he said. "I'm glad for your day of happiness."

"Thank you, sir. I am, too," she said, but there was no happiness in her voice.

"I'm glad for you, too," I said, but still she ignored me. Perhaps I was merely a shade of the darkness around her.

"I best get to Saint Bride's," she said. "Don't want to keep William waiting."

"Go, then," Mr. Merrick said. "Godspeed, Polly."

She nodded and smiled, though her eyes remained the same mournful gray, and turned toward the open door. "It's so black out there. But I don't want William to think I jilted him." She stared a moment longer and then moved toward the portal, and once she'd passed through, the door closed behind her, leaving behind a wake of pained memory in the room. Mr. Merrick and I were both silent for a long time.

"It's almost unbearable, isn't it?" he finally said. "I feel so sad for her."

"I think she's beyond anyone's help, Mr. Merrick. God rest her soul."

"But she's clearly not at rest."

I agreed with him on that, but I could not think what she needed, for I'd only just accepted without doubt the fundamental reality of ghosts, and that she was truly one of them. There were Spiritualists and others who held convocations with the dead, but I had always dismissed them as charlatans and mountebanks, and still put no faith in *their* parlor tricks.

"You listened to her," I said. "Perhaps that's enough."

"I don't think so," he said. "I think she'll return. But I no longer fear her."

I also took consolation in that, at least.

"You asked her if she was murdered," Mr. Merrick said. "Why?"

"Because she was," I said. "Haven't you heard? There's a madman loose in Whitechapel. They say he's killed three women. Polly's soul was set free the very same morning she first came to you. She was killed but one street away, not far from this very spot. If you think on that, is it any wonder she's haunting?"

"I think her murder was the end of her pain," Mr. Merrick said. "Not the beginning."

"Clearly not the end," I said.

He nodded. "True. But what I mean is, I don't think that's why she haunts."

As my fear abated, a weakness crept up and began to overtake me by the limbs, and I didn't want to think on the encounter any longer. "I don't pretend to know what desires and compulsions govern the affairs of ghosts."

"Nor I," Mr. Merrick said.

"The fire's almost out," I said. "I'll fill your coal hod straight-away, so you won't be cold."

He nodded. "Very well."

I went for the bucket, feeling grateful he hadn't protested, and left his room quickly. Outside, I found the morning was in earnest now, the sky possessed of a faint light that quietly flushed out the abandoned quality of the courtyard. Everything that had just transpired grew distant with each step, as though a dream upon waking, and, believing it impossible to convince myself none of it had happened, I hoped I could at least push it far out of mind. Now that I knew Mr. Merrick didn't seem to be endangered by this ghost, I didn't want any part of the undead world. One experience with it was quite enough for me.

After I'd gone to the coal shed and filled the hod, I lugged it back to Mr. Merrick's room, where I found he'd moved himself from the armchair to his bed.

"I could have helped you get situated, Mr. Merrick," I said as I fed the fire, trying to keep any trace or weight of the last hour from my voice.

"There are times I prefer to manage on my own," he said. "Is there really a madman murdering women?"

"Yes."

"How dreadful," he said, and it was almost a moan. "Those . . . those poor women. Poor Polly."

A different pain afflicted him upon hearing the news than I supposed the rest of us felt. He looked at the world in a way I still did not fully understand, but it seemed to me that he found a semblance of his mother in every woman he met, and the murder of any was the murder of her. He closed his eyes, brought his legs up, and bowed his head upon his knees.

"Would . . . would you like to get some sleep?" I asked.

He looked up at me. "Yes, I think I would."

"Very good, then. I'll make sure it's a late breakfast for you."

"Thank you, Evelyn."

"You're welcome." I curtsied, something I had not done for Mr. Merrick in several days, so familiar had we become. But I did so then perhaps to remind myself that I was a servant, and his affairs were his affairs, and I had no rightful part in them—nor did I want a part in them. I went for the door, hoping that I also might reach my bed and find as many moments of rest as I could before an accusation of dereliction.

"Evelyn," he said as I reached the door.

"Yes, Mr. Merrick?"

"Thank you."

This time, his words conveyed all those things I was trying not to think on, and I could only allow myself to acknowledge his appreciation with another curtsy, and then I left his room. Back in my own, with Becky and Martha still sleeping, I fell into my bed and closed my eyes, but I was still haunted. The ghost of Polly Nichols hadn't left my mind as surely as she had Mr. Merrick's room, and it took some time to fall asleep, but when I did, my rest was deep and deathly.

I awoke with the other staff, and throughout that morning, I kept myself somewhat aloof from Mr. Merrick and performed my duties with formality, but he seemed quite preoccupied with his own thoughts and failed to make note of it. Such was his distraction that he hadn't eaten a bite of his luncheon when I returned later in the afternoon with his tea. Ordinarily I would have asked him what was the matter, but I knew too well the answer to that. I did feel a measure of guilt at not asking after him, but I also knew that nothing I could say would afford him any comfort.

Later in the evening, he ate his dinner and had his bath, and afterward asked if I would read from *Emma*. That, I was grateful to do, and we sat with Miss Austen by the fire well into the evening, until my eyes grew heavy-lidded and I had to close the book.

"Thank you," he said. "That is much better."

"Better?"

"Than *Northanger Abbey*. Now you know why I wanted to stop reading from *that* book. I thought perhaps it had summoned Polly."

My body became tense at the mention of the ghost, a subject I had successfully avoided all day. "I see" was all I managed to say, and I rose to leave before he could draw me into that conversation further. "Will you need anything else tonight, Mr. Merrick?"

He regarded me for a few long and uncomfortable moments, and I wished his rigid face could intimate at least a hint of what he was feeling inside.

"Are you cross with me?" he asked.

"Oh no." I shook my head vigorously. "Not at all, Mr. Merrick. But even if I were, it's not my place to say so."

"Your place? I think of you as my friend. I hope you would express whatever you might feel."

"I . . . thank you for that," I said, feeling badly that he believed I was cross with him.

"Do you think of me as your friend?"

"Yes. Of course." Which I found was true as I said it.

He nodded his great head. "I am happy to hear that." Then he paused. "I believe Polly will return. But . . . I no longer fear her."

I grew wary. "That's good, Mr. Merrick."

"What I mean is, I will not ask you to be here again when she comes. If that is troubling you. So you need not maintain this distance, and we can be friends again."

"I—" He had noticed my aloofness, after all, and his words set the hound of guilt upon me. "I'm sorry, Mr. Merrick. I didn't mean for you to think me cross with you. I suppose I was frightened."

"I see," he said. "But now that we've aired it all out, we don't need to speak of it again. Can we return to how we were?"

"Yes," I said, relieved to have that settled.

"Good. Now I will answer your question, and that is no, I will not need anything else. Good night, Evelyn."

"Good night, Mr. Merrick."

I left him then and went to my bed, where I slept well, and the next morning I arrived at his room feeling a great deal more settled in my nerves than I had been the day before. I was thankful to Mr. Merrick for putting me at ease by speaking openly about the ghost, for in guessing accurately my fears, he'd been able to partially alleviate them.

He ate his breakfast, had his bath, then had a visit from Dr. Treves, who came most every day to see him for at least a few moments, if not longer.

"You're looking tired," Dr. Treves said to Mr. Merrick. "Are you sleeping well?"

I stood at the mantel, arranging a few recently delivered pictures and cards, but I felt Mr. Merrick look in my direction.

"As well as can be expected," he said.

"Your rest is important, John." Dr. Treves walked toward Mr. Merrick's bed. "Perhaps we could fashion you a better arrangement."

"No, thank you," Mr. Merrick said. "It's not the bed."

"I see." Dr. Treves frowned, a movement accentuated by his mustache. "Well, do let me know if there is anything we can do. There are funds enough, so don't worry yourself on that score."

"Thank you," Mr. Merrick said. "I do have one question."

"Of course. What is it?"

"Do you believe in ghosts, Doctor?"

I froze where I stood, while Dr. Treves's frown dug even deeper toward his chin. "Ghosts, you say?"

"Yes," Mr. Merrick said.

"I don't—that is, I hold no personal belief in them. I've opened countless human bodies in surgery and I've yet to locate the seat of the soul. But there are some who study Spiritualist phenomena. I've a few friends among the Society for Psychical Research."

"A society that studies ghosts?" Mr. Merrick asked.

"Among other subjects. Thought transference. Mesmerism. That sort of thing. Their president is a man named Sidgwick. A professor at Cambridge."

"Do you suppose I could meet him?" Mr. Merrick asked.

Dr. Treves raised his eyebrows. "I think that may be possible. He lectures in London on occasion. I could write an invitation to him, if you'd like."

"I would like that," Mr. Merrick said.

"Very well," Dr. Treves said. "But might I ask, why the sudden interest in ghosts?"

Mr. Merrick looked in my direction again. "I want to know what happens when we die."

Dr. Treves chortled. "As do we all, I should think. Mortality is our collective obsession." He strode toward the door. "I'll let you know as soon as I receive a reply from Professor Sidgwick. Meanwhile, enjoy the rest of your afternoon."

After he had gone, Mr. Merrick fell silent, but not in melancholy or sullenness. He seemed contemplative, and though I'd decided I didn't want to know any more about his ghostly dealings, I nevertheless found myself curious whether she had returned—or perhaps I was anxious, for I said nothing.

CHAPTER 8

For the next few days, Mr. Merrick and I resumed what had briefly been our customary pattern of activities. Between his meals we would talk, read, and work on his model church, which seemed to rise up at the same centurial pace as an actual stone cathedral, due to the cumbersomeness of his hand and his desire to do as much of it by himself as he could. He did not seem to mind the slowness of progress, but applied himself with the same deliberate care he took with his speech, and a stubborn resolve to get it right.

Late Thursday morning, I returned to Mr. Merrick's room with fresh bedding from the laundry and found Charles there, already playing his violin. My arrival caused not a pause or a missed note in the lovely song he played, which had no words, and would have sounded quite out of place in the sort of establishment where I assumed Charles normally performed.

When he finished playing, I asked him, "Is that a classical piece of music?"

"Not quite," he said. "It were a *romantic* tune. Mendelssohn wrote it for pianoforte, but I made better use of it, wouldn't you say?"

"You made a worthy use of it," I said, not wanting to agree with his conceit.

"Yes," Mr. Merrick said. "It was very pleasing, Charles."

"I thank you both most graciously." He bowed his head. "How about another?"

Mr. Merrick agreed, and Charles played a second song, and a third, both again romantic and somewhat mournful, like the first, and by their end it felt to me as if a solemn draft of church air had wafted into the room. In the silence that followed, Charles knelt to put his instrument away.

"I best be going," he said. "Good to see you, Joseph, my ugly bloke."

"Thank you for coming, Charles," Mr. Merrick said. "As always."

"Miss Fallow," Charles said, "always a pleasure to see you, too."

"Thank you, Mr. Weaver."

"Fancy a walk with me sometime?"

I felt warmth bloom in my cheeks. "I've already answered you. No, I'm sorry."

"Right, then." He smiled and crossed to the door. "But I'll keep asking, you know."

"Why?" His obstinate confidence irritated me. "Do you not believe me?"

"Oh, I believe you," he said, and then laid a hand on his chest. "But you see, I'm a God-fearing man, and I also believe in miracles. You might yet have a change of heart. Good day to you both." He opened the door and left.

His invitation flustered me, and I set about tidying Mr. Merrick's room, though there was no disorder.

Mr. Merrick let out a sigh. "That music he played . . . I feel as if it should have reminded me of something."

"Oh?"

"A place. Or a person, maybe."

I could not say whether Mr. Merrick was unaware of Charles's flirtation with me or if he simply chose to ignore it.

"Perhaps it simply reminded me of a feeling," he said.

"Perhaps so, Mr. Merrick."

"Why do you not go walking with Charles?"

He was aware of it after all, then. I planted my hands on my hips and said, "I do not want to."

"Are you not fond of him?"

"No, that isn't—I mean . . ." The truth was that I still felt uneasy around Charles, but I was becoming increasingly confused by why that should be, and I had no rational reason for it, to say nothing of the idea of leaving the hospital grounds, which frightened me all on its own. "I don't know him well enough to feel any way toward him," I finally said, hoping that would suffice.

"Then, why—"

"Mr. Merrick, would *you* go out walking the streets of London looking as you are?" My question came out more sharply than I intended it.

"Perhaps not," he said, his voice low. "But I wish that I could."

"I . . . wish I could, too," I said. "But that isn't to be. I am the way I am. It can't be changed, and there's no sense pretending otherwise. I've no intention of returning to those streets, for Charles or anyone."

"Are you going to stay here in the hospital the rest of your life?" he asked.

I hadn't thought on the matter in quite those terms. "I don't know what the future holds for me. All I know is what's right now."

"I suppose that's all any of us knows," he said.

"Mr. Merrick, I know Charles is your friend." I stopped short of saying that I didn't trust Charles, with his easy charm, or to ask what sincere interest he could possibly have in me. Instead I simply pronounced, "I won't be accepting his invitation, and I'd appreciate it if we said no more on the matter."

"Of course," Mr. Merrick said. "I meant no offense."

"And I've taken none. We're friends, remember?"

"Right. Friends."

"Friends. Now, shall we work on your model for a bit before I fetch your luncheon?"

He agreed, and we spent some time with the church, and then he ate, and then we read, and soon the day was at an end. The following evening, Dr. Treves returned with a letter from Professor Sidgwick stating that he would be honored to come into London to visit with Mr. Merrick.

"That is most generous of him," Mr. Merrick said.

"You are worthy of all generosity, John," Dr. Treves said. "But it certainly doesn't hurt that you are also something of a celebrity."

"When will he come?"

Dr. Treves checked the telegram. "Wednesday next. Sometime around three o'clock."

Mr. Merrick nodded, and after the doctor had fulfilled the obligation of his daily visit and left, my friend seemed quite contented. "How fortunate I am," he said, both to me and, it seemed, to himself.

I marveled at his good cheer. "Begging your pardon, but that's not a word many would use for someone in your condition."

"True," he said. "But consider that I have but to ask for a thing, say, a visit from a Cambridge professor, and it seems the world stands ready to deliver it to my door. Consider the friends I have. Consider the generosity shown to me."

"I suppose that's true."

"Are you not fortunate to have your position here at the hospital?"

"Indeed, I am," I said. "But I can't easily forget the *unfortunate* circumstances that made it necessary in the first place."

"I'd rather not balance life as a ledger," he said. "I prefer to attend to the gains and ignore the losses."

"Some losses can't be ignored," I said, suspicious of his optimism even as I wished for it.

He chuckled. "Then perhaps I would have made a dreadful clerk."

"Perhaps," I said, and smiled back at him. "But I suppose your method of accounting is a part of what draws so many to visit you. Like the professor."

"Hmph," he said.

Or like the ghost of Polly Nichols, I thought, but left unsaid.

After that, I saw to his dinner, the nurses bathed him, and I bade him good night. Rather than go back to my room, I decided to take a stroll through the hospital gardens, as Mr. Merrick said that he had done. The sun had set, but the sky hadn't completely given itself over to the stars, and I enjoyed a twilit walk along the gravelly paths, a few of the flowers still clinging to their stems against the autumn death. I thought myself alone, and had brought down my shawl to enjoy the air, but as I neared a tall oak tree a figure emerged from behind it, startling me a few steps backward.

"Good evening," the figure said, a man. "Forgive me, Miss Fallow, is it? I didn't mean to frighten you."

He stepped out of the shadows, and I recognized him as the blond doctor who'd admitted the patients at the gate on my first day at the hospital. "Oh, Doctor, it's quite all right," I said, then curtsied. "Yes, I'm Evelyn Fallow." I moved to raise my shawl.

"Oh, no need to trouble yourself with that on my account," he said. "Phossy jaw, yes? I've treated much worse."

His rough honesty snagged me mid-act. I paused, considered what he must see in the normal course of his occupation, and then lowered the shawl back to my shoulders. So far, the hospital had offered me the acquaintance of several people with whom I felt I could be open. That was part of what I'd hoped for in coming here, and it meant a great deal to me. I could feel less singular—more like a normal woman.

"I'm Dr. Tilney," he said. "Francis Tilney."

"Pleasure to meet you, Doctor." I curtsied again and moved to go around him. "Good night—"

"Wait a moment," he said, and stepped in front of me. "I . . . How do you find him?"

"How do I find who, sir?"

"Merrick."

I wondered at the source of his curiosity. "I find him most agreeable."

He nodded. "He is that. But his appearance ... it doesn't disturb you?"

"I ..."

"Oh, come, come." He looked around us, his blond hair a ribbon of bronze in the gloaming. "We're alone on a garden walk at night, Miss Fallow. I can think of no better circumstance for confessions, and your secret shall be safe with me."

His brusque affability put me at ease, and somehow, I believed I could trust him. "I was quite disturbed at first. But not anymore."

"Truly?"

"No, sir."

He leaned away from me. "You impress me, Miss Fallow. Took me the better part of three months to grow accustomed to the man."

"Do you know him well? I've never seen you—"

"Oh, I haven't been to his quarters for some time, since before the high society ladies started calling on him. Merrick was even more pitiful back then. Practically mute. Lonely. He'd tried walking about the hospital corridors, you see, but gave such a terrible shock to the other patients, Treves asked him to stay in his rooms. Some of us were then ordered to go and provide him with regular company."

"That was kind of you."

"It was kind of Treves, to be sure. But I was never quite up to the task, to be honest." He paused, his eyes vacant, as if caught up in a memory. "The Elephant Man. Always looked more like . . . I don't know. A tapir or somesuch, to me. But anyway, his fame spread, and soon he had no further need for the likes of me."

"I'm sure he appreciated you."

"I'm sure I made no impression on him, whatsoever."

"You might be surprised, Doctor. I'm certain he would enjoy another visit from you."

"Yes, well." He coughed. "I'm very busy with my duties, and I've just been invited to lecture at the medical college, which is quite an honor, but demanding, and will be, um . . ."

I shook my head a little at his excuses.

He seemed to notice, and paused for a moment, looking into my eyes. "Do you know," he then said, "perhaps I will. You inspire me, Miss Fallow."

"Thank you, sir," I said.

He stepped aside, opening the path for me. "I won't delay you any further, but I trust you will maintain the utmost secrecy of our conversation."

I curtsied. "Of course, Dr. Tilney. Good evening."

"Good evening to you."

I strolled past him, a smile stretching my scars tight, and a moment later I heard him whistling away behind me into the night. I resisted the temptation to turn and look, and went to my room, where I readied for bed and then lay there thinking of Dr. Tilney. I was very aware he wasn't interested in me beyond my connection to Mr. Merrick. Yet, I appreciated that during our conversation he had taken no particular notice of my scars. He hadn't stared at them or averted his eyes from them. In his presence, I very nearly felt as though they didn't matter at all. And I don't think I'd ever felt that way around anyone else before.

It occurred to me that was likely the most I could ever expect from a man, but it was far more than I'd dared hope for until then. I tried to content myself with this notion, even though it still left a painful longing that followed me into sleep.

The next morning, I found Mr. Merrick pallid, his disposition worsened considerably from the day before, reminding me of his state following Polly's first visitations, but this time it didn't require a great deal of inducement for him to confess the reason.

"This morning a second ghost came," he said quietly from his bed, and I saw his slender arm quivering.

My body went rigid. "A second?"

"Polly came at the time she usually does. She said the things she always says, about William and her father. Then she left, and I went to sleep and—" His voice collapsed to silence, and few moments later, tears fell from both eyes. "But then . . ." His body began to rock back and forth. "*She* woke me."

My mouth had dried out. "Who?"

He shrank from me. "She was leaning right over me, her mouth wide open, as if she meant to devour me. And she was wailing . . . the sound . . . Oh, God. I cried out, but no one came."

"Oh, Mr. Merrick—"

"I hoped you would come. Maybe you would know, somehow, and maybe if you came, she would leave me."

"How long was she here?"

"I don't know. But after she screamed at me, she started sobbing, and that was when she finally departed."

"Mr. Merrick—"

"I don't want her to return," he said. "I—I can accept Polly, but not her. Not her."

"That Professor Sidgwick will be here Wednesday," I said. "That's but four days off. Surely he'll know something you can do."

"But what until then?" His cries had assumed the quality of a young boy that his innocence often suggested, pathetic and small. "I can't bear it, Evelyn. I can't!"

"I'll be with you," I said, before thinking better of it, and felt regret coming swiftly on. "I'll . . . sit with you."

His sobbing lulled. "You will?"

I found a resoluteness, or perhaps simply resignation. "Yes."

"Oh, Evelyn, thank you. Thank you."

"You're welcome, Mr. Merrick." I cleared my voice. "But let's—let's go about our day and try not to worry ourselves, right?"

He sighed. "Yes. You're right. Let's try not to worry."

"Very good. This day won't be unlike any other. Starting with your breakfast."

"I'll try to eat."

"That's good, Mr. Merrick," I said, and for the rest of that day I did my utmost to hide my fear and maintain an air of confidence that could not have been more false. I was nearly frightened out of my senses at the thought of what awaited me at Mr. Merrick's bedside, but I would not abandon him to face the spectres alone. I wondered who she might have once been in life, but it wasn't until the afternoon that I considered the possibility that the leather-aproned demon prowling Whitechapel had claimed another victim. Beatrice confirmed that suspicion later in the evening over our dinner as she read from the *Star*.

"Cheese and Crust, he's killed another one," she said.

"He never!" Martha said.

Becky sat beside her, eyes wide, shaking her head.

"Says it were over on Hanbury Street near Osborn," Beatrice said. "Says her throat were cut and her abdomen—oh . . . oh dear Lord in Heaven."

"What is it?" Martha asked, leaning forward.

Beatrice covered her mouth. "Her—her viscera were—"

"Stop it!" Becky shouted. "Stop it, stop it! It is too dreadful!"

"Easy now," Beatrice said. "I'll not read on if it upsets you so."

I felt my gorge rising, as much due to what I imagined Beatrice had been about to read as to the surety that Mr. Merrick's new visitor was in all likelihood the very same woman whose murder Beatrice detailed, and I'd promised to be there when she came to haunt. I resolved to find out what I could about her before she came.

"What time was she murdered?" I asked Beatrice, for if she followed after Polly's manner, she would arrive upon the hour of her death.

"Uh . . ." Beatrice looked the paper over. "Between a quarter to five and a quarter to si—Cheese and Crust, them's daylight hours!"

"What was her name, Beatrice?" I asked.

"Annie," she read. "Annie Chapman."

"What does it say about her?"

"Let's see. She'd quarreled with a woman who kicked her breast. Didn't have enough money for her lodging last night. She was seen drinking at the Ten Bells pub with a man. He was five foot six with a dark mustache and—"

"Does it say anything about *her*?" I asked. "Her family? What sort of woman she was?"

Beatrice shook her head. "No, nothing like that."

I nodded, feeling frustrated and afraid of the unknown.

Beatrice went on. "But they's charging a penny for those what wants to get a look at the scene of the crime. The dried-up blood is still there, it says. Twenty-nine Hanbury Street, behind the—"

I rose from the table with a suddenness that stopped her speaking. "I'll hear no more of this," I said, and stalked away, down the corridor to my room, where I lay down in exhausted horror. It didn't shock me that someone would charge for such a thing, nor that others would pay, but it disgusted me.

A few moments later, Becky rushed in after me and flopped onto her bed, followed by a trudging, sullen Martha. "I wanted to leave, too," Becky said to me. "Martha didn't. Beatrice is back to going on about it."

"Ain't you curious at all?" Martha asked, still standing by the door.

"No," Becky said. "I got no desire to have that in my head. And if you do, you can go back to Beatrice by yourself."

"Right, then," Martha said, pointing her nose up. "I will." After which, she did, leaving me and Becky alone in the room.

"That Martha," Becky said, lying on her back, staring at the ceiling. "She don't have no sense or thoughts of her own. Let's not talk about it, eh? Let's not say one word about it."

I closed my eyes. "Very well."

"It's not right, dwelling on it. It's like thinking on the Devil."

"I suppose," I said.

"Not supposed to think on the Devil. Gives him power over you."

"I've heard that."

"I'm not gonna think on this—this *maniac*, either."

"Good."

"My head don't need filling with . . . with blood and entrails and—and let's not think on it."

"Let's not."

"Why Martha wants to hear about all that, I'll never know."

"Likely not."

"She do well to put it out of her mind. Like us."

So it went for some time, until Becky had talked her way out of her fear, and Martha had returned to the room, her curiosity likely unsatisfied, for I doubted it was curiosity about the mud that drove a hog to wallow.

After they'd both gone to sleep, I lay awake in an unremitting state of disquiet, both from this monster, Leather Apron, who might even now be skulking just outside the hospital walls, and from the ghost of his latest victim—Annie Chapman—whom it seemed I was shortly to meet.

CHAPTER 9

It was a cold night with but a thin, soap shaving of a moon that could barely light my way across the courtyard. I reassured myself that, brazen as he seemed, Leather Apron would not dare ply his death trade within the hospital grounds. I was safe, at least, from him. I did not know if I was truly safe from the ghosts of his victims.

When I reached Mr. Merrick's room and entered, I found him in his armchair near the fireplace, his good hand resting atop his other. "Thank you for coming," he said, but his voice sounded as though it had reached me from someplace much farther away than his body.

"Of course I came, Mr. Merrick." I took a seat next to him, my exhausted body all ahum with unease. "Did you still doubt I would?"

"I never doubted it," he said. "But I'm grateful."

"You won't be alone," I said. "No matter what comes through that door."

He seemed to be as tired as I was, anticipation as hard a work as any factory labor, and we said nothing more as the minutes seemed to creep around us in their slow passage through the room. I gradually acclimated to my fear as one might to a chill, and soon found myself somewhat entranced by the undulating shadows smeared from the coals across the floor. The pipes and musculature within the hospital walls creaked and trembled around us, as if the building understood what was coming, echoing the state in which we waited and waited.

Polly appeared at her usual time, and though Mr. Merrick seemed quite undisturbed by her arrival, I was not so accustomed as he, and I startled when the door opened, seemingly of its own accord. When Polly drifted into the room in her gossamer wedding gown, the pain flared up in my jaw as though the white phosphor still burned my marrow. The ghost's complexion had sickened since the last time I'd seen her, her cheeks sallow, her eyes diminishing into sockets of black.

"Hello, Polly," Mr. Merrick said.

She came right toward him without granting me a glance or nod, though I sat but a foot away from him, and as she passed me her dress brushed against my knee. The shock of that touch stripped me of all warmth, and I gasped. I felt no more maliciousness from her than from a child carrying the plague, but she nevertheless had brought death with her.

"You know me?" she asked Mr. Merrick.

"We have talked before," Mr. Merrick said. "It is your wedding day."

"It is," she said. "I'm on my way to Saint Bride's. And I do feel I know you."

Mr. Merrick leaned toward her. "I want to tell you something. I want to tell you that William will not leave you, even if he knows the truth about what your father did to you."

Polly retreated from him, seeming to lose some of her substance. "How do you know about that?"

"You told me," Mr. Merrick said. "It wasn't right, what he did. It was his wrong, not yours."

"You haven't told William, have you?" she asked, and her voice became a wind in my ears. "You mustn't tell him! He'll toss me over!"

"I haven't told him," Mr. Merrick said calmly. "And no, he won't forsake you."

"He will!" she shouted, and I felt her distress crash over me.

"He won't," Mr. Merrick said again.

"He will! And he's waiting for me! He'll think I've jilted him!" With that, she turned and rushed from the room, the short train of her gown a wisp of mist, and the door shut behind her. The pain in my jaw subsided with her departure.

"Why does she come?" Mr. Merrick reached his good hand toward the door, as though he would pull her back. "I can do nothing for her! It does not matter what I say to her. She is inconsolable."

"I don't even know if a spirit *can* be consoled," I said.

He shook his head and then he closed his eyes. "The other one will be here soon."

I checked the time on his mantel clock. It was a little after half past three in the morning. Annie Chapman had been murdered between quarter to five and quarter to six, according to what Beatrice had read. "I believe we have perhaps two hours, Mr. Merrick, before she comes."

He opened his eyes. "How do you know that?"

I reluctantly told him about the murder, during and after which he sat forward and became quite agitated. He blinked repeatedly and waved his good hand as his mouth opened and closed like a stuck hinge. "What is . . . this . . . this monster? How can he . . . how can *it* . . . do such evil?"

"I think that's the question every decent soul in London is asking."

"But these poor women. Is nothing being done? Does no one care about them?"

"People care," I said, but I knew the truth of it to be more complicated. The writers of papers and broadsides cared about their circulations, and the coppers cared whether they looked like fools, and the rest of Whitechapel cared if they had gossip-fodder, but whether anyone actually cared for the murdered prostitutes? "They're looking for a man called Leather Apron."

"Leather Apron," he whispered. "And the spirit's name is Annie?"

I nodded.

"Two hours," he said. "Perhaps we might do something to pass the time? Or else I shall go mad."

I was grateful for any distraction, as the talk of murders and Leather Apron had beat my nerves out of the bushes, so we went first to his model church, which looked nearly complete enough to hold services, and then we read from *Emma*. I found it difficult to keep my mind on the words, and though they left my lips I did not taste them, my attentions instead on the tolling of the mantel clock. An hour passed, and a half hour after that, the coming of the screaming spectre imminent.

Eventually, my gaze left the book for the clock face in a glance that stayed, and Mr. Merrick noticed.

"We can stop reading," he said.

"Very well," I said, and closed the book without even marking the page with the ribbon.

"Evelyn?" Mr. Merrick said a moment later.

"Yes?" The clock's steadfast little heart beat on, and I wondered how it could remain so calm.

"I do not want her to come."

"I don't, either," I said.

"Perhaps she won't come."

"She will come," I said. I knew it was better to expect the worst than to hope.

When the clock struck half past five, I turned my eyes toward the door, and I ceased to breathe. I stared so forcefully at the door my vision failed at the edges, and there were moments it seemed the wood grain shifted and swirled, but I blinked and it returned to where it had been.

Moments passed.

Then I felt the pain in my jaw and sensed a presence moving out in the courtyard the way one feels an omnibus thundering by.

"She comes," I whispered.

Mr. Merrick brought his good hand up to cover his eyes. "Please. No—"

The door burst open as if kicked, and I nearly fell from my chair as a woman in black rushed into the room wailing. Before I could recover myself, she was upon us, filthy fingers reaching, her high shriek deafening and unceasing, her mouth gaping. I covered my ears and shrank from her, which only brought her closer and closer until I could see the fissures in her tongue, her face as twisted a mask of fear and torture as would be drawn on the cover of a penny dreadful.

I wondered if she would snatch me, claw at me, or bite me with her teeth.

Beside me, Mr. Merrick grabbed my arm and squeezed so tightly it hurt, but it reminded me that he was there.

The ghost of Annie Chapman had seemed to drag in a surging shadow behind her, but I realized it was a cloak she wore, which billowed as though she were wandering a windswept moor. On she wailed at us without pausing for a breath, her voice violent, and I felt buffeted and powerless against it, filled with its anguish to my utter extremities.

Her mouth seemed to stretch over me, her eyes shot with red, her dark hair writhing in the same invisible wind as her cloak, and in the moment I wondered if her voice alone could tear me asunder, I thought I heard a word in her screaming, or rather a name.

John-ny.

I could not be certain of that, for in the next moment she turned and rushed from the room in the manner she had come, and the door slammed shut behind her, leaving behind a wounded and violated silence.

Mr. Merrick sobbed beside me, still clutching my arm. I turned toward him. "She's gone."

He said nothing back to me, but simply sobbed and whimpered. I let him go on, and I didn't take my arm from his hand, though I could feel he'd bruised it. Eventually, his crying ebbed and he released me in his own time.

"Did you feel it?" he asked.

I thought I knew what he meant, for her pain had made me as empty as a used eggshell. "It's like she's missing something. Someone."

"I cannot bear that again." He clutched the less corrupted side of his face. "Am I cursed? Why do they come to me?"

"Perhaps that is a question Professor Sidgwick can answer."

"That is still three days away," he said.

That meant three more visitations. "I'll be with you, Mr. Merrick. You won't be alone."

He sighed. "Thank you, Evelyn. You are an angel."

The word fit me all wrong, especially knowing what it meant to him, and I wriggled out from under it. "I'm not that, Mr. Merrick," I said, for I knew better than anyone I hadn't always acted divinely, and I certainly didn't look it, as Matron Luckes had made quite clear.

"You're an angel to me," he said.

"If you knew what I've done—"

"What have you done?"

"What have I done?" I did not like to think on what I'd had to do. "I've lied. I've stolen. I've cheated. And I've hurt people." My confession sounded almost belligerent. "I'm not proud of it. I did what I had to do. But I am no angel."

He closed his eyes. "And yet you are here with me now. That is what I know."

I couldn't argue that, even though I wasn't as ready as he was to believe that a single, possibly selfless choice could outweigh a plentitude of ignominious acts in the final reckoning.

"Do you think anyone else in the hospital heard her?" he asked.

"If no one heard her yesterday, I doubt anyone heard her today," I said.

He nodded. "I think I would like to rest now."

"Can I help you to bed?"

"No, thank you. I'll sleep here in my chair by the fire."

"Very good," I said, then brought him a blanket and tucked it around him. It caused me not a moment's pause to touch him thus, which caused me a brief moment of surprise. With all the time we'd spent in each other's company, the landscape of his abnormal features had become familiar to me. "I'll return with your breakfast later."

"Thank you," he said.

I left his room, and out in the courtyard greeted a day fully risen. Though cast with clouds, the sky shone with weak light from a hidden sun, which gently burned away the dread and pain from Annie Chapman's haunting. I returned to my room, where I washed and dressed, and then went to breakfast with the rest of the maids. Their conversation still dealt almost entirely with the topic of murder, but had moved into the territory of speculation as to the motive and character of this Leather Apron.

"I think he's got himself a lame cock," Beatrice said. "So's he takes out his anger on the bunters. Why else he choose them?"

It did seem possible to me that impotence could so frustrate a violent man.

"Them ladies of that sort gets what's coming to them, don't they," Beatrice said.

"Or maybe it don't have nothing to do with his lobcock," Becky said, cheeks a bit flushed with embarrassment, it seemed, or perhaps anger. "Maybe he's just evil, and he picks the women no one cares about so's he gets away with it."

That made equal sense to me.

"And why should I care about them, eh?" Beatrice said. "You ask me, they's as much a part of the problem as the maniac. There's a reason all he picks is whores."

"Thus far," I said.

The table fell silent for a moment at that.

"They say he's a Jew," Beatrice said. "Police had a man in custody, and a violent mob nearly took him by force to hang. But turns out he were arrested on unrelated charges."

"Is the whole world going mad?" Becky asked.

We separated shortly after that to our duties, and I waited some hours before I took Mr. Merrick his breakfast. He was still asleep when I reached his room, but he woke as I entered, and we passed the day somewhat subdued by the experience of that morning and the awareness that we must endure it again. When Dr. Treves came for his daily visit, Mr. Merrick said but little to him, which seemed to concern the surgeon, and he suggested that perhaps it might be time again for a thorough medical examination. The matron even came that day, to my dismay, for I did not feel myself to be at my best, as I hadn't slept at all the night before and felt the high tax on that.

Nevertheless, the matron seemed pleased with me. "I hear good reports from Miss Flemming and Miss Doyle," she said as she proceeded through an inspection of the room's cleanliness. "As well as Dr. Treves."

"Thank you, ma'am," I said, feeling very relieved.

"Thus far," she said, "I believe I made the right decision in hiring you."

"I'm glad you feel that way," I said, though my own thoughts and feelings on the matter had become quite tangled and convoluted by the presence of the ghosts.

"Might we speak outside?" she said, but did not wait for my reply before she turned toward the door. I followed behind her, and out in the courtyard she spoke in a hushed tone. "And how do you find Mr. Merrick?"

"Well, ma'am," I said.

"What I mean is, are you able to tolerate his condition?"

"Yes, I am."

"Are you really?"

"Yes, ma'am."

"You do seem to have a fortitude your predecessors lacked."

"Thank you."

She nodded as if at some silent appraisal. "I am impressed by you, Miss Fallow."

It was the second time someone had said as much to me, and I curtsied. "I'm flattered, Matron."

"Continue in your duties as you have been, and your position here at the hospital can be assured should . . . circumstances change."

I wondered what she meant by that, but merely thanked her once more.

Matron Luckes nodded toward Mr. Merrick's door. "As you were."

"Yes, ma'am." With that I curtsied and returned to my duties.

Later that evening, I ate my dinner quickly and hurried to bed to catch what little rest I could before Polly's coming. With the certainty of it, and knowing what to expect, I was actually able to sleep. I did not even stir when Becky and Martha came in, and later awoke to a feeling of utter disorientation of the hour and the day. Following that sensation, I suffered a panic that I had overslept, but it faded at the realization it was but two thirty. I rose and decided to bathe.

"Evelyn?" Becky whispered from her bed in a voice both rasped and confused.

"All's well," I said. "Go back to sleep."

Her head fell back to her pillow, and I went out into the corridor toward the bathroom.

Our wing of the hospital, at that hour, was utterly silent, save the echoes of my own footsteps that followed me, making it sound as though I were being stalked. I even thought I sensed someone behind me and turned back to look, but found myself alone in the dim light.

It then occurred to me that if ghosts were real, as I had learned they were, then the hospital might be haunted by other spirits and apparitions, and some of them might be dangerous.

I felt a chill, then, and hurried on to the bathroom, where I closed and locked the door, and thereafter I moved very quietly, so as not to wake the dead. I filled the tub with hot water, which seemed to splash thunderously, and quickly submerged myself in it, feeling quite alone and vulnerable.

Every drip of water from the spout and every slosh I made echoed loudly in my ears, and with my eyes closed against the soap and water I imagined phantasms stalking the edges of the room, bandaged patients with horrific injuries. I even thought I heard someone take a grunted breath behind me, and the water went frigid, but when I craned slowly to look, holding my breath, I found no one there.

After bathing, I dried myself and dressed quickly, shivering in my gooseflesh, and then hurried to Mr. Merrick's room, where we took up our vigil. The waiting, though I knew what to expect, still was not an easy thing. We distracted ourselves once again with reading, but the effort was halfhearted, and after but a few pages Mr. Merrick interrupted me.

"Did you hear Annie's spirit say a name?" he asked.

I placed my finger on the page and looked up from the book. "I did."

"Johnny?"

"Yes."

"I wonder what that means. Could that be the name of the monster who killed her?"

I thought about that a moment, and then decided against it. "I don't think so. She cries in longing. We both felt that. I think she mourns for this Johnny."

"I wonder who he is."

"Her husband? A beau? The paper said little about her."

"Perhaps I can ask her."

"Mr. Merrick . . ." I thought of Annie's wailing and her tortured face, very frightened at the thought of trying to communicate with her. "She doesn't seem like Polly. I know nothing about ghosts, but she seems a different kind of revenant. I doubt she'll speak with you."

"I can try," he said.

He tried again with Polly when she appeared, but his consolations and assurances once again seemed to have no power to comfort her, and she vanished with the same despair as she had come. When Annie Chapman came raging into the room, I could but recoil from her screaming, open mouth as I had before, but Mr. Merrick somehow bravely raised himself and his voice.

"Annie Chapman!" he shouted.

At the sound of her name, her screaming ceased, and she stared at him with eyes afire, her mouth still agape.

"We want to help you," he said. "Who is Johnny?"

"John-ny!" she wailed. "I didn't want to leave you! Forgive me!"

"Who is he?" Mr. Merrick asked. "Is Johnny your husband?"

Her wailing ascended to screaming once more, and Mr. Merrick collapsed away from her into his chair. We endured her torment for a few, endless moments, and then she tore from the room, her black cloak flapping behind her, and we were alone.

"You are right," Mr. Merrick said, breathing hard. "She is . . . quite unlike Polly."

"Are you all right?"

"I am," he said. "But it saps my strength somehow. I think I would like to sleep."

"Of course," I said. "But should I fetch Dr. Treves?"

"No, I'll be set right if I but rest."

"Very well," I said.

He slept most of the morning, and did not wake until I brought his luncheon. I was tired as well, but his weariness seemed to have a different quality than mine, and I grew more and more concerned for him.

That evening, over our dinner, Beatrice related the newest developments in the hunt for the murderer, as reported in the *Star*. It seemed the man called Leather Apron was a Jew, after all.

"Goes by the name of Pizer," Beatrice said. "They apprehended him . . . but he ain't the murderer."

"What?" Martha asked.

Beatrice slapped the paper with the back of her hand. "It weren't him. He got alibis, it says, and they let him go."

"Then who is it?" Becky asked. "Who's the maniac?"

"Some other Jew," Martha said. "Right? The witnesses seen a Jew?"

"Listen to this," Beatrice said. "A man wrote to the paper and says the removal of the viscera and such suggests it be the work of a medical man. Says we should scrutinize all the nearby hospital porters."

A horror seized the table as the import of that statement settled over us. The London was the only hospital of note within Whitechapel, and certainly the hospital nearest the crimes. The author of that suggestion in the *Star* could've had no other institution in mind but ours, which meant the deranged maniac would've been one of us. I'd assumed the hospital walls would keep the murderer out, but what if he were already inside them? No one said anything for several moments. It seemed the table had lost its communal appetite, and that included myself.

I rose to leave.

"You going to bed?" Becky whispered to me. "Why so early?"

"I rise early to help Mr. Merrick," I said.

"Help him with what?"

I sighed. "With whatever he needs."

She cocked an eyebrow. "You ain't his slave," she said. "But you're smart. You keep this up and they'll *never* sack you."

"That's my hope. Good night, Becky."

"G'night, then."

I went to bed and rose a few hours later to go to Mr. Merrick's room, where we repeated our ghostly ritual with Polly and the terrible Annie Chapman. Afterward, Mr. Merrick needed rest, and worried me when he slept most of the next day. Dr. Treves repeated his desire for an examination, against which Mr. Merrick meekly protested, and though I inwardly agreed with the doctor's concern, I doubted whether his medical instruments could uncover the true drain on Mr. Merrick's vitality.

Then Wednesday arrived, and the knowledge of Professor Sidgwick's coming somewhat eased the burden of Polly's fear and Annie's grief, and both Mr. Merrick and I looked forward to the afternoon with great hope that the learned man might be able to help.

CHAPTER 10

Professor Sidgwick was a slender man in a fine wool suit, with long smooth hair that curled about his ears, and a wide fleecy beard the color of steel that reached his chest. I resisted the desire to lift my shawl and hide my face, remembering the matron's orders, but other than an initial, lingering glance, the professor gave me no special attention. After making the introduction to Mr. Merrick, it seemed that Dr. Treves planned to stay in the room for the interview, for he sat himself in a chair.

Mr. Merrick looked at him in what I recognized to be distress, and then at Professor Sidgwick, and I blessed the new, strange man, for he appeared to readily appraise the situation.

"Dr. Treves," he said, his voice clear and slightly nasal. "Might I speak with Mr. Merrick alone? The type of conversation you intimated in your letter is often best undertaken in private."

"Oh," Dr. Treves said. "Well, his speech can be quite difficult to understand, you see."

"I can translate," I said.

Mr. Merrick nodded his approval.

"A perfect solution," Professor Sidgwick said to me, and then to Dr. Treves, "I would not want to take your valuable time away from your patients or the management of this hospital."

"I see." Dr. Treves looked about himself as if he'd forgotten something, and then rose to his feet. "I thank you again for coming, Sidgwick." He offered the professor a tip of his head. "I shall be in my office when you are concluded."

"I shall seek you out there," Professor Sidgwick said, returning his nod.

Dr. Treves left the room, and Professor Sidgwick turned his gaze on us with a gentle smile. Then he took the seat the doctor had just vacated. "I am no medium or psychic," he said. "But one does not need to be to feel the fear in this room, or to know that you did not summon me to discuss philosophical questions on the afterlife."

"No," Mr. Merrick said. "I asked you here because I am haunted."

"He says—" I began, but Professor Sidgwick held up his hand. "I understood that, Miss . . . ?"

"Fallow," I said.

"I understood that much, Miss Fallow." He turned back toward Mr. Merrick. "Do you mean to say that ghosts or spirits have made their presence known to you in some way?"

"Yes," Mr. Merrick said.

"In what manner?" he asked. "Is their presence observed indirectly, through the manipulation of objects, or is it direct? Do you hear or see them?"

"It is quite direct," Mr. Merrick said. "I hear and see them as I hear and see you."

There, the professor turned toward me for interpretation of Mr. Merrick's speech, which I provided.

"I see," the professor said. "You must forgive me for the following questions, but I am a philosopher, and we of the Society for Psychical Research approach these matters with scientific rigor."

"I understand," Mr. Merrick said.

"Did anyone else perceive these spiritual manifestations?"

I spoke up. "I did, sir."

"And are your perceptions in agreement with each other?"

"They are," I said.

"Were any hallucinatory or inebriating substances in use at the time by either or both of you?"

"Not at all," Mr. Merrick said, sounding a mite affronted.

"My apologies, once again," Professor Sidgwick said. "But such questions must be asked. Now, what time of night was this?"

"How do you know it happens at night?" Mr. Merrick said, which I then translated.

"While ghosts and haunted houses are not my area of specialty within the society," he said, "I am familiar with the common features of the phenomena. Hauntings almost universally occur at night."

"Why is that?" Mr. Merrick asked.

"I suspect it can be attributed to our greater attention to fears at night." The professor straightened his back against his chair. "A particular noise—a creak on the landing, let's say—which is considered banal during the day, becomes suddenly ominous at night. Doors that slam during the day are attributed to a draft, but at night they are blamed upon ghosts."

"It sounds as if you don't believe in spirits," Mr. Merrick said.

After I'd translated, the professor frowned. "It is not a matter of belief," he said. "It is a matter of evidence. I am a skeptic, and in my experience nearly all psychical phenomena are proved to be the result of willful deception, a desire to be deceived, or an overly fertile imagination."

"We did not imagine these ghosts," I said. "And they don't both come at night."

The professor angled his head toward me. "No?"

"No," I said. "One comes at half past three, but the other after half past five in the morning, when the sun is up."

"I see," he said. "Those times specifically?"

"Yes," Mr. Merrick said. "As if on a schedule."

"I see." Professor Sidgwick pulled a small notebook out of his pocket along with a pencil nub. "And how often do they come?"

"Every morning," I said. "Since the first murder."

"Pardon me, *murder*, you said?"

I nodded. "Yes. These ghosts are the victims of Leather Apron. Well, whatever he's called now."

"You refer to the recent Whitechapel murders?" The scratch of the professor's pencil in his notebook was quite loud. "You think these apparitions are the ghosts of the victims?"

"They are," Mr. Merrick said.

"You seem quite certain," the professor said.

"We are," I said.

"Why might that be?" the professor asked.

"Because they answer to their names," I said.

Professor Sidgwick ceased writing and looked at me directly. "Am I to understand you have *communicated* with these spirits?"

I was growing somewhat irritated at the slowness of the

interview. "Mr. Merrick speaks with Polly Nichols quite a bit. Annie Chapman is a different matter."

"This whole affair seems a different matter than what I typically encounter." Professor Sidgwick stroked his beard in an absent way. "Let us adjust our method of inquiry. Why don't you first tell me about these visitations as you have experienced them, and I will ask my questions afterward."

That seemed a more sensible approach to me, so Mr. Merrick and I together related the details of the haunting, how Polly had come first, and the repetitive conversations with her that had followed, and then Annie Chapman's alarming appearance. Throughout our narrative, Professor Sidgwick nodded and scribbled more notes in his little book. Even after we'd finished, he went on writing for another moment or two before returning his attention to us.

"This case of haunting is quite unique in many regards," he said. "The first is that it does not seem tied to a specific location. Neither of these women had connections with the hospital, correct?"

"As far as we know," Mr. Merrick said.

The professor continued. "It seems, then, that this is a haunting of a person, rather than a place. I would assume that person to be you, Mr. Merrick."

"Why me?" Mr. Merrick asked.

"Let us hold that question for a moment." Professor Sidgwick glanced back at his notes, as if finding his thoughts there. "Another unique aspect of this case is the level of awareness the spirits seem to possess. In my experience, the only ghosts who converse are those who speak through a medium, and those tend to say exactly what the listener is hoping to hear. Ghosts in haunted houses are often more . . . inscrutable."

"I'd say *these* ghosts are inscrutable," I said.

"But are they?" Professor Sidgwick leaned forward excitedly. "This Polly seems to know exactly what she's about. It's her wedding day. Likewise, Annie is missing someone named Johnny. That is already a great deal more than many apparitions reveal. Most seem content to simply knock stuff about and otherwise cause a racket."

"But why do they haunt *me*?" Mr. Merrick asked.

"They are drawn to you, Mr. Merrick, like a moth is drawn to a flame."

"But why?" Mr. Merrick's tone had become plaintive.

I looked at the mantel, with its hoard of cards and portraits, and especially the portrait of his mother. I thought of the way I was drawn to Mr. Merrick, not by his looks, but by the gentleness of his soul, and the way he refused to believe the girl in Charles's song could be in the wrong.

"I would assume an affinity of some kind exists between you and the spirits," the professor said. "But what that might be . . ." He shrugged.

In that moment, I thought I knew, and believed it had something to do with what Matron Luckes had said about Mr. Merrick's general infatuation with women. In a manner of speaking, he loved them all, quite innocently and perhaps even worshipfully, and he assumed the most nobility and grace of them, always. That, it seemed to me, could explain why the spirits of these women were drawn to him, for among all the dark souls in Whitechapel, his was inclined to be the kindest toward them.

"What can I do for them?" Mr. Merrick asked.

"I should like to stay and observe," the professor said. "I would see these spectres for myself before I make any recommendation to you. If you are amenable to my presence here."

"Of course," Mr. Merrick said. "Please, stay. I will be glad for any wisdom you have."

"I take it you haven't mentioned these visitations to Dr. Treves?"

"No," Mr. Merrick said.

"I assume you would prefer to keep him in ignorance?"

"I would," Mr. Merrick said. "He is a very practical man, and I doubt he would encourage this."

"You confirm my own assessment of him," the professor said. "In that case, I shall simply tell him I wish to continue our discussions into the evening. I am only in London for a short time, you see." He gave us a conspiratorial wink. "Meanwhile, I shall go and procure some instruments that I'll need. I wish there were sufficient time to enlist a photographer. Or perhaps even acquire and test one of Charles Hinton's tesseracts."

"What is a tesseract?" I asked.

"A crystal cube through which ghosts are said to become visible in the fourth dimension." He waved his hand dismissively. "I would not expect you to understand—"

"A *fourth* dimension?" I said. I remembered some of my mathematics from school, as well as the lessons given me by the tutors my father once hired, knowledge I hadn't once needed in my life on the streets. "There are but three dimensions, are there not?"

Professor Sidgwick's eyebrows jumped. "You surprise me, Miss Fallow. I'd not expected a maid to know of such things."

"I was not always a maid," I said.

"Apparently not," he said. "Yes, we perceive three dimensions. But imagine how we, in our three dimensions, would appear to something or someone possessing only two." He tore a blank sheet from his notebook and handed it to me. "For example, what impression would a sphere leave as it passed through this two dimensional piece of paper?"

I looked at the paper, and imagined it bisecting a sphere. "The sphere would appear as a circle."

"Precisely!" Professor Sidgwick said. "Someone or something in two dimensions would have no way of perceiving an object in three dimensions. So it goes with a fourth dimension, which is outside our normal perception. A fourth dimensional being passing through our plane of existence would appear to us as possessing only three dimensions. A tesseract is a tool for visualizing the world in four dimensions."

In my attempt to comprehend what he was saying, I roused the old machinery of my mind that I'd long since left to rust, and found it still worked. "Then . . . do you suppose ghosts are four-dimensional beings?" I asked.

"Some suspect that," he said. "But if they are, I highly doubt a crystal cube would reveal them. I mentioned using the tesseract only because I wish to disprove it as a legitimate tool of psychical research."

"I am quite lost," Mr. Merrick announced.

"Not to worry." Professor Sidgwick chuckled and stood. "It

isn't at all important to our purpose here, really." He strode toward the door. "I am meeting some associates for dinner, but I shall return afterward, and we will wait together for these ghosts to make themselves known."

"Thank you," Mr. Merrick said. "Thank you for coming."

"Not at all, my dear fellow. I hope our efforts might bring you some relief."

That was my hope as well, for I worried over the continued toll of the haunting on Mr. Merrick's health. The interview had seemed to invigorate him, though, and in the hours following the professor's departure, Mr. Merrick was in much better cheer than I had seen him in several days, and we passed the time in our usual way before the hauntings had started.

Then, as he had promised, Professor Sidgwick returned after dinner, exclaiming as he stepped into the room, "My, God! The whole city's gone mad! Policemen everywhere! Mobs calling themselves 'vigilance committees' roaming the streets, going on about the Jews. These murders are a ghastly business to begin with, but why is mankind's response to a bad situation always to find a way to make it worse?" He had brought with him a few newspapers, along with several instruments wrapped in cloth. These he carefully laid out on Mr. Merrick's table, after he had calmed, and I inquired as to their functions.

"This is a barometer," he said, indicating a device like a large pocket watch. "It measures air pressure. Some believe spirits have an effect on the density of air in a room. This here is a thermometer, of course."

"The ghosts do cause a chill in me," I said.

The professor nodded. "That is quite commonly reported."

"And when they appear, my . . . my jaw hurts. My scars."

He looked at my disfigurement then, finally giving it the scrutiny others gave continually, and I felt suddenly quite conscious of my ugliness. "Are there other times it hurts in this way?" he asked.

"When the weather turns," I said.

"My, my. That *is* quite fascinating." He gently tapped the barometer's glass face. "Weather changes are also associated with changes in air pressure, you see. Perhaps you are a human ghost detector, Miss Fallow."

It amazed me there might've been a scientific reason for the pain I'd experienced, but also reassured me that I could perhaps anticipate a ghostly presence in that way.

Mr. Merrick called from his armchair, "Might I see these instruments?"

"Of course," Professor Sidgwick said, and carried each of them over in a cradle of cloth between his hands. "I borrowed these, so I must be careful with them."

Once Mr. Merrick's curiosity had been satisfied, the professor arranged the instruments around the room and took readings from them, which he scratched into his notebook. "We must establish a basal measurement," he said, "against which we will monitor for changes."

It did not appear that the threat of haunting frightened the professor at all, but rather energized him.

Once he had established the tools of his science, we settled in to wait, and Professor Sidgwick handed me the newspapers. "I thought the current facts on the murders might inform our investigation of the ghosts of their victims."

I accepted the papers from him, though I had no desire to read them for the bloody and sensational. The only question I wanted answered just then was who Johnny might be. I started with the *Evening News*, and then moved on to the *Star*, and finally the *Times*. Not one of them reported anything about Annie Chapman's life. They mentioned that her funeral had taken place, but said nothing about the family and friends who might have attended it. Instead, the editors railed against the incompetence of the police and speculated on suspects the coppers had either questioned or taken into custody; that poor Jew Pizer had been released from jail but not the public's mistrust; and the fictional character of Mr. Hyde had even been accused. The papers did recount the most gruesome aspects of the murders, as if their readers needed reminding, on the very same page that they denounced the city's high society for not caring about the murdered, claiming that if the first victim had been a true lady instead of a streetwalker, the maniac would not have had the opportunity for a second.

I closed the papers in disgust.

"Is there nothing in them?" Mr. Merrick asked.

"Nothing worth mentioning," I said.

"That banker Samuel Montagu has offered a reward of one hundred pounds for the capture of the killer," Professor Sidgwick said. "Probably as much an attempt to restore the city's goodwill toward his Jewish brothers and sisters as it is an incentive for justice. Not that there was ever a just amount of goodwill to restore.

Simply a ghastly business, all the way 'round." He stroked his beard for a few moments. "Does that phonograph work?"

"It does," Mr. Merrick said. "It was a gift from the famed actress Madge Kendal."

"Indeed?" Professor Sidgwick crossed the room and looked at the device. "This is Edison's design, if I'm not mistaken," he said. "What is on the cylinder?"

"It is Handel," Mr. Merrick said. "An oratorio called *Israel in Egypt.*"

"I've not heard a phonograph before." Professor Sidgwick reached for the hand crank. "Would you permit me?"

"Of course," Mr. Merrick said.

The professor turned the crank and the cylinder rotated in reply, and out of the flaring horn emerged the sound of music and singing, but it was muffled and distant. At the first few notes, I felt a wonder and delight at the sounds emerging from this machine, but soon the lack of natural, vibrant beauty in the music struck my ear as though someone had canned the concert like so much pea soup.

When the cylinder ended, the professor ceased cranking the handle and stepped away from the phonograph. "That is the closest thing to a ghost I've encountered," he said. "That is the sound of someone reaching out to us from the past. Haunting, is it not?"

"I do not care for it," Mr. Merrick said. "I much prefer Charles's music. But please do not tell Mrs. Kendal. I would not want to seem ungrateful."

I had to interpret those words for the professor, who then reassured Mr. Merrick that he would keep his confidence. Mr. Merrick asked if I would read to him, which I did, while Professor Sidgwick went about fussing over his instruments. The night progressed at an adequate pace, its mood lifted over previous nights by the professor's presence, and at midnight I felt fatigue setting in. My eyes tried very hard to close against my will, while Professor Sidgwick's energy appeared boundless, and he prodded me awake when I began to drift to sleep.

"Tell me about your upbringing," he said. "Your schooling, specifically."

"There isn't much to tell." I tried and failed to suppress a yawn. "I received a quality instruction until my father could no longer afford it. He believed firmly in the education of women."

"As do I," Professor Sidgwick said. "Wholeheartedly. Indeed, thirteen years ago I founded Newnham College at Cambridge. It is a women's only college, and a fine institution."

"That is . . . wonderful, I'm sure." I didn't know why he was telling me this. It did not strike me as a boast, but I could think of no other reason for him to say it, and anyway I was too tired to give it much care.

"A college for women?" Mr. Merrick said. "What a marvelous thing."

"I quite agree," the professor said.

A few minutes went by in which I once again felt sleep overtaking me, and Mr. Merrick went equally quiet.

"I can see these nightly visitations have thoroughly exhausted you," Professor Sidgwick said. "I shall stay awake if you would like to sleep. We have a few hours, yet."

Mr. Merrick and I both complied with his suggestion, and though my sleep was fitful in the upright chair, it did me good, for when the professor roused us at three that morning, I felt somewhat refreshed. I blinked and rubbed my eyes, and then added some coal to the fire. The professor made another circuit around the room, checking his instruments and scratching in his book, his eagerness for Polly's arrival palpable. We said little as the minutes went by, each of them bringing us closer to the appointed hour.

When the clock tolled half past three, I readied myself, as did Mr. Merrick. I quivered a bit, still nervous, but I felt no ghostly presence move outside the door.

Professor Sidgwick looked at me. "Your scars?"

I shook my head, feeling no ache there.

Before long, it was a quarter to four, and Polly had failed to appear. Then it was four, and still she kept away.

"This is most unexpected," Mr. Merrick said.

Professor Sidgwick frowned, but continued to monitor his instruments and wait.

The minutes multiplied upon themselves and became hours, still absent Polly, and soon absent Annie as well. Professor Sidgwick had spent an entire night without witnessing those things he had stayed over to see, and therefore had gleaned no answers to our questions or his. Disappointment rounded his shoulders as he gathered his instruments and rewrapped them.

"I'm sorry," I said, unsure of what to make of this development. I desperately wanted someone more learned than myself to witness the ghosts. It wasn't that I doubted my own senses, but I wanted answers. I wanted a way to stop the hauntings for Mr. Merrick and myself. "We have wasted your time, Professor."

"Think nothing of that," he said. "This sort of thing happens with some regularity. Ghosts hate to be studied, it seems, and become shy around scientists. I'm only sorry that I can't be of more help to you. But perhaps the ghosts have gone and will trouble you no more."

"But what if they return?" Mr. Merrick asked. "What do we do?"

I felt sure they would return, and still feared them as greatly as I had before.

The professor paused. "Those who claim to know of such things often say that spirits who haunt are suffering under the tyranny of powerful emotion. The young widow stricken by grief over the death of her soldier husband, for example. The emotion is the engine of their haunting, and must be resolved if they are to find peace."

"How can their emotion be resolved?" I asked.

"That depends upon the source of it, I suppose. Someone living must do what the ghost would do were they alive." He shook his head. "I'm sorry I can't tell you more, but this truly is not my area of expertise. I'd hoped that if I could see these ghosts I might better understand it all. But now I must return to Cambridge."

"I thank you for coming, at any rate," Mr. Merrick said.

"I was glad to, and hope to come visit again. It was a pleasure to meet you." The professor shook Mr. Merrick's good hand and then asked if I might join him a moment outside. I followed him, and in the courtyard he brought up the subject of his women's college once more. "You could attend," he said. "I could see to it that you're admitted."

"Me, sir?" It seemed absurd enough to be a mockery.

"Why, yes. From our conversations last night, I can see you have the intellect, as well as a previous education."

He made it sound as though those things were all that was required. He did not understand how it was for me, the eyes on me always full of loathing and fear. He did not understand how painful it would be for me to attend his college, day after day bearing the weight of knowing that I was not wanted there. If the streets had rejected me, what chance did I have in a lofty place of learning?

"Why not consider it?" he asked.

I wanted to tell him to look at my face, but he had seen it all night and still he'd extended this invitation.

"No, sir," I said. "I thank you most gratefully, but I am content in my position with Mr. Merrick."

"Yes, of course," he said. "I would not ask you to leave him now, certainly. He clearly relies on you, and your service to him is admirable. But what about . . . after?"

"After?"

"After he passes from this earth."

He made Mr. Merrick's death seem imminent. "Sir?"

"Treves informed me he's not sure how much longer Merrick has to live. When the hospital first took him in, no one believed the lad would survive this long."

It had not occurred to me that Mr. Merrick's condition might shorten his life, and I wondered if these were the changing circumstances to which the matron had alluded. That realization shocked the breath out of me for a moment, and replaced it with grief.

"You might give a thought to your future, Miss Fallow," the professor said. "I see potential in you. With that, I bid you good day."

CHAPTER 11

The hope that Professor Sidgwick's visit had brought vanished quickly, and by the afternoon an oppressive melancholy had returned to claim Mr. Merrick. He did not eat, and did not wish to engage in any of his usual activities. Instead he sat by the fire, alternately staring blankly into the coals and dozing, and I didn't know what I could do for him.

"Maybe they won't return," I offered. "They didn't last night."

His response was very slow in coming, and weak when it finally emerged. "They will return. I know it. But there is nothing I can do for them."

"Let's just wait and see," I said.

"Will you be with me?" he asked.

Though I had no wish to be, for myself, there was only one possible answer I could give him. "Of course I will."

His forecast proved accurate, for that night Polly and Annie came back, and their visitations proceeded as if indelibly recorded on a phonograph cylinder, to be turned again and again in perpetual, haunting repetition. It was indeed a kind of tyranny, just as Professor Sidgwick had described it, from which neither they nor we could escape. That night, and the next, and the next after that, they came, and with each successive appearance Mr. Merrick grew weaker. At times I tried to convince myself it was simply the exhaustion from his lack of sleep, but more often found I could not deny the *unnatural* aspect of his decline.

On the Sunday following Professor Sidgwick's failed investigation, Dr. Tilney came to visit Mr. Merrick. I felt glad to see him again, for our encounter a few nights earlier had been pleasant. Upon entering the room, he stood by the door, wearing his long coat, his top hat in hand, looking at his shoes, in obvious discomfort he attempted to hide.

"Dr. Tilney, it has been a long time," Mr. Merrick said. "It is good to see you."

"Yes . . . um." Dr. Tilney turned to me, clearly flummoxed, and so I interpreted Mr. Merrick's speech. "Yes, Joseph," he then said. "It has been a long time. I've been quite busy, you see. I lecture now at the medical college."

"Congratulations," Mr. Merrick said. "I'm sure the students learn much from you."

This I also translated.

"I trust they do," Dr. Tilney said, finally lifting his eyes to Mr. Merrick where he sat in his bed. The doctor then took a step farther into the room. "Are you well, Joseph? You do not look it, old chap."

"I doubt I ever look well, Dr. Tilney." Mr. Merrick attempted a chuckle.

"Right, of course." Dr. Tilney crossed the room and placed his hat on the table next to the model church. "What I mean is, your complexion is quite peaked. Are you eating?"

"Some," Mr. Merrick said.

Dr. Tilney looked to me, and I answered honestly. "He eats but little."

"And are you sleeping?" the doctor asked.

"Some," Mr. Merrick said.

This, too, I corrected, though naturally I omitted the cause.

Dr. Tilney pulled me away for a hushed aside. "How long has he been in this condition?" he asked me.

I lowered my voice. "Two weeks now."

"Is Dr. Treves aware of it?"

"He has spoken of performing another medical examination, yes."

"A medical display, you mean," Dr. Tilney said.

I detected disapproval in his voice. "Pardon me, sir?"

"What Treves refers to is a display of Joseph naked before the medical body of the hospital. It isn't about the man's health, it's about the mystery of his condition." He shook his head. "Never sat right with me, to be perfectly honest. How different is such an exhibition from Merrick's freak show days? It'd be better to let the man live out his remaining days in peace."

"Are his remaining days so few?" I asked. Professor Sidgwick's words had sat heavy with me, and I felt both worried and sad.

"It's impossible to know for certain, of course," he said. "Before, I would have expected him to reach at least thirty-five years of age. Seeing his condition now . . ."

"How long, sir?"

He simply shook his head and said, "Treves must know of this. But what of you? You do not look well, either. When was your last day off?"

"I've not taken one," I said. "I've no wish to leave the hospital."

"Do," he said. "You need it." He then retrieved his hat from the table and raised his voice. "Joseph, it was wonderful to see you!"

"I'm sorry you must leave so soon," Mr. Merrick said, but Dr. Tilney didn't wait for me to interpret his speech.

"I'll try to come again soon," the doctor said, heading toward the door. "In the meantime, eat and sleep more, yes? Doctor's orders."

"I'll try," Mr. Merrick said.

"Good man." Dr. Tilney gave me a nod. "Miss Fallow, good day."

Then he was gone, and Mr. Merrick blinked at the door. "That was a surprising visit. I didn't know Dr. Tilney still worked at the hospital."

"Like he said, Mr. Merrick, he's an important man now, and quite busy."

"What were you both whispering about?"

"Oh . . ." I attempted a casual lie, something I'd not had to do recently. "Nothing to trouble yourself over."

"You were speaking of me, were you not?"

"It was nothing," I said, and attempted a change to the subject. "What will you do with this model church when it's finished?"

He swung his prodigious head toward his table. "I think I shall give it to Mrs. Kendal, to thank her for everything she has done for me. Did you know she once arranged for me to have basket-making lessons?"

"I didn't."

"Yes. I wrote to her that I should like to know how it was done, and a man came to teach me."

"And where are these baskets that you made?" I asked.

He tapped his tuberous hand. "It will probably not surprise you to learn that I was not very accomplished at it."

I thought he meant that as an attempt at humor, and I smiled.

"I've been thinking about what Professor Sidgwick told us," he said. "About what the spirits want."

"Oh?"

"Yes. I wish that I could do for them what they cannot, because they are dead and I am living."

Once again, I marveled at the kindness in his nature, how a man could be so pitiful and despised, and not grow angry and hateful of the world in return, but rather show it such charity and compassion. "Would that all men were like you, Mr. Merrick," I said, and immediately knew how he would respond to that.

"Most men would—"

"I don't mean your face, you joker. I mean your character."

He laughed, and the sound warmed me through. "I know," he said, but within a moment had grown somber again. "But I am in earnest about what I wish."

"I know," I said.

"I wonder . . ."

"You wonder what?"

"It . . . might be too much to ask of you."

I was seized then by a fear quite different than that which I felt in the presence of the ghosts. This was not a fear of the unknown, but a fear of what I knew all too well, and if Mr. Merrick was about to ask me what I thought, I wanted no part of it. I would not venture back out into the streets of Whitechapel, not for myself and certainly not on a spirit's errand.

"Would you do for me what I would do for the ghosts?"
he asked.

"Mr. Merrick . . ."

"Please, hear me out. I've been thinking about Polly. She seems
·to be under a tyranny of fear that William would abandon her.
Perhaps if I—that is, perhaps if you find her William and tell him
about her father, she would know William loved her in spite of it
and be at peace."

What he suggested seemed both overly romantic and impossible, like something from a novel. "Mr. Merrick, you're saying
you want me to track down a strange man of unknown quality
to deliver a message from his dead wife that's very likely to
upset him?"

"Yes."

My fear mounted higher, especially at the thought of Leather
Apron on the loose. "No," I said. "I'm sorry, Mr. Merrick, but I cannot do what you ask."

"I know it is difficult—"

"It's not *difficult.*" My voice quavered. "It's *unthinkable*, Mr.
Merrick. You of all people . . . you know what it is like out there.
You came here to hide, the same as me. I beg you, don't ask me."

He said nothing for several moments, and then he extended
his good arm toward me as near as he could reach, and I met him
the rest of the way and took his hand in mine, which he gently
squeezed. "I understand," he said. "I am sorry to have asked."

My fear diminished, and I softened toward him. "It wasn't
wrong of you to ask," I said. "I just can't do it."

"I know." He released me and slumped backward against his

pillows. "It isn't something anyone can do," he said with a sigh of utter surrender.

I thought about what Dr. Tilney had told me, and I felt a constriction of grief in my chest that nearly stopped me from breathing. "We don't even know if that would help Polly, do we? I mean, Professor Sidgwick didn't even know."

"I suppose that's true."

In honesty, I was trying to reassure myself. The thought that I might be able to do something to stop the hauntings and thereby relieve Mr. Merrick's suffering but chose not to filled me with guilt. So I instead relied entirely on a faith that the doctors would find a way to help him, and I strained toward a hope that with time, perhaps the spirits would simply leave him in peace of their own accord. They did not leave him in peace that night, though, but I was with him at least as he sought vainly to comfort Polly and understand Annie through her endless screaming. Dr. Treves came the next day to examine him, during which I left his room, motivated more by a respect for Mr. Merrick's privacy than by my previous fear of his body. After the examination, Dr. Treves sought me out and found me in the laundry.

"I am at a loss," he said. "I've not seen him this low since he first came to me. I don't understand this sudden decline, but then, we know little about his condition. He is simply wasting away. Can you not get him to eat, somehow?"

"I provide his meals, sir," I said. "Beyond that—"

He stopped me short with a flick of his hand. "Yes, yes, I know. It's not as if you can force the food into him, now can you? I didn't mean to suggest any negligence on your part."

"What can be done for him?" I asked.

"Well, I must give some thought to a more suitable bed. Perhaps if he could sleep more comfortably, he might regain some strength. As for this melancholy, I may solicit a few more visits from the society women I know. And he has wanted to go to the theater for some time. Perhaps Mrs. Kendal could use her connections to arrange it. A pantomime, I think. That would give him a reason to look ahead and get his strength back."

I knew Dr. Treves meant well, but his efforts on behalf of Mr. Merrick seemed to me somewhat patronizing, in the same way as the nickname he'd given him. Mr. Merrick was a man worthy of forthrightness and respect, not a child to be sheltered and indulged, but I simply said, "I'm sure he would enjoy all those things."

He nodded. "In the meantime, do what you can to encourage him to eat. Make him as comfortable as possible. See that he rests."

"Yes, Doctor."

"And if you should uncover the source of his melancholy, please inform me of it. I think that may be at the root of his poor health."

"Yes, Doctor," I said, wincing inwardly at a twist of guilt.

"In the coming weeks, I shall present him before the medical college. It has been some time since we made a study of him."

I did not want to seem brazen, but I thought about what Dr. Tilney had said and felt driven to protect Mr. Merrick. "Sir, do you think him well enough for that?"

Dr. Treves scowled. "It is because of his condition I feel it necessary. For the betterment of our medical profession. I am duty-bound to take what opportunity we have to study him, and if he is coming to the end of his tragic life, we must act quickly. We may not have another chance."

His calculation possessed the scientific indifference of a balance scale, and even had I been willing to risk a further impertinence, I had no argument against his logic. He left me then, and after I'd finished taking care of Mr. Merrick's bedding, I went and filled his coal hod.

On the way back, I chanced to meet a porter about some hospital errand. He was a brutish-looking fellow with a simian's brow and a bricklayer's hands. I was alone with him, and now the newspapers had insinuated a suspicion into the mortar of the walls I'd thought would protect me.

Any one of these men moving about the hospital so freely and easily could've been a murderer in healer's clothing. By his appearance, I could believe the man before me capable of terrible violence. He looked up at me askance as I drew near him, and I let go of the cumbersome hod with one hand to pull my shawl tighter around my face.

He stepped to the side of the corridor to let me pass. "Miss," he said with a nod.

"Thank you," I said, and slid by him with my head down, giving him as much distance as I could manage.

"Where you going with that coal?" he asked my back, his voice hollow and rough.

"Mr. Merrick's rooms," I said without turning.

"I could help you."

"No." It might have simply been my nerves, but something about his offer felt wrong. "But thank you."

"Looks heavy for you," he said, with some insistence.

I stopped and looked back. He hadn't moved from the side of the corridor, and he stared at me from under that prominence of a brow. A chill overtook me, and my breathing stopped in fear.

"It's my duty," I said. "I can manage it."

"Suit yourself," he said, but he didn't move from that spot for several moments, watching me until I'd rounded a corner.

I hurried back to Mr. Merrick's room, shaking, where I confined myself for the next two days, unless my leaving were absolutely necessary to fetch his meals and see to his needs. Though haunted, that place had become my final safe harbor, save the few hours I spent each night with the other maids around the table and then in my room.

On Thursday the following week, though I'd watched Mr. Merrick decline in that time even further, Dr. Treves came as planned and brought with him Miss Flemming and Miss Doyle. The nurses took Mr. Merrick into the back room to bathe him and dress him, and while I waited with the doctor I wondered how Mr. Merrick felt about this primping and imminent exhibition.

When Mr. Merrick emerged from the bathroom, he looked even more pitiful than was usual for him. His head swung low enough I feared it would drag him to the ground, and he looked paler than I had ever seen him. Again I felt a deep ache in my chest from my guilt.

"Are we ready, then?" Dr. Treves asked.

"I am ready," Mr. Merrick said, his voice almost a whisper.

Dr. Treves produced an enormous and curious cap with a wide hood attached to it, which Mr. Merrick allowed to be placed over his head. It covered his face to the shoulders in the manner of a potato sack, with a slit cut in the fabric before his eyes.

"Would you walk with us, Evelyn?" Mr. Merrick asked me.

"Of course," I said.

Dr. Treves led the way outside, where Miss Flemming and Miss Doyle left us to return to their duties. We then went through the east wing into the hospital gardens, our progress quite slow due to the laborious nature of Mr. Merrick's gait. I walked beside him, my arm linked with his to lend him both support and my companionship. He drew much attention from those patients we passed, but less from the staff who had no doubt been warned not to stare—but with the hood covering his face, those who did watch him showed expressions of curiosity rather than horror or fear.

"I used to walk here at night," Mr. Merrick said to me just before we'd reached the far side. "I like these gardens."

I nodded. "They're quite lovely."

"I should like to see them better," he said. "Without having to look through this mask."

"Perhaps we can arrange for another private walk sometime," Dr. Treves said.

After the gardens, we crossed the grounds to the medical college where I'd found the library and borrowed *Northanger Abbey*. Dr. Treves stopped us at the steps up to the front doors.

"Wait here a moment," he said. "I'll just go in to make sure they're ready for John in the theater."

After he'd gone, I could not resist asking, "Does this bother you at all, Mr. Merrick? Being displayed like this?"

His expression had always been difficult to read, but with the hood over his face, it was utterly impossible, and I didn't know how to interpret his silence that followed my question.

"I'm very grateful for everything the hospital has done for me," he said at last.

"I don't doubt that," I said.

"I shouldn't complain," he said.

"So it does bother you, then?"

"I do feel . . . like an animal at a cattle market. All those doctors prodding and whispering."

"Why don't you tell Dr. Treves you don't want to do it?"

Another silence followed. "I shouldn't complain."

"The way I see it, Mr. Merrick, you don't owe them this." I heard the anger in my voice, and I knew it to be half directed at myself.

"Don't I?"

"No. Just because they're taking care of you doesn't mean they own your dignity."

"They're ready for you, John," Dr. Treves called as he came back out through the doors. He descended the steps and took Mr. Merrick's arm from me. "Thank you, Miss Fallow. He'll be back in his room in two hours or so."

I waited to see if Mr. Merrick would go with him, and he did.

"Very good, Doctor," I said through clenched teeth, and after they'd gone inside I marched back to the nurses' house and downstairs toward my room. As I passed near the kitchens, I saw a newspaper lying on the dining table and assumed Beatrice must have left it there after breakfast or luncheon. It was a copy of the *Times* from the previous week, and I fought with myself over whether to pick it up and read it. There were things I absolutely did not want to know about the killings, but I also considered there might be further information about the victims. I wondered if I might learn something to stop the hauntings, without leaving the hospital as Mr. Merrick had asked me. I decided to look through the paper, for his sake.

Most of the text concerned itself with new clues, new witnesses, and new theories, none of which seemed relevant to the lives of Polly or Annie. But some pages in, the editors printed a letter from someone identified as "S.G.O." In the letter, S.G.O. expounded at great length on the sins that had been allowed to proliferate throughout the East End, and went so far as to claim the recent Whitechapel murders were only the natural result of this iniquity, to the point of nearly blaming the victims for their own deaths, because of their disrepute. Upon reading this, I slammed the paper down in anger and leapt to my feet.

"Mad as hops, you look," someone said, and I turned to see the cook standing in the corridor, her arms folded across her narrow chest.

"What do you want?" I asked.

"Easy now," she said. "What's got into you?"

"It's nothing," I said, not because it was, but because I didn't want to discuss it with her.

"It's something," she said.

I pointed at the paper. "Do you know what they're saying about the murders? That it was those women's own fault getting themselves killed."

"Well," she said, "if they hadn't been out swiving, they wouldn't be dead. Can't argue that, now can you?"

She angered me as much as the paper, and I stalked away from the table to rid myself of both their presences.

"But they also wouldn't be dead if that maniac hadn't killed them," she said. "Can't argue with that, neither."

I stopped and turned. "So what are you saying?"

She unfolded her arms. "There's blame to be laid, that's for certain, but you can be sure it'll fall where it keeps the upper crust feeling safe." With that, she returned to her kitchen.

I stood by the table, pondering what she'd said, imagining the rich swells quaking in fear at Leather Apron and desperate for any cause to say he wouldn't come for them or their ladies.

"Evelyn!" Becky charged suddenly down the stairs into the room, her breathing quick and ragged, her eyes wide.

I stepped toward her. "What is it?"

"It's Mr. Merrick," she said. "He fell."

CHAPTER 12

I found Mr. Merrick in bed with his eyes closed, propped upright against a mountain of pillows, as still as a frozen rain barrel. Deathly still. Dr. Treves and Dr. Tilney tipped their heads together at his side, but both turned to look at me when I entered. I'd run to Mr. Merrick's rooms even though the matron expressly forbade running, even at times of emergency, but now that I felt the doctors' eyes upon me I adopted as decorous an approach as I could manage across the room toward them.

"What happened?" I asked them. "Is he . . . ?"

Dr. Treves spread his mustache wide with his thumb and forefinger. "He is alive. But he is very unwell. He collapsed in the theater, and has yet to regain consciousness."

"He collapsed?" I asked.

"I was conducting my lecture," Dr. Treves said, "and partway through he simply fell."

"For God's sake, Freddy," Dr. Tilney said. "It was obviously too much for him. I could see that plainly from my chair."

A flare of anger burned through my pain, for I had voiced similar concerns before Dr. Treves had taken him.

"I find your recriminations unhelpful, Francis," Dr. Treves said. "But . . . perhaps you are right."

"Will he recover?" I asked.

"We've done everything we can," Dr. Treves said. "There is no cure for his condition. He has no infection, no secondary disease. It seems his body is finally succumbing to the travails of his life."

That didn't answer my question, and his evasion only worsened my panic. I knew the source of his weakness, because I had refused to do what Mr. Merrick had asked me to do. "Will he recover?" I asked again, my voice louder.

"We don't know," Dr. Tilney said. "There is too little medical precedent. But it doesn't look hopeful."

"Miss Flemming and Miss Doyle will take shifts watching over him," Dr. Treves said. "Miss Fallow, I'd like for you to be here as well. It may be he has some degree of awareness, in which case your presence might prove a balm to him."

"Of course, Doctor," I said, trying to steady my voice. "I shall stay at his side."

"Good, thank you." Dr. Treves then looked at Dr. Tilney, and a nod passed between them. They left the bedside and moved toward the door, and as they reached it, Dr. Tilney allowed Dr. Treves to pass through first.

"I'll join you in a moment, Freddy," he said, and when he and I were alone he shook his head. "I'm sorry," he said. "I should have checked on him sooner. I should have kept visiting him."

I appreciated his remorse, but I knew the cause of Mr. Merrick's decline, and it was not Dr. Tilney's fault. Nor was it actually Dr. Treves's, though he certainly hadn't helped. "You must not blame yourself for this," I said. "You could not have prevented it."

"Even so," he said, and frowned at the floor. Then he looked up at Mr. Merrick for a moment. "My wife is expecting me. But I'll return soon."

I hadn't known he was married, but it made sense that a handsome doctor such as he would be, and even though I had not truly allowed myself to consider him in any romantic way, I felt a small disappointment shatter to pieces inside me. "Good day, sir," I said.

He departed, and I sat down alone beside Mr. Merrick's bed, nearly collapsing under the ponderous burden of my remorse. I feared that if I had acted according to his request and sought to help those spirits find peace, Mr. Merrick might've been recovering even in that moment, but I'd been a coward. Low as the chances of success in finding Polly's husband had seemed, surely it would've been better to have tried *something*.

Somehow, the serenity of his syncope rendered his features less monstrous. By then, the topography of his form had become a familiar landscape to me, and I looked on the mass and growth of his face with a kind of affection, for the first time recognizing his deformity not as something to look past, but as a part of who he was. I wondered if the spirits would've come to him for comfort had he not developed a sensitivity toward their sex because of his mother and his affliction, and I sat there for several moments letting guilt flog me, feeling powerless and afraid, until the arrival of Miss Doyle.

"How is he?" she asked, but in a perfunctory manner that seemed to already know the answer. She took his wrist gently with the tips of her fingers and checked the rhythm of his heart against her pocket watch, after which she wrote something down in a notebook she kept in her apron. "Sad, isn't it? His life?"

"It is," I said.

"I took a solemn oath to save life," she said. "But there are cases where I wonder if death would be the kinder mercy. For some patients I find myself wishing for it even as I'm fighting against it."

"Are you wishing for it for Mr. Merrick?" I asked.

"I don't know," she said. "I truly can't imagine the tragedy of his life. He's here now, and I've no doubt his life is better for it, but is he out of pain?"

Much of my pain had only begun after I'd healed from my surgery, and I'd accepted I would never be free of it.

"I suppose it's in God's hands," she said, the words and the sigh that followed them sounding well used.

She stayed a short while, and then left, and then returned, and then left again. Miss Flemming then came in the same pattern. I assisted them when necessary, at one point rolling his great frame to change his bedding, and they taught me how to measure the rate of his heartbeat. It felt odd to count the pulses of blood through the vessels of his delicate wrist, for though they were driven by Mr. Merrick's noble heart, they were silent on the matter of his kindness and innocence found there.

When evening fell, I went to the dormitory for a quick meal and received a round of distant sympathy from the other maids, then returned to his side. I stayed there in that chair into the night, dozing off and startling awake to check Mr. Merrick's breathing. As I rounded the midnight bend, my awareness shifted to the door of the room and the courtyard beyond, for I wondered if the ghosts would still come.

A few hours later, Polly did, entering the room as she always had in her wedding gown, but she stopped just inside the door. Her hollow gaze then swept the room, and her eyebrows met in worry.

I rose from my chair, but dared not approach her. "He is dying," I said. "You are killing him. Please, if you can understand me, you must leave him in peace."

She ignored me as she always did, and instead of leaving, she drifted to the mantel and seemed to study the cards and pictures there.

"Please!" I called to her. "You must go!"

She turned about slowly and came over near me to the bed, while I did my best to keep my feet under me and my wits about me. Without Mr. Merrick awake, I felt much more vulnerable, and feared this apparition might yet turn malevolent and violent. She leaned in close over Mr. Merrick and watched him for several moments, her worried expression somewhat childlike and more lost than she had ever seemed to be.

When she reached up to touch Mr. Merrick, I shouted, "No!"

I even extended my hand to shield him, but she reached straight through my wrist, sending a freezing convulsion up my arm, and I recoiled. After laying her palm against his cheek, she turned and glided toward the door.

"D-don't come back," I said, though I knew she would ignore me, and she did. Then she was gone, and I dropped hard into my chair, rubbing my icy wrist where she had befouled it with her touch. "Oh, Mr. Merrick," I said. "I don't know if you can hear me, but I'm sorry. Sorry I didn't do what you asked me. I'm going to make it right. Somehow."

The next two hours felt strained and tortured on the rack. But they passed, and then came the pain in my jaw, and I knew Annie had appeared.

When the door flung open and she stormed into the room, I let out a scream of my own, but I couldn't even hear it over her terrible sound. She charged directly at me, and I quaked and shielded my head with my hands and arms, my eyes squeezed shut. Without looking, I knew she stood over me, her mouth open, forming the same name.

John-ny!

"Please go," I whispered as tears leaked out of my closed eyes. "Please. Please go."

No soul heard my plea, and the screaming continued for an eternity. When it abated, I opened my eyes slowly and looked up to find that Annie had gone, and though my tears did not then stop, my sobbing was not for myself. I sat hunched over, crying for Mr. Merrick. I didn't understand how I could so care for a man I had only known for a few weeks, and I realized then that perhaps all those women who'd sent him cards and photographs truly had been sincere. Perhaps he had touched their lives in the same way he had mine, and for the same reason that drew these spirits to him.

When my crying subsided, I washed my face in Mr. Merrick's bathroom and then went about the ordinary duties of the day. Miss Flemming and Miss Doyle continued their observance of the signs of his vitality, and Dr. Treves and Dr. Tilney came as well.

After their examination, they pronounced him slightly worsened, and spoke with a solemnness that seemed to have already accepted Mr. Merrick's death as inevitable.

Around ten o'clock Charles came to visit, ignorant of Mr. Merrick's condition. Upon learning it, the knowledge seemed to deflate his posture and humble his demeanor.

"Poor ugly bloke," he said. "Will he recover?"

"The doctors aren't sure," I said.

"What can be done?"

"Perhaps you might play for him? The doctors believe he may have some awareness."

Charles took a deep breath. "Right, then." He went for his instrument and tuned it as he brought it to the foot of Mr. Merrick's bed. "What should I play?"

"Whatever you think he'd like to hear."

He paused, looking up at the ceiling, and then launched into a beautiful tune. It had the sound of a country ballad, and though Charles sang no words, a sad and mournful quality hung about the music's beginning. As the notes progressed, the song found hope and laughter, a little at first, and then a great swell of rising happiness. By the time Charles finished, the song had come to a joyous ending, and I applauded when he played the last note.

"That was lovely," I said. "What is it called?"

"I haven't named it."

"You mean . . . did you compose that?" His talent impressed me.

"It were me, indeed," he said. "That give you cause to rethink your appraisal?"

"Not at all," I said.

"Maybe I'll call it 'Joseph and Evelyn,'" he said, and that actually brought a smile out of me. "But now," he said, grinning, "I'm wondering what a song 'Charles and Evelyn' would make—"

"Do not flirt with me," I said. "Not now, of all times." It offended me he would even try.

He dipped his head. "Of course. My apologies."

"He is *dying*," I said. "How could you even think—"

"I'm sorry," he said.

I didn't know if he truly was or wasn't, but it felt unfair to give him any further attention for it while Mr. Merrick lay there.

"Before I go," Charles said, "is there anything else I can do for Joseph?"

I thought of what really needed to be done, namely the action Mr. Merrick had asked me to make on behalf of the spirits. Such a thing would require me to go into the city to first find the friends and associates of Polly and Annie, and from them learn where I might find William and discover the identity of Johnny. I grudgingly admitted it did not seem to be a task I could undertake alone.

"There may actually be something you can do, Mr. Weaver."

"Name it," he said.

"You might . . . find it hard to accept."

"I'll accept anything you tell me."

"Do you remember Mr. Merrick asking if you believed in ghosts?"

He cocked his head. "I do."

"He had reason to ask it," I said, and then explained to him all the details of the haunting. Through my tale he remained stoic, nodding here and there, but otherwise refrained from commenting, and I had no sense of whether he believed me or not. I thought it likely I sounded quite mad, but pressed through until I had caught him up to the present circumstances.

When I'd finished, Charles stood a moment rubbing his knuckles. "So you're saying you been seeing ghosts?"

"Yes."

"And you never run away? You stayed with Joseph?"

"I did."

"Bricky bit o' jam, you are, you know that? Bricky bit of jam."

I took his compliment with a slight blush in spite of myself.

"And now," he said, "you needs to find this William bloke, and this Johnny bloke?"

"That's right."

"Then what?"

"I don't know. But I must talk with them. Perhaps they'll have some answers."

He kept rubbing his knuckles a moment or two longer, and then dropped his hands to his sides. "Right. Let's do it, then."

"You mean you'll help me?"

"Of course," he said. "But I must confess, I'm hoping this'll earn me the privilege of a walk with you." My indignation at that must have been apparent to him, for he held up his hands in mock defense. "Only having some fun with you."

"Once again, now is not the time."

"I see that plainly enough, and regret my mistake." He lifted his violin case. "Where do we start?"

"I don't know." I lifted my shawl up to cover my face and

pulled it tight. "The paper said Annie Chapman drank at the Ten Bells."

"I know that pub," he said. "Up in Spitalfields by Christ Church. So we ask around there, then?"

"I suppose it's as good a place to start as any." I headed for the door.

"Hang on. You need to let them know you're taking off or something?"

"Oh." In my hurry and eagerness to help Mr. Merrick, I had given almost no thought to the matron's expectations of me. But she could've been anywhere in the great hospital, and it would've taken time to seek her out. Time was something I didn't feel I had to spare, for Mr. Merrick's life seemed measured by the hour. "I've not taken a single day off since I came here," I said. "I'm owed the time. I'll leave a note for Miss Flemming and Miss Doyle on the table." I hoped that would be sufficient.

"Fair enough," he said.

After doing so, I cast Mr. Merrick a long glance and silently renewed my promise to him. Then I went with Charles from the room out into Bedstead Square. Instead of exiting through the wards, we turned east and crossed the courtyard, passing the hospital's workshops, and left the grounds through a tall gate manned by a porter on East Mount Street. From there, Charles led the way north to Whitechapel Street, where wagons full of crates and barrels, carts with livestock, hansom cabs, and omnibuses packed the street. The sound of horses, the smell of dung, and the shouts of drivers, vendors, and pedestrians assaulted me.

"Let's ride the tram!" Charles said, lifting his voice above the din.

We jostled between porters unloading whiskey barrels from a couple of wagons, walked to the rail lines embedded in the street, and Charles waved his hand to flag down an approaching omnibus. The driver pulled the horses to a stop before us, and the conductor motioned us to the rear of the bus and up the circular staircase to the garden seats atop the vehicle. I went up first, and made sure to clutch tight my skirts to keep Charles from getting a view of my drawers, but he waited until I'd decently ascended before climbing up after me. We then claimed two seats next to each other on the right side, and the omnibus resumed its trundle down the tramway, the hospital on our left.

Our vantage offered a view of the street below, but also made me feel somewhat displayed to those we passed, and I checked my scarf to make sure it was in place.

"I haven't ridden a bus in quite some time," I said.

"I like to when my pockets ain't empty," Charles said. "But I've stepped off a bus to find my pockets emptied, anyways. Bloody dippers."

Omnibus passengers were a favorite target among pickpockets, which was another reason I'd avoided the vehicles, aside from the cost of riding. Maltoolers went for women in particular.

Within a few moments, we passed the greengrocer I'd stood before on my first day at the London Hospital, and next to it hunkered the same boarded-up waxworks, which must've been the very same place Mr. Merrick had been exhibited, and where Dr.

Treves had first seen him. It was very strange and sad to think of him in there instead of the hospital, frightening matchgirls from a dark and dusty room.

At the end of the block we came to Court Street and the Star and Garter pub, and but two doors on, we passed Thomas Barry's Live Entertainments, and next to it Thomas Barry's Waxworks. A crowd had gathered around the latter, and I leaned toward it to see what was of so much interest.

In the window of the waxworks hung a long painting depicting a woman. I had to blink at it twice for the image to settle upon my senses, and once it did I gasped and looked away in horror. The woman was obviously supposed to be one of Leather Apron's victims, and from what the papers had said, and the quantity of red and severity of injury depicted, I guessed it to be Annie Chapman.

"You all right?" Charles asked.

"They're putting the murdered women on display?" I said.

Charles nodded toward the establishment. "For a penny you can go in and see the bodies made in wax. Just as they were found murdered. The painting's a grab to get you in the door."

"I don't want to go near that place," I said.

Charles shrugged. "I'd go in."

"It's ghoulish," I said, and shuddered.

"I'm rightful curious is all."

I decided to drop the matter as I had with Martha, and on we rode down Whitechapel, which cut a wide arc southward as if it meant to reach the Thames. We passed the St. Mary's Station of the Metropolitan Underground Railway, opened but four years previous, and soon after rode by St. Mary's Church, all steeple and newly rebuilt after a fire had gutted her. A short distance from there we came to the frantic crossroads at Commercial Street, where different lines of the tramway came together near the Aldgate Station of the underground railway. Vehicles, pedestrians, horses, merchants, and vendors all choked the street as surely as consumption of the lungs.

Here, we paid the conductor our two farthings and disembarked from the omnibus, then boarded another heading north, up Commercial Street. This took us out of Whitechapel toward Spitalfields, into the Evil Quarter Mile, a warren of back slum alleyways, rookeries, doss-houses, and brothels. My father's body had been found in one of the alleys that we passed, and I tried not to look too long at any of them. Commercial Street was itself wide and busy with traffic, but from it reached narrow avenues like Flower and Dean, which was known as the foulest and most dangerous street in all London, with Dorset Street perhaps competing with it for the distinction.

I peered down both of them as we passed, Flower and Dean on the right, then Dorset on the left, both dark, narrow, and teeming with whores, house-breakers, lurkers, and bludgers, where children crawled naked in the filthy street, and in the face of evil the only two responses were to cheer it on or look the other way.

Charles leaned closer to me. "You ever been in there?"

I nodded but didn't want to say anything more to him about it, because I had no desire to remember. "And you?" I asked.

He shook his head. "Mutton shunters won't even go in there."

He was right. For a policeman to enter either street, he needed at least half a dozen compatriots at his side if they hoped to get out alive and unmaimed, and even then it would be a close thing. There would always be someone waiting in the shadows to serve out a crusher and damage any policeman for life. Kill a policeman, it'd be the gallows, but break a leg so the copper never walks right again, it'd be only twelve months hard labor, which to many was a dirty cheap price for the pleasure.

Past Dorset, we rolled up to Christ Church and disembarked with another two farthings paid to the conductor. The white building gleamed before us, the six thick columns at its feet bearing up the tall steeple with its clock face.

"Ten Bells is over there," Charles said, pointing across Fournier Street at a corner pub. "Shouldn't be too rough this early in the day."

I inhaled deeply to steady my nerves, then checked my shawl. I'd gone into such pubs as a girl, looking for my father. I didn't know exactly what I would find inside this one, but I knew I had to begin somewhere, and if this tavern had been frequented by Annie Chapman, it seemed a good enough place to start asking questions. I was afraid, but I had only to think of Mr. Merrick wasting away in his bed to find my courage.

"You sure about this?" Charles asked.

"Yes," I said. "Let's go."

CHAPTER 13

Even given the time of day, the Ten Bells had a bit of a crowd inside. Charles had been right, though. This wasn't the rough gathering it would be that night, but rather a collection of laborers and tradesmen taking a beer before they settled into their afternoon's work. The pub wasn't large, just one room with a horseshoe bar along the far wall to the right.

The barkeep was a black man, his graying hair in a terrier crop, wearing a white shirt, black waistcoat, and an apron, and he offered us a nod as we entered and approached. "Good afternoon," he said. "What do you fancy?"

"Wondering if we might ask you a few questions," Charles said, leaning forward against the bar.

"Depends on the question," the bartender said, "and if you're buying."

Charles nodded. "Right. Gin for me, beer for the lady."

I shook my head. "I don't want—"

"Allow me," Charles said, and paid the bartender for the drinks.

I was no teetotaler, but I had watched drink destroy my father, and on the streets I had seen how vulnerable a drunken state could make a person. Though there had been times I'd certainly desired the sweet oblivion of alcohol, or opium for that matter, I'd never succumbed to such temptations.

Charles, on the other hand, tossed back his gin in an instant and ordered another. "What do they call you?" Charles asked the bartender.

"Flat Michael," the bartender said.

Charles nodded. "Flat Michael, I'm Charles Weaver. We're wondering about this Leather Apron business."

Flat Michael's eyes went dark and he leaned forward over his bar. "Bad business, that. Why you here asking me about it?"

"We heard Annie Chapman drinks here," Charles said.

"Not no more," Flat Michael said. "And unless a ghost can drink, I don't expect I'll see her again."

I felt a shiver as he said it, as if his words might summon Annie to that spot.

"Of course," Charles said. "My mistake, God rest her soul."

"I already told the police," Flat Michael said. "I didn't hardly know her."

"Don't sell me a dog," Charles said. "You know everyone who comes through that door."

"Why would I lie, eh? This maniac is bad for my business." He jabbed his own chest with his thumb. "Keeps the women away and brings in mobs hunting Jews. If I had information would catch him, believe me, I'd shout it. Why're you asking?"

"We simply want to know more about her," I said.

Flat Michael looked at me, then down at the beer I hadn't touched. "Something wrong with your drink?"

"Does she have any kin around?" Charles asked.

"None she spoke of," Flat Michael said. "Her husband's dead."

"Who was he?" I asked.

"A coachman," Flat Michael said. "John Chapman."

I thought of the name that Annie always screamed when she came—Johnny—as well as the black clothing she wore, and thought perhaps that mystery had been solved. But I had not a single notion of what could be done to assuage her spirit's pain if the man she mourned was dead. "When did he die?" I asked.

"On Christmas Day, it'll be two years," Flat Michael said. "But they'd not been living together before that."

"You know anyone else on terms with her?" Charles asked.

"Nah," Flat Michael said. "She sold things she crocheted or somesuch, and when that weren't enough, she sold her cunny. Kept with the Pensioner, at times."

Just then, a tall, blue-eyed woman with blonde hair poked her head through the door of the pub. "Michael," she said, "have you seen Barnett?"

"Not today, Mary Jane," Flat Michael said, after which the woman thanked him and left.

"The Pensioner?" Charles asked.

"Oh. That's what they call him. Military man. Lives on Osborn Place."

"Do you know what he drinks?" I asked.

"Anything he got the coin for," Flat Michael said. "Why?"

"I'll take a bottle of gin," I said, and paid him for it. Charles eyed me sidelong but said nothing as we thanked Flat Michael and left the Ten Bells. Out on the street, I tucked the bottle into a pocket in my skirts and led the way east along Fournier Street, down the length of Christ Church. Charles waited until we were a few paces on before asking me about the liquor I'd purchased.

"Planning to boil an owl, are you?"

"It's not for me," I said. "It's for the Pensioner."

"I see," Charles said. "So that's where we going, then?"

"It is," I said, feeling emboldened by our success thus far. I hadn't yet discovered how I might aid the spirit of Annie Chapman in her torment, but I knew more than I had when we'd left the hospital a short time earlier, and felt sure we might yet uncover the answer.

"I still don't understand what we're looking for," Charles said.

"I believe we'll know it when we find it," I said.

Osborn Place lay just opposite the far end of Flower and Dean, across Brick Lane, and a direct route to the Pensioner's might've taken us through the black heart of the rookeries. By traveling down Fournier and then turning south, I avoided that danger, though with its Jewish residents, Brick Lane was filled with an explosive air. On our way south, Charles and I passed several mobs armed with clubs and iron bars marching down the street, shouting and cursing, some wearing sandwich boards proclaiming LEATHER APRON IS NO ENGLISHMAN!

"I thought they cleared Pizer of suspicion," I whispered to Charles.

"Then it must be some other Jew," he whispered back, his voice sharp with cynicism.

We passed Heneage Street, with its stinking Best and Co. brewery, the pungent sour of fermentation mixed with smoke in the air all about the block, and came to Osborn Place. Across from it lay the other dark entrance to Flower and Dean. Osborn was not much better in character, but Charles stepped forward to approach a coster wearing a blue velveteen coat and a yellow kingsman about his neck. His boy next to him called out his oysters at a penny a piece and winkles at a penny a pint.

Charles bought a bag of winkles and asked the man if he knew where the Pensioner lived.

"Number one," the coster said, his hoarse voice ruined by a lifetime of barking. He pointed at the first door on the south side of the street.

We thanked him and approached the address. Charles knocked upon the door, and I withdrew the gin bottle from my skirts. Moments passed without a reply, and I'd almost reached the conclusion the Pensioner was out when I heard the key in the lock on the other side of the door. It opened to reveal a balding, farthing-faced, muscular man in shirtsleeves untucked from his trousers.

"Who're you?" he asked, with that deadness in his eyes I had come to recognize in men who'd lost all conscience.

"Charles Weaver." He gestured to me. "Miss Evelyn Fallow."

The man shifted his weight and leaned against the jamb. "Get on with it, then."

"We've come to speak about Annie Chapma—"

"Shove off," he said, and went to slam the door, but I stuck out my hand and stopped it from closing. The Pensioner responded to this by throwing it wide and stepping out aggressively toward me, but Charles leapt between us.

"Easy, there," he said. "We got no quarrel with you."

"Then what're you doing on my doorstep asking about Annie?"

"We just want to talk," Charles said.

I held out the bottle of gin. "For your trouble," I said, and then Charles lifted the bag of winkles.

The Pensioner eyed the bottle longer than he did the sea snails, and after a moment he turned back inside. "Come on, then."

Charles looked at me and his eyebrows gave a quick little hop, to which I nodded, and so we followed the Pensioner through the door, though if I had been alone I never would have done so. We came into a single cramped room, with a little kitchen off to one side from which a rancid smell emanated, and a staircase that was more of a ladder climbing up a bare wall in the far corner. A table stood in the middle of the room, surrounded by a chair and a couple of stools. The Pensioner motioned for us to sit and shuffled off into the kitchen, then returned a moment later with two mismatched tin mugs. He extended his hand toward me and snapped his fingers impatiently, so I gave him the gin bottle, which he opened.

"Thanks for talking with us," Charles said.

The Pensioner splashed some gin into the two cups, pushed one to Charles and the other to me, and then took a drink for himself right from the bottle. "Who said I was talking?"

Charles tossed the bag of winkles onto the table, and they landed with a rattle of their shells. "People been harassing you?" he asked.

The Pensioner plucked a pin from the bag and scooped a handful of the little snails out onto the table. "More than that. I lost my job."

"How?" I asked.

"They called me to testify at the inquest." He stuck the pin

into the opening of the winkle's shell and dug out the curling little bit of meat. "Had to take the whole day for it, and my employer
gave me the sack."

"What do you do?" Charles asked.

"I was a bricklayer," he said, and took another swig from the
gin bottle.

Charles went for a pin and winkle, and I decided to as well.
Though dead and cooked, the little snail seemed reluctant to give
up its armor, but once I'd tugged it free I relished the briny, chewy
morsel, and flicked the empty shell onto the table.

"You knew Annie Chapman," I said. "That's why you spoke at
the inquest."

"I know lots of women," he said.

"What can you tell us about her?" Charles asked.

The Pensioner picked another few winkles. "She were a good
woman. Good teeth. Strong legs. Drank too much at times." He
took another swig.

"What else?" I asked.

"Tell me what you want to know," he said, sounding irritated.

The problem was, I didn't know what I wanted to know. We'd
come to the part of the plan for which I hadn't prepared, having
hoped the necessary action would present itself. But sitting there
in that hovel, looking into the eyes of a man I wouldn't have
trusted with a casual greeting on the street, I was at a loss.
"Can . . . can you tell me about Johnny?" I asked.

"Don't know much about him. She never talked about him
unless she were near shipwrecked with drink."

"She took his death hard, then?" I said.

"Johnny ain't dead," he said. "Far as I know."

"I thought he died on Christmas Day," Charles said.

"Ah, you be thinking of John, her husband. No, Johnny's her son, John Alfred."

"Her son?" I said, and the sound of her spirit's screaming echoed in my mind from an entirely different, motherly direction. "Where is he?"

"Saint Vincent's School in Dartford," the Pensioner said. "He's a cripple, see? She had to leave him there."

"When?" I asked.

"Don't know. I told you, she never talked about him. But I think it were about the same time her daughter died."

"She lost a daughter?" Charles asked.

The Pensioner shrugged. "Infection or some other."

I sat back in my chair with the overwhelming sensation that Annie Chapman's deepest wound had right then been laid bare before me. It didn't surprise me that she'd turned to drink to extinguish her pain, in the same way my father had, and I knew the dissolution to which that path led. Unlike my father, her self-destruction had been slow, and Leather Apron was not the author of it, but merely its finisher, and I now knew I had to seek out Johnny in Dartford.

"Thank you for your time," I said.

The Pensioner took another gulp of gin and picked a winkle. "Time's *all* I got," he said, and didn't even rise for us as we went to the door, and bade no farewell as we stepped through it.

Outside, we returned to Brick Lane and turned south, passing Thrawl Street, with the Frying Pan pub on the corner, then Old

Montague Street, and from there wended down to Whitechapel. It was now just after two in the afternoon, which meant I had time enough to take the train to Dartford. I turned to my right to head for the Aldgate Station of the underground railway.

"Hold on, where you going?" Charles asked. "Hospital's the other way."

"I'm going to Dartford."

"Dartford?" Charles shook his head. "You're not bricky, you're mad."

"Why?"

"You're going all the way to Dartford chasing a wild goose."

"I know it's what I need to do," I said, and felt it surely. "It's but, what, fifteen miles away?"

"Even so," he said. "I have to play this evening."

Even though I feared the loss of him at my side, I'd gained just enough confidence to proceed alone. "You don't have to come with me, Charles. Keep your concert."

"It isn't that . . ." He held his hands up in the manner of surrender. "Just wait until tomorrow. I can go with you tomorrow."

Confidence or not, I was frightened enough of the streets and Leather Apron that I considered his suggestion for a moment, but then dismissed it.

"Mr. Merrick doesn't have any time to waste. I'm grateful for all your help, truly, but I must do this. If Johnny is there, I need to speak with him." At that point, I turned and walked away, leaving Charles standing on the sidewalk. I wondered if he would follow after me, but he didn't, which, I was surprised to acknowledge, disappointed me.

I checked my shawl and made my way down several blocks to the end of the tramway, where Whitechapel Street became Aldgate High Street, and there I passed under a broken section of the ancient stone wall that once surrounded the City of London. Halfway down the next block, I arrived at the Aldgate Station, where a length of the underground railway lay exposed below and perpendicular to the street before vanishing back into its subterranean lair.

I entered the station and purchased a ticket to Cannon Street. I knew from there I could board the aboveground railway to the London Bridge Station and the North Kent Line, which would take me out to Dartford. Beyond the ticket booth, I descended the staircase to the train platform in the cavern below. Having never ridden the underground before, I found the scene before me a phantasmagoria. Gaslight and some sunlight filtered through air, suffused with dust and smoke, not fully illuminating the vaulted space, while shadowy travelers flitted into view and out, and the steam engines huffed and growled along their tracks with glowing eyes like fabled dragons of old.

A conductor directed me toward my line, and after a wait of but ten minutes or so, my train arrived out of the mist and darkness. I'd purchased a third-class ticket, and I boarded a wooden car at the rear, which was open to the smoke and soot. Wealthier travelers boarded bright, contained cars with velvet seats, lit within by gas lamps. I found most of my fellow passengers were men, but there were a few women. I claimed a bench and tried to calm an unease that I realized had been growing in me since I'd entered that subterranean realm.

The train moved down the track with a curious undulation, gently up and down, with almost no side to side swaying. The roar of the engine filled the tunnel completely with endless echoes, and the gaslight in the cars ahead glowed around us, turning the train into an island of light moving through a black void. The smoke at times seared my eyes and nose, and all of us in the third class coughed and covered our mouths.

It felt unnatural to be belowground, away from the sun, rooting about beneath the city streets. Those tunnels did not seem to welcome woman, man, or child, and as my disquiet went deeper, I wished for the train to hurry along so that I might be out of them.

We stopped at several stations along the way but still reached Cannon Street within twenty minutes, a trip that would have taken much longer aboveground. Despite the convenience, I nevertheless hurried from the car and rushed across the platform, then up the staircase to the surface, where I gratefully found the sun waiting outside and brushed the ashes from my dress.

The proper, aboveground railway station waited for me not far from the Metropolitan Underground. I went inside the main entry and purchased a round-trip ticket to Dartford. The next train didn't leave for some fifteen minutes, so I bought myself a meat pie from a vendor and ate it while I waited under the arching glass ceiling. As the time for departure neared, the crowd around me on the platform thickened, and I checked my shawl in the jostle, imagining what it must have been like for Mr. Merrick to be besieged in a much bigger station like Liverpool.

When the train arrived, I boarded and found a seat in the third-class car, blessedly contained this time, and before long we pulled out of the station and lumbered on our way. This train seemed much older than the underground, its upholstery worn to a polish, its wood and brass dented and gouged. I counted the five granite arches of the London Bridge to our left as we crossed the wide Thames, and then we stopped at the London Bridge Station for more passengers. That was my first time across the river in my life, and indeed my first time beyond the borders of the East End since I'd been a child, and I felt a child's rush of giddiness as the countryside soon whipped past me at the speed of a greyhound.

The railway followed roughly the course of the river eastward into Kent, first through Greenwich, after which passing the vistas of farm, hamlet, and smoke-belching factory that alternated in my window like a zoetrope. That fleeting show and the motion of the railway car lulled me into a stupor, and the time barreled as quickly for me as the distance beneath the iron wheels of the train, such that I was surprised when the conductor made his walk through the cars shouting Dartford as the next stop.

I rose from my seat and made my way to the door, disembarking as the train came to a squealing, lurching stop. I asked an attendant at the ticket counter if he knew where in Dartford I might find St. Vincent's.

"The Catholic Industrial School, you mean?" the man asked, looking over the top rim of his spectacles. "It's on Temple Hill. That way."

I thanked him and out in front of the station hired one of the waiting hansom cabs to take me there, another luxury I had not afforded for myself nor enjoyed since my girlhood. Though I found my saved wages rapidly diminishing, it would all be worth it if my efforts somehow ceased the haunting and restored Mr. Merrick's health.

The hansom cab smelled of the cigar smoked by its previous passenger, but I ignored the odor and paid mind to the road ahead as we bounced and drove through the city, which was a great deal smaller and greener a metropolis than London. Tall trees grew everywhere, and I realized how much I'd missed them in the city, and in my pastoral reverie neglected to plan what I might say upon my arrival at St. Vincent's until we were already there.

I climbed out of the cab, then paid my driver and sent him on his way back down the hill, while I surveyed not only the school but also the view of the surrounding countryside, including a vast heath to the southwest. The school appeared quite new, both long and spacious, built of brown brick that rose two stories to a roof lined with multiple peaks. Hedges and shrubs surrounded it, and ivy had already begun its slow and persistent conquest of the walls. I didn't know who I might meet inside, nor how I would explain to them my presence here, for I thought it best to leave out any mention of ghosts. The only armature I carried with me was the name of a crippled boy housed somewhere within.

John Alfred Chapman.

I repeated that name to myself as I approached the door, ready to go inside and find him.

CHAPTER 14

The door to the school lay open, and I walked into a barren lobby not nearly so well appointed as the London Hospital, with nary a side table, vase, or plant in sight. A great carved wooden crucifix, quite old by all appearance, adorned one wall, flanked by icons of Catholic saints gilded with gold leaf. Behind a long desk opposite the cross sat an attendant in a high-necked white blouse with a cameo at her throat, her graying hair pulled up loosely, and behind her stood a bank of file cabinets and drawers. Upon my entrance, she looked up at me and smiled. "Can I help you?" she asked.

I stepped toward her. "I'm here to inquire after one of the boys in your care."

"Are you a relative?"

I considered lying, but thought against it. "I'm not. But I'm concerned for him."

"I see," she said. "And what is the boy's name?"

"John Alfred Chapman."

She repeated the name to herself as she spun around on her swivel chair to the file cabinet behind her, and after flipping through several inches of papers she said, "Here we are," and withdrew one. Her expression as she scanned it quickly fell, though, from her brow to her frown. "Would you wait here a moment?" she asked.

"Of course," I said.

She rose and retreated through a door behind her desk, taking the sheet of paper with her, and was gone for quite some time. I waited on a bench beneath the heavy presence of the cross, my hands in my lap. When the woman returned, she brought with her a white-haired priest in his long black robes. He carried with him a small wooden box, and came around the desk to sit beside me on the bench, placing the box next to him.

"Good afternoon," he said, his accent Irish. "I am Father Cogan. You're here about John Alfred Chapman?"

"I am," I said.

"But I'm told you're no relation to him."

"I know—" I started, but corrected myself. "I knew his mother, who died recently."

"Died, you say?"

"Murdered. Have you by chance heard about the recent evil in the East End?"

"I have, indeed," he said. "A *great* evil."

"The boy's mother, Annie Chapman, was one of the victims."

Father Cogan crossed himself. "Oh, sweet mercy. What a dreadful, dreadful end!"

I nodded. "Would it be possible to speak to John Alfred?"

"Oh, my dear child, I'm afraid that's not possible. John Alfred is dead, you see."

My initial confusion at what he'd just said turned quickly to harrowing disappointment. If the boy was dead, then how was I to end the haunting? Charles had been right, and I'd wasted the trip out there chasing a wild goose and was no closer to helping

Mr. Merrick than I had been that morning. I felt my frame buckling under the strain of my failure.

"We've had no word from the lad's mother in some years," Father Cogan said. "We sent letters but never heard back. But she's dead you say? You're sure of it?"

I stared hard at the stone floor, having gone a bit numb in my extremities. "Quite sure," I said.

"Poor woman." Father Cogan shook his head. "After she left him here, I heard she wandered out on the heath for two days, refusing to leave. As lost a soul as ever there was."

"You speak the truth, Father," I said, imagining her billowing cape, though he could not have known just how lost was her windswept spirit. "Why did she bring him here?"

"He was a cripple. His affliction was beyond her ability to care for."

"I see. And when did the boy die?"

"Oh, it's been nearly a year now. The lad would have been eight years old in November."

"How did he die?"

"His defect kept him frail. A fever took him in the end, and by God's will."

"I see. Thank you, Father." I nodded deeply and marshaled myself to rise from the bench and make the return journey to the hospital, but the priest held out his aged hand.

"Wait a moment," he said, and brought the box onto his lap. "The boy is buried down in the churchyard, paid for by the school. But we kept this out of the coffin, thinking his mother might want something to remember him by, should she ever return." He lifted the lid of the box away and pulled out a red crocheted scarf. "It's fine work."

"It is." I remembered the bartender at the Ten Bells had mentioned that Annie crocheted.

"I wonder if you'd like to have it?" the priest said.

I faltered in my reply. "M-me?"

"You are the only person who's ever come asking after him. His father's gone, and now his mother, God rest their souls, the two of them. I don't know what else to do with it."

I accepted the scarf from him and found it very fine indeed, for it seemed there was a love I could touch in its weave. "I . . . yes, Father. I'll accept it. If you're sure."

"I want it in the hands of someone with love for the boy."

"But I never knew him."

"And yet you're here. That is enough for me."

I nodded again, this time in gratitude. "Very well, Father, I accept it."

"Thank you." He slapped his knees. "Will you be heading back into London today?"

"Yes."

"You best hurry on, then, if you're to catch the last train."

I thanked him and departed from the school, returning the way I'd come, back down the hill by foot. In a particularly quiet and empty lane, I took off my shawl and replaced it with the red scarf, which did not quite hide my face as well, but felt as soft as snow against my skin. I reached the train station just as the bell tolled the locomotive's imminent departure, and I scrambled aboard almost in the same instant the wheels jolted forward. The ten miles to London passed quickly, but it was nevertheless approaching evening when we pulled into Cannon Street Station. I was not eager to once again descend beneath the streets to the Metropolitan Underground, but did so, and once more found myself traversing that unreal realm that was the surface's forsaken twin.

As the train pulled into the dark tunnel, I noticed a fiddle-faced man staring at me from across the car. He was dressed well enough, but the look in his eyes felt both hostile and frightening. I summoned the resolve to do what needed to be done, and returned his glare with force and menace, the image of a leather apron foremost in my thoughts. In response, he nudged the passenger next to him and pointed at me. The other man glanced up but immediately looked away, and his gaze turned desultory.

"Bloody hell, she got a face on her," a third man whispered from my side, and I realized the cause of the attention.

John Alfred's scarf had slipped, and one side of my face lay exposed. I quickly covered myself, but the damage had already been dealt, and the whispers quickly spread throughout the car. On the street, I could've escaped from such a situation easily enough, but I was not on the street. I was trapped with all those strangers on a moving train, under the ground.

Their stares pecked at my neck feathers, and my chest emptied of blood and breath. I had to get off that train, for there wasn't any way to know who aboard it might turn violent. It was rare for the hostility against me to surpass the verbal, but it had happened, once when I rounded a corner right into a gang of bruisers, and once when I entered Flower and Dean and ran afoul of a particularly vicious prostitute. Both times they'd knocked off my corner pieces and left me bashed and purple. I didn't know why they so hated me on sight, but they did, and there were some who could do naught but attack what they hated.

The silence in the train car had gone to church, but I kept my chin up and my eyes forward on nothing as that short ride back to Aldgate Station became the seemingly longest segment of my entire journey that day.

When we finally emerged into the gaslit oasis and eased to a stop, I stayed in my seat until the other passengers had disembarked, for it was better to have them ahead of me than at my back. I likewise proceeded carefully from the platform and up the stairs to the surface, believing every stranger around me not only capable of striking me, but of gutting me as Polly and Annie had been.

I turned up Aldgate High Street, the roadway now lit by gas lamps and storefronts, for the sun had abandoned the world while I'd been underground. The traffic in the street had coarsened in aspect and temperament, no less congested with vehicles and pedestrians, but bawdier and more drunken. I'd hoped to be back at the hospital by then, but aboard an omnibus it shouldn't have taken much longer to reach it. I passed back under the ancient, broken wall and reached the beginning of Whitechapel Road and the tramway.

An omnibus waited on the rails, but when I approached the conductor, he waved me away. "Tramway is blocked," he said. "A wagon up ahead lost an axle. Tipped its load onto the tracks. You be better off walking."

I wasn't sure I agreed with that. "How long 'til it's cleared?"

He shrugged. "How should I know?"

I contemplated waiting, but as I looked around me at the crowd I noticed the fiddle-faced man from the Metropolitan Underground. He stood some yards off, but he seemed to be watching me. I didn't want to loiter under his gaze, so I nodded to the conductor, adjusted John Alfred's scarf, and set off on foot. Over my shoulder, I saw that the fiddle-faced man moved with me, following at a distance, so I hurried my pace in an attempt to disappear into the crowd.

I hadn't been out at night in some weeks. Wood smoke and the savory aroma of charred fish and meat wafted about me. In the glow of gas lamps, barrel fires, and even torches, vendors barked their wares, and pedestrians stopped and ate sheeps' trotters, donkey milk, herring bloaters, and plum duff. Here and there a small crowd gathered watching street entertainments: acrobats, fire-eaters, sword swallowers, musicians cranking hurdy-gurdies, and numerous others who made the entire roadway into their stage and every pedestrian a momentary member of their audience. I even passed a man with a dancing bear on a leash near Great Garden Street as I made my way eastward through the throng.

A block later, near St. Mary's Station, I chanced to look back and noticed the fiddle-faced man behind me, but closer now than he had been before. It seemed he was following me, and at that realization I would have run from him, had the congestion on the street permitted it. Instead I had to duck, slide, and weave my way along the sidewalk, all the while keeping him in the tail of my eye.

He stayed with me, quite brazenly, the crowd oblivious to my plight, and I understood then how it was Leather Apron had committed his crimes in much darker and lonelier places, especially if I'd been a known streetwalker like Polly or Annie. I hadn't yet let myself believe the fiddle-faced man to be Leather Apron, but the fear and doubt were there, for I could think of no virtuous reason he would follow me. Sweat chilled my brow, and my heart hadn't truly slowed since I'd risen from the underground.

I nearly panicked when up ahead of me I noticed a large gathering completely blockading the walkway in front of the Pavilion Theatre, for if I were to stop or slow, I feared the stranger would reach me. I decided to step out into the street and go around them, unwise as it seemed in the dark, when I heard a voice call out up ahead.

"Evelyn!"

I peered across the faces in front of me while still pressing forward in my intended escape.

"Evelyn, wait!"

It was then I saw Charles emerge from the crowd and stroll toward me, his normal swagger a bit slipshod, and I would've known he'd been drinking even before he reached me and spoke.

"You missed it. I was just playing not half an hour ago." He wore a silly grin. "Are you back from Dartford, then?"

Drunk as he was, I was relieved to see him, for his presence seemed to have stalled the fiddle-faced man, who'd ducked backward against a storefront. "Yes, Charles, I'm back."

"That's right bang up to the elephant, that is." He leaned toward me, and I smelled the piney scent of gin on his breath. It called my father to mind, the memory of that last night he went out, already drunk. I'd grabbed hold of him and begged him to stay with me, and he'd hugged me. But then he'd pushed me firmly away without looking in my eyes. They later told me the man who'd killed him had done it for the five shillings my father carried, and then left his body in an alley off Commercial Street.

"Did you speak to the boy?" Charles asked.

"No," I whispered.

"Why not?"

"He . . . he died a year ago."

"Died, you say?" Now he offered an exaggerated frown. "Then what're you going to do?"

"I don't know." And I still worried about the fiddle-faced man. "Listen, Charles, would you walk with me back to the hospital?"

"Can it be you fancy a walk with me?"

"No," I said. "Yes. Tonight only, yes. Please, Charles."

"Very well." He gave me a lazy wink and extended the crook of his arm, and I placed mine through it with another backward glance, dismayed to see the fiddle-faced man dislodge from his hiding place and follow. Whatever the stranger wanted with me, he did not seem to be giving up the chase.

The hospital was only a couple of blocks away, but Charles proved to be somewhat of a hindrance in navigating the crowd. He bumped along casually, and I had to pull him with me by his arm, much as I'd dragged my father to his bed, watching the stranger behind us drawing nearer. The western edge of the hospital did eventually come into view across the street, but the front gates were now locked. I needed to reach the far eastern side through which we'd left that morning, and I feared I wouldn't make it in time.

"Charles," I said. "There's a shady man following us. He's been with me since Aldgate Station."

"What?" Charles stood up straighter and spun around. "Where? I'll take him!"

"Don't stop," I said. "You're in no state for that. We just need to hurry."

"I've a better idea," he said. "Is he watching us right now?"

I looked. "I don't see him right—"

"This way." He pulled me suddenly to the side, through the open doors of the nearest building. I'd lost sight of the fiddle-faced man, which I hoped meant he had also lost sight of us, and I thought perhaps Charles had just done well.

"I'll pay your way," Charles said, and gave the doorman two-pence. "And next door, Miss Juanita will box any man weighing less than ten stone whilst wearing only fleshings."

"Where are we?" I asked, even as Charles pulled me deeper into the building, through a press as thick as it had been on the street. We made our way down a corridor of red velvet curtains, the light quite dim. "Charles, where are we?" I asked again.

"I wanted to see 'em," he said, and we turned a corner into a chamber of horrors, and I knew then where we were.

"No," I whispered, and turned around instantly, but the image I'd glimpsed had already lodged itself.

Nearby me was the crude form of Annie Chapman, shaped in wax, lying on a table. A deep gash to the figure's throat nearly separated the head from the body, while the abdomen had been opened, and the figure's waxen red viscera thrown up and over her shoulders as though in ghastly imitation of a scarf. Her features had been stretched into a rictus of pain no natural, fleshen face could make.

"Charles," I said, pain and anger in my voice.

"What?" His head wobbled back and forth. "Oh, that's right! You didn't want to, did you?"

"No!"

"Why're you so soft?" he asked with an irritated scowl.

"I have to leave," I said, nearly unable to breathe, and pressed forward the way we had come in. I didn't even care if Charles were exiting with me, and I didn't care if the fiddle-faced man waited for me outside. I only knew I could not stay in that building a single moment longer.

When I reached the street, I inhaled and clutched my chest with one hand, my scarf with the other, then turned up the street and ran. I saw no sign of the fiddle-faced man, and when the traffic in the street broke, I dove across it to the hospital's side of the thoroughfare. Though the front gates were closed, the hospital windows glowed in welcome as I raced along the building's length and then turned down East Mount Street.

As soon as I'd entered the shadows, a figure stepped out of them in front of me. It was the fiddle-faced man, and I halted and shouted, "Stay away from me!" I had no weapon, and nothing around me on the street to use as one.

The stranger stood where he was and held up his empty hands. "I'll not come closer," he said. "I just needs to talk with you's all."

"Who are you?"

"They call me Jimmy Fiddle, on account of my face," he said. "I work for the Silver King."

I remembered that as the name of the showman who'd exhibited Mr. Merrick. "Why are you following me?" I asked.

"I had to make sure you's the one," he said. "The Silver King got word the Elephant Man had a new maid without no jaw. I seen you on the train in your maid's apron, and then I seen your face, and I says to meself, that's her. That's the one. But I had to make sure, see?"

"What do you want with me?" I asked. This strange man may not have turned out to be Leather Apron, but that didn't mean I was about to trust him. "How does this Silver King even know about me?"

"There's porters and scrubbers will talk if you buy 'em a drink," Jimmy Fiddle said. "The Silver King has kept an interest in Mr. Merrick, but the hospital won't let him in. The Silver King wants you to give a message for him."

"I doubt I'm allowed to do that," I said, but I felt intensely curious. "But tell me the message."

"Oh." Jimmy Fiddle removed his bowler and clutched it in front of his chest. "The Silver King would like Mr. Merrick to know that if he ever wishes to return to the stage, he can be assured he'll have the very best halls, the very best food, and a generous split of the proceeds."

"Mr. Merrick has no wish to return to that life," I said, but with less certainty than I would have liked.

Jimmy Fiddle replaced his hat and pulled it down tight over both ears. "But you'll give him the message?"

"I make no promises."

"You might could be on the stage, too," he said. "Looks like you got most of your jaw, but they could still call you the Jawless Lady."

His suggestion enraged me, even though I knew he had said it without mockery. "I'll thank you to keep such vulgar ideas to yourself," I said.

"Meant no harm," he said, walking around me. "Could earn yourself a decent living's all. You give that message to Mr. Merrick, though, will you? The Silver King would love to have him back."

He continued down the street, and I watched him go, shaking. I had at one desperate time considered taking to the stage as a freak. It was only the last scrap of pride left to me that'd prevented it. But I knew that's what others saw when they looked at me, and I knew that's where they thought I belonged. I recoiled from that, telling myself they were wrong, and Jimmy Fiddle was wrong. I'd found the place where I belonged, which was in the hospital, at Mr. Merrick's side.

I had no intention of relaying the Silver King's message to him, but I truly wondered what he would say to it should he recover, for was it really so different to be on the stage than to be displayed before the medical college?

The porter at the gate recognized me and let me through. "You all right there, Miss Fallow?" he asked.

"Yes," I lied.

"That's good. I think they been looking for you."

"They have? Who?"

"Nurse asked me if I'd seen you leave."

A knife of worry caught me between the ribs. "Thank you."

I passed the workshops and entered Bedstead Square, and only then did I allow myself to slow to a normal walk. As I crossed the courtyard, I labored to drive the image of the waxwork from my mind by instead imagining the living Annie Chapman, the grief-stricken mother wandering the windy heath, unable to depart the place she'd left her child.

When I reached Mr. Merrick's door, I opened it slowly.

"Please do enter," came a woman's voice.

I stepped in and saw Miss Doyle sitting by the fireplace, looking calm everywhere except her tapping toe. I nodded to her and then went to Mr. Merrick's side, where I found his skin had gone from pale to gray, but I did note the barest movement of his chest. "How is he?" I asked.

"He continues to decline," Miss Doyle said, rising from her chair. "The doctors believe he could pass at any time."

I nodded, feeling once again powerless to help him, and now tormented by the knowledge that I had failed in finding a way to free Annie from the tyranny of her grief. "Y-you were looking for me?"

She nodded and stepped toward me. "Where were you?"

"In the city. I took a day off."

"I saw your note," she said. "Were you not aware that the matron must approve *all* leave taken?"

"I didn't know that for certain," I said. "But it was urgent for me to go."

"I doubt that will save you."

"Save me?" Her words took that knife of worry and twisted it.

"I mean, save your position. You're sure to be sacked."

Panic ravaged me, both for myself at the thought of returning to the streets, and also for Mr. Merrick. "Miss Doyle, I left a—"

"You left a note, yes, I saw it. The matron did not."

"Why?"

"Because I did not show it to her," she said, raising her voice. "You left without giving word to anyone, which meant that I, along with Miss Flemming, had to do your job. I am a nurse, and I had to carry coal, Miss Fallow. *Coal.*"

"I'm sorry," I said. "I didn't mean to inconvenience you."

"The last time we spoke, I warned you, but instead of heeding me, you left your post and went . . . shopping. With that Charles fellow, the porter tells me." She tipped her head to the side and folded her arms. "That is a lovely scarf. I hope it was worth the price."

"Please, Miss Doyle . . ." I said, but I didn't know how to plead my case with her a second time. I couldn't tell her about my real reason for my leaving, or she would think me mad, and then I certainly would lose my position.

"It is in the matron's hands," Miss Doyle said. "She will speak with you tomorrow morning." She turned her back on me and marched toward the door. "For now, do your duty and watch him."

"Yes," I said. "Of course, I—"

But she had already left through the door and shut it behind her, and I was alone with Mr. Merrick, perhaps for the last time.

CHAPTER 15

After Miss Doyle had left, I lowered the red scarf to my shoulders and sat down next to Mr. Merrick. I took hold of his left hand, his fingers frightfully cold, and upon closing my eyes, imagined the rest of him, the body that had so thoroughly turned against him, as finely formed as that delicate hand. I imagined his face without its growths, his arm and his legs of normal shape and size, and found him to be quite handsome in my mind's eye. But I was also aware that the virtues of an attractive figure were as nothing compared to the virtues of his soul. When a few moments later I opened my eyes and he returned to his monstrous form, he was no less a man to me.

"Joseph," I said. "I don't know if you can hear me, but Dr. Treves thinks you might, so I'm going to talk to you." I cleared my voice. "I went searching for Annie Chapman's family today. All over London, it felt like. I even rode the Metropolitan Underground and went out to Kent. I was trying to do what you wanted me to. I learned that Johnny is her son, and she had to give him up, because he was crippled. But he died, you see. So now I don't know how to help her, and I feel that I failed you."

He said nothing back to me, nor fluttered an eyelid, nor twitched a muscle.

"I have no idea where to start looking to help Polly, but even if I did, I fear it would be another wild-goose chase, just as Charles said." I shook my head at his name. "He was half-rats tonight. He took me to see the waxworks, against my will, but you'll forgive me for not giving you any details about that. So I'm cross with him over it. But I suppose I must give him credit for accompanying me most of the day."

The room had become a bit chilly, so I rose and fed the fire some coal, a task Miss Doyle had apparently thought beneath her.

"I don't know what to make of Charles," I said, returning to my chair at Mr. Merrick's bedside. "He persists in flirting with me, but he can't mean it. He can't. He says he wants to take me for a walk, but how could he want such a thing?" I looked at Mr. Merrick's motionless face. "I know what I am," I said. "*You* see it. How can Charles not see it? How could he want me?"

It didn't upset me to finally say such things aloud, for they'd filled my mind often enough, under the breath of my thoughts. In the past weeks I'd learned well the extent to which I was wanted, and in what capacities; I was wanted as a maid only if hidden from sight, and if not hidden from sight, I was wanted by showmen as a freak. The ways that men, when sufficiently drunk, had wanted me back on the street, I chose not to think about.

"I don't trust him," I said. "You ask me, he's a performer who never leaves the stage. But I know he's your friend, and I don't mean to offend you, so that's all I'll say about the matter." I covered my mouth to hide an expansive yawn. "I don't know what else to talk about, but I want you to hear my voice, so I think I'll read from *Emma*. Would you like that?"

I found my book on his table and opened it. With all the reading we'd been doing, we had only a few pages left to turn, but before I'd made it through them I felt the exhaustion of the day catch up with me. The words on the page began to dodge my eyes, or switch places, playing tricks on me, and I soon gave up trying to hunt them down and fell asleep for some hours in my chair.

A pain in my jaw woke me, and then Polly entered the room. She did as she had done before, and I whispered, "I'm sorry, I'm sorry," during her whole visit, though I knew she wouldn't hear me. Then she was gone, and it seemed Mr. Merrick looked even grayer from her ghostly touch.

I knew Annie would be along in her time as well, so I resumed reading to pass the hours, and finished *Emma* before her arrival. "I'll read it again once you're awake," I said to Mr. Merrick. "All the parts you don't remember."

When the pain in my jaw returned, I sat up straight in my chair and shuttered myself against the oncoming storm. Annie came in screaming as she always did, and I closed my eyes and palmed my ears to keep out the sound, but within a moment of her entering, the wailing ceased.

I looked up to find the ghost standing still, staring at me, her mouth closed, something she hadn't ever done in any of her visitations. I had no idea what to think of it, whether it was a good or evil sign. Then she flew at me, and I jolted backward from her so hard I almost overturned my chair, but she stopped short of touching me. Instead, her face hovered but inches from mine, insubstantial but undeniable, her eyes roving over me. When they stopped at my neck and lingered there, I cursed myself a fool for having forgotten about the scarf. I lifted it from around my neck, and her eyes widened.

"Do you know it?" I asked.

She spoke then, her voice a breath over a bottle lip. "Here, Johnny, to keep you warm."

"Yes," I said, blinking at sudden tears.

"Johnny," she whispered. "Johnny, my boy. My beautiful boy." She held her hands out to me as if to receive a newborn infant, and into them I placed the scarf, careful not to touch her, after which she drew it unto her chest. The scarf appeared to become one with the incorporeal matter of her spirit, and she looked heavenward with a smile that spoke not so much of joy, but of relief and the end of pain. "I missed you so," she said, crying. "My boy. You're perfect to me. I'll see you again, I promise, I swear it."

She vanished, one moment standing there, the next moment not, and the scarf fell softly to the floor. The instant in which it happened passed so quickly it took several more instants for me to realize it.

Annie had gone, and not in her usual way. The ache in my jaw had ceased almost immediately with her departure, and I hoped that somehow the sight and touch of the scarf had released her from the tyranny of her grief. Perhaps she had simply needed the farewell she'd never bade her son, and with a piece of Johnny in her hands she'd finally said her good-byes and found her peace.

If nothing else, that was what I wanted to believe, but the test of it would be whether Mr. Merrick recovered any strength. In those first moments since her leaving, he looked unimproved, but I reassured myself it might take time for the effects to manifest.

It wasn't much later in the morning that the door opened again, only this time it was the matron who strode into the room. Any sense of accomplishment I felt in aiding Annie fled before the severity of her expression, and I rose from the chair to curtsy.

"Miss Fallow," she said. "I see no reason for pleasantries. I have been informed of a serious dereliction in your duties yesterday."

"Yes, ma'am."

"You admit it?"

"I admit I took the day off, ma'am."

"The day *off*?"

"Yes, ma'am. Until yesterday, I'd not taken a single day off."

"Why did you not inform me of your desire and ask my permission?"

"It was a matter of some urgency, Matron. I left a note on the table, there."

"I saw no such note."

"I regret it never reached you," I said, aware that it would serve no purpose to blame the nurses she undoubtedly trusted more than me.

"And what, pray tell, was urgent enough that you would risk losing your position over it?"

"I . . . I had to . . ." I considered telling her something of the truth, for I felt then I had nothing to lose by it. It seemed Miss Doyle had been right, and I was about to be sacked. Even so, I found the words of my confession difficult to assemble, and in the brief time I took to contemplate my answer to her question, Dr. Treves entered the room with Dr. Tilney at his heels.

"Ah, Miss Fallow," he said. "You've returned."

"Perhaps not for long," the matron said. "I am still waiting for her to explain her absence."

A thorny silence followed.

"Well," Dr. Treves said, gripping the lapels of his coat. "The maids are your responsibility, Matron Luckes, and I'll leave the matter to your unimpeachable judgment." He then swiveled toward Dr. Tilney. "Francis, shall we?" he said, and they both went to Mr. Merrick, though Dr. Tilney did smile at me before going.

"Miss Fallow?" the matron said. "Are you going to inform me of your urgent matter, or are you not?"

"I . . ." My resolve to tell her of the haunting had weakened in the presence of the doctors. "I regret that I can't say, Matron."

"And why can you not say?"

"It is a private matter."

"Private?" Matron Luckes shook her head. "I'm unaccustomed to such obstreperousness. I do not *want* to dismiss you, but you have given me no justification or reason not to."

"I understand, ma'am," I said. "I'm asking that you trust me that it was absolutely necessary for me to leave the hospital. Please don't send me from Mr. Merrick. Not now. Not until he's well."

"He may not ever be well," she said, her voice lowered, but she appeared to be thinking about my plea as she rubbed with her thumb one of the many rings she wore. When she stopped rubbing, I knew she'd reached a decision. "No. I am sorry," she said. "I wish that I could simply trust you at your word, but the staff of a hospital cannot be run in such a way."

I noticed Dr. Treves and Dr. Tilney looking at me, perhaps with sympathy. "Ma'am," I said, "I beg you—"

"My decision is final," she said. "Miss Fallow, your employment at the London Hospital is hereby at an end. You will gather your—"

"No," came a weak whisper from the bed.

Everyone in the room turned toward it, and a wave of elation carried me to Mr. Merrick's side. His eyes weren't open, but he had spoken, and I felt overcome by joy.

"Mr. Merrick?" I said, with laughter in my voice. "Can you hear us?"

Dr. Treves and Dr. Tilney had their hands upon him, measuring his temperature and pulse. "This is remarkable," Dr. Treves said.

"Evelyn," Mr. Merrick whispered, "stay."

Dr. Treves leaned in closer and raised his voice to nearly shouting. "What's that you say, John? You want Miss Fallow to stay?"

"Yes," he whispered.

Dr. Treves turned to Matron Luckes, who'd come to stand at the foot of the bed and was showing as much surprise as I suspect she ever allowed herself.

"What do you think of that, Eva?" Dr. Treves asked. "I know I said I wouldn't interfere with your management, but I must consider my patient. I think it unwise to send Miss Fallow away. At least for now. It seems to be doing John some good."

Matron Luckes gave a reserved nod. "I . . . agree. I suppose she may stay on for the time being. But make no mistake, Miss Fallow. You are here only as a comfort to Mr. Merrick, and once he is recovered you *will* be dismissed. I give you my word on that."

"I understand," I said. "I do. Thank you, Matron, and thank you, Dr. Treves."

"Begging your pardon," Dr. Treves said, "but I wasn't speaking on your behalf. Nor do I believe the matron was thinking on it."

That, too, I understood, but in that moment I did not care. I knew my time in the hospital was now bounded and I would one day be sent back out into the streets, but the only thing of importance to me then was Mr. Merrick's recovery. "I shall do my best for Mr. Merrick," I said.

"I trust you will," the matron said, and after that she left the room.

Dr. Treves and Dr. Tilney stayed on, conversing with each other in their medical tongue, asking brief questions of Mr. Merrick, which he answered even more briefly. Eventually, Mr. Merrick opened his eyes, and I sat by and waited until the doctors had gone. When we were alone, I took Mr. Merrick's hand, eager to finally talk with him about Annie Chapman.

"She is at peace, Mr. Merrick." I gave his hand a gentle squeeze and told him about what Charles and I had learned, and what had happened with her ghost and her son's scarf.

"May I . . . hold it?" he whispered.

"Of course!" I placed the scarf beneath his good hand, and he caressed it with his fingertips.

"Soft," he said.

"It is very fine," I said. "I learned she sometimes sold her crochets."

He gathered a length of the scarf into his fist and held on to it, but there was a weakness in the gesture. Annie's release had only restored a measure of his health, and to bring him the rest of the way I had to somehow do for Polly as I had done for Annie. That I didn't know anything about Polly did not seem so great an obstacle as the fact that I hadn't actually meant to help Annie in the way I had. The scarf had been nothing more than a gift by a kindly priest, and I had accepted it as such.

"Can you eat anything?" I asked him.

"Perhaps," he said.

I went to the kitchens and returned with a cup of strong beef tea, made by one of the cook's assistants. Mr. Merrick was able to drink it down, and it seemed to so fortify and vitalize him I brought him another cup. Afterward he slept, and I busied myself with cleaning his room and filling the coal hod. Then Miss Flemming and Miss Doyle came to see if he were up to a bath, and with my help we were able to walk him to the bathroom and get him into the tub. This time, I did not flinch or run at the sight of him but conducted myself with the same air of respectful decorum as the nurses. Miss Doyle actually offered me a slight nod of approval, which I appreciated, even though I knew an improvement in her opinion of me would not save my position. Partway through Mr. Merrick's bath, I left to change his bedding and fetch him clean clothes, and once he was dressed and back in his bed, he slept again.

Later that afternoon, Charles came for a visit, his neck stooped in contrition as he entered the room. His expression brightened when he saw Mr. Merrick awake. "Joseph!" he said. "How are you feeling, my ugly bloke?"

"Better," Mr. Merrick said. "How are you, Charles?"

"Never mind me," Charles said. "I'm always well enough. I'm just happy to see my chum on the mend."

"Thank you," Mr. Merrick said.

Charles bowed his head toward me. "Miss Fallow," he said. "You're owed an apology, and that's a fact. I was already half a brewer when I saw you, or else I wouldn't have treated you as I did."

"Your drunkenness was plain to see, Mr. Weaver. But it must be said, I appreciated your help prior to that, nonetheless."

"Least I could do," he said. "And our efforts seem to have helped, eh, Joseph?"

"I appreciate you both," Mr. Merrick said, and though I did not appreciate Charles putting his assistance on the same level as mine, I did not want to appear proud and said nothing. Mr. Merrick's health was the most important thing to me.

"Shall I play for you?" Charles asked.

"Yes, please," Mr. Merrick said.

"Perhaps you might play the song you composed," I said.

Charles nodded. "Very well." Then he lifted his violin to his chin, and the tune he played sounded as beautiful the second time hearing it as it had the first. Mr. Merrick thought it very lovely, too, and was quite impressed that Charles had created it. My own displeasure with Charles dissipated somewhat at my renewed appreciation of his talent, which consternated me, for it happened quite easily and against my will, when I wasn't looking. Charles, it seemed, was one of those infuriating characters with whom one could not stay angry for long.

When he was finished, he asked, "So what do we do next? For the other one?"

"Polly," Mr. Merrick said.

"Yes, Polly," Charles said. "What do we do for her?"

"I don't know," I said. "We need to find her husband, a man named William. I need to give him a message from her."

"Excellent," Charles said, and clapped his hands. "Another day on the hunt."

"I'm afraid I can't go with you," I said.

"Why not?" Charles asked.

"I'm to be sacked for leaving yesterday. The matron let me stay on 'til Mr. Merrick is well, but if I leave again today, I don't think she'll spare me that much. She'll toss me out for sure."

"Right," Charles said, nodding. "So what can I do, then?"

"Perhaps you could make inquiries and find her husband," I said. "William Nichols?"

"Easy enough," he said. "I'll be like that Sherlock Holmes bloke and track him down for you. What then?"

"Wait by a moment," I said, and found some of Mr. Merrick's stationery and a pen. I thought some moments about what I should write, and then I wrote it.

Dear Mr. Nichols,

I am most sorry for the circumstances that require me to write this letter to you, but I hope it might be received in the spirit of kindness in which it is sent. Though we have never met, I was acquainted with your late wife, Polly. I hope my mention of her does not cause you pain. I only wish to make known to you what your marriage meant to her. She told me that day at St. Bride's was the happiest of her life, for you were saving her from a pain she feared even to mention. She was afraid if you knew the truth about how her father had ill-used her, you would no longer wish to marry her. I trust that is not the case, but perhaps knowing it now, you might understand what turmoil it was that drove her to the life she had on the streets. May God keep you, sir.

> *Yours very truly,*
> *Evelyn Fallow*

When I finished, I folded the letter into an envelope and handed it to Charles. "When you find Mr. Nichols, will you give him that?"

"Done," Charles said, first slipping the letter into his coat pocket, and then replacing his instrument in its case. "Good day to both of you. Joseph, you stay on the mend, eh?"

"I'll do my best," Mr. Merrick said.

"Good day, Charles," I said.

He tipped his cap and left, and I went back to tending to Mr. Merrick. Though it comforted me that he had recovered some of his vitality, he had not yet returned to the state of health he had previously known.

That night at dinner, the other maids gathered around me, desiring gossip.

"You're here!" Becky said. "We heard you was almost sacked!"

"I *was* nearly sacked," I said.

"How'd you stay on?" Martha asked.

"Mr. Merrick asked for me," I said. "So the doctor asked the matron to keep me."

"What happens when he gets better, then?" Becky asked.

"He ain't getting better," Beatrice said from the head of the table, her newspaper spread wide. "That's what I heard."

I ignored her. "As soon as he's recovered, I'm to be dismissed." The weight of that was still falling upon me, the dread and terror of it not yet fully settled, though I knew they were coming for me.

"So," Martha said, "we . . . *don't* want him getting better, then?"

"What?" I said. "No, of course we want him to get better."

"But what about you?" Becky asked.

To answer Becky's question I had to think about my prospects, which were as few and bleak as they had been on the day I'd come to the hospital. "I don't know what I'll do," I said. "But Mr. Merrick is my concern right now." I threw a glare in Beatrice's direction. "And he *will* get better."

"Lord willing," Beatrice said from behind her paper, and a moment later she cursed. "Another suspect released! It says here John Fitzgerald's confession to Annie Chapman's murder was all bung and he's been liberated!"

"Why would he confess to such a thing if it weren't true?" Becky asked.

"Must not have his right change," Martha said. "He's barmy's all."

"Well," Becky said, "I suppose it's better a madman confess to something he didn't do than do it."

"But now the worthless mutton shunters are empty-handed," Martha said. "When are they going to catch this devil?"

It had been three weeks since Annie Chapman's murder, and there'd been no new crimes, which seemed to me enough of a reprieve to hope Leather Apron's mania had been satisfied.

"All the liars and fools out there don't make it easy work for the police," Beatrice said. "Says here someone wrote a message in chalk on the pavement by some lamppost. 'I am Leather Apron,' they wrote. 'Five more and I will give myself up.' Now, if the police has to investigate every prank like that, they'll never catch the demon!"

After dinner, I went to my bed and slept but a few hours before waking to a pain in my jaw, which confused and frightened me. It hadn't the intensity of my previous ghostly encounters, but it pricked as though from a distance. I checked the time and found it to be but one o'clock in the morning. That meant the ghost I felt wouldn't be Polly, not at that hour.

A new spirit had come into the hospital. Outside my window, I could see and hear rain, and it felt as though the icy droplets were running down my back. It seemed Leather Apron had not finished with his depravity, after all.

CHAPTER 16

The rain had quieted to a mutter by the time I entered Bedstead Square. Moonlit steam rose here and there from iron grates where the hospital exhaled its heat, and as I walked through those low-born clouds toward Mr. Merrick's door, the ache in my jaw surged. The pain had its own quality, different from that of either Polly or Annie, the way a bruise felt different from a cut, and both of them from a burn. The new pain was deeper than the other two, and not quite as insistent, but rather dared me to ignore it.

But I could not ignore it. *Something* was inside Mr. Merrick's room even then, and if I was right about it, that meant somewhere out on the streets lay the ruined body of a woman, opened up and still warm, and somewhere else a monster made his escape. When I reached Mr. Merrick's door, I felt the apparition move on the other side, and I entered holding my breath.

The woman stared at me from the middle of the room, her hair in dark, rich curls around a pale face, her back rigid. Mr. Merrick's open eyes stared in her direction, but I could not tell if he was seeing her, and I worried he had gone senseless.

"Please help me," she said upon my entrance, her words sweetened slightly with the accent of the Swedes, but then she lurched toward me. Her steps came in twists and jerks, her limbs at severe and unnatural angles, and a loud cracking sound issued from her spine, as though it fractured her very bones to move. "My husband and children are drowned! The water took them when the *Princess Alice* sank!"

"I'm sorry," I said, dodging away from her, holding my hands against the air before me as I would a door. "Please, don't come any closer."

"But you must help me!" She came again toward me, bones snapping, and again I leapt clear of her.

"How?" I said. "How can I help you?"

"Money!" she said. "I need money!"

I reached into the pocket in my skirt and pulled out all the money I had, but I could not bring myself to hand it to her. Instead, I let the coins fall through my fingers to the floor, where they clinked, bounced, and rolled in her path, while I scuttled out of her way.

She dove to her knees before the money, scooping it up frantically. "Thank you, miss!" she said. "Thank you!" After she'd gathered it all to the last farthing, she let out a sigh and rose to her feet. "I'll be going now," she said, and bowed her way backward out of the room. "You are kind. You are very kind. I thank you." She reached the door, and with one final, deeper bow, she left.

I rushed to Mr. Merrick and took hold of his hand, the chill in which brought a gasp out of me. "Mr. Merrick?" I said. "Joseph? Can you hear me?"

He seemed lifeless. His glassy eyes remained fixed on a point on some distant plane I could not see or know. I patted his cheek, his hand, his arm, but received no response from him, and I feared his soul had fled his body. A feeling of devastation brought me to my knees, still holding his hand, and I buried my face against the side of his bed, caught between a curse and a prayer.

"I had no money for her," Mr. Merrick whispered.

I looked up, and then scrambled to my feet. "Oh, Mr. Merrick! You—I thought you'd left me."

"I'm . . . sorry I gave you . . . a fright."

I laughed even as tears fell. "Don't you dare apologize to me, you beautiful man."

His hand stiffened in mine. "Beautiful—" He started, but his voice faltered at the end of a breath. "You . . . you said . . ."

"Beautiful, yes. You are, Mr. Merrick, even if only the ghosts and I are honored to see it."

He closed his eyes then, and I saw tears leaking from them as they still did from mine. Neither of us spoke for some time, and then Mr. Merrick asked me if I'd given her the money she'd asked for.

"I did," I said. "All that I had."

"Do you suppose that's what she wanted?" he said. "Just . . . money?"

"She certainly seemed grateful and relieved," I said.

"Did she take it with her?"

"Yes, she . . ."

She had taken it, but not in the same way Annie had taken the scarf, and neither had this new spirit vanished in the way Annie had when set at peace. I let go of Mr. Merrick's hand and he asked, "What is it?"

"I'm not sure," I said, and followed a slithering trail of doubt to the door, which I opened, and then stepped out into the stairwell. The night had become cold with the passing of the storm, the stars like white chips thrown from the ice seller's cart. I climbed the cement staircase until I stood in the courtyard, finding it as empty as I expected to, but then I looked down at the ground around my feet.

There lay a pile of my coins. I stared at them a moment, loath to touch them, but eventually I stooped to reclaim them, and the cold in them hurt my hands. Once I'd deposited them back into my skirt pocket, I returned to Mr. Merrick's room.

"What is it?" he asked again.

I shook my head. Upon reflection, and unlike Annie, there had been no sense of peace in the new spectre's departure, and I likewise realized the pain in my jaw hadn't ceased abruptly, either, but faded away by degrees. "Mr. Merrick," I said, "I fear she will return. But I will put her to rest just as I did Annie, and as I will Polly. Charles will help me. You shall see, Mr. Merrick. You shall see."

He took on the quiet stillness of a churchyard, but not yet the grave.

"Let's warm it up in here," I said, and moved some coal from the hod to the fire. "Perhaps I can read to you?" I sat down in a chair by his bed, my back to the fireplace, and opened my copy of *Emma*. "Let's see now, what is the last thing you remember happening in the novel?" He offered me no answer, so I looked up from the pages. "Mr. Merrick?"

A jolt of pain exploded in my jaw, and my hand flew up to the side of my face.

I did not want to look behind me. Mr. Merrick's eyes had become fixed again, and he trembled as he whispered my name. At last I forced myself to slowly turn, and there on the ground before the fireplace sat a woman with her back to us. She appeared small and slender, hunched over something in her lap, with a slight convulsion in her shoulders. Unlike the previous visitations, she ignored not only me, but Mr. Merrick as well, and I clutched my stomach as the import of her presence froze the room beyond the power of any coal to overcome.

Two women had been murdered that night, in less than an hour's time of each other. Two more victims of Leather Apron, that butcher of daughters, sisters, mothers, and friends. Two more lives ended in agony and terror I could not but imagine, and the attempt to do so broke me up and scattered my pieces.

"Evelyn," Mr. Merrick said.

"Mr. Merrick," I whispered, unsure of where my voice had come from.

"Evelyn, go to her."

I nodded, but had to reassemble myself before I could attain my feet. Once there, I made my way toward the apparition, considering each step whilst keeping my eyes squarely upon her heaving back. I drew closer to her, and within a few paces, her auburn hair came into my sight, spilling down over her shoulders and face so that I had no view of what she hunched over. I sidled around her, my ragged breathing loud in my own ears, but over which I came to hear the spirit's muffled sobbing.

"He-hello," I said, from a distance as near to her as I wanted to be.

She didn't look up at me, but continued to worry over whatever she had in her lap.

I swallowed and took another step closer to her. "Can . . . we help you?" I asked, but received no reply. I stepped toward her again, and then again, craning to see what she had, and then I finally caught a sight of it.

Her left forearm lay limp and torn open in her lap, and with the fingernails of her right hand she raked through her own flesh. Amidst the blood and tatters of skin I glimpsed the blue of what I guessed had once been a tattoo.

I covered my mouth and stepped away. "Mother of God," I said. "Don't—don't do that to yourself!"

She looked up at me then, a woman of at least forty years of age, grunting and grimacing even as she dug deeper into her arm. "I'm sorry," she whimpered. "So sorry."

"Stop!" I said.

But that only seemed to spur her into a more frenzied and aggressive attack on herself, and she clawed away her own tissue until the yellow of her bones lay exposed. I believed she meant to keep going until she had no arm left at all, and I dared not consider what she would tear into after that.

"You must stop!" I said, and in desperation reached my hand toward her shoulder. As soon as I touched her, my stomach wrenched so hard it drove the air out of me, and I thought I might vomit, but she flinched away and broke our contact.

"I'm sorry!" she screamed. Then she leapt to her feet and streaked from the room through the door. I expected to see her blood on the floor where she'd been sitting, but there was none, all evidence of her having been there gone.

"Mr. Merrick," I said. "Are you—"

A gurgling sound came from his bed, and when I looked toward him I saw one of his pillows had fallen out from behind him, and his head tipped backward, straining his neck and cutting off his breathing.

"Mr. Merrick!" I shouted, and flew to him. Without any strength of his own to aid me, I had to lift the whole weight of his massive head on my own, but the cumbersomeness of its shape made it difficult. His gurgling continued, his eyes wide and rolling, looking up at me as I strained. "No," I whispered through clenched teeth. "Not like this."

I wedged both my arms behind him, up to my shoulders, and then I heaved his head forward. Once upright, his air passage unobstructed, Mr. Merrick sucked in a desperate breath with the whine of a torn bellows, while I retrieved his fallen pillow and returned it to its rightful place. I then laid him back against it, his support once again made sure.

"Mr. Merrick," I said. I was out of air myself and felt a sudden faint wearing away at my sight. I let myself collapse into the chair, and after a few moments of deep breathing, my faculties were somewhat restored, and I leaned toward him. "Are you all right?" I asked, blinking.

He appeared to have lapsed back into a state of unconsciousness, but in that moment he was breathing evenly, and I felt a prayer of gratitude in my heart for that, at least.

His torpid condition left me alone to ponder what had happened and sort through the rapid and disturbing events. Two strange ghosts had appeared in succession, undoubtedly the victims of two fresh murders. Though neither apparition had spoken her name to me, I would learn who they were within a matter of hours when news of them appeared in the papers.

The first spirit, the Swede, had needed money, and had spoken of losing her family in the sinking of the *Princess Alice.* I'd been a girl of seven or eight years of age when that calamity had befallen the city and didn't remember it well. I recalled only that a collision had taken place on the Thames between a passenger ferry and a coal freighter, and that many had drowned. The spirit had begged for money, but I wondered whether the boat tragedy had more to do with her torment, and felt I had a direction in which to begin my hunt.

The other spirit troubled me more, not only in my shock at the violence she'd done to herself, but because I knew even less about her. All she'd said was that she was sorry, but to whom and for what I had not a single notion. The blue tattoo, though obliterated as it was, remained the only detail of any peculiarity that might guide my way.

A few hours later, Polly appeared, but against the two wraiths that had preceded her, I welcomed her anxious joy, and even smiled at her familiar wedding gown. I wished she would talk to me, but in her manner she merely stood over Mr. Merrick for several moments, and, finding him unresponsive, went to inspect the cards and photographs along the mantel as though she had no memory of having done so many times before. Night after night she had repeated the same actions, as had Annie, the dominion of these ghosts one of amber, wherein past events and emotions had become trapped in a world unto themselves.

After Polly had gone, I waited to see if Annie would return, no longer fully convinced I had succeeded in liberating her. But when her appointed hour came and went without any sight of her open mouth or sound of her wail, I sighed and smiled for her soul. The assurance that a ghost could be freed, and that I had done it, were all I needed to continue in my Spiritualist enterprise.

Miss Doyle and Miss Flemming came before long, and finding Mr. Merrick again insensate, fetched Dr. Treves.

"Damn," he said, following his examination. "I thought perhaps we'd turned a corner somehow. But it seems we were right in our first conclusion."

"He was well enough yesterday," Miss Doyle said, and then she turned to me. "Did something happen during the night?"

Much had happened, but nothing I could speak of with her. "No, miss," I said.

She turned her body away but kept her eyes on me a moment longer in obvious suspicion. I knew very well she had no idea what had transpired, but under her scrutiny, I felt a bit of perspiration forming along my brow.

Dr. Treves held a fist to his mouth as though he meant to blow into it. "Watch him closely," he said. "I fear we're truly near the end, this time." He shook his head on his way out of the room, repeatedly growling, "Damn."

Miss Flemming left soon after him, but Miss Doyle remained behind with me. I was about to ask if she needed anything more, but she spoke first. "When you took your day off without permission, where did you go?" she asked.

"I— Why do you ask?"

"Mr. Merrick seemed to recover the following morning. Unexpectedly. Did you perhaps purchase a remedy for him on the street?"

"What?" I said, indignation lifting my chest. "Of course not!"

"Dr. Treves is a man of science," she said. "He holds no regard for the quacksalvers and charlatans."

"Neither do I."

"I've watched you, Miss Fallow. I believe you truly care for Mr. Merrick, and I can't imagine why you'd leave him the way you did. Unless you did it *for* him."

To that I had no reply. Though wrong in her theory of what I had done in my absence from the hospital, she'd uncovered my motive for leaving.

"I know you don't trust me," she said. "But I promise I'll not snitch on you. Whatever you acquired for Mr. Merrick while you were out, it seemed to help him. Perhaps you might get him some more of it."

"I got him nothing," I said. "I gave Mr. Merrick no remedy—"

"Whatever it was," she said, and firmed up her bearing, "whatever it was, it can't be a bad thing now if it prolongs his life or eases his passing."

"He is *not* passing," I said.

I could sense her growing impatient with me. "Did you know Dr. Treves performed an appendectomy earlier this year? You're ignorant of what that is, of course, but it was the first surgery of its kind in England, and he saved a boy's life doing it. The Queen herself named him Surgeon Extraordinary. So you'll pardon me if

I take the good doctor's judgment over yours." She shook her head at me and went to the door. "Just think on what I said, and do what you need to do for Mr. Merrick. I care about him, too."

Whether I agreed with her about Mr. Merrick's condition or whether she believed I'd given him some patent medicine didn't really matter. What mattered was that Miss Doyle had just offered me her approval to leave the hospital, which was nearly the same as receiving it from the matron, for there was no one else from whom the matron would learn of my absence. Before I undertook another such expedition, however, I had to learn more about the murdered women.

I pulled on my shawl and walked through the hospital to the front gate, and within a few minutes I was able to purchase an array of the morning's newspapers from passing peddlers. I carried this haul of gossip back to Mr. Merrick's room, and there I pored over the sensational details of the crimes.

There'd been two women murdered, just as I'd already concluded. They had met their ends within a short walk of each other, and within the same hour, and, much to the continued humiliation of the police, Leather Apron had accomplished his purpose seemingly beneath the coppers' very noses.

The *Echo* reported the first of the victims as a Swede named Elizabeth Stride, and indeed her husband was said to have shipwrecked and drowned. Since then, she'd lived in a lodging house in Flower and Dean, and went by the name Long Liz. I shuddered to think of entering that place in search of information, and hoped that would not be necessary. Of the second victim, nothing was yet known, but her inquest had been scheduled for Thursday, four days hence, at eleven o'clock at the City Mortuary on Golden Lane. I felt a pressing need to be present for it, though I feared Mr. Merrick would not live that long.

I waited out the rest of that day impatient for more news, for I still had little knowledge with which to make a pursuit. I hoped that Charles would come with word from William Nichols, but the day came and went without the musician's return.

That evening, I repeated my morning excursion and collected another assortment of papers, hoping the day's investigation had brought the reporters more revelations. I was quite hungry by then, so rather than take that new stack back to Mr. Merrick's room, I carried it to the servants' table for dinner. I arrived before everyone else, which afforded me the opportunity to read through them, and I did so as quickly as my eyes could gallop.

When Beatrice came in with her copy of the *Star*, she appeared to notice my collection of papers, and scowled. I wondered if she felt annoyed at having someone else at the table as informed on the events as she. Later, as the maids gathered 'round eating, Martha asked if there were any news on the murders.

Beatrice opened her mouth to speak, but my voice outpaced hers. "The second victim is still unidentified," I said. "Though she has a unique tattoo on her arm in blue ink. The initials *T* and *C*." That detail matched what I had glimpsed on the arm of the second spirit before she'd ruined her flesh.

Beatrice's scowl deepened as I spoke.

"Well, that's something," Becky said. "Someone ought to know her from that."

"What of the first murder?" Martha asked.

"Long Liz," Beatrice said, loudly asserting herself. "A street-walker, like the others, all four of 'em gin bottles, too."

I spoke up then, for that was not the whole character of the woman whose ghost had come into Mr. Merrick's room. "She also lost her husband and children when the *Princess Alice* sank," I said. "Those who knew her said she was kind and would do a good turn for anyone."

"Aw," Becky said. "That's nice, isn't it?"

Beatrice thinned her eyes at me. "She had a taste for grapes," she said, it seeming more important that she know *something* than know something of importance. "Says she ate them right before she had her throat cut."

"That's not true," I said. "At the inquest, the coroner stated emphatically she'd eaten no grapes."

"Perhaps the coroner got it wrong, then," Beatrice said, her lips stitching tightly together, as if cinched by a needle and thread.

"More likely the reporter making the claim got it wrong," I said.

"Why do grapes matter?" Becky asked.

"It's a murder investigation," Beatrice said. "Everything matters." Then she looked hard at me. "That's why it do matter if she were a prostitute."

"She was also a charwoman," I said. "Which isn't so different from us, now is it? Is that important to you?"

Beatrice slapped her paper down upon the table. "You think these women were like us? Well, I think maybe they got what's coming to them. I think maybe this Leather Apron is a religious fanatic trying to rid the city of sin."

"Or maybe he's a Jew," I said. "Or maybe he's an American from Texas. Or maybe he's this mysterious lodger. Or maybe he's an escaped lunatic." I'd read numerous theories that day, some quite outlandish, all written by readers to the editors of the papers, as though it had become a hobby among the wealthy and learned to speculate on the crimes. "A theory is not a truth," I said. "Though it may satisfy some as one."

"Whoever he is, he can hold a candle to the Devil," Beatrice said, and rose from her chair. "I think we can agree on that."

"We can," I said.

CHAPTER 17

That night, when Long Liz came calling with her tortured movement and the sound of a butcher snapping joints apart, I tried to obtain more information from her ghost. "Tell me about your husband, Elizabeth," I said. "The one who drowned."

"My husband drowned," she said. "He was aboard the *Princess Alice*."

"I know," I said. "I'm terribly sorry. But will you tell me about him?"

"My husband?" she said. "He—he drowned on the *Princess Alice*."

"I know," I said.

"With my children," she said.

"Tell me about your children, then."

"They drowned when the *Princess Alice* went down in the river."

Her thoughts seemed caught in an eddy, swept 'round and 'round the same rocks by the current of her grief. Annie had been similarly trapped, and it was the scarf, a piece of her son, that had finally allowed her to escape. Perhaps Long Liz needed something of her husband and children to be free. From the papers, I'd learned of only one place where I might find such an article, and that was her lodging in Flower and Dean.

"Do you have money?" she asked me, cracking again. "Please, I need money."

"I have money," I said, and again tossed what coins I had to her, and then later, after she'd gone, I went out into Bedstead Square to retrieve them freezing from the ground. The second, nameless spirit soon appeared, more quietly than the others, suddenly before the fireplace. I went to her side sooner then, and before she'd had a chance to deface it with her clawing, I saw the tattoo, *TC*, in blue ink, just as the paper had reported it. I wondered if the letters were her initials.

"What is your name?" I asked.

She shook her downward-cast head, sobbing. "I'm sorry. So sorry."

"I know," I said. "But please, you must tell me your name."

She ignored me, and the destruction of her arm began in earnest. I had to look away, but I could hear the slippery sounds of her flesh tearing, her grunts and whimpers, until at last she screamed, "I'm sorry!" and once again ran from the room.

I stood shaking in her aftermath, no closer to knowing who she was or why she haunted or why she did such injury to herself. Unless someone came forward in the papers to identify her, the upcoming inquest presented perhaps the only opportunity I would have to discover the key to free her from her pain.

When Polly came a few hours later, I'd fallen asleep in Mr. Merrick's oddly canted chair and woke only to the ache in my jaw announcing her presence. She hovered by the mantel near me, surveying the cards and photographs, and then she was gone, off to St. Bride's.

When Dr. Treves came later that morning, he reported Mr. Merrick's condition worsened, both in his breathing and the strength of his heart, and Miss Doyle gave me a knowing look and nod. I knew what was needed to restore him, but a later search of that day's papers offered nothing useful to my purpose, and it became clear I would have to do what I had been avoiding. I needed to venture out into the city once again, to Flower and Dean and the former lodging of Long Liz, if I was to help Mr. Merrick in time. Such a thing would've been extremely foolish and dangerous on my own, so I waited and hoped for Charles's return to ask him to accompany me.

He failed to return that day, during which I watched Mr. Merrick's skin grow grayer, the draft of his breathing driven further over the shoals. Dr. Treves came frequently with Miss Doyle, and I felt crestfallen each time the door opened on them and not Charles.

I slept the first few hours of that night in my bed, and a few more in Mr. Merrick's chair after Long Liz and the nameless spirit had come. Neither of them had offered any further revelation, and I resolved to go out the following morning into the city on my own whether Charles returned or not, for Mr. Merrick's life would not wait for him.

Fortunately, Charles did come the next morning, and he had located William Nichols.

"Sorry it took me so long," he said. "Chap was hard to track down, but I found him working as a printer's machinist at Perkins and Bacon, over on Whitefriars."

"You delivered my letter to him?" I asked.

"That I did."

"And what was his reply?"

"He wrote a letter of his own." Charles reached into his coat pocket and pulled out an envelope, which he then handed to me. "Seemed a decent enough man, to me."

I took the letter from him and rushed to open and read it.

Miss Fallow,

I thank you for your letter. I wish you had no cause to write it. Polly left me and her children three years ago. I have not seen her since, but I did not wish her any harm, and certainly not the evil that found her. Regarding her father, that is something I suspected when I married her, but it would not have stopped me from joining with her. I could not make her speak of it, just as I could not make her leave the drink alone. If she had stopped drinking, we might have got on all right together. But it has come to a sad end at last.

Sincerely,
William Nichols

His mention of her drinking snagged me, pulling on the barb in my chest. I hadn't been able to make my father stop, either.

"What's he say?" Charles asked.

"He would have married her anyway," I said. "Just as Mr. Merrick has tried to tell her."

"Pity the man can't come and tell her himself. Can't think how I'd convince him to, though."

I didn't know how I might persuade him, either, but I put his letter on the mantel, hoping to read and contemplate it again later. Before that, there lay an urgent task ahead. "We need to go to Flower and Dean, Charles."

"Bloody hell. You going to make this worth my while?" His voice had lost the lilt of flirtation, laden now with a true expectation.

"It isn't enough you do it for Mr. Merrick?" I said. "Your friend?"

"Sure it is," he said. "It's just a bit unfair you still think so little of me, is all."

"I don't think little of you."

"Oh no? So you'll go for a stroll with me? We'll be filly and foal, we will."

"No," I said.

"Why?" he said.

I had no answer for him, other than the disquiet he caused me. The reasons I had built into a wall no longer fit together as securely as they had when I'd first refused him, but I wasn't yet ready to bring the ramparts down. "Charles, I . . ."

"Fine," he said, with stony anger. "Let's go, then. For Joseph."

I nodded, grateful to let the matter drop, and we left the hospital, taking the omnibus as we had before. We spoke little as we rode down Whitechapel, for Charles had fallen into sullenness, and as we passed Thomas Barry's establishment, advertising two new waxen corpses, I found my own anger at him renewed.

So I peered down at the street traffic, which had become more taut and hostile since my last excursion. Nearly every person we passed wore an expression of anger, fear, or suspicion, and abundant coppers strolled along the street, more numerous than I had ever seen them. Signs, posters, and graffiti shouted about the murders from every side, blaming the Jews or blaming the police, offering rewards, and inciting general paranoia. Evangelists preached fiery religion from the corners, lambasting the vices and moral ailments of the East End. Even the Socialists and Anarchists were out distributing pamphlets, though I failed to see how their politics related to the situation, beyond a general desire for an audience.

We traded omnibuses at Commercial Street once more, and rode up to Spitalfields and into the Evil Quarter Mile. Fear and nausea turned my stomach with each passing block, bringing us closer to the cursed place. We disembarked at Thrawl Street and walked up the rest of the way to Flower and Dean. I kept my head bowed and my shawl pulled tight, the mood on the street here more menacing than it had been on Whitechapel, and nearly walked right into a blackened coal heaver.

"Watch it, girl," he said.

I roused the old bullyragging cat I'd left behind and snapped at him, "Next time, you mind the grease and make way for a lady." I moved to go around him, but he stepped into my way. When I tried the other side, he again placed himself in my path.

"You got a mouth on you," he said.

"Oi!" Charles said to him. "Step aside."

"Make me, meater," the coal heaver said, "unless you mean to shake a flannin'."

"I've no quarrel with you," Charles said. "And neither does the woman."

Charles may have been willing to back down, but I was not and could not. "Well, *I've* a quarrel if you don't move out of my way," I said, and reached into my skirt pocket, a risky move to make him wonder what I might be hiding.

He noticed it and looked into my unblinking, unflinching eyes. I brought all my anger and will to bear on him, and his buckled before me. I could see it by the drop in his shoulders, and he stepped back and to the edge of the sidewalk. But I wasn't finished with him.

"You don't doff your cap to a lady?" I said.

His face went red, but he tipped his bowler, spilling coal dust from the brim. Charles and I strolled by him, and once a safe distance away, Charles whispered to me, "I know you're cross with me, but do you have to get me thrashed?"

"He didn't want *you*," I said, thinking perhaps Charles wouldn't be as useful as I'd hoped.

We entered Flower and Dean, a dim and narrow cranny choked with smoke, where it seemed the sunlight couldn't reach. Refuse and waste of all kinds gathered in piles along the sides of the street. I stepped around a naked child eating something she'd dug out of the street muck and pressed forward. The wood and brick lodging houses reached up four stories to either side of the slum, and its occupants thronged the street. We passed a couple of prostitutes standing outside a brothel, their hulking minder standing near even as their abbess leaned out a window to keep watch.

"Hey there, pretty fellow," one of them called to Charles. "What's in the case?"

"A violin," Charles said, tucking it tighter against himself. I didn't think it wise of him to have announced that. A violin could be sold for a lot of money.

"Oh," the other one said, "I'll bet you got a real fine instrument. Come inside and let me play it." They both giggled.

"Not today, ladies," Charles said, blushing a little in his ears.

They both pouted and simpered, and the first one said, "Oh, come on. Bring your lady friend, too! Play us a tune and we'll dance!"

"I'd sooner see you both dance upon nothing," I said, a reference to the gallows that seemed to stun the playfulness right out of them. They looked at each other with mouths agape, and even their minder took note of me.

"Besides," Charles said, "ain't you two worried about Leather Apron?"

"We ain't no bunters like them he's murdered!" said the second. "We're high-class toffers, here!" She looked up toward her abbess, but the woman had left her window perch.

"Sure you are," Charles said, and on we walked.

"We're looking for number thirty-two," I said.

We passed more prostitutes and a couple of bruisers I knew would need little provocation to attack either of us, even as filthy urchins scampered around our feet. Fortunately, it was still morning, and that time of day would find most lurkers, cutthroats, and bludgers still abed, sleeping off the last night's drink.

When we reached the address the papers had given as that of Long Liz, Charles rapped upon the door. A giantess opened it, obviously the deputy of the house. She wore her cloak and bonnet as if she meant to go out directly.

"We got no beds," she said.

"We're not here about lodging," I said. "We're inquiring about Long Liz."

"On my way to the inquest just now," she said, ducking through the door to join us in the street. "Why you asking?"

"I'm wondering about her husband," I said. "The one who drowned."

The formidable woman nodded. "You ain't the only."

"What do you mean?" Charles asked.

"She been telling that story to everyone, even her man, Michael Kidney. But some of us been talking, and it don't sound right."

"How so?" I asked.

"Mind you, I make no habit of speaking ill of others," she said, leaning down toward me. "Leastwise the dead. But Liz seemed to like the attention she got for being disaster's widow. And one night when she was low, I asked her, I says, 'Liz, if your husband was drowned, why don't you try for some of that *Princess Alice* subscription money they raised for the families?' She says to me she applied, but there was some problem, because another bloke with the same name as her husband had died of consumption in an asylum on Devon's Row, so they wouldn't give her no money." The deputy stood up straight again, nodding. "Tell me that's not skilamalink."

"It does sound odd," I said.

"Odd is right. You ask me, I think that bloke in the asylum *were* her husband, and she cooked up the other story for God

knows why. And I'm not the only one who thinks so. Her chucka-
boo, Catherine, agrees it don't all come together. But mind
you, we won't speak any of this at the inquest. No, I'll not say
anything to harm her memory. She were a good, kind, hardwork-
ing woman."

I found her protestations to be at odds with how willing she
was to gossip with me, a stranger, about her former tenant, but I
thanked her, and she walked away toward Osborn Street, towering
over the road.

"She's a Maid Marian, isn't she?" Charles said.

"She's not quite that large," I said.

We turned in the opposite direction and made our way back
through the slum. As we approached that first brothel, almost at
Commercial Street, I was disconcerted to find the two ladybirds
had gone inside and had been replaced by three brutish minders.
One of the mobsmen had a pipe between his teeth and wore a fine
top hat. When he saw us, he removed his hat and set it carefully on
the brothel's stoop, along with his pipe, after which the three of
them stalked into the street to block our path. They meant to
accost us, that was certain, but I didn't know what type of violence
they intended, for Charles, or for me.

"Should we go the other way?" Charles whispered.

I looked around us. Everyone else who'd been in the street had
turned away or scattered. "Won't do any good," I said.

"We heard about your violin," the pipe-smoking bludger said.
"I'd like to make you an offer."

"Your judys already made me a generous one," Charles said. "If
I turned them down, it's not likely I'll accept an offer from you."

The man chuckled and stepped right up to Charles, close enough for me to see the red in the whites of his eyes. "Think me a mandrake, do you?"

"Not at all," Charles said. "I was—"

The leader struck him in the face with his fist. The blow sent Charles sprawling, and his violin case tumbled away. I dove to his side as he attempted to raise himself, bleeding profusely from his nose, but before I could get him up, the other two bludgers rushed around and grabbed him from behind.

"Leave him be!" I shouted as they hauled him roughly to his feet.

Their leader strode up, shoved me out of the way, and struck Charles again, and again, in the face and in his gut. I raced to the edge of the street, grabbed a broken chunk of brick, and flew at Charles's assailant from behind. I landed a blow against the back of his skull, which caused him to stagger, but didn't drop him as I'd hoped. Instead, he recovered his footing and palmed his head, and when his hand came away red, he snarled at me. I went deathly cold at that, and attempted my earlier ploy by reaching into my skirt pocket.

"What you got there?" he asked.

"Come one step closer and you'll find out," I said.

"All right, then," he said, and barreled toward me.

My bluff had not worked, and the monster met my eyes with the level of rage I imagined drove Leather Apron's mania. Charles hung limp and broken between the other two bludgers, and I was about to be raped, killed, or both, but all I could think was that I had failed Mr. Merrick.

Just then, a copper sauntered into view on Commercial Street, his peak-hatted silhouette crossing the entrance to Flower and Dean. He was close enough to hear me, but I had to get his attention in a way he couldn't ignore. An idea occurred to me then.

"LEATHER APRON!" I screamed. "IT'S LEATHER APRON!" I pointed at the mobsman charging at me, which halted him instantly in his steps.

The copper took one glance at us and blew his whistle, and within moments, three of his comrades had rushed to his side. Then the four of them advanced into the slum toward us, appearing cautious but determined.

"Bitch," the mobsman said as he backed away. He nodded to his associates, and they dropped Charles to the ground, and then the three of them turned and fled down the street. To my dismay, one of them snatched up Charles's violin along the way.

"Stop right there!" yelled one of the coppers, but halfheartedly. They gave no chase, and though I was grateful to them for coming to our aid, I scoffed at their seeming ineptitude and cowardice. "Are you all right, miss?" the same copper asked me, while the others went to Charles.

"I'm well enough," I said. "But what of my friend?"

"He's coming to," announced one of the coppers, bearing him up. "But we best get him to the London."

"What makes you think that man was Leather Apron?" the first copper asked me, sounding almost irritated.

"He was about to kill me," I said. "You need more than that to go arrest him?"

The man looked deeper into Flower and Dean but said nothing, his silence an indictment against the whole bloody city. I realized then that he would have ignored my plea had it not been for the spectre of Leather Apron I'd summoned, and I would've ended up like so many other nameless victims of the East End, my life of little account, my fate but what I deserved according to those with privilege and wealth. That was the existence I'd but briefly escaped. That was the life that waited for me after I helped Mr. Merrick recover.

The coppers helped us to Commercial Street, where one of the policemen ordered us into a hansom cab. The horse and driver carried us more swiftly than the omnibuses, until we hit a blockade of traffic that slowed our pace. Along the way, Charles continued to rally and was soon sitting upright. I used my apron to wipe away the blood from his face and examined his injuries. The mobsman had blackened both his eyes, broken his nose, and collapsed a cheekbone, and that was just the damage done to his face. Still, it could have been much worse if they'd had a knife.

"How ugly do I look?" he asked.

"Still not as ugly as me," I said.

"Stop with that. Did you—" He winced. "You get my violin?"

I paused before telling him. "No, I'm sorry. They grabbed it."

He let out a moan as though that loss caused him more pain than any of his physical wounds, and said nothing else to me on our journey to the hospital. When we arrived, the hansom driver discounted the fare, due to the emergency, and I paid him. Then I helped Charles to the front gate and waited until a porter took him inside and I knew he would be cared for. I didn't go into the receiving room with him, for fear that would invite too many questions about where I'd been, and instead hastened down and around to the gate on East Mount Street.

From there, I crossed Bedstead Square and went to Mr. Merrick's room, where I found his condition no worse than it had been earlier that morning, which brought its own kind of relief. After that, I could but sit and wait, trembling as I recalled all that had just happened, and contemplated what had nearly happened.

CHAPTER 18

It seemed a great deal of time passed before Dr. Treves came with Miss Doyle, and I greeted them eagerly. I had no expectation that anything might have changed for Mr. Merrick, but I wanted to know about how Charles was getting on. After Dr. Treves had conducted his examination and gone, Miss Doyle sat me down at Mr. Merrick's table, the model church nearby close to completion. I made a silent vow in that moment that Mr. Merrick would finish it before I left.

"You were absent the earlier part of the day," she said. "I made sure it went unnoticed."

"Thank you," I said.

"I did not do it for you. Were you . . . successful?"

"I don't know yet." I didn't know if I'd gleaned anything useful from the day's inquiry. "But time will prove it."

She nodded and pushed away from the table to leave.

"Miss Doyle?" I said.

She paused. "Yes?"

"I believe Charles Weaver was admitted to the hospital earlier today. He's the violinist who comes to play for Mr. Merrick."

"Yes, I know of him," she said. "But I didn't know he was admitted. Is he ill?"

"He was attacked in the street and took a thrashing."

"How awful," she said. "Male physical trauma and injury are typically placed in Gloucester Ward. Would you like me to inquire about him?"

"No, thank you," I said. "I can go to the ward myself."

"I hope his injuries weren't serious," she said. "I know Mr. Merrick considers him a friend."

I found to my surprise that I had come to consider him a friend, too. "I hope so as well," I said, and a short while later I put on my shawl, left Mr. Merrick's room, and entered the inner lobby of the East Wing. On my first day at the hospital, Matron Luckes had pointed Gloucester Ward out to me, and I entered there with some trepidation.

The ward was a long room, both of its sides lined with iron bed frames like those I'd seen being scrubbed out in the square. A row of tall windows on the right let sunlight in, which reflected dully against the polished wood of the parquet floor, while potted plants and nurses' desks sprouted up and down the middle of the room.

The male patients sat up or lay in their beds, some of them reading newspapers, some of them playing chess or cards with one another, others simply staring with blank expressions. I scanned the nearest of them but didn't see Charles.

One of the nurses approached me in her white apron and dress of sky blue. "Yes, what is it?"

"Is Charles Weaver here?" I asked.

"He is," she said. "Were you sent on an errand?"

"No," I said. "I wish to see him for personal reasons."

"These are not visiting hours," she said. "But . . . since you are staff, I suppose I'll allow it. He is in bed nineteen, on the left."

"Thank you, miss," I said, and walked down the row of bandaged patients, nodding at them with my face covered by my shawl, until I saw Charles. His appearance clenched my chest. One of his eyes was completely swollen shut, the other nearly so, with his cheek painted crudely with a bruise.

"Charles," I said. "Oh, Charles."

He grinned as I sat down on his bed near him, and I noticed a chip in one of his teeth. "Not to worry," he said. "This will all heal. Only got one broken rib, and my cheek. They's keeping me over one night, to make sure there's no sepsis."

"I'm so sorry."

"It were my fault. Shoulda left the violin in Joseph's room." He shook his head. "That's what hurts the most. My father saved and bought me that instrument, which is no small thing for a bricklayer. Don't know what I'll tell him."

"I wish I'd tried to grab it."

"Not your fault," he said. "You were right bricky." He grinned, and I smiled at his double meaning, though I hadn't felt very brave when I'd grabbed that brick, merely desperate. "Don't remember what happened after that," he said. "Thought they was going to send me home."

"I called a passing copper," I said.

"And he came? Into the rookery?"

"He couldn't ignore me. I accused the bludger of being Leather Apron."

Charles snickered at that. "Proper bit of frock, you are," he said, and I felt a bit of blush heat my cheeks. "So tell me true," he said. "How do I look?"

"*Now* you're as ugly as me," I said, and I laughed, but alone.

"Why don't you fancy me?" he asked.

The boldness of his question flustered me, and also angered me. "Why would I? Do you truly fancy me?" I immediately regretted the question, for I suddenly found I didn't want the answer.

"Why you asking me that?" He looked at me for a moment out of his swollen eyes, his gaze cold. "I reckon it's not actually because you don't trust I fancy you. It's because you don't trust yourself to be fancied. And that's a bloody shame."

I didn't know how to reply to that. I didn't think he was right, but I also couldn't say he was wrong. It was true that I still did not fully trust him, but I had to admit I didn't trust anyone, save Mr. Merrick. It was also true I didn't think myself a woman anyone could desire. I had long since settled that matter for myself, and even though it pained me, I accepted it, but then Charles had come stirring up trouble.

"Evelyn," he said. "What are you doing?"

"I'm listening to myself," I said.

"No," he said. "I meant for Joseph. What're you doing next? About the ghosts?"

"Oh," I said. "I don't know." But I felt relieved for a change in the subject of our conversation. "There's an inquest on Thursday for the other victim. I plan to be there, and perhaps I'll learn what I need to help her ghost."

"And Long Liz, with her *Princess Alice* story?"

"She's still a fifteen puzzle," I said. "I don't know what to think of her. I agree with that Maid Marian, though. I think Liz made that whole story up, about her husband and children drowning. Why else wouldn't she collect the money from it, if money's what she wants so badly?"

"I had the same thought." He tipped his head back against the bedstead. "My eyes will still be in slings on Thursday, but I'll go to the inquest with you."

"Thank you, Charles."

"When this is over," he said, "and Joseph is on the mend, you might consider a career as a ghost hunter. I think you've a knack for it."

I laughed. "When this is over, I want no more truck at all with the unquiet dead."

He nodded. "Then may it be so."

"You need rest, and I should be getting back to Mr. Merrick."

"Go on, then. Give him a punch in the arm for me. And thanks for checking on me."

"You're welcome." I rose from his bed, but he reached out and seized my hand, not roughly, but firmly. "Think on what I said, eh? A man's pride can't abide being denied."

"That's a pretty turn of phrase," I said. "You should put that in a song for the stage."

"You think?"

"Indeed. Because you'll get no sympathy from the audience before you now."

He let me go with a wry smile, and I left the ward and returned to Mr. Merrick's room. There I busied myself with all my usual chores, dusting and cleaning. When Miss Doyle and Miss Flemming came, we all worked together to change his bedding. The sour smell about him worsened during those days when he lay unconscious and unwashed, but it helped to clean what we could. When evening came, I put on my shawl to join the other servants at dinner, and this time let Beatrice hold court as both Queen of Gossip and Prime Minister of Scandal, wielding all the authority of her *Evening News*, though for several minutes she only related things already known.

"They're still saying he's a medical man," she said. "A doctor perhaps, who has epileptic fits, and he has it out for streetwalkers."

"I still say his weapon is dull," Martha said.

"Will you stop with that?" Becky said. "Honestly, Martha, you spend altogether too much time thinking on the maniac's manhood."

"Look who he's murdering!" Martha said. "What else could it be about?"

Beatrice leaned forward with a sudden gasp. "Cheese and Crust, there's been another woman murdered!"

I nearly dropped my fork in alarm, for if a fourth ghost came it would surely be too much for Mr. Merrick in his state, not to mention my own nerves, which could handle no more. But I quickly realized the body must've already been found, for the news to have made the paper, which meant the ghost would've already come, were she going to.

"A torso found wrapped up in a parcel in Westminster," Beatrice said. "Head, arms, and legs cut off."

"It's too much," Becky said, sounding as fragile as a porcelain shoe. "It's like the whole world's gone mad."

"Is it Leather Apron?" Martha asked.

"They don't know," Beatrice said. "But I'd wager a month's wages it is."

"It isn't," I said, and everyone turned toward me.

"And how would you know that?" Beatrice asked.

I couldn't tell them the truth, so I said, "None of the others were . . . cut up in that way."

"They was disemboweled, weren't they?" Beatrice said. "Butchery is butchery."

I pressed harder against her argument. "But Leather Apron doesn't wrap up his victims in parcels. He leaves them in the open. Like he wants them found."

"Oh, you a detective now, are you?" Beatrice ladled ice into her words. "Scotland Yard must be so grateful for your talents."

I ignored her. "It's like he's . . . taunting the police."

"That makes sense to me," Becky said.

"'Course it does." Beatrice turned the anger toward Becky. "But you Africans know all about savages, don't you?"

"Beatrice!" I shouted, and stabbed my finger at her. "Shut your sauce-box."

"Don't trouble yourself," Becky said to me, rising from the table. "And Beatrice, I'll remind you there ain't one single witness saying this Leather Apron is a black man. You ask me, you white folk got your own kind of savage to worry about." She left the table then, and Martha hurried after her.

A moment after they'd gone, Beatrice laughed in an embarrassed way that flapped her lips and sounded false. "I don't mean *she's* a savage. Becky's a nice little Hottentot."

I stood then, and my voice became a hiss. "She's a far better woman than you'll ever be, you miserable old haybag."

If I'd been closer to her, Beatrice might have slapped me, such was the fury that crossed her face, but I merely turned my back on her and left her steaming. In our room, I found Martha sitting next to Becky on her bed, and Becky looked up when I came in.

"Thank you," she said.

"Pay her no mind," I said, ripping off my shawl. "She's nothing but a vile church-bell."

"Oh, she don't bother me," Becky said. "I've heard worse."

"I'd still like to batty-fang her," Martha said.

"You'd lose your position and so would I," Becky said.

"Maybe I'll thrash her," I said. "I'm as good as sacked, anyway."

Becky chuckled. "Go on, then. Have at her."

"Just as soon as Mr. Merrick is recovered," I said, returning her laugh. "Speaking of which, I must get back to him. Will you be all right?"

"Oh, yes," Becky said. "That old blowsabella don't matter a whit to me."

I bade them both good night and left, disturbed for some time by what had happened. My distress and anger on Becky's behalf did not arise only from the attitudes my father had taught me, though, but from my own experiences. The matron wouldn't hire a black woman as a nurse any sooner than she'd hire me, and that was far from the only time my appearance had been so judged. I meant not to compare burdens, but felt that when Beatrice insulted Becky, she may as well have been insulting me or any of us that were overlooked and disregarded.

I reached Mr. Merrick's room, and having already cleaned it thoroughly that day, there wasn't much I could do to pass the time or distract myself out of the dark mood Beatrice had caused. The anger I'd felt at the coppers earlier in the day became an overwhelming rage at the city for all its daily injustices, not just to Becky but to me and Charles and Polly and Annie and Long Liz and countless others who got worse than they deserved. Even well-meaning souls like Matron Luckes were complicit, and had my fury taken physical form that night it would have burned the whole of bloody London to the ground.

The spirits upset me, too, for they had offered no explanation for their demands but had demanded them nevertheless. They were all of them flayed to the deepest part of their pain, and I could not help but feel some of it with them, along with a helplessness at being unable to relieve it. Perhaps that was what exhausted Mr. Merrick and brought him low, because he felt for them in a way I still couldn't understand.

Gradually, my seething wrath boiled down to a single name—*Leather Apron*—and in that moment I wished I could somehow seek him out and believed myself capable of tearing him apart. But I could not sustain such a state indefinitely, and as the hours of haunting approached, I felt a devastating fatigue set in.

When Long Liz came bent and breaking into the room, I found it difficult to even rouse myself from my chair in fear as she approached in her fitful way, crying, "I need money!"

"No," I whispered.

She stood up straight, cracking all the way. "Please! I need money!"

"No," I said, raising my voice in anger.

"My husband and children! They drowned on the *Princess Alice*!"

"No, they didn't!" I shouted back. "I think you are a liar. Your husband died in an asylum."

Her mouth snapped shut, she stared at me, and I knew I was right. In the waters of her eyes I saw no depth, nothing but a slick of pain at the surface. "My husband . . . he drowned." Her voice sounded weak.

"He didn't," I said. "I'm not sure why you tell this lie. Maybe you want pity. Maybe you just wanted a different life. But no one here believes you. No one will give you money. You best move along."

"Please—"

"No," I said. "Not one farthing."

She trembled as a spiderweb in a breeze.

"Unless you tell me the truth," I added.

A moment passed.

"The truth," she said.

Then the spirit's posture relaxed and she paced about the room, cracking less. Her movements eased as she let go of the rigidity in her joints, and the breaking of her spine ceased. "My husband was John Stride," she said. "We kept a coffeehouse once, and he sometimes was good to me. But we had no children. My life was not what I wanted."

"I'm sorry," I said. "My life has not been what I wanted, either."

She let out a sigh that lasted longer than any mortal breath.

"But why did you tell that story?" I asked.

"For pity and charity, at first," she said. "But soon . . . I suppose I just liked to believe it myself. But it weren't the truth."

"You've told me the truth," I said. "And you have my respect for it." I reached into my skirt. By then, I'd spent most of my money, but I pulled out the coins remaining. "Here, Liz. All that I have."

"No, but I thank you," she said.

"Please, Liz," I said. "Let me give this to you."

She bit her lip, then nodded and held out her hands, and I dropped the coins into them one at a time. They fell into her substance without a sound, and as the last one reached her, she said, "Thank you," again, and vanished. The coins fell to the floor with a clatter, and the pain in my jaw ceased. The scene called to my mind that verse in the Bible. The truth had set her free, but I had little time to revel in my success, for the tattooed spirit soon appeared.

This time, I didn't look away as she tore into her own flesh, but forced myself to engage with her.

"Who are you?" I asked.

"I'm sorry," she said.

"What is your name?" I asked.

"I'm sorry," she said.

"What do those letters on your arm mean?"

"I'm sorry! I'm sorry! I'm sorry!" she screamed, bloodied by her own doing. I had no notion of what could make a person turn on herself in such a way, but then she was gone, and I cursed Leather Apron once again.

When Polly entered a few hours later, her gladness lifted some of the darkness from my mind, even as her fear broke my heart. She strode to Mr. Merrick's weakening body, and thence to the fireplace, where she scanned the mantel. Partway down it, she seemed to grow especially curious about an item, and leaned in closer.

"That's William's hand!" she exclaimed.

I'd forgotten about his letter, which I'd left there earlier that morning. Polly plucked it from the mantel and took a long time reading it. I watched her, wringing my hands as I waited and hoped. When finished, she looked in Mr. Merrick's direction and spoke to him as though he were awake.

"He knows," she said, blinking in surprise. "I don't know how, but he knows." She looked back down at the letter. "And still he wants to marry me. Can you imagine that?"

"Of course he wants to marry you," I whispered.

She folded the letter back into its envelope and glanced toward the door. "I best be going. He's waiting for me at Saint Bride's, and I don't want him to think I've jilted him. I—I'm scared to face him, knowing he knows, but he's there, ain't he? He's there."

"He's there," I said. "Godspeed, Polly."

"Happiest day of me life," she said, and then she vanished in the manner of Annie and Liz, and the letter she'd been holding fluttered down into the fireplace. I didn't move to retrieve it, but instead watched it flare up on the coals and go to ashes, which then rose up on drafts of heat into the chimney.

That was two ghosts I'd helped put to rest in one night. I hoped the departures of Polly and Liz would at least be enough for Mr. Merrick to recover his consciousness by morning, and then I had but one more spirit to deal with, and after that he would be free of them altogether, so long as Leather Apron took no more victims.

CHAPTER 19

Mr. Merrick did return to us early that morning, to the joy of Dr. Treves. Though weak and reticent, Mr. Merrick was nevertheless able to sit up on his own, drink more beef tea, and even sit by the fireplace. His strength returned by degrees, and when we were alone, I related all that had happened, from the assault in Flower and Dean to the departure of the two spirits.

"Will Charles be all right?" he asked.

"Yes," I said. "He will heal, and hopefully replace his violin soon."

"I'm so sorry for what befell him."

"It was not your fault."

"I feel it was. This is all my fault, somehow."

"Mr. Merrick, we'll have none of that," I said, scolding him. "Charles wanted to help. You must allow people to care for you."

"Do you allow other people to care for you?" he asked, but with curiosity rather than a barb.

"I . . . yes," I said, but the question frightened me as I really considered it. I rarely allowed myself to trust anyone, and I certainly hadn't let myself believe that Charles fancied me. "If a person *truly* cared for me, I'd accept it. I accept your care, don't I?"

"But not from Charles," he said.

It seemed our time together had given him the ability to hear my thoughts. "You seem awfully concerned about Charles and me." I did my best to keep my irritation to myself. "I think it'd be better if you applied your concern to getting better."

"There is only one spirit left? The one whose name you don't know?"

"I shall find it out today at the inquest."

"But Polly is gone?" he said. "You're sure of it?"

"Quite sure, Mr. Merrick. Why?"

Even through the rigid mask of his flesh, I'd begun to discern the subtle ways in which his emotions manifested, by the twitch of his lip, the wrinkles around his eyes, or the angle of his gaze, and in that moment, he seemed quite sad about something.

"Mr. Merrick, what is it?"

"It's just . . . I didn't say good-bye to her."

His sensitivity still had the ability to surprise me, especially in contrast with the callousness of the city around us. I believed there were very few besides Mr. Merrick who gave Polly any thought at all. "I'm sorry, Mr. Merrick."

"Well, she is at peace, and that is what matters." He sighed, and then he slowly looked about the room. Then he pointed at the table where I'd left some of my newspapers. "What are those?"

"I was trying to learn more about the spirits," I said.

"May I see them?"

"Of course," I said, and handed them to him.

He spent the next several minutes perusing them, until he stopped on one page and tore a section from it.

"What is it you have there?" I asked.

He showed me an advertisement for a men's dressing case, which included a hairbrush, toothbrush, and hat brush, all silver-backed, as well as an ivory-handled razor. He needed none of it, of course, but I imagined he admired it for the same reason he'd kissed my hand upon our first meeting. He liked to imagine himself a proper gentleman, and to that end he saved the clipping.

He then felt up to laboring on his card model church, and with the raising of its final spire, he finished it. I thought it quite lovely in its completion, and all the more impressive for how he'd built it with but one good hand. But the experience was also a melancholy one for me, for as we'd worked I remembered my status at the hospital, and I felt very glad to have spent the time with him and seen the model completed before the matron sacked me. Now that Mr. Merrick had recovered, I expected that to happen at any moment.

"I shall give this to Mrs. Kendal," Mr. Merrick said, sounding quite pleased with how the church had turned out. "As a token of my thanks for all she has done for me."

As he spoke, my stomach turned and turned as I thought about what waited for me. "I believe Dr. Treves is going to ask her to arrange an outing to the theater for you."

His expression brightened even more. "Truly?"

"That is what he said."

"Will you come, too?" he asked.

"I doubt I shall be invited," I said. "If they take any of the staff, it will likely be Miss Doyle or one of the other nurses." I did not mention to him that I would surely be gone by then.

He humphed. "I shall ask for *you* to accompany me."

"That is most kind of you," I said.

Dr. Tilney entered the room then, and brought with him a jovial air. "Ah, Joseph!" he said. "Dr. Treves told me you'd rebounded. I'm pleased to see he was right."

"You sound surprised," Mr. Merrick said.

"And I'm happy to be so," Dr. Tilney said. "Be a good chap and keep on surprising us, won't you?"

"I'll do my best, Dr. Tilney. But praise must be given to Evelyn. I would not have recovered without her care."

"Indeed," Dr. Tilney said, appraising me with a knowing smile. "I've observed her ministrations to be most admirable and devoted."

"Thank you, Doctor," I said.

"Might I speak with you, Miss Fallow?"

"Of course," I said, not sure what he could want to speak with me about. The Leather Apron theories from the newspapers insinuated themselves into my mind—"the maniac must be a medical man"—but I did my best to brush away the unease.

Outside in Bedstead Square, Dr. Tilney lost a shade of his cheer. "Why are you here?"

"Sir?"

"I have been watching you, and for the life of me, I can't understand why you're a maid when you could be a nurse. You *should* be a nurse."

He sounded almost angry with me, and it threw me off my balance. "Dr. Tilney, I applied to the matron for a nurse's position, but she refused me."

"What? Did she give a reason?"

"My age." I looked down at my feet. "But, sir, I think you must be aware of the true reason."

"What? Your scars?"

I said nothing.

"But that's ridiculous," he said. "I am a skilled surgeon. If I were injured, would the matron prevent me from doing my work saving lives?"

"You would have to put that question to her," I said.

"I just may," he said. "She's wasting your talents and abilities where you are."

"I appreciate your concern," I said. "But I'm happy where I am, serving Mr. Merrick. Though I'm afraid I won't be for much longer. Now that Mr. Merrick is better, the matron will dismiss me."

"Nonsense," he said.

"You were there, Dr. Tilney. Her threat was not idle."

"Perhaps not, but I'll raise Cain if she tries to sack you."

I'd not had someone speak so defensively of me since my father was living, and it rendered me speechless for a moment, confused almost to the point of tears. "I . . . appreciate that. Truly. But Dr. Tilney, why are you so confident in me?"

"I will answer that with a question of my own," he said. "Why are you not confident in yourself?"

His words echoed something of what Charles had said to me, and what Mr. Merrick and I had just been talking about, and even what Dr. Sidgwick had told me. Though I inwardly resisted all of them, I had no reply for Dr. Tilney, other than to ask, "What good would it do?"

"What do you mean?"

"Confidence cannot change my appearance."

"It may not change your appearance, but it can change how you are perceived."

Again I had no response, for I'd told Mr. Merrick something similar, and I had believed it to be true for him.

"Think on it, Miss Fallow," he said.

I nodded, and he left, and then I went back into Mr. Merrick's room unsettled by the conversation. I felt I should have been grateful and comforted by it, and I was, but I was also made quite anxious and didn't know why. It felt as if Dr. Tilney, like Professor Sidgwick, was inviting me to cross a crowded public market without my shawl, and no amount of confidence could take away my fear of that. They had no idea what they were asking of me.

When Miss Doyle and Miss Flemming came shortly to give Mr. Merrick his morning bath, I pulled Miss Doyle aside and asked her if I might leave the hospital for a few hours.

"But Mr. Merrick is doing quite well," she said. "You need more of the . . . remedy?"

"I just want to make sure," I said.

"I see." She gave me a little frown. "Very well. I'll cover for you."

"Thank you," I said, but couldn't leave until Charles arrived. I hadn't seen him since he'd left the hospital, and I hoped he would come soon. The paper had said the inquest would begin at eleven, and the Coroner's Court on Golden Lane was in the City of London, in Cripplegate. I'd been there once before in my life, and I knew it would take time to reach even by way of the Metropolitan Underground. When Charles did finally come, he looked a little worse than he had on Tuesday. The bruises around his eyes and cheek had gone mottled and green, and he moved as if his broken rib caused him considerable pain.

"Joseph, my ugly bloke," he said. "I wouldn't take a wager on who looks worse, me or you. I'd play you a song, except I've lost my violin, and truth be told"—he pointed to his battered face—"they gave me what Paddy gave the drum, as my Irish friends say."

"You do not look well, Charles," Mr. Merrick said. "I am sorry."

"You should be," Charles said. "Even as those bludgers was slugging me, I was saying to meself, I says, 'Charles, where's that ugly bloke, Joseph? Could sure use an ally right about now.' You missed a proper thrashing, you did."

"It seems so," Mr. Merrick said, laughing weakly. "But I am especially sorry for your violin."

At the mention of his instrument, it didn't seem Charles could varnish the pain with humor, and his nod grew heavy. "I thank you for your sympathy, Joseph." Then he turned to me and said, "We should get underway."

"Right," I said, and tied my shawl around my face. Thus far none of Leather Apron's killings had taken place during the broad day, but my nerves quivered nevertheless.

We bade good-bye to Mr. Merrick and left the hospital grounds through the gate on East Mount Street, and from there we made our way by omnibus down the Whitechapel Road tramway until it reached the old city wall. Then we walked to the Aldgate Station of the underground railway, the same station I had used earlier. I did not like to go down belowground again, but to reach the inquest in time we had no other choice, and besides, Charles was in no condition for a lengthy trip. We bought our tickets, but whereas my last journey had taken me south from the station, we now boarded a train heading north. Columns of brick arched over us like the rib cage of some long-dead serpent buried beneath the city's foundations, through the remains of which we now coursed.

When we stopped at the Bishopsgate Station, passengers got on and off, while we kept our seats and did the same at Moorgate Station, but at Aldersgate Station we disembarked, and the underground railway disgorged us on Aldersgate Street at its crossing with Barbican. We took Barbican east, by foot, for two blocks, passing warehouses and train yards, until we arrived at Golden Lane and turned north.

It was easy to spot the Coroner's Court because of the crowd already gathering outside. Some would be reporters for the newspapers, a few would be family or friends perhaps coming forward to testify at the inquest, but most were curiosity-mongers and bystanders seeking scandal.

The court itself was a fairly large building of brick and stone, housing the courtroom, mortuaries, offices of the coroner and attendants, as well as the shelter block where families found temporary living quarters if infection rendered the cleaning of their residence necessary.

I hadn't adequately prepared to see the place again, and its appearance nearly overturned me on my wheels. "I don't know if I can do this," I said.

"What do you mean?" Charles asked.

"This is where I came to identify my father." I shuddered at the image. His body, lying there on the table, covered by a white sheet, had been purpled and bruised about his face and looked all wrong to me, like a waxwork. I'd held my nose against the sharp sting of disinfectant in the air, wanting to tell the policeman the body couldn't possibly be that of my father, as if that could make it so. But I knew it was, and he was gone.

Charles looked again at the building. "You want I should go in without you?"

I shook my head. "No. I must see this thing done."

"Bricky girl," he said.

We drove our way through the crowd to the front doors, though with Charles's broken rib, I was the point of the wedge.

We'd arrived but a few minutes early, and when the doors to the court opened, we filed in through a plain foyer, pressed on all sides, and then into the courtroom. There, we took our seats in the public gallery, while to our right sat the twelve members of the jury in two rows on their stand. Opposite them ran a long row of desks where reporters had already begun scribbling notes, and in the middle of the room stood a witness box. The solicitor handling the inquest sat behind his bench at the front of the room where he could preside over all, the same smell of disinfectant around us, and overtop, the subtle reek of decay, while the coroner stood near a desk of his own before the jury.

Charles jostled a bit next to me on the hard wooden bench, as if trying to ease his discomfort, his face the worse side of a joint of meat, but he didn't complain. I looked around the room at those who had come to observe the proceedings.

"Do you think her family is here?" I asked Charles.

"Maybe," he said. "If she had any. But it's a million to a bit of dirt you's the only one here about a ghost." He chuckled, and then ceased abruptly with a wince.

When the coroner brought the inquest to order, the solicitor, a Mr. Crawford, said to the coroner, "I appear here as representing the city police in this matter, for the purpose of rendering you every possible assistance. The jury has already viewed the deceased in the mortuary?"

"They have," the coroner said.

"Then," Mr. Crawford said, "let us begin this inquest. You may call up your first witness."

A woman in her cape and bonnet stepped forward from the gallery and approached the witness box with reddened eyes, clutching a handkerchief to her lips, and identified herself as Eliza Gold.

"I live at six Thrawl Street, Spitalfields," she said. "I recognize the deceased as my . . . my poor sister." She sobbed suddenly and quite loudly into her handkerchief, and continued to do so for a few moments.

Feeling hopeful, I whispered to Charles, "Her sister should know much about her."

He nodded.

When Eliza Gold recovered enough to proceed, she said, "Her name was Catherine Eddowes. I cannot exactly tell where she was living. She was staying with a gentleman, but she was not married to him. Her age last birthday was about forty-three years, as far as I can remember."

The fact that she didn't accurately know her sister's age did not bode well for the closeness of their relations.

She continued, "She has been living for some years with Mr. Kelly. He is here in court. I last saw her alive about four or five months ago. She used to go out hawking for a living, and was a woman of sober habits. Before she went to live with Kelly, she had lived with a man named Conway for several years, and had two children by him. I cannot tell how many years she lived with Conway. I do not know whether Conway is still living. He was a pensioner from the army, and used to go out hawking also. I do not know on what terms he parted from my sister. I do not know whether she had ever seen him from the time they parted. I am quite certain that the body I have seen is my sister."

"When did you last see this Conway?" Mr. Crawford asked.

"I have not seen Conway for seven or eight years. I believe my sister was living with him then on friendly terms."

The coroner then asked, "Was she living on friendly terms with Kelly?"

"I cannot say. Three or four weeks ago I saw them together, and they were then on happy terms. From that time, until I saw her in the mortuary, I have not seen her."

One of the jurymen motioned for the coroner, who went and received a muttered communication into his ear. The coroner then returned to Eliza Gold and said, "You saw them together three or four weeks ago?

"Um. Yes."

The coroner frowned. "But you earlier said you had not seen your sister for four or five months. Was that a mistake?"

"Yes," the woman said, twisting the handkerchief between her hands. "No. That is, I—I am so upset and confused." She commenced to sob again, and after a glance between the coroner and magistrate, was allowed to leave the witness box.

"She don't seem reliable," Charles whispered next to me.

"Perhaps not," I said, but at least she'd provided a possible name. *Catherine Eddowes.*

The next witness called was a strong-looking, ruddy man named John Kelly, the man mentioned by Eliza Gold, who identified the victim not as Catherine Eddowes, but Catherine Conway, which I found confusing.

"I have been living with her for seven years," Mr. Kelly said, "at a common lodging house in Flower and Dean Street. I last saw her alive about two o'clock in the afternoon of Saturday in Houndsditch. We parted on very good terms. She told me she was going over to Bermondsey to try and find her daughter Annie. Those were the last words she spoke to me. Annie was a daughter whom I believe she'd had by Conway. She promised me before we parted that she would be back by four o'clock, and no later. She did not return."

Thus far, I'd learned the ghost's name was Catherine, possibly Eddowes or Conway, and that she had a daughter named Annie, but nothing yet about the tattoo or what she so consumingly regretted as to injure herself over it.

"When she failed to return," the coroner said, "did you make any inquiry after her?"

"I heard she had been locked up at Bishopsgate Street on Saturday afternoon," Mr. Kelly said. "An old woman who works in the lane told me she saw her in the hands of the police."

"Did you know why she was locked up?" the coroner asked.

"Yes, for drink. She'd had a drop of drink, so I was told. I never knew she went out for any immoral purpose. She occasionally drank, but not to excess. When I left her she had no money about her. She went to see and find her daughter to get a trifle, so that I shouldn't see her walk about the streets at night."

If she didn't drink to excess, I had to wonder why she'd been locked up for drunkenness, but this discrepancy was never resolved, for after a series of questions establishing the precise hour and circumstances in which Mr. Kelly had last seen Catherine, he was dismissed.

The next witnesses included the deputy of the lodging house where Mr. Kelly and Catherine had been staying, followed by those who'd found her body, and then the policemen they'd called, their testimonies serving primarily to establish a timeline of Catherine's whereabouts prior to her murder. Then the coroner summoned the surgeon who had examined the body, a bread loaf of a man with a long and flaring mustache, Dr. Frederick Gordon Brown.

"I was called shortly after two o'clock on Sunday morning," he said, "and reached the place of the murder about twenty minutes past two. My attention was directed to the body of the deceased. It was lying on its back, the head turned to the left shoulder, the arms by the side of the body, as if they had fallen there. Both palms were upward, the fingers slightly bent. A thimble was lying near. The clothes were thrown up. The bonnet was at the back of the head. There was great disfigurement of the face. The throat was cut across . . ."

I did not want to hear any of that, and feared where the surgeon's testimony would yet go, but I could not escape the crowded gallery the way I had the waxworks, and this time had to endure the details of violence and depravity.

"The upper part of the dress had been torn open," Dr. Brown continued. "The abdomen was exposed. The, um, that is . . ." He glanced between the coroner, the reporters, and those of us in the gallery, as though unsure how to measure his words for the varied audience. "The intestines were drawn out to a large extent and placed over the right shoulder."

A few gasps and murmurs rose up around me, but I was not as shocked as they, for such had been depicted by the waxworks.

"The intestines," Dr. Brown continued, "were smeared over with—with some feculent matter. A piece of intestine about two feet was quite detached from the body and placed between the body and the left arm, apparently by design."

"God blimey," Charles whispered.

"The lobe and auricle of the right ear were cut obliquely through. The body was quite warm. No rigor mortis. The crime must have been committed within half an hour, or certainly within forty minutes from the time when I saw the body. I made a postmortem examination on Sunday afternoon." He paused a moment to wipe sweat from his brow, the silence in the courtroom one of both horror and anticipation. "The clothes were taken off carefully from the body. A piece of the deceased's ear dropped from the clothing. The face was very much mutilated, the eyelids, the nose, the jaw, the cheeks, the lips, and the mouth all bore cuts. There were abrasions under the left ear. The throat was cut across to the extent of six or seven inches."

The coroner spoke up then. "Can you tell us, what was the cause of death?"

After learning the extent of the mutilation, it was a question I had avoided asking, for I didn't want to know how much of that had been done to a living woman.

"The cause of death was hemorrhage from the throat," Dr. Brown said. "Death must have been immediate."

The whole courtroom seemed to exhale then, and sigh, including myself.

"I understand that you found certain portions of the body removed?" the coroner said.

"What does he mean?" I asked Charles, who shrugged.

"Yes," Dr. Brown said. "The uterus was cut away with the exception of a small portion, and the left kidney was also cut out. Both these organs were absent, and have not been found."

"The devil took the organs with him?" Charles whispered.

I understood Becky then, for like her, it was all too much for me, and I wanted to cover my ears.

The coroner put his hands on his hips, spreading his coat. "Would you consider that the person who inflicted the wounds possessed anatomical skill?"

Dr. Brown nodded. "He must have had a good deal of knowledge as to the position of the abdominal organs, and the way to remove them. The kidney would require a good deal of knowledge, because it is apt to be overlooked, being covered by a membrane."

"What would he want with her *organs*?" Charles whispered.

I could not and had no desire to imagine what vile and evil

uses Leather Apron might have for such things, and because of
that did my best to bar the rest of Dr. Brown's testimony from
traveling to my ears, until he was mercifully dismissed from the
witness box.

The coroner then called up the next witness, a young woman
appearing just north of twenty years of age, with auburn hair and
wearing black. She stepped into the box and identified herself as
Annie Phillips.

"Annie. That's her daughter," I said to Charles, hoping I might
finally learn something useful.

CHAPTER 20

Annie Phillips began her testimony. "I reside at number twelve Dilston Road, Southwark Park Road, and am married, my husband being a lamp-black packer. I am daughter of the deceased, who formerly lived with my father. She always told me that she was married to him, but I have never seen the marriage lines. My father's name was Thomas Conway."

I realized Thomas Conway's initials were the same as those tattooed on the spirit's arm.

"What calling did your father follow?" the coroner asked.

"That of a hawker," she said.

"What became of him?" the coroner asked.

She looked downward at the witness box railing. "I do not know."

"Did he leave on good terms with you?"

She hesitated. "Not on very good terms."

"Was he a sober man?"

"He was a teetotaler," she said. "Quite fervent."

"Did he live on bad terms with your mother?"

"Yes," she said, "because she used to drink."

The coroner then asked, "Did your mother ever apply to you for money?"

He was referring to what Mr. Kelly had said about Catherine going to get a trifle from her daughter.

"Yes," Annie Phillips said, in a weary way that suggested it had been a common occurrence.

"When did you last see her?" the coroner asked.

"Two years and one month ago," she said, which revealed a great deal to me about the state of their relations.

"Have you any brothers or sisters by Conway?"

"Two brothers," she said.

"Did your mother know where to find any of you?"

"No," she said.

"Were your addresses purposely kept from her?"

Annie Phillips failed to respond.

The coroner stepped toward the witness box. "I said, were your addresses purposely—"

"Yes," she said.

"Why?"

"To . . ." Her grip on the handrail of the witness box showed the whites of her knuckle bones. "To prevent her applying for money."

"When did your mother last receive money from you?" Mr. Crawford, the solicitor, asked.

"Just over two years ago," she said. "She waited upon me in my confinement, and I paid her for it."

"Is your father living with your two brothers?" the coroner asked.

"He was," she said.

"Where are your brothers residing now?" the coroner asked.

She shook her head. "I do not know."

"When did you last see them?" the coroner asked.

"About eighteen months ago. I have not seen them since."

The coroner glanced toward the jury. "Are we to understand that you had lost all trace of your mother, father, and two brothers for at least eighteen months?"

"That is so," she said.

It seemed to become clear, then, to myself and the members of the court that Annie Phillips would have little useful information about her mother's death, but for my purposes, she had given me much to think on. It was obvious her family had experienced a terrible discord, for they were all of them estranged, and it did not seem unreasonable to suppose the spirit's regret somehow related to that. An urgent need came over me to speak with Annie before she left the inquest, and I rose from my bench as she left the witness box.

"We going?" Charles asked, and slowly eased to his feet.

"Yes," I said, feeling impatient of him. "I'm sorry, we must hurry." Annie had already reached the gallery aisle.

When Charles was ready, we squeezed our way down the row, bumping and jostling the knees of those still sitting. Some decent men rose to let me by, while others seemed to enjoy my posterior in their faces and let me stumble along before them. I mostly ignored them and kept my eyes upon Annie, and she soon reached the courtroom door and exited. A moment later, I reached the aisle and hurried after her, Charles limping along behind me. Out in the foyer, which was as packed with spectators as the courtroom had been, I caught sight of her leaving through the court's main door. I feared I would lose her as I pressed through the gossiping mass, and as I came out onto Golden Lane, also congested with gawkers, I saw Annie had already traveled half a block south.

"Mrs. Phillips!" I called, but she seemed not to have heard me.

"Go," Charles said behind me. "Catch her up."

I left him hobbling along and ran after her, calling her name repeatedly. Eventually, she heard me and turned to look back. I checked the placement of my shawl even as I came to a stop before her.

"I apologize," I said, panting, "for running you down like this."

"What can I do for you?" she asked, and up close I saw her mother's features in her face.

"I wish to speak with you about Catherine," I said.

She looked over my shoulder, back toward the Coroner's Court. "I have said all there is to say."

"I don't wish to speak about her death," I said. "I wish to speak about her life."

"It's easier to speak of her death than that."

"Your mother had much to regret."

Annie's eyes flicked open an eyelash wider. "That she did, but her lips never tasted an apology. Not to anyone for anything. You knew her, then?"

"I did."

"I trust she treated you fairly. Good day to you." She turned away and resumed her path down the street.

"Wait," I called, and once again she stopped. "What would you say if she did apologize?"

"Pardon me?"

"If your mother had ever apologized, what would you have said to her?"

"I haven't any words, after all she did to me and my brothers.

And to my father, not that he were any saint. We all suffered from her drinking and her scrounging, and it broke our family apart. Not once did she repent of any of it." Her heavy sigh settled her like a sack of grain on the pavement. "Well, I've made a good life for myself now, and I wasn't about to let her destroy it with her intemperate ways. Who could expect me to, I ask you? How could I have known she would . . . that this maniac . . . ?"

Dr. Brown's testimony had surely been harder for her to bear than it had been for me. "So," I said, "you would forgive her?"

"Of course I'd forgive her," she said. "As the Bible says I ought. But she was far too proud to ask it of me."

"But if she asked it now—"

"What's it matter?" She paused, pursed her lips, and then asked, "How did you know my mother?"

She seemed to have become suspicious of me. "I—I knew her from the lodging house."

"Which lodging house?"

Mr. Kelly had named it in his testimony, but in that moment, I couldn't recall it to my mind, and I stammered, "It was, uh—"

Her eyes narrowed by more than a few lashes. "Tell me how you knew her."

I offered no answer.

"You're hiding something," she said. "What is it?"

I did not suppose another lie would be more successful or improve the situation better than the truth, so I gave it to her, fully expecting her to dismiss it. "I believe I have seen your mother's ghost," I said.

Annie Phillips opened her mouth, and that way it silently stayed.

"Her spirit haunts the London Hospital where I am a maid," I said. "During her visitations, she says one thing, and one thing only."

"That so?" She kept her tone quite flat, so I couldn't tell what she made of my claim. "And what does she say?"

"'I'm sorry.'"

Annie stayed quiet for several moments. "You say that as if it's the truth."

"It is," I said.

"It is," Charles said, finally reaching us. "It is your mother's ghost, Mrs. Phillips. Down to the tattoo on her arm. TC."

"Are you a medium?" she asked me, but before I could answer, she said, "I have known some Spiritualists, and they have always struck me as believable. But I never thought . . . May I see her?"

"What?" I asked.

"May I see my mother's spirit?"

That was not an outcome I'd anticipated, and I didn't know how to reply.

"I will pay you," she said. "But I must speak with her. I can't help but feel if I hadn't turned her away, if I'd but opened my house to her, perhaps she wouldn't have . . . perhaps it wouldn't have ended this way. It's my fault, and I must ask her forgiveness."

"I don't know," I said.

"Might be worth a try," Charles said to me. "Maybe her daughter can bring the ghost some peace."

"Please," Annie Phillips said.

I saw then how Spiritualists and mediums and charlatans successfully preyed upon others' grief, for I doubted there existed a person who would not feel some secret regret upon the death of a loved one and wish they could converse with them but one more time. "I cannot promise she will appear for you," I said.

"I understand," Annie Phillips said. "But if she appears for you, I believe she will for me."

It seemed a better notion than anything I had arrived at. "Come to the hospital at one o'clock tonight," I said. "There is a gate on East Mount Street. I'll have the porter let you in."

"Thank you," she said, clasping my hands. "Thank you, I will." With that, she hurried on her way, while Charles and I took the road more slowly.

"I hope you're right, Charles."

"I haven't seen her ghost," he said, "but from what you say, that Catherine Eddowes or Conway or whatever her name is needs to eat the leek before she can move on, and it won't do, her apologizing to *you*."

At the bottom of Golden Lane, we turned west on Barbican and returned to the Aldersgate Station. With our descent below the streets, my fourth such subterranean sojourn, the railway proved to be not as disquieting as it had been. I began to understand how so many travelers had grown accustomed to it and made use of its convenience each day, for Charles and I were back at the hospital before dinner.

He walked me to the East Mount gate, and there I thanked him and bade him good evening.

"Wait, Evelyn," he said. "I was wondering if you'd given any thought to what I said."

"You mean, when I visited you on the ward?"

"Precisely that," he said.

I'd given it no direct thought, but his words had echoed about me since then, along with Mr. Merrick's, and to a lesser degree Dr. Tilney's, all of them challenging my doubts about myself. "I'm sure you'll understand that my mind has been quite preoccupied," I said.

"Of course," he said. "Of course. But might you give it some thought now?"

"Charles, please—"

"You confound me, woman," he said, each word a stamped boot. "I've never met your like."

"But you don't know me," I said.

"Surely I do."

I shook my head. "Our familiarity over Mr. Merrick is one thing, but I feel I barely know you at all. I don't even know where you live, or how you live—"

"I'll show you," he said. "Come out with me, and I'll show you whatever you wish."

I was about to rebuff him again, but the way he stood there, bruised, swollen, and favoring his rib, summoned my pity toward him, as well as a measure of guilt over his condition. I thought perhaps I should ignore my own warnings and listen to Professor Sidgwick and Dr. Tilney and Mr. Merrick. A thundering sounded in my ears as I fought through the terror over going out into the city again, not on some errand, but with Charles. Perhaps it was time to take that risk.

"When the spirit of Catherine Eddowes is gone," I whispered, "I will go for an evening with you."

"Truly?"

"Yes," I said.

He laughed, and immediately grunted and doubled over, clutching his side. "You please me so it hurts," he said.

"Perhaps we should wait until you're mended," I said.

"No," he said. "I'll not wait that long. Don't you fret a whit about me. Just send that ghost on home."

"I'll do my utmost."

"I knew you couldn't resist me." He tipped his cap to me. "G'night, then, Evelyn."

"Good night, Charles," I said, and watched him go with a flurry of fear and excitement, but that blew away almost as soon as he'd turned the corner onto Whitechapel, and I was left with the same dreadful uncertainty I'd felt before, and even then regretted having said yes to him.

I left all that on the stoop, though, and went in to tend Mr. Merrick as I always did. I brought his dinner, helped with his bath, and then ate my own evening meal with the other maids. Beatrice hadn't yet recovered her previous bluster, for which I—and I suspected the rest of the servants—was grateful.

After dinner, I told Mr. Merrick about the inquest, and that Annie Phillips would be coming that night to see the ghost of her mother.

"All did not seem right between them," I said. "I think there was a great rift in their family."

"What if the spirit doesn't appear?" he asked. "They didn't for Professor Sidgwick."

"I'm hopeful that she will appear to her daughter."

"Does this Annie Phillips know about me?" he asked. "Does she know who I am?"

I was surprised to realize I'd neglected to mention Mr. Merrick to her. But a few weeks ago, I could not have forgotten him. "No. She doesn't."

His nod was nearly imperceptible. "I do not want to alarm her," he said. "Perhaps I shall sit in my bathroom while she is here."

"Mr. Merrick, I'll speak with her. I'm sure it will be all right."

"Perhaps," he said. "But I would rather not have my appearance jeopardize our purpose. What if she should see me and flee?"

Since I knew that had happened to him, likely many times, I understood his fear and decided against challenging him further. "All right," I said. "But let's put your armchair in there so you have a place to sit."

"Yes, thank you. Let's do that."

Of course, that meant me doing it, but I didn't mind, and after some heaving and shoving, I'd managed to get the odd piece of furniture through the bathroom door and situated next to the bathtub. As the night approached one o'clock, I helped him out of his bed and made sure he was comfortable in his chair before I left to meet Annie at the hospital gate.

As I waited for her, I noted how pleasant the night air felt, and in fact it had been an unseasonably warm autumn. Had it not been for the scourge that then brought the spirits to me, I might've noticed it sooner. When Annie arrived, I had the porter let her in, and we silently crossed Bedstead Square to Mr. Merrick's room.

"What is this place?" she asked.

"A patient's residence."

"You have patients residing in the hospital?"

"Only one that I know of," I said, hoping she wouldn't pursue the matter too closely.

We entered the room, the appearance of which struck me as wrong, due to the absence of Mr. Merrick and his chair.

"Who lives here?" Annie Phillips asked.

"I'm not at liberty to discuss our patients," I said.

"What is that smell?"

She must've been referring to Mr. Merrick's odor, which I hadn't noted at all when we'd come in, so accustomed had I grown to it.

"The room is due for a cleaning," I said.

She wandered over to the mantel and glanced across the photos and cards. "Gracious, that's the princess!" She reached for the portrait, but I interrupted her before she'd taken it in hand.

"Please leave those be," I said. "I'll get in trouble. I've taken a risk bringing you here."

She stepped away from the mantel. "Yes, of course. My apologies." Then she frowned and looked around the room. "Why *are* we here?"

"This is where the ghost of your mother comes," I said.

"It is? Why here?"

I could not easily answer that question. "You would know your mother better than I."

"Those cards on the mantel. They're written to Joseph Merrick. That name is familiar to me, but I can't think why."

It seemed she hadn't yet given up her pursuit of the matter, but I decided not to give her any aid. "I feel I should prepare you in some way. Your mother's spirit will come soon."

"How do you know?"

"She comes at the same time every night. The time of her death."

"The time of her murder, you mean," she said, touching her stomach. "May I sit down?"

"Of course." I had no desire to shock her, but I decided it would be easier if she knew ahead of seeing her mother what to expect. "When she comes, she . . . injures herself."

She took one of the chairs at Mr. Merrick's table. "What do you mean?"

"She—she claws at her tattoo, doing great damage to her arm."

"I see." She inhaled with a shudder, and a few moments passed. Then she noted the objects resting on the table with a nod, the phonograph and the model church. "These are fine and swell," she said. "This Joseph Merrick have time and money, then?"

I was conscious that Mr. Merrick sat just in the next room and could likely hear our conversation, and I didn't like to think of her saying something that would upset him. "Please understand," I said. "I'm truly not at liberty to discuss the patients."

"You can understand my curiosity, though," she said. "My mother's spirit chose this place, it seems."

"That she did."

"I just want to know—"

A sudden pain stabbed the roots of my remaining teeth, even as Annie's eyes widened, and I knew Catherine had arrived. I looked toward the fireplace, and there she sat, hunched over as she always was, grunting. Annie looked to me, and the fear I saw there suggested she hadn't really understood what it would mean to see her mother's spirit.

"Go to her," I whispered. "Say what you wish to say."

Annie shook her head, pale-faced, and I thought she meant to bolt.

"This is what *you* wanted," I said firmly. "Go to her."

She swallowed. Then she nodded and rose from her chair, crossing the room with hesitant steps.

"Mum?" she said.

The spirit stopped doing what I knew she was doing to her arm and looked up. "Annie?"

"Yes," Annie said, and a sudden sob erupted from her. "Oh, Mum, it's me."

Catherine cried out, too. "Annie, my girl!"

Annie dropped to her knees beside the spirit. "Wh-what are you doing? Good Lord, your arm . . ."

Catherine looked down and tipped her head as though in confusion. "Them's your pa's initials," she said. "I weren't a proper wife to him, nor mother to you and your brothers."

"That's all done with now," Annie said.

"But I'm sorry, you see. So sorry."

"I'm sorry, too," Annie said. "I shouldn't have turned you away. I should have opened my door to you."

"No, it were my doing," Catherine's ghost said. "I ain't done nothing right in me whole life. When you was but one year old I sold gallows-ballads at me own cousin's hanging. I ask you, what kind of judy does a thing like that? I ain't never been right with myself, nor right with you."

"Oh, Mum," Annie said.

"I'm sorry, Annie. So sorry. Will you let me make it right? I swear I'll make it right."

"Yes," Annie said. "Of course, Mum. Of course."

Catherine opened her arms wide, whatever wound she'd given herself now vanished, and it seemed Annie lost the years of her womanhood and fell against her mother as a little girl. They embraced for some time, and the pressure of it filled the room. I found myself wishing in that moment for my own mother with an ache that took my heart in its fist. But I yearned for my father, too. I longed to hold him and beg him to stay with me, to leave the drink by and come home.

Then, without warning, bye, or leave, Catherine vanished. The pain in my jaw ceased, and Annie sat on the floor hugging herself.

"Mum?"

"She's gone," I whispered, wiping my eyes.

Neither of us spoke for some time.

"Was that real?" Annie finally asked.

"It seemed so to me," I said. "They've all seemed real."

"All?"

"Each of Leather Apron's victims has come here. I've done what I could to bring them all peace. For your mum, that meant bringing you, it seems."

"I needed peace, too," she said. "I don't know if I've found it, but it's a start." She rose to her feet. "I thank you. Tomorrow, I'll probably doubt my own senses about what happened here tonight. But I thank you."

"You're welcome, Annie," I said.

"I should get home," she said, and walked to the door. As she reached for the handle, her gaze flicked up and she said, "Hang on . . . he's the Elephant Man. Isn't he?"

Again I thought of Mr. Merrick listening in the next room. "He is," I said. "He didn't want to frighten you, so he stayed away."

"That's right considerate of him," she said, and then gestured toward the mantel. "He must be quite the gentleman to have the princess sending him a portrait."

"That he is," I said, smiling.

"You tell him thank you for me, won't you?"

"I will," I said, and then she was gone.

CHAPTER 21

The next morning, Mr. Merrick seemed even more improved, well enough that Dr. Treves reported he no longer felt it necessary to examine him quite so regularly. That day, Miss Doyle and Miss Flemming also reverted to their normal duties of simply bathing him, and I resumed the pattern I'd begun before the first ghost appeared, tending to his meals and his room. All morning, I worried the matron would seek me out and sack me, now that it seemed Mr. Merrick had recovered, but she didn't, though Charles came in the afternoon, eager to know what had transpired the night before.

"Did the ghost get sorted?" he asked.

"She did," I said. "I think so did her daughter, in a way."

"Right bang up to the elephant, that is," he said. "Well done. Well done, indeed."

"Thank you," I said, though I knew his enthusiasm to be for more than our successful resolution of the hauntings. By my own word, Catherine's departure meant I would now be free to go out with him, though I wished for a way to undo my promise.

"Do you suppose this maniac is finished with his evil?" Mr. Merrick asked.

"Who knows?" Charles said. "Even if he is, I'm sure another will come along to take his place. This is Whitechapel."

Though there was no doubt some truth to what he said, I

didn't like to hear such pessimism, and I didn't believe Mr. Merrick liked it, either, but he said nothing more on the subject, and Charles moved on to the subject of our outing.

"Do you think you could get tomorrow night off?" he asked.

"It might be possible," I said, without any eagerness.

"What is this?" Mr. Merrick asked.

Charles puffed up, the effect of which was somewhat lessened by his battered face. "Evelyn has finally consented to an evening on the town with me. We shall go to a coffeehouse, and a night market, and perhaps a music hall."

Mr. Merrick stared at Charles.

"You have it all planned out," I said.

"You gave me plenty of time to think on it," Charles said.

"Perhaps the matron won't give her the night off," Mr. Merrick said.

"Perhaps," Charles said. "But now you're on the mend, I can't see why she wouldn't allow it."

My thoughts went to her promise to sack me, which would make time off rather irrelevant. It also put me in mind of the workhouse, and the freak show, and the other possibilities before me if I was to live out there again. I doubted Charles would have any further interest in me once my state had fallen.

"What if Leather Apron murders again?" Mr. Merrick asked. "And another ghost should appear?"

"I'll return her to you in good time," Charles said. "You'll not even miss her."

"I think I shall miss her a great deal," Mr. Merrick said. "I am not comfortable with this. I do not want you to go, Evelyn."

I couldn't decide what had agitated him. It may have been simple jealousy, or perhaps and more likely he had come to depend on me and felt anxious without me near. I leaned toward him. "Mr. Merrick, I told Charles I would," I said, and patted his arm. "It's just one evening. I'll be back before you notice I'm gone. You'll be all right."

"I will not," he said.

"Easy, my ugly bloke," Charles said. "We're good friends, ain't we?"

"Of course," Mr. Merrick said.

"You wouldn't deny your good friend an evening with the girl he fancies, now would you?"

I tried to believe he meant that, though I still found it difficult.

"Good friends cheer their blokes on, see?" Charles said. "Are you my bloke?"

Mr. Merrick stared at him. "I suppose so." He paused, and I noted a minute crease in his brow. "But is it not dangerous? With Leather Apron still on the loose?"

That was a fear of mine, too.

"Not at all," Charles said. "He prowls the back slums and byways, looking for ladybirds. We'll not even draw his eye."

Mr. Merrick did not appear convinced, but said nothing more, and I assumed he'd resigned himself to it. Charles tipped his cap and departed, while I went and sought the matron to ask her permission. It seemed foolish of me, given her promise, but I didn't like the thought of hiding from her anymore, and if she were to sack me, a part of me wanted to just be done with it.

I hadn't been back to her office since the day I'd applied for a position. Though nothing about the room had changed, I'd come to better know the woman who occupied it, and I saw anew the objects she'd chosen for the shelves behind her desk. The delicate pen-and-ink drawing of a girl with a puppy, for example, struck me as incongruous with the woman who now looked up at me from a stack of papers.

"Yes, Miss Fallow?" she asked.

"Ma'am," I said with a curtsy. "I was wondering if you might let me take a few hours off tomorrow night."

"Mr. Merrick is doing quite.well, I hear." She looked back down and resumed writing, the scratch of her pen the only sound in the room.

The floor beneath me felt as if it swayed. "He is, ma'am."

"Dr. Tilney tells me that is largely because of your care."

"Dr. Tilney is very kind," I said. "Miss Flemming and Miss Doyle did much more than me, ma'am."

"Of course they did," she said. "I trained them."

"They're a credit to you," I said.

"Dr. Tilney also told me it would be unwise to send you away. He says I ought to give you a probation and make a nurse out of you."

"I appreciate his confidence in me," I said.

"I do not share it," she said, "so far as any thought of nursing is concerned. But he has a point about your current position. You are by far the best maid we've yet had working for Mr. Merrick, and I doubt I shall easily replace you. Consequently, I've decided to let you stay on."

I felt such relief then I nearly lost my composure. I wanted to laugh and cry and pull the matron into an embrace, but I kept my bearings and curtsied instead. "Th-thank you, ma'am. I'm very grateful to you."

"Thank Dr. Tilney as well."

"I will, ma'am."

"As to your other request, you may have a few hours' leave tomorrow evening. So long as Mr. Merrick's health stays improved."

I curtsied again. "Thank you, ma'am."

"Good day, Miss Fallow."

I left her office and returned to Mr. Merrick, and as I removed my shawl and entered Mr. Merrick's room, he leaned forward in his armchair and asked, "What did Matron Luckes say?"

"She gave me leave," I said.

He slumped backward. "So you mean to go with Charles."

"Mr. Merrick," I said, and pulled a chair over to him and sat down. "What is it that so distresses you about my outing?"

"It is what I already said."

I looked at him a bit askance. "Is it really?"

"Yes," he said.

I still suspected he might've been feeling some jealousy. "Mr. Merrick, you're my friend and there is nothing in this world could change that. You know that, don't you?" I leaned over and kissed his cheek, without even thinking about it, and that set the left side of his bottom lip quivering. "So you see," I continued, "there is nothing to fear in my going on an outing with Charles. Nothing at all. When I'm back, I'll come tell you all about it."

"Very well. You are my friend," he said. "And nothing will change that."

"I'm so glad to hear it," I said, and we passed the rest of the afternoon and evening pleasantly, and that night, when I left him to go to my own bed, it was the first time in weeks I didn't need to rise in the ungodly hours for a haunting. I slept soundly until morning, awoke in my bed at the same time that Becky and Martha did in theirs, had breakfast with the other maids, and remembered what it had been like before the ghosts had come.

The rest of the day did not pass as easily, for each hour brought me closer to my outing with Charles, and thoughts of that whipped my stomach to a froth and wrecked my nerves. I felt like a policeman entering Flower and Dean, and I was doing so willingly. But unlike a policeman, I'd already been maimed for life. What more could be done to me?

After I'd taken care of Mr. Merrick's dinner and settled him for the evening, I left him to change into the better of my two dresses.

Charles came for me at the East Mount gate before the sun had gone down, wearing a better coat and trousers than I'd seen on him before, but with the same bowler, his swollen eyes opened wide enough to see his whites again.

"Miss Fallow," he said. "You look lovely this evening."

"Thank you, Mr. Weaver," I said.

"You've not called me Mr. Weaver for some time," he said.

"That's true," I said, but could not remember when I'd made the switch. "So where are we going?"

"Thought we might go down to the Saturday market by Mile End Gate."

"All right," I said, pulling my shawl tightly about my face.

We rode the omnibus down the tramway several blocks, and as we drew near the market, the light from the multitude of naphtha lamps set the sky above it ablaze. At the same time I saw the light from the market, I heard the sound of it, the cacophony of competing musicians, performers, costers, and vendors.

The omnibus deposited us where the street had been given over entirely to a slow-moving flood of pedestrians, the muddy roadway lined two and three deep with wagons, carts, and stalls. Even when I'd lived on the streets and even when I'd had a little money to spend, I'd zealously avoided such places.

"Come on!" Charles said, raising his voice above the din to be heard, and took my arm in his. He then led us forward into the thick of it, right up to a potato man and his wheeled hot cart. "Philosopher Jack's baked potatoes!" the vendor shouted, the bright red kingsman about his neck at odds with his blue-striped shirt.

"We'll have two," Charles said, and paid him.

Philosopher Jack reached through a cloud of steam into his cart and pulled out two potatoes wrapped in paper. "Salt?" he asked, and Charles and I nodded yes. As he seasoned our food, the coster shouted, "Two potatoes, two philosophies! First! Neither a borrower nor a lender be, for loan oft loses itself! Second! If the missus won't eat what she's cooked, best test it on the dog!" He handed us our potatoes, and we carried on through the market as we ate them.

My potato was dry and turned my mouth into a desert, and Charles's must have done the same to him, for as soon as we came across a ginger beer seller, he bought us two bottles. Next to where we stood to drink them, something huge and black filled a cage nearby. I peered closer and realized it was a gorilla, and next to its cage stood an Aztec. I moved toward the beast for a better look but was stopped by a showman's cane.

"A penny to approach," he said, which Charles paid. "Put nothing you value between the bars."

I'd never before seen a gorilla in the flesh. I could sense the strength in its long arms and thick neck, quite sure the beast could've easily broken out of its prison, and I was surprised that it smelled much as a man might if he'd not bathed in a month. The spectators next to me shouted at the animal and jeered and taunted it with leaps and whoops, but the beast barely regarded them with its small, forlorn black eyes, and I could see that the cage had thoroughly dashed whatever spirit it had once possessed.

Charles barked and shouted at it, waving his arms and laughing. Then he turned to me. "There's a monster for you."

"Is it?" I asked.

"Look at it," he said. "Imagine that thing roaring at you from the trees."

"I pity it," I said, and on we moved.

We passed acrobats and flame-eaters, a hairy man with a hairless dog that greatly amused Charles, and even a giant who claimed to stand seven feet and six inches tall. We next came to the quack doctors who stood by diagnosing every ailment and disease, and likewise had the cures for those afflictions conveniently for sale. From there we reached the more general merchandise, where the cheapjacks shouted their wares on all sides.

"Carpets from the Orient!" called a vendor, the intricate patterns in his rugs a maze to trap the eye.

"Secondhand boots and clothes!" called a man next to him. "Barely worn!"

"Toys and diversions!" shouted a woman with a few dolls and figures carved in wood, as well as a cage of sparrows to which tethers had been tied so that children might enjoy the frantic flapping of their wings until the birds were either set free or finally gave out and died.

"Paintings by the famous artists!" shouted a dealer. "Portraits! Landscapes! Here we have a painting of Christ healing the sick! And here's a portrait of Benjamin Lincoln, President of the United States!"

Hatchets, jewelry, oilcloths, furniture, artificial flowers, lamps, and nearly anything else one could wish for we passed and could be purchased at the market.

"Would you like ice cream?" Charles asked.

"All right," I said.

He bought us two, which were more ice than cream, but sweetened with honey, and then he led us over to a public house. "I need a beer," Charles said. "You want one?"

"No, thank you," I said, remembering his earlier drunkenness. "And I'd rather not go—"

"Come on." He tugged on my arm, and in we went anyway, the establishment even more crowded than the street. I adjusted my shawl and waited for Charles to order his drink, which seemed to take him as long as it had taken us to traverse the market. He ended up with a gin, rather than a beer, and he downed it fast.

"Ready?" he asked, as though I'd had a drink with him and actually wanted to be there in that place.

"Of course I am," I said.

He led us out onto the sidewalk, and we went by foot up the back side of the market, passing more pubs, as well as music halls, theaters, and other live entertainments. Signs in their windows proclaimed the melodrama, violence, comedy, and bawdries to be found within. We hadn't said much to each other thus far, and I suspected we were both aware of the awkwardness hanging between us like damp clothes on the line.

"I've played on most of these stages," Charles finally announced.

"Oh?"

"I have."

"I see. And do—do you have a favorite?"

"Uh, the Pavilion, up closer to the hospital."

"Do you play by yourself, or with others?" I knew the question to be trivial, and wondered if Charles felt as I did about this forced conversation.

"I play what's wanted and earns me coin," he said. "The musician's life is at the whim of the audience." He pointed up ahead. "There's a fine place full of proper donas and rorty blokes. Let's see who's on stage tonight."

I followed him to the music hall, where the doorkeeper greeted him by name. "Blimey, what happened to you?"

"Fell off a bus," Charles said. "Good crowd tonight?"

"Aye, good crowd. Got your fiddle?"

"Not tonight," Charles said, and nodded toward me.

The doorkeeper looked at me and tipped his head. "Welcome,

miss." Then he turned back to Charles and winked. "In you go, then."

The music hall was quite expansive, with a wide stage at the far end of a long, terraced floor jammed full up with tables and chairs. The audience occupying them seemed a raucous mixture of the middle and lower classes. Overhead, second and third tiers of seats wrapped around us, looking out over the floor and the stage. The ornate columns and balconies had been carved with the shapes of nearly naked women, devils, satyrs, and serpents. Charles found us two seats off to one side, and a waiter soon approached our table.

"Would you like something to drink?" Charles asked me.

"Another ginger beer would be nice," I said.

He nodded and said to the waiter, "A ginger beer for the lady, and I'll smother a parrot."

"Absinthe?" I asked, after the waiter had gone.

Charles smiled. "You think me a Bohemian?"

I was more worried about how hard the drink would hit him. "Do you think yourself a Bohemian?"

He shrugged, and a few moments later, the gaslight dimmed and the stage brightened. What followed was a series of singers, musicians, dancers, and acrobats. Some of the women wore scandalously few clothes, or wore fleshings that made it seem they wore no clothes at all, provoking much reaction from the men in the audience. Some of the performers I found entertaining, but others struck me as vulgar and unfit for the stage. Two men dueled with swords and produced a profusion of fake blood, some of which sprayed in the air.

Act after act took to the stage, but before long I lost interest in them and turned my attention to Charles, who laughed and clapped enthusiastically with each performance. I could see this was the world he loved and he was at home in it, while I definitely was not. I wasn't enjoying the outing with him at all, actually, and didn't expect that to change, for aside from our mutual friendship with Mr. Merrick, we obviously shared little in common. We'd proceeded that evening from one thing to the next, as though Charles were merely enacting the steps of some plan he'd worked out. In fact, he'd paid less attention to me and become less flirtatious as the night had passed, as though having obtained my company, he no longer desired it.

It flattered me to be fancied by him, if in fact I was, but that wasn't a sufficient reason for me to fancy him in return, and I realized in that moment I didn't and never would.

He continued to drink a great deal more after the green absinthe, both beer and gin, and before long showed the signs of obvious drunkenness, reminding me of the night he'd tricked me into the waxworks. It likewise disturbed me to think of being with another person so consumed by drink.

"Charles," I said, leaning close to him.

"Yes, my fairest flower?"

I didn't care for the double meaning of that, whether he intended it or not. "I'd like to go back to the hospital. The matron only gave me a few hours' leave."

He smirked at me. "She'll forgive you being late."

"Please, Charles. I must go. Now."

"But—" He pouted at the edge of anger. "I've *waited* for this."

"I'm sorry. I'm expected back."

He leapt to his feet with his hands balled into fists and said, "Let's be off, then!" and kicked a chair over as he stormed away from the table, drawing stares from the men and women around us.

I followed him timidly from the music hall, but once outside he immediately draped his arm over my shoulder as though he didn't even remember his outburst from the moment previous, which set a squirm loose in my neck.

"Off to sail the storm of heaves?" the doorkeeper asked, and I could hear the leer in his voice.

"If the lady be willing!" Charles replied, and I blanched, wondering if bedding me had been the whole reason for this orchestrated outing from the start.

I wriggled out from under his heavy arm and stepped away. "The lady is *not* willing," I said. "You've had too much to drink, Charles. I'll walk myself back." With that, I turned and marched away from him for the second time, the sound of the doorkeeper's laughter following me.

Crowded though the streets were, I knew I wasn't safe walking alone, so I hurried as fast as I could up Whitechapel Road, ignoring the bustle I made my way through. I occasionally glanced back over my shoulder to see if Charles was following me but saw no sign of him, and I assumed that meant he'd been too drunk either to give chase or to care. The walk felt less dangerous in the light of the street's gas lamps, but I passed numerous alleys and back lanes that fell away from the road into endless pitch. If Leather Apron were lurking anywhere, it would be in one of those dark places.

At last I came to East Mount Street, but as I made to turn

down it, I heard someone call my name, and then Charles rushed half stumbling from the crowd toward me.

"Evelyn, stop! I thought you wanted to see where I live!"

"Go home, Charles," I said, and continued on my way down the side street toward the hospital gate, but alone in the shadows he caught up with me and seized my arm in a painful grip.

"Evelyn—"

"Let go!" I shouted. "You're hurting me!"

"What's your game?" he said, his words a slurry, his breath strong enough to carry coal. "You toyed with me!"

I yanked my arm free of his hand. "I have *not* toyed with you."

"After all I've done," he said. "My violin is gone! My . . . my . . . Can't you see how hard I've been trying to win you over?" He closed his eyes and shook his head. "You . . . you think you're too good for me? Is that it? You?"

"Not at all, Charles."

"Well you're not!" he said. "I'm too good for *you*. Just have a look at your face." The sneer he gave made me feel as though I wore no shawl. "Just look at you! Who could fancy you? I never fancied you; I just told you that so you'd fancy me. You've got nice round bubbies and a pretty back avenue, but you'd have to wear a sack on your head for me to bed you."

Each of his words lashed, and each tore right through whatever feeble confidence I'd managed to gather about myself, leaving me without protection or any words to throw back at him. I had thought I couldn't be maimed again, but it turned out I could. My legs weakened beneath me, and I found it hard to breathe. I turned toward the gate, desperate to get away.

"Don't you turn your back on me!" he said, his voice a hiss, and he grabbed me from behind.

"Let go!" I shouted again, but he spun me around and drove me up against the wall, smothering my mouth with his hand, and for a horrifying moment I wondered if he was Leather Apron.

He came in close enough for his lips to graze my ear and whispered, "I'm owed . . ." Then he grabbed my breast and squeezed it hard, bringing tears of pain to my eyes, and then his hand slid down my body, over my belly, and snatched at my skirts, trying to gather them up.

For a few endless moments, fear and confusion immobilized me, and it was as though I were watching Charles assault a waxwork figure of myself, but before he was able to have his way with me, a primal will to fight rose up through me. I slugged him, driving my fist deep into his broken rib. I heard his grunt, and then he staggered away from me and dropped to one knee, gasping for breath and clutching his side.

I ran from him, straight down the road to the hospital gate, where the porter, unaware of what had just happened, let me through.

"You all right, Miss Fallow?"

"Don't let Charles in," I said. "Whatever you do. He's not himself. He's crazed with drink."

"Very good, miss," the porter said, and without hesitation he locked the hospital's gate.

CHAPTER 22

I stood shaking in the middle of Bedstead Square, crying, and then I dropped to the ground and shook on my hands and knees. In the time I'd lived on the streets, I'd come that close to such intimate violations before, but never by someone I'd let myself trust, even a little. Though I hadn't ever fully believed Charles's sincerity, I also hadn't suspected him capable of harming me in such a way. He may not have been Leather Apron, but there'd been a monster lurking inside him, and I should've heard it rumbling in its den.

That mistake was mine. I shouldn't have trusted Charles. I shouldn't have listened to Professor Sidgwick, or Dr. Tilney, or Mr. Merrick. None of them knew what they asked of me. *I* had known, but I had ignored what I knew, and I vowed never to let that happen to me again. The streets had tried to reclaim me, but they had failed, and I would not give them another chance. I would stay hidden away in the hospital with Mr. Merrick, and I wanted no pity from anyone for that. I simply wanted to be left alone where I belonged.

I took several long breaths, and after the shaking in my body had subsided, I got back up on my feet. I knew Mr. Merrick would be up worrying, and I didn't want that, so I wiped my eyes dry of tears and went to his room.

He was reading in his armchair when I entered, but immediately closed the book and set it aside. "How was your outing?" he asked.

"It was . . ." I wrestled with myself over which words to use. For Mr. Merrick to learn of his friend's betrayal would undoubtedly cause him pain, and I didn't want to bring additional pain to a man who'd already endured more than anyone should. "It was fine, Mr. Merrick," I said. "But I shall not be going on another outing with him."

"Oh?" Mr. Merrick said, with noticeable cheer in his voice. "Why is that?"

"I don't fancy Charles in that way."

"You don't?" he said. "But I thought—"

"He . . . was helpful to me in his way," I said, though it galled me to speak of him even that favorably. "I know he is your friend, and I don't want to disappoint you. But Charles and I will never see eye to eye."

"I'm not disappointed," he said, quietly, and his skin flushed in those parts of his face without his growths. "I wish you and I could go on an outing."

I took his hand in mine. "I wish that, too," I said, and I meant it with all sincerity, for there could not have been a more gentlemanly figure in all of Whitechapel that night than he. "In fact," I said, as an idea formed in my mind, "why don't we? Let's have an outing of our own."

"What? How . . . how could we do that?"

"You leave that to me," I said. "For now, it's late, and we should both get to sleep. You're still getting your strength back, remember?"

I helped him into bed, and then I went to my own, though it took me some time to fall asleep, and even then I woke frequently from nightmares about Charles. In my dreams he *was* Leather Apron, and with a surgeon's scalpel he stabbed into me and sliced me open. The only way I found any true rest was to think of Mr. Merrick and the outing I wanted to plan for him.

The next day, when Dr. Treves came for a short visit with Mr. Merrick, I pulled him aside and spoke of the plan I'd conceived.

"Are you suggesting we turn the hospital into a common street market?" he asked.

"I thought perhaps we could simply bring a few sellers and performers into Bedstead Square. They could use the gate on East Mount Street. It would not disrupt the hospital, sir, and I think it would help Mr. Merrick continue his recovery. I believe it would mean a great deal to him."

Dr. Treves fiddled with the topmost button on his coat. "This is highly irregular, Miss Fallow."

"Yes, sir," I said.

"But it seems you feel strongly about it."

"Mr. Merrick desires more than anything else to live life as a normal man and do those things a normal man does. I shouldn't think the cost would be too extravagant."

"There are certainly funds enough, but I must act as a wise steward," he said. "I shall consider your request."

"Very good, sir," I said. "If you decide in favor of it, I was thinking it might be best a surprise."

"Noted," he said, and then he left.

That night at dinner, Beatrice returned to her old habits of recounting what the papers said about the murders, cursing the police for incompetence, and speculating wildly as to who or what may have committed the crimes.

"He must be supernatural," Beatrice said with a shrug. "That's the answer. He's got satanic powers."

"He doesn't have satanic powers," I said.

"Then how do you explain it?" Beatrice asked. "He's doing these deeds with the police around the corner! Is he invisible? Is he some demon?"

"He's an evil man," Becky said. "Ain't that enough?"

"Coppers catch evil men all the time," Beatrice said. "But you can't catch the devil, now, can you?"

It did surprise me that after so many weeks and four victims, Scotland Yard and the police seemed no closer to apprehending the fiend than they had been with the first murder. That meant Leather Apron was still out there in the city somewhere, perhaps stalking another victim even then, and I carried with me the silent prayer that I wouldn't ever feel another pain in my jaw, nor Mr. Merrick endure the torment of another haunting.

Two days passed before Dr. Treves came to me privately and announced he would agree to the market in the square, and he would make the arrangements. He did stipulate Mr. Merrick would have to wear his special cap and hood, for the vendors and performers couldn't be trusted to react with decorum upon seeing him. That did not seem too great a concession, and we set a date for our ersatz market the following week.

My excitement for the event mounted as a few of those days

went by, brought low only when one evening Mr. Merrick inquired about Charles.

"He hasn't been to visit in some time," he said. "Ever since the two of you went on your outing."

"That's true," I said, wondering what he suspected or implied. The mention of Charles's name and the memory of that night had turned me cold with sweat, and caused my breathing to fray.

"Why do you suppose he hasn't come?" Mr. Merrick asked.

"I'm . . . afraid I don't know his mind," I said, the lie quite comfortable in the coat of truth it wore.

"I hope he is well," Mr. Merrick said, "and that he has got himself a new violin."

"That is thoughtful and kind of you," I said, and moved the topic away from Charles, but I knew the matter would not lay dormant for long, and two days later, Mr. Merrick brought up the subject of his friend once again.

"I do hope Charles is well," he said. "Perhaps his injuries were worse than we knew."

"I don't think it's that," I said, although I had no idea how my blow to Charles's rib might have further wounded him.

"Then what is it?" Mr. Merrick asked.

I sensed his worry, and I wasn't free of guilt over it. I had it in my power to relieve some of his distress, but I'd refrained from answering him for fear of causing even greater distress with the truth.

Mr. Merrick asked, "Do you suppose it's something I said to him?"

"Not in the least," I said. "You put that thought right out of your head."

"But perhaps I offended him in some way. My manners are poor."

"Mr. Merrick," I said. "Your manners would surpass those of the highest-born gentleman, and that's a fact."

He ignored me. "I can see no other reason for his not coming," he said, and then he looked directly into my eyes. "You would tell me, wouldn't you? If you knew what it was I said or did? Perhaps . . . did Charles say anything about it?"

"No, Mr. Merrick," I said, "there is nothing you did to keep him away, nothing at all," but I could plainly hear in my voice the turmoil I felt. I could still feel Charles squeezing my breast, and his breath burning my ear.

"Evelyn," he asked, "what is the matter?"

"I don't . . ." It was still true that I didn't want to cause Mr. Merrick pain, but it seemed to be causing him pain regardless by withholding the truth, and I respected him too much to lie to him. "The night of my outing with Charles, he . . . did an evil thing."

Mr. Merrick paused a moment, and then asked, almost in a whisper, "What thing?"

"He became drunk and he . . ." My throat tightened and my voice broke. For Mr. Merrick's sake, I did manage to put down the rebellious tears that fought their way outward. "He laid his hands on me," I said, crawled over by revulsion. "Against my will."

Mr. Merrick touched his malformed lips. "Charles?"

"Yes."

"Charles did this?"

"Yes," I said.

I watched Mr. Merrick as the revelation seemed to settle over him, and then he made a fist with his good hand at his side. The fury I saw in him had the same purity and innocence as every other feeling he'd demonstrated. It was the righteous and certain anger of a child. But then he started punching his head with his own hand. "He is a *wicked* man. A wicked man!"

"Mr. Merrick, stop!" I said, reaching for his fist.

He let me pull it away from his head, which he hadn't bruised too terribly, and then he looked up at me in utter confusion.

"He has wickedness in him," I said. "But he was always kind to you, and you ought not to forget that." It angered me to defend Charles in that way, but that anger didn't make what I had said untrue, for I still believed Charles's friendship with Mr. Merrick to be real in some manner I didn't understand anymore.

Mr. Merrick let out a sound like a growl. "If you should see Charles again—"

"I very much doubt Charles will ever come back here," I said. "And now you know why."

"Let us hope not," he said. "But if you should see him, when you're out—"

"I'm never leaving the hospital again," I said.

He loosened the fist he'd made. "Do you mean that?"

"There's nothing for me out there," I said. "Would you leave the hospital, if you could go back to the showman's stage?"

"No," he said. "But . . . that is a strange question."

I hadn't yet shut the sluice against my honesty, so I went on. "Jimmy Fiddle gave me a message for you. The Silver King sent him."

"What was the message?" Mr. Merrick asked.

"I gathered he wants you back with his show, and he promised you the best halls, the best food, and a generous share of the proceeds."

Mr. Merrick chuckled, and there was a wistfulness to it. "The word *generous* means something different to the Silver King than it does to you and me."

"Does the offer tempt you?" I asked.

He appeared to be thinking about it. "No," he said. "But I suppose it feels good to be valued."

"I suppose it would," I said. "But look around at all the cards and gifts. You are certainly valued here."

"And so are you," he said. "This is where we both belong."

Again he had read my thoughts.

The rhythm and routine over the next several days bore that out, and Mr. Merrick and I settled again into our easy way, rising in the morning, taking meals, bathing, cleaning, day after day, putting away all thoughts of ghosts and Leather Apron and Charles, until the time came for Mr. Merrick's private night market.

When the sun had gone down, I told him there was a surprise waiting outside in Bedstead Square for him, and then I helped him dress in his suit, along with his long coat and the cap and hood specially made for him. Not once did he object, but he did seem somewhat quiet and nervous.

"What is the surprise?" he asked.

"You shall see," I said. "Don't be frightened."

"But what will I see?"

"You'll know it when you see it," I said, pulling on my shawl to hide my face.

When we left his room, I helped him labor up the steps into the courtyard, where Dr. Treves stood waiting for us, the market spread out behind him. The surgeon had created a wonderful parallel to the street I'd seen the other night. His bazaar was smaller, naturally, but just as vibrant, with perhaps half a dozen stalls and carts arranged in a crescent moon around the middle of the square. Naphtha lamps burned bright among them, and the smells of cooking meat and sounds of buskers filled the square. Some of the other hospital staff already milled about among the vendors, no doubt invited by Dr. Treves so as to give the tableau a natural quality and provide the sellers more customers. Upon seeing the display, Mr. Merrick stood perfectly still, and beneath his hood I imagined his astonishment.

"What is this?" he asked.

"It was Miss Fallow's suggestion," Dr. Treves said. "A proper market experience for you."

"You said you wanted an outing," I said. "Since that isn't possible, I decided to bring the outing in."

"Do you like it?" Dr. Treves asked.

"This is . . . for me?" Mr. Merrick asked.

"Naturally," Dr. Treves said. "Do you like it?"

Mr. Merrick's head nodded. "Oh yes. I like it very much."

"Wonderful," Dr. Treves said. "Here is some money for you to spend." He placed a handful of bills and coins into the palm of Mr. Merrick's good hand.

"Well?" I said.

"Well, what?" Mr. Merrick asked.

"Aren't you going to ask me to walk with you?" I asked.

"Oh yes. I'm sorry." He extended the crook of his arm. "Evelyn, would you do me the honor of a stroll about the market?"

"Of course," I said, linking my arm with his. "I would be honored."

With that, we made our way slowly to the first vendor, a man selling oysters, and with my aid in translation, Mr. Merrick bought us a dozen to share. The coster eyed Mr. Merrick warily but not too obviously, and I was sure Dr. Treves had done work to prepare those vendors he'd invited in. After we'd eaten the relishes, we moved on to a man playing on a hurdy-gurdy, a small monkey dancing at his feet wearing a blue vest. Mr. Merrick laughed with delight at the antics of the little animal, and after several tunes tossed a generous coin into the performers' hat. Next, we came to a potato man, and we each ate one, which brought back an unpleasant memory of Charles for me. Mr. Merrick, however, seemed to fall easily into the fiction that had been created for him, and before long his back appeared a whit straighter, as though he walked as tall as he could, and his garbled speech took on the lofty tone of a man about town. I could but smile at his earnestness and do my best to join his fantasy.

The next coster wore boots stitched with red hearts and flowers, and sold sausages about which Mr. Merrick said, "We used to call these bags o' mystery in my days on the stage. The kinds of sausage we could afford, at any rate. But these are good."

"They are," I said, eating one.

After that, we came to a man selling shoes and other leather goods. Mr. Merrick purchased a pair of shiny riding boots, even though they would never be used or even fit his feet, and after that we stopped at a woman with a cart of jewelry and fancies. Here, Mr. Merrick paused and leaned in close to examine the wares with a grave interest.

"I would like to buy something for the lady," he said to the seller.

I shook my head. "Mr. Merrick, I—"

"Please, Miss Fallow," he said, "allow me." He then repeated himself to the woman, who looked baffled, obviously unable to understand his speech.

I could not let him be embarrassed, so I said to her, "He wants me to choose something," at which she smiled and nodded. I looked down at the pendants and brooches, the rings and other trifles, their cheap jewels of glass catching the sharp naphtha light. "Mr. Merrick," I said, "I truly don't need anything."

"Nonsense," he said. "We're on an outing, and I will buy you a gift. Do you not see anything you would like?"

Among the ornaments I found an inexpensive ring, likely made of tin, embellished with a simple filigree. Mr. Merrick bought it for me, and when I put it on, he asked, "Do you like it?"

"Very much," I said.

"It is butter upon bacon, on your hand," he said.

"Thank you, Mr. Merrick." I then spied a man's dressing case not unlike the one in the advertisement he'd clipped from the newspaper. When I pointed it out to him, he purchased it immediately. To conclude our market stroll, so like and yet utterly unlike my time with Charles, we ate some ice cream and drank a ginger beer as we watched a man swallow swords, and then an Italian man perform a fantoccini puppet show. Mr. Merrick enthusiastically applauded the latter's outsized drama overflowing its miniature stage.

Dr. Treves walked up beside us, also clapping his hands. "I thought you would like the marionettes," he said to Mr. Merrick. "I wonder if you'd like to go to a real theater?"

"Oh yes," Mr. Merrick said. "Is it possible?"

"It is," Dr. Treves said. "I spoke with Mrs. Kendal about it, and she has used her connections on your behalf. We shall attend the Theatre Royal in Drury Lane and watch the pantomime from the private box of the Baroness Burdett-Coutts, who has graciously allowed us its use."

"That is most kind and generous of the baroness," Mr. Merrick said.

"That it is," Dr. Treves said. "I understand the novelist Charles Dickens used the same box, from time to time. No one shall see you or disturb us."

"I . . . I am overwhelmed," Mr. Merrick said, softly enough to only barely be heard over the noise of the market.

"It is as I've told you, John," Dr. Treves said, smiling. "You are beloved of London."

"When will I go?"

"Some weeks hence. The eighth of November."

"May Evelyn come with us?"

Mr. Merrick had earlier said he would ask for me to accompany him, and he'd stayed true to his word, but I did not wish for it in the least. After what had happened, I didn't want to leave the safety of the hospital again, even for such a fine evening, and even for Mr. Merrick.

"I see no reason why not," Dr. Treves said. "But the decision lies with Matron Luckes, of course. I shall speak to her about it."

"Begging your pardon, sir," I said, "but that won't be necessary."

"Oh?" Dr. Treves said.

"I thank you for the invitation, but I've little interest in the theater, I'm afraid."

Dr. Treves bore a frown and spoke with indifference. "Suit yourself, Miss Fallow." Then he returned his attention to Mr. Merrick. "Have you enjoyed your evening?"

I could discern Mr. Merrick nodding beneath his cap and hood. "More than I can say."

"Splendid, splendid," Dr. Treves said. "I'm pleased."

After a stroll back through the market, our outing at an end, I walked Mr. Merrick to the stairway and down to his door, and once inside I helped him prepare for bed. He chose to sleep in his chair that night.

"Where would you like me to put your new boots?" I asked.

"By my bedside," he said.

"And your dressing case?"

"Perhaps on the table, there."

I did as he asked, the effect of which seemed to please him enormously from his armchair. The more the appearance of his room approached that of a gentleman's, the more he seemed to think of himself as one.

"Do you really not have interest in the theater?" he asked me. "I thought you wanted to accompany me."

"That was before."

"Before Charles?"

"Before everything, Mr. Merrick."

"I wish you would come," he said.

"I know. But you shall go with Dr. Treves, and I'm certain you shall have a grand time."

The left side of his lips drooped in his subtle rendering of a frown, and though he said nothing more that night, I knew the matter wasn't settled.

October's remainder passed with the ominous tension of a humming omnibus rail, the news and rumor of Leather Apron ever present and unremitting. The police took suspects into custody and released them at a rate suggesting they wanted to simply appear to be doing *something*. Not even the sizable monetary rewards, offered from all quarters, managed to produce an arrest, and letters from someone calling himself Jack the Ripper had become so commonplace a hoax as to be worthless for anything other than wild speculation and controversy.

One day, Beatrice closed her newspaper, slapped it on the table, and declared, "He's dead."

"Who's dead?" Becky asked.

"The Ripper," she said.

"Do it say that?" Martha asked, looking at the paper, her voice rising in hope.

"No," Beatrice said. "But that's why they haven't nabbed him. If he ain't supernatural, then he's dead. Has to be."

"It were a month almost between the other murders," Becky said. "They say there's a pattern to 'em. That's why the police take precautions every Saturday and Sunday. The Ripper's bound to kill again."

"Unless he's dead," Beatrice said with a quick nod.

"We can only hope," I whispered, to which everyone agreed.

The conversation moved on to a cryptic message that had been written on a wall next to the body of Catherine Eddowes, something about the Jews being blamed. The message had been erased, apparently, so as to prevent more of the violence and hatred already escalating along Brick Lane and other Hebrew enclaves. Other papers had moved on to blaming a German, as it seemed there passed a superstition among German thieves that the light from a candle made from a woman's uterus would have a soporific effect, and this presented a motive for the mutilations. From there, the table's discussion moved to a group of Spiritualists in Cardiff who'd gone to the police purporting to know the identity of Leather Apron, while a competing séance in Bolton had supposedly achieved the same aim, both of which claims amused me.

"The medium in Bolton says the murderer is a middle-aged navvy with a mustache, living on Commercial Road," Martha said. "She summoned the spirit of Elizabeth Stride."

I chortled. "No, she never summoned Long Liz."

"Oh, Long Liz, is it?" Beatrice said. "You have tea with her or something?"

"That's what they called her," I said. "And no one has summoned her spirit."

"How d'you know?" Becky asked.

I had not the will nor desire to convince her. "Because I know," I said with a sigh.

The others carried on chattering in their ignorance of the spectral realm, but a moment later, Becky turned to me and whispered, "You all right?"

"Yes, why?" I said.

"You been so touchy lately," she said. "You got your shawl pulled tight so I can't hardly see you. For weeks you been . . . disappearing."

I wanted to tell her she was right. To disappear was exactly what I wanted. "Everything is as it should be," I said.

She frowned and worry creased her eyes, but she kept whatever remaining concerns she had to herself. Another week passed after that with no capture of Leather Apron, in spite of the information supplied by the supposed Spiritualists, but also with no murder. I wondered if Beatrice were right, and somehow the fiend had met his end in a way that would forever leave the mystery of his crimes unsolved.

In the afternoon on the day Mr. Merrick was to go to the theater in Drury Lane, Dr. Treves brought him a new suit to wear, and Miss Flemming and Miss Doyle bathed him early for the occasion. Throughout his preparations, which did not involve his boots or his dressing case, Mr. Merrick asked me repeatedly to reconsider my decision, but each time I refused him as politely as I could.

When he and I were alone, in the hour before his departure, he finally declared, "I don't understand! Do you not wish to be seen with me? If that is so, rest assured, Dr. Treves told me the whole affair will be conducted in secret—"

"Mr. Merrick!" I said. "I assure you, it is not that! If anything, you have greater cause to not be seen with me."

"You know that is not true."

"I know no such thing," I said. "What I do know is that I do not belong out there."

"Then . . ." He looked down at his new suit. It was of fine gray woolen fabric and had been tailored to his irregular form, which served to accentuate his deformity rather than hide it, and gave him the appearance of pitiful imitation, a boy in a man's clothing. "Then do I not belong out there?" he asked.

My heart fractured in the way of ice beneath a warm kettle. "Mr. Merrick, you belong anywhere in this world you choose to be."

"But you do not?"

"No."

"Why?" he said. "Why, Evelyn?"

"I am a monster," I said, remembering the gorilla Charles had mocked. "And I have accepted my cage."

"Am I not a monster?"

"No," I said. "Look around you at all these gifts. At your suit. At the theater where you go tonight. Others do not see you as a monster, Joseph. They see you as a man. Unfortunate and deformed, yes, but a man. I'd begun to hope others might see me as a woman, but I know now that will never be so. Not really."

"You say this because of Charles?"

"Charles merely confirmed what I already knew but had forgotten."

He bowed his head low enough I wondered if he would be able to raise it again, but he did, and he spoke in his beautiful voice. "I look at my body, and I know my life will be short. I know there is much I will never do as a normal man. You read to me from *Emma*, but I know I will never . . . love . . . a woman. But if I could, you—your scars . . . such a thing would not prevent me . . ."

Whatever he had been about to say, he seemed to have lost the nerve to say it, and I felt so overthrown by his sentiment I could but stand in silence as I fought to keep the beating in my heart confined to my chest.

"Do you understand?" he asked.

Each time I tried to open my lips to speak, I felt certain a sob would escape, so I kept them closed until I could safely manage a halting reply. "Mr. Merrick, there isn't a woman good enough to deserve you." Then I turned away from him. "Dr. Treves will come for you soon. He said he will look after you upon your return from the theater, so I'm to go to bed. I shall see you in the morning."

"Evelyn . . ."

"Good evening, Mr. Merrick." I hurried from the room without his farewell and ran to my own bed, but the tears had sprung free before I reached it. I cried into my pillow for some time, beset on all sides by angry echoes, each attempting to shout above the others in my mind. I listened hard for Mr. Merrick's gentle voice, but could not hear it over that of Charles and the matron and every other man and woman who had told me exactly what I'd daily held myself against. I had come to the hospital believing the streets had not really changed me. They had tried, but I thought I'd been stronger, even as unbeknownst to me the harsh words and violence had eaten away at my soul just as the phosphorous had my bone. Now I knew the truth of it. The streets had changed me. They had shown me who I was, and still waited for me even then, cursing me.

At some point, I fell asleep to that vicious sound, and did not awaken even when Becky and Martha came in to bed. Instead, it was the pain in my jaw that woke me.

CHAPTER 23

I lay abed with my eyes pinched shut, quaking, the pain somehow deeper than the roots of my teeth, deeper even than what was left of my jawbone. It stopped my breath and caused me to groan, worse than it had ever been, worse even than after the surgery to cut out my glowing, phosphorus-poisoned bone. I could barely rouse myself through the agony, but thoughts of Mr. Merrick eventually opened my eyes.

A figure stood in a far dark corner of the room, vague, looking like the shadow of a woman who wasn't there, its breathing a gurgled sucking.

I sat up and scrambled backward on my bed into my own corner, curling my legs up, my hands flailing before me. Becky and Martha appeared to sleep on soundly, even as the shadow stepped toward me, dragging the darkness of the corner with it, as though pulling a moldering shroud over the room.

"P-please," I whispered, my voice nearly inaudible. "What—"

The ghost was not like the others. It had not gone to Mr. Merrick. It had not been drawn to him. It had been drawn to me, and from it I felt nothing but hatred and malevolence. I couldn't shrink far enough away from it. I couldn't escape it, and as it drew nearer, I saw its pale face and looked into the pits of its eyes, the darkest two points in the room, into which all light fell.

It stretched its hand toward me and pushed the tips of its wispy fingers into my mouth. I tasted nothing, but choked and gagged as it seemed to reach its hand down my throat and pull the air from my lungs.

It made no sound, but somehow smothered all other sounds to become the loudest silence in the room. I closed my eyes again as it came close enough for an embrace, the pain in my jaw severe enough to loosen my hold on consciousness. I retained enough of my shattered senses to know when the ghost touched my chest with its other hand, like the sharp tip of an icicle, and then it stabbed that icy dagger into my belly and sliced upward.

My eyes shot open, and I kicked and convulsed, feeling my skin tear as the black, icy woman burrowed inside me, stretching into my gut, my chest, and then my arms and legs, as though I were its clothing. It strained me so taut I couldn't even scream, and felt I would surely be ripped asunder. But after a few moments' struggle, the ghost settled, and I blinked my eyes and found my chest and the rest of my body intact. I lay there in my bed as I had been when I'd awoken to the figure in my room, only it was no longer standing in the corner.

It was inside me. I could feel it stirring, like bubbles rising from the sewage-laden Thames. I could hear it hissing and whispering insistently at the back of my thoughts, but I had to listen carefully to understand its meaning, and within a few moments, I was able to discern words and phrases.

Kill her.

"What?" I said.

Kill her.

The sensation of these utterances inside my own head set me writhing, and I leapt from my bed as though to escape it, but the voice followed me.

Kill her.

I quickly dressed and pulled my shawl about me.

Kill her.

I fled the room, raced up the dormitory stairs, then through the foyer and out into Bedstead Square. It was four o'clock in the morning, made darker and colder by a mizzle that wet every stone, cobble, and brick, but the shock of the chill in my nose and lungs restored some clarity to my mind.

Kill her.

The voice still followed me, and I quickly settled on the idea that I had become possessed by the ghost, much as the Spiritualist mediums professed to be. I fought the urge to tear at my chest as Annie had torn at her arm, to pry the spirit out of me. "Who—who are you?" I asked it, my voice still quavering.

The ghost went silent within me for a moment, and then said, *I am Black Mary.*

"Who?"

I saw you.

I didn't know what that meant. "You saw me? Where?"

The Ten Bells.

I shook my head, trying to clear away enough fear to remember. I recalled that was the name of the pub in Spitalfields, near Christ Church, where I'd gone with Charles in search of someone who'd known Annie Chapman. That establishment had been nearly empty, but there had been a young woman who'd poked her head in, asking the barkeep if he'd seen a man.

"I remember you," I said.

Kill her.

Her teeth bit me anew. "What do you mean? Who?"

She who killed me.

I struggled to make sense of that, for I'd assumed the ghost inside me to be another of Leather Apron's victims, and yet she spoke of a woman having killed her. "Who has killed you?" I asked.

She who killed the others killed me.

"Others?"

Kill her!

I clutched my head against the loudness of the voice, but could not avoid it by closing my ears or stepping away from it. "Please," I said. "I don't understand."

The others came.

"The others?"

The others came and you aided them.

My confusion spread wider and reached deeper, for Black Mary seemed to be saying the other ghosts that had come to Mr. Merrick, the four I had helped, had been murdered by the same person who had murdered her. Such a conclusion would mean Leather Apron was not a man at all, but a very different kind of fiend.

Kill her.

"You want me to kill . . . Leather Apron?"

Yes.

Kill her.

"No," I whispered. I'd already done much more than I would've thought I could, and endured more than I would've thought I could bear. To think of going back out into the city, to confront the murderer, the one who had evaded capture and slain five women in so brutal a fashion, was enough to bring me to the edge of madness. "I won't do it," I said. "Don't ask me."

Kill her!

"No."

Kill her! Rip her! Bleed her!

"No!" I shouted, my voice resounding up the walls of the hospital to either side of the square.

I will leave you, Black Mary said, and I sensed her sliding and tugging on my sinews, in the direction of Mr. Merrick's door. *I will go to him instead.*

"No, please!" I said. "I beg of you. He can't take anymore. Leave him be!"

Kill her.

I looked from Mr. Merrick's door toward the hospital gate through which I had thought never to leave again. I felt the city brooding beyond its bars, waiting for my return, eager to reclaim me as its own, and I realized then my stay in the hospital had been but an indulgence, a delusion I had been allowed, but it had now come inevitably to its end, and I was to return home. I had thought I could escape my death there, but the truth was that my fate had long since been decided.

"This will be my end," I said.

Go. Kill her.

I knew Mr. Merrick might be awake, perhaps still bedazzled by the spectacle of the Drury Lane pantomime, but I did not wish to burden him with a farewell he could not understand. My refusal of him the night before had only brought him pain and confusion, and I could explain this no better. He had always walked above the streets, whilst I had been made by them, as had Leather Apron, and that remained the difference between Mr. Merrick and me that he would never see, because of who he was.

I turned toward the gate and roused the porter to let me out.

"Bit early for an errand, eh, Miss Fallow?" he said. "Not quite five yet."

"Some things must be done when they must be done," I said.

"True enough," he said. "Mind yourself, though. That devil ain't caught yet."

"Not yet," I said as I passed through the gate. I then turned up East Mount Street toward Whitechapel.

Hurry, Black Mary said.

"I don't know where I'm going."

I will lead you.

A subtle strumming on my fibers and tendons propelled me forward, guiding me along the street. At the end of East Mount, it pulled me west, and since it was too early yet for the omnibuses to be running and I'd left my money behind in my room, I walked. The crossing of Whitechapel proved perilous, for rain had slicked it with mud, and the carts and wagons careened, but on the other side, next to the greengrocer's, I came to the boarded-up waxworks where Mr. Merrick had been displayed. There I stopped, kissed the tips of my fingers, and laid them against the mildewed wood.

Hurry.

"Farewell, Joseph," I said, and then followed the prompting of the ghost I carried inside me as it led me past Thomas Barry's Waxworks, soon to have another gruesome display, and then the Pavilion Theatre. The city seemed to rouse with a predator's quality at my passing, though the rain kept hats down and collars up, turning all men into anonymous skulkers.

Hurry.

The possession of my body had left me with some volition, even as I was led. It was as though I were adrift in the current of a stream, but not one so strong I couldn't plant my feet and stop my progress if I chose to do so. It was simply easier to let myself be carried, as though I were the passenger in the third-class compartment of my own body.

Hurry! She is still with me.

"With you?"

With my body. She still . . . works on me.

I stopped in the middle of the sidewalk, forcing the traffic to flow around me. "You mean she's . . ." I couldn't bring myself to say the rest of it. "How do you know?"

I feel it.

My innards coiled up tight. "I'm so sorry."

Hurry. Please.

I resumed my walk down the street, my only consolation the fact that I was leading the spirit farther and farther from Mr. Merrick. I still had no idea what I would do when I was brought before the demon of Whitechapel that so many had hunted, nor how that confrontation might end. I still had no idea why I'd been chosen.

"Black Mary?"

Yes.

"Why do you haunt me when the others haunted Mr. Merrick?"

No.

"No?"

The others did not haunt him.

"But they did."

No.

It was you.

We passed by St. Mary's on the far side of the street, and my pace slowed as I thought about what she'd just said. "No, I am certain—"

All is dark, but here there is light.

Again her words brought my march to a halt, for that was what Polly had said to Mr. Merrick. "But I thought . . . I thought she meant *him*."

No.

You.

The city rushed away from me, and I no longer felt the frigid touch of the rain, no longer smelled the manure of the horses, and no longer heard the bellow of the traffic. "But I am not—I am a . . ."

Yes. You know of loss. Our loss.

I knew not what to say. *We are grateful. So grateful.* I felt Black Mary's malevolence returning, a heaving and terrible rage. *But we must hurry.*

"Yes," I whispered. "We must hurry."

We reached Commercial Street, and here the ghost guided me north into Spitalfields and the Evil Quarter Mile, a direction in which nothing in Heaven or Hell could have induced me to travel the day before. With Black Mary inside me, full of dire vengeance, I now proceeded without hesitation or fear.

I passed the entrance to Flower and Dean without even giving it a glance, and soon Christ Church and the Ten Bells pub came into my view. Black Mary led me down Dorset Street, which was as narrow and vile a rookery as any of its neighbors, and then through an even narrower passage, into a tight courtyard perhaps ten feet wide and fifty feet long. A single, sickly gas lamp sputtered in the rain to my left, stretching my faint, early morning shadow across the flagstone pavers and up the side of the nearest lodging. I was wet through from the drizzle by that point, and shivering.

She is gone.

"What?"

She is gone.

"How do you know?"

That is my room. That is where she left me.

Black Mary pointed me toward a low doorway that my shadow then crossed, but I took not one step toward it. The door appeared old and perfectly ordinary, but I tried not to imagine the horror and ruin of Black Mary's body, just on the other side. I knew well what mutilations Leather Apron had wrought when risking capture in the open streets. A wave of nausea crested near my throat when I imagined what depravities the murderer might have inflicted on the tissues and organs of Black Mary's body while undisturbed in the privacy of her lodging.

"Whatever is on the other side of that door," I said, "I will not see it."

It doesn't matter.

I took another look around me at the shabby tenements, a common outdoor pump their only source of running water, refuse and filth choking the corners of the court, the squalor in which Black Mary had lived and died.

"What was your real name?" I asked the ghost.

Mary Jane Kelly. But she is destroyed. I am Black Mary, and I will have my revenge.

I cast a final look at that desolate place and fell back through the passageway onto Dorset.

Evelyn!

"What is it?"

She is near. She flees.

"Where?" My gaze flicked to and fro, up and down the street, even as my heart launched upward. "Where is she?"

This way.

The pull on my sinews felt more urgent than it had at any point thus far, almost painful, and I sensed Black Mary's fury mounting.

Kill her. Rip her. Bleed her.

I reached Commercial Street and let the ghost draw me back down it, struggling then to keep my pace commensurate with her strength and ferocity. The city had fully awakened by that time, though it still yawned and trudged heavily in the rain and mud. I kept my gaze forward, scrutinizing the swelling crowd, expecting the ghost to alert me to the one she sought.

Hurry. Kill her.

"I am hurrying," I said, and quickened my gait to a trot. We had nearly reached Whitechapel when I noticed a bent old woman shambling along, and Black Mary yanked me toward her.

There.

"Where?"

Kill her!

I disbelieved it. "Her?"

Yes! Kill her!

I hastened to a sprint and charged up behind the old woman, compelled without thought, my heart a tinker's hammer stroke. As I caught her up, I grabbed her shoulder and spun her around to face me with such force it nearly tipped us both over.

I knew her face, its leathery skin and severe frown intimidating and familiar from the night of the dock fire.

"The midwife," I whispered, the import of the revelation creeping over me.

Kill her!

"Oi," the old woman croaked. "Why you accosting me?"

She had dried blood caked beneath her fingernails, and a single brown droplet stuck to her craggy brow near her hairline, almost hidden by her cap. Others who chanced to notice those stains upon a midwife would have no cause for suspicion. The facts of the murders flew about me, assuming their formation. The victims, all women; their organs removed; a maniac with medical knowledge.

Kill her! Kill her! Kill her!

Black Mary thrashed within me as if trying to seize control of my arms, hands, and fingers. If I allowed it, I knew she would have them at the old woman's throat, and if that happened, no one would have power sufficient to pry them loose.

"You an imbecile or something?" the midwife asked. "Speak!"

"I know who you are," I said.

The old woman's frown cut low enough to sever her chin. "Do you, now? You look familiar to me as well."

"No," I said, and lowered my voice so she actually leaned in toward me. *"I know what you've done, you devil."*

She leaned back then as a shroud fell away from her, a kind of invisible veil I hadn't known she was wearing, the last shred of humanity she wore like a garment, and beneath it I glimpsed something darker even than Black Mary's eyes, darker even than the foulest back slum of Whitechapel.

"Do you, now?" she said again.

I stood there in the rainy, crowded street, unarmed before a murderer who had slaughtered and butchered five women and would no doubt think it an insignificance to do the same to me. It occurred to me that her long knife might've even then been secreted away about her person somewhere.

Kill her! Let me kill her!

"Ah," the midwife said, with a grin even more terrible than her frown. "Now I know you." She leaned in toward me again and whispered, "That's a pretty scar you've got."

Before I could react, she grabbed my head and jerked it downward with shocking strength, wrenching my neck. My arms flew wide to keep my balance, and I felt an intense pain as she tore my shawl away with a fistful of my hair. Then she charged off into the crowd.

I watched her go, my scalp afire, my face exposed to the world.

She flees!

I needed to hide myself away or find something to cover my face, but I was out in the open with nothing to use as a shield. Had I the ability, I would have clawed up the cobblestones and bricks to bury myself in the street. The people around me who had seen the midwife's attack stared at me. They pointed at me and leered with the expression Charles had worn as he'd assaulted me. I felt hatred and disgust from each of them, exactly what I had known and feared and fled.

Chase her! Kill her!

"I can't," I whispered, and I hurried into the nearest alleyway between two buildings to hide myself away. The corridor sloped downward into the shadows, and I followed it to its fetid bottom, as if swallowed by the street, and there I huddled behind a stinking fish barrel, clutching my head and rocking back and forth as I had seen Mr. Merrick do.

You must move!

I shook my head frantically, eyes wide as shame and pain immobilized me and ate me alive.

She will kill again! She will not stop until she has ripped the world apart!

"I can't."

You can.

"No," I whimpered.

Yes.

"Don't you see? I'm a monster. Charles—"

No.

"No?"

That is not why you hide.

"Yes, it is. My scars—"

No. He left you before your scars.

I knew of whom she spoke, and the pain inside turned my guts out, becoming unbearable. I could not face it, nor could I escape it, and I wanted to die to end it. "Please . . ."

You hide your pain behind your scars.

"Yes," I said.

He is here. This is where he died.

I went as quiet as I had ever in my life been. Nothing in my body moved, and no breath passed through my lungs. I was there in an alley off Commercial Street. It did not seem possible, and yet I wished with all my strength it was.

"Father?"

A figure stepped toward me out of the darkness at the alley's end. He moved in a way so familiar, yet forgotten, that it broke my mind open and spilled all my memories out onto the ground. The man I saw before me was the one who had left me that night. He had the same eyes, encircled by dark red, the same bend in his back, the same weariness in his stride. He came toward me without looking up to meet my eyes.

"Father!" I raced forward to embrace him, but Black Mary yanked me back.

Not yet.

"What? Please, let me—"

She yanked me back again, harder.

No.

"But why?"

You must ask him first.

"Ask him what?"

You know the question, and you must ask him. You must bring him peace.

I stared at my father's spirit, so unchanged though I had grown, trapped by the tyranny of his own emotions. But I carried my pain as well. I had buried it deeper than my scars and deeper than my bone, and I had left it there. I waged a war with my scars instead of that pain, hoping to forget why it was there, blaming my disfigurement and the city instead. But the pain could no longer be ignored. It rose to the surface like a coffin in a flood, and I realized that pain was the true, deep reason for my fear of everything else.

I looked at my father's spirit and I asked him, "Why?"

My father looked up at me. "Why what, daughter?"

"Why did you leave me?" I was a young girl again, holding on to him with my eyes shut tight. "Why could you not stop drinking for me?"

"Oh, my daughter," the spirit said, and his chin quivered. "How can you ask me that? How can you think it was you?"

"But you left me."

"I had my own demons, it's true. But you, daughter, you were my angel. Even so, there wasn't anything you could've done. It wasn't your fault I was lost. But you found me now. Can you ever forgive me for leaving you?"

"Of course, Father. I love you. All I wanted was for you to stay with me."

"I wish I had," he said. "More than anything, I wish I had."

My vision blurred with tears.

"I lost you," he said.

"You didn't lose me." I wiped my eyes, and when I blinked them open, my father had changed. He resembled the younger, happier man in the locket portrait hanging from my neck. "I love you."

Now I was allowed to rush into his arms, and he embraced me with his warmth. I cried and squeezed him hard.

"I love you, my beautiful girl. Be happy."

With that, he was gone, and I was left holding myself in the alley. Black Mary allowed me to sob for a few moments more before she spoke.

Now you must hurry.

I took a deep breath and exhaled slowly through my pursed lips. The old pain I'd just unearthed was gone, the hole left behind filled in, and now I found I had less fear of the crowd and less shame for my scars. I looked back out of the alley, toward Commercial Street.

Hurry.

"Right." I took a step toward the light. "Let's go after that old bitch."

CHAPTER 24

The stares and whispers continued as I walked down the street, but I ignored them, and I disregarded even the curses that occasionally landed upon me and fell away. I still felt somewhat naked without my shawl, out of habit, but my appearance actually had the effect of making my passage easier, for the crowd parted around me.

"Where is she?" I asked Black Mary.

Ahead. Keep going.

I scanned the pedestrians' backs ahead of me, searching for the bent shape of that midwife. When I reached Whitechapel, I found it jammed with early morning delivery vehicles of all kinds, and the omnibuses had begun operating, the metal railways glistening in the rain. Then, in the same moment Black Mary whispered in my thoughts, I spotted Leather Apron standing there, waiting for a break in the endless traffic to cross the street.

It is her.

"I see her," I whispered.

The old woman still clutched my shawl in her gnarled hand as I moved silently toward her, stalking through the traffic with my glare locked upon her. She occasionally turned and looked over her shoulder, but each time I managed to slide from her view, and before long stood but a few feet away from her.

Kill her.

I wanted to. My anger and hatred of her were undeniable, but when I thought about actually carrying out an act of murder, even of her, I faltered.

Kill her!

"I don't think I can," I said, low enough to pass under the sound of the rain.

You must!

"I am no killer," I said.

Then let me do it!

"What?"

Give me your arms. Your hands. Let me take my revenge!

"That will not bring you peace," I said.

I am not like the others, Black Mary said. *I did not come to you for peace.*

A break in the traffic appeared in the distance, which would soon make the midwife's escape possible. I trembled as I watched the opening drawing closer, and saw the murderess move a step to meet it. Another moment would've given her the opportunity to flee, and make it necessary to hunt her down again. Even then, I wondered what I would do, for I doubted I would find myself any more capable of murder at the second opportunity, or the third, than I was in that moment.

She will escape! Black Mary's voice became a ferocious snarl. *Let me slay her!*

The tension in the ghost surged, vibrating my whole being as though the stream had become a torrent, and I felt my feet slipping on the river rocks below. To resist the force of her required all my strength, which I couldn't sustain, and in a moment of doubt

I gave a fraction of myself over to her. She seized this power as one seizes a doll by the arm, and with that I surrendered the rest of me, retreating to the back of my own mind.

Now I will kill her, Black Mary said.

A large omnibus drew near, fully laden with at least thirty passengers, both atop and within. Just as it reached us, Black Mary dove forward as if stumbling, slamming hard into the midwife's shoulder. The old woman lurched forward and spun around, arms outstretched, but lost her balance and fell on her back, onto the metal rail directly before the omnibus wheel. The vehicle lurched as it ran her over, and she howled, sitting nearly upright, watching the metal grind through her belly, leaving her nearly cut in half. It had happened so quickly, only then did someone scream, and the driver had already stopped the omnibus.

The midwife's blood filled the railway channel, her gut a mess of torn flesh and fabric. Her legs twitched a little, but she flailed her arms, her neck strained upward, her mouth opening and closing, looking and sounding like a fish flopping and dying on a dock. Blood soon spouted from her mouth, and she collapsed, convulsing but a few more times before going still.

Black Mary relinquished my body then, and I took back my faculties and the power over my limbs.

It is done, the ghost said.

I could barely breathe, let alone speak. Many of the passengers of the omnibus had disembarked, and the crowd circling the vehicle and the corpse had multiplied. Shouts went up for the police, and for a stretcher, but it was plain to everyone there that such efforts would be to no avail.

"She just fell on the tracks!" the driver shouted, sounding frantic.

"She was pushed!" said a man nearby me. "I saw it happen with me own eyes!"

I wanted to turn and run, but the calm voice of Black Mary said, *Be still.*

"But they saw me!" I shouted inwardly, knowing my singular features would make it impossible to hide.

No. They saw me.

She was right, for when a policeman arrived a moment later, the witnesses all reported seeing a blonde or red-haired woman who had since vanished. I gradually got away from the scene of the accident, fighting through an unceasing tide of blood-spectators that poured in to catch a glimpse of the body. Once free of it, I turned up Whitechapel, toward the hospital.

I will leave you now, Black Mary said. *We are all grateful to you, Evelyn.*

"And I am grateful to you," I said, for I still strode without a shawl or covering of any kind to hide my scars.

Farewell, Black Mary said, and then her presence rushed out of me.

The absence of her left me somewhat thrown, and I gasped. I'd grown accustomed to her strumming my sinews, the whisper of her voice against my thoughts, and the sudden stillness of my body and silence in my mind required that I stop in the sidewalk to recover my footing.

A few moments later, I resumed my walk back, and before long came to the same gate I'd left through that morning. The porter nodded as I entered. "Welcome back, Miss Fallow," he said. "You get done what you needed?"

"Yes," I said.

"Glad to hear it," he said. "Shoulda taken a rain napper, though. You're wet through."

"I'm afraid you're right," I said, and only after I'd reached Bedstead Square did I realize he hadn't remarked or stared at my scars.

Before going to Mr. Merrick's room, I bathed and dressed in a clean uniform and took my breakfast with the other maids, though I ate not a single bite. I waited for Beatrice to report news of Black Mary's murder, but the papers said nothing about it. It seemed the remains of her body hadn't yet been found. Nothing was said of the omnibus accident, either, and I doubted anyone would ever forge a connection between the dead midwife and the sudden cessation of Leather Apron's evil work.

When I went to Mr. Merrick, he seemed to be completely unaware that a fifth ghost had come to the hospital at all. From the moment I entered his room, he spoke of nothing but the pantomime he'd attended the night before.

"Oh, Evelyn," he said. "You should have been there!"

"Tell me what I would've seen," I said.

"You would have seen the way the cat, Puss, outwitted that Ogre and gobbled him right up! And the King and Queen, with their court of knights all dressed in silver and gold, and the fairies in their realm . . . it was simply perfect."

"You make it sound enchanting," I said.

"It was," he said.

"I wish I had been there," I said. "If you go again, I hope to attend with you."

"Truly?" he asked.

"Yes, Mr. Merrick."

"Then I shall ask Dr. Treves! This is wonderful! Perhaps we can go to another pantomime at Christmastime, and then we can find out what the Prince did after we all left the theater."

"That would be lovely, Mr. Merrick."

"May I ask," he said, "what has changed your mind?"

I considered telling him about what had happened with Black Mary that morning, but thought better of it, for I didn't want to disturb his reverie and joy. One day, I would tell him everything and let him know Leather Apron was dead and there would be no more hauntings, but that day I simply said, "A change of heart is all."

"I am so glad," he said. "It was so kind of Madge Kendal to arrange it for me."

"Yes, it was."

"I would like to write to thank her, and send my model church as a gift."

"I think she would appreciate that," I said.

I helped him move to his table, where he sat with his stationery and wrote a letter with his good hand in pleasing script. When he was finished with it, he asked, "Would you read it? To make sure it is well written?"

"I'm certain it is thoughtful and kind," I said. "That is what matters."

"But I want it to be as it should. Will you read it?"

"Yes, Mr. Merrick," I said, and picked up the piece of his

stationery, in the corner of which was printed the small picture of a nobleman and lady dancing.

Dear Mrs. Kendal,

Many thanks indeed for the pantomime at the theater which you so kindly arranged for me to attend. The performance left me spellbound, and is not something I shall ever forget. As a token of my appreciation, I have sent along this model church, which I hope shall bring you joy and remind you of my admiration. I am yours very truly,

Joseph Merrick
London Hospital
Whitechapel

"Mr. Merrick, it is a perfect expression of thanks," I said.

"You think so?" he said.

"I do," I said, and noticed that he had written something on the back side of the paper as well. "What is this?"

"It is a poem," he said. "I often include it in my correspondence."

"May I read it?"

"Of course," he said, and so I did.

'Tis true my form is something odd,
But blaming me is blaming God;
Could I create myself anew
I would not fail in pleasing you.

If I could reach from pole to pole
Or grasp the ocean with a span,
I would be measured by the soul;
The mind's the standard of the man.

I put the letter down upon the desk, the paper quivering with the shaking of my hand. Tears wet my eyes enough to glisten, but not enough to fall with a blink. "It is beautiful. Did you compose that?"

"No," he said. "I adapted it from a poem called 'False Greatness' by Isaac Watts."

"It is perfect."

"Thank you," he said.

"*You* are perfect," I said.

He shook his great head. "I am not, Evelyn."

"You say you want to be measured by your soul and your mind, Mr. Merrick. Well, that is my standard, too."

He reached out his good hand, and I took hold of it. "Would you like to know how I think of you?" he asked.

I laughed. "Of course I do."

"I think of you as my mother."

"What?" I let go of his hand, feeling somewhat affronted. "Mr. Merrick, you think me your mother? That all my care for you makes you my—my child?"

"No," he said. "You misunderstand. Do you not remember what I told you? My mother is an angel, Evelyn."

His meaning finally reached me, and then my tears fell freely. "Mr. Merrick," I whispered.

"You are an angel, Evelyn," he said. "You are light to me."

EPILOGUE

I breathed deeply before rapping my knuckle upon the matron's door, and she then called for me to enter. Her office still remained as it had been on my first time entering it, though it had been nearly two years since that day.

"Miss Fallow," she said from her desk, setting aside the papers she'd been reading. "Please, won't you sit down?"

"Thank you, Matron," I said, and took one of the seats in front of her.

She interlaced her jeweled fingers. "Miss Ireland of Blizzard Ward tells me you have been a great asset to them."

"Thank you, ma'am," I said. "Miss Ireland is a very good nurse."

"She is, indeed. With good judgment, I should add."

I accepted that compliment with a bow of my head.

"I also hear that the absence of your shawl has not caused an unacceptable degree of alarm or disruption."

"I hope that is so, ma'am, for I've no wish to wear it."

"How are you getting on, Evelyn?" she asked. "It was hard for all of us, but you had a special friendship with him."

I checked the stanchions around my heart for weakness before I spoke. The matron allowed for emotion, but to cry in her office would be seen as unprofessional. "I miss him, ma'am," I said. "I still wake up some mornings and walk to his room. I stand there at the top of those stairs, like I'm lost, and then I remember he's gone . . ."

"I am sorry," the matron said.

Mr. Merrick's death had happened so suddenly, and had shocked everyone. I'd thought nothing at all amiss that day as I'd taken him his lunch. He complained he hadn't slept well the night before, and wanted to nap, so I'd left him alone. Dr. Hodges had found him a little over an hour later, and the doctors determined that somehow, his head had fallen backward as he slept, and he had suffocated.

"He had a kind soul, did he not?" the matron said.

"Very kind," I said, and felt the braces groaning, my throat constricting.

"It has been quite difficult for Dr. Treves," she said. "He insisted he alone be the one to mount Mr. Merrick's skeleton. Some might think that ghoulish, but I think we both know it to be a sign of affection, for there isn't anyone else to whom Dr. Treves would entrust such a task."

"No, ma'am," I said. I'd heard they were preparing Mr. Merrick's bones for future scientific examination, but I'd vowed never to look upon them. It did not seem right to me that, even in death, he would be on display. For my remembrance of him, I'd asked for but one thing, which Dr. Treves had given to me, and that was the portrait of Mr. Merrick's mother.

"What was it you wished to speak with me about?" the matron asked.

I sat forward, both sad and grateful to speak of something else. "I was wondering if you might write me a letter of reference."

"And for what would I be recommending you?" she asked.

"I plan to apply to Newnham College at Cambridge."

"The women's college?" the matron asked.

"Yes. Professor Sidgwick once invited me to attend."

"When was this?"

"A year and a half ago, now."

Her eyes flicked as if counting back the months on a calendar. "Ah, yes." She nodded. "I remember him coming. An unpleasant time."

"Yes, it was, ma'am."

"I must confess, Miss Fallow, I am disappointed."

"Ma'am?"

"You have impressed me greatly. Upon the recommendations of Dr. Tilney, Miss Doyle, and now Miss Ireland, and based upon my own observations, it is my intention to admit you with the next class of probationers. If memory serves, that is what you wanted when you first came to me."

"It was, ma'am."

"And now?"

"I . . . I don't know, ma'am." I'd not thought it possible for me to be a nurse. Though I had made peace with my scars, I'd not expected the matron ever would, and after Mr. Merrick's death, I'd decided to attend the women's college to make something more of myself than a maid.

"You don't know?" the matron asked.

"It's just that . . ." Even as a nurse, I still didn't think I could stay there, where memories hung as thick as carbolic in the air, burning my eyes with tears at unexpected turns. "He was . . . more than a patient to me."

Matron Luckes propped her elbows on her desk and raised her many rings to her chin. "I see. And you think it would be too painful to remain here. Is that it?"

"That is it exactly. But I am grateful for your offer, Matron. Truly."

"I am sorry to lose you, Miss Fallow. But I think I understand. I shall write a letter of reference to Professor Sidgwick directly."

"Thank you, ma'am."

"It is my pleasure."

I rose from the chair to leave, but as I reached her door, she called to me, "Miss Fallow?"

"Yes, ma'am?"

"He was quite singular, wasn't he?"

I smiled, wishing that all grief could be so alloyed with joy. "He was, ma'am," I said. "In every way."

Acknowledgments

It would not have been possible for me to write this story without the help and support of many. First, I would like to thank the large community of "Ripperologists," and in particular the casebook.org website, which was an invaluable and inexhaustible resource. My editor, Lisa Sandell, first heard me describe the idea for this book in 2010, and she knew when the time had come for me to write it. As always, I'm grateful to her for her friendship, wisdom, and guidance, and also to my copyeditor, Starr Baer, and to our production editor, Rebekah Wallin, for their careful insights. Many other friends at Scholastic have supported me over the years, including, but not limited to, David Levithan, Ellie Berger, Lizette Serrano, Emily Heddleson, Charisse Meloto, Monica Palenzuela, Tracy van Straaten, Caitlin Friedman, Bess Braswell, Lauren Festa, Ed Masessa, Emma Brockway, and Lauren Felsenstein Bonifacius. Utah's community of writers, the Rock Canyon group, remains something completely unique and deeply meaningful to me. I would also like to thank my family, extended and immediate, by birth and by choice, for their ongoing support. I couldn't do this without the love and patience of my wife, Jaime, and my stepkids, Stuart, Sophie, and Charlie, who understand when I have writing to do.

Finally, I would like to thank Joseph Merrick, whose brief life touched and inspired so many, including me.

About the Author

Matthew J. Kirby is the critically acclaimed author of the middle-grade novels *Icefall*, which won the Edgar Award for Best Juvenile Mystery and the PEN Literary Award for Children's and Young Adult Literature; *The Clockwork Three*, which was named a *Publishers Weekly* Flying Start; *The Lost Kingdom*; *Cave of Wonders*, the fifth book in the Infinity Ring series; The Quantum League: *Spell Robbers*; and *Last Descendants*, an Assassin's Creed novel. He was born in Utah and grew up in Maryland, California, and Hawaii. Matthew lives in Utah, where he is currently at work on his next novel. Learn more about Matthew at www.matthewjkirby.com.